BORN IN DEATH

Nora Roberts writing as J. D. Robb

ISIS

LARGE PRINT

Oxford

First published in Great Britain 2007
by
Piatkus Books
An imprint of Little, Brown Book Group

Published in Large Print 2011 by ISIS Publishing Ltd.,
7 Centremead, Osney Mead, Oxford OX2 0ES
by arrangement with
Little, Brown Book Group
An Hachette UK Company

British Library Cataloguing in Publication Data
Robb, J. D., 1950–
 Born in death. - - Large print ed. ~
 1. Dallas, Eve (Fictitious character) - - Fiction.
 2. Policewomen - - New York (State) - - New York
 - - Fiction.
 3. Murder - - Investigation - - New York (State)
 - - New York - - Fiction.
 4. Detective and mystery stories.
 5. Large type books.
 I. Title
 813.5'4–dc22

 ISBN 978–0–7531–8688–6 (hb)
 ISBN 978–0–7531–8689–3 (pb)

Printed and bound in Great Britain by
T. J. International Ltd., Padstow, Cornwall

I am Alpha and Omega,
the beginning and the end,
the first and the last.

-REVELATION

Love begets love.

-ROBERT HERRICK

CHAPTER
ONE

The ways and means of friendship were murderous. In order to navigate its twisty maze, a friend could be called upon to perform inconvenient, irritating or downright horrifying acts at any given time.

The worst, the very worst requirement of friendship, in Eve Dallas's opinion, was sitting through an entire evening of childbirth classes.

What went on there — the sights, the sounds, the assault on all the senses — turned the blood cold.

She was a cop, a Homicide lieutenant with eleven years on the job protecting and defending the hard, merciless streets of New York. There was little she hadn't seen, touched, smelled, or waded through. Because people, to her mind, would always and could always find more inventive and despicable ways to kill their fellow man, she knew just what torments could be inflicted on the human body.

But bloody and brutal murder was *nothing* compared to giving birth.

How all those women with their bodies enormous and weirdly deformed by the entity gestating inside them could be so cheerful, so freaking *placid* about what was happening — and going to happen — to them was beyond her scope.

But there was Mavis Freestone, her oldest friend, with her little pixie body engulfed by the bulge of belly, beaming like a mentally defective while images of live birth played out on the wall screen. And she wasn't alone. The other women had more or less the same God-struck look on their faces.

Maybe pregnancy stopped certain signals from getting to the brain.

Personally, Eve felt a little bit sick. And when she glanced over at Roarke, the wince on his angel-kissed faced told her he was right there with her. That, at least, was a big red check in the Pro-Marriage column. You got to drag your spouse into your personal nightmares and into that twisty friendship maze right along with you.

Eve let the images blur. She'd rather study a crime scene recording — mass murder, mutilation, severed limbs — than look up some laboring woman's crotch and watch a head pop out. Roarke had horror vids in his collection that were less gruesome. She could hear Mavis whispering to Leonardo, the entity's expectant father, but blocked out the words.

When, dear God, when would it be over?

Some setup here, all right, she thought, trying to distract herself by evaluating the birthing center. The whole damn building was a kind of cathedral to conception, gestation, birth, and babies. She'd managed to duck Mavis's attempt to give her a tour of the entire place by pleading work.

Sometimes a well-placed lie saved friendships, and sanity.

The educational wing was enough. She'd sat through a lecture, several demonstrations that would haunt her dreams for decades, been forced as part of Mavis's coaching team to assist in a mock birth with the labor droid and squealing droid infant.

And now there was this hideous vid.

Don't think about it, she warned herself, and went back to studying the room.

Pastel walls covered with pictures of babies or pregnant women in various stages of bliss. All filmy and rapturous. Lots of fresh flowers and thriving green plants arranged artistically. Comfy chairs, supposedly designed to aid the women in hauling their loaded bodies up. And three perky instructors who were available for questions, lectures, demos, and serving healthy refreshments.

Pregnant women, Eve noted, were constantly eating or peeing.

Double doors at the back, one exit in the front, left of the vid screen. Too bad she couldn't make a run for it.

Eve let herself go into a kind of trance. She was a tall, lanky woman with a choppy cap of brown hair. Her face was angular, and paler than usual, with whiskey-brown eyes currently glazed. The jacket she wore over her weapon harness was deep green and, because her husband had bought it, cashmere.

She was thinking about going home and washing the memory of the last three hours away in a full liter of wine when Mavis grabbed her hand.

3

"Dallas, look! The baby's coming!"

"Huh? What?" Those glazed eyes popped wide. "What? *Now?* Well, Jesus. Breathe, right?"

Laughter erupted around them as Eve lurched to her feet.

"Not this baby." Giggling, Mavis stroked her basketball belly. "*That* baby."

Instinct had Eve glancing in the direction Mavis pointed, and getting a wide-screen blast of the bellowing, wriggling, gunk-covered creature sliding out from between some poor woman's legs.

"Oh, man. Oh, God." She sat down, before her own legs went out from under her. No longer caring if it made her a sissy, she groped for Roarke's hand. When he gripped it, she found it as clammy as her own.

People applauded, actually clapped and *cheered* when the wailing, slippery-looking form was laid on its mother's deflated belly, and between her engorged breasts.

"In the name of all that's holy . . ." Eve muttered to Roarke. "It's 2060, not 1760. Can't they find a better way to handle this process?"

"Amen" was all Roarke said. Weakly.

"Isn't it beautiful? It's the ult, the extreme ult." Mavis's lashes — currently dyed sapphire blue, sparkled with tears. "It's a little boy. Awww, look how sweet . . ."

Dimly she heard the lead instructor announce the end of the night's coaching class — *thank God* — and invite people to stay for refreshments or questions.

"Air," Roarke murmured into her ear. "I'm in desperate need of air."

"It's the pregnant women. I think they suck up all the oxygen. Think of something. Get us out of here. I can't think. My brain won't work right."

"Stand with me." He hooked a hand under her arm, pulled her up.

"Mavis, Eve and I want to take you and Leonardo out for a bite. We can do better than the offerings here."

Eve could hear the strain in his voice, but imagined anyone who didn't know him as well as she would only hear that easy, fluid stream of Irish.

There was a lot of chatter going on and women were making a beeline for the food or the bathrooms. Rather than thinking about what was being said or done, Eve focused on Roarke's face.

If it couldn't distract a woman, she was too far gone to worry about it.

He might have been a little pale, but the white skin only intensified the wild blue of his eyes. His hair was a black silk frame around a face designed to raise a woman's heart rate. And that mouth of his. Even in her current state it was tempting to just lean in a little and take a good bite of it.

And the body only added to the fantasy: tall, leanly muscled, and slickly presented in one of his perfectly tailored business suits.

Roarke wasn't just one of the richest men in the known universe, he also looked the part.

And at the moment, because he was taking her arm and leading her out of that nightmare, he was her ultimate hero. She grabbed her coat on the fly.

"We're sprung?"

"They wanted to see if a friend of theirs could join us." He still had Eve's hand, and was rapidly walking toward the exit. "I told them we'd get the car, bring it around to the front. Save them steps."

"You're brilliant. Freaking white knight. If I ever recover from this trauma, I'll screw your brains out."

"I hope, eventually, my brain cells regenerate enough to make that possible. My God, Eve. My God."

"Total tandem here. Did you see how it sort of slithered out when —"

"Don't." He pulled her into the elevator, called for their level of the parking garage. "If you love me, don't take me back there." He leaned back against the wall. "I've always respected women. You know that."

She rubbed at an itch on the side of her nose. "You've nailed plenty of them. But yeah," she added when he just gave her a bland stare. "You've got respect."

"That respect has now risen to admiration of biblical proportions. How do they *do* that?"

"We've just seen how. In graphic detail. Did you see Mavis?"

Eve shook her head as they walked out of the elevator. "Her eyes were all glittery. And it wasn't fear. She can't wait to do all that."

"Leonardo looked a bit green, actually."

"Yeah, well, he's got that thing about blood. And there was blood — and other *stuff*."

"That's enough. There'll be no talk of other stuff."

Because the late January weather was lousy, he'd driven one of his all-terrains. It was big and black and

6

muscular. When he uncoded the locks, Eve leaned back against the passenger door before he could open it.

"Look here, ace. We gotta face this, you and me."

"I don't want to."

Now she laughed. She'd seen him face death with more aplomb. "What we did in there, that was just a preview. We're going to be in the room with her when she pushes that thing out. We have to be there, counting to ten, telling her to breathe, or to go to her happy place. Whatever."

"We could be out of town, or the country. No, we could be called off planet. That would really be best. We'll be called off planet to save the world from some criminal mastermind."

"Oh, if only. But you know and I know we're going to be there. Pretty soon, probably, because that bomb inside her's just ticking away."

He sighed, then leaned down to rest his brow to hers. "God pity us, Eve. God pity us."

"If God had any pity on us, He'd populate the world without the middle man. Middle woman. Let's go drink. A lot."

The restaurant was casual, a little noisy, and exactly what the midwife ordered. Mavis sipped some sort of exotic fruit punch that was nearly as sparkly as she was. Her riotous silver curls were tipped in the same sapphire as her lashes. Her eyes were a vivid, unearthly green tonight to match — Eve supposed — the tone of the sweater that fit over her breasts and belly like neon elastic. Numerous loops and squiggles hung from her ears and shot sparks of light as she moved her head. Her sapphire blue pants fit like a second skin.

The love of Mavis's life sat beside her. Leonardo was built like a redwood, and as he was a fashion designer neither he nor Mavis were ever at a loss for an eye-popping ensemble. He'd gone with a sweater as well, a crazed and intricate geometric pattern of colors against gold. Somehow — Eve could have said — it suited his strong form and burnished copper complexion.

The friend they'd brought along was every bit as knocked-up as Mavis. Maybe even more so, if such things were possible. But in contrast to Mavis's out-of-orbit style, Tandy Willowby wore a simple black V neck over a white tee. She was a tea-and-roses blonde, with pale blue eyes and a blunt-tipped nose.

During the drive over, Mavis had chattered out introductions, explaining that Tandy was from London, and had only been in New York a few months.

"I'm so glad I saw you tonight. Tandy wasn't there for class," Mavis continued as she mowed through the appetizers Roarke had ordered. "She dropped by toward the end to give the midwife the vouchers for the White Stork. It's this completely mag baby boutique where Tandy works."

"It's a lovely shop," Tandy agreed. "But I didn't expect to drop by, then get fed and watered." She offered Roarke a shy smile. "It's awfully kind of you. Both of you," she added to Eve. "Mavis and Leonardo have told me so much about you. You must be so excited."

"About what?" Eve wondered.

"Being part of Mavis's coaching team."

"Oh. Oh, yeah. We're . . ."

"Speechless," Roarke concluded. "What part of London are you from?"

"Actually, I'm from Devon originally. I moved to London as a teenager, with my father. Now here I am in New York. I must have a bit of the wanderlust. Though I expect I'll be grounded for a while now." Dreamily, she stroked a hand over her belly. "And you're a policewoman. That must be brilliant. Mavis, I don't think you ever told me how you and Dallas met."

"She arrested me," Mavis said between bites.

"You're having me on. No?"

"I used to work the grift. I was good at it."

"Not good enough," Eve commented.

"I want to hear all about it! But now, I have to make my way to the loo. Again."

"I'll go with you." Like Tandy, Mavis levered herself up. "Dallas? Coming with?"

"I'll pass."

"I remember — vaguely — what it's like not to have something planted on my bladder." Tandy sent the table a smile, then waddled off with Mavis.

"So . . ." Eve turned to Leonardo. "You met Tandy in the class?"

"Orientation," he confirmed. "Tandy's due about a week before Mavis. It's nice of you to let her come along. She's going through all this without a partner."

"What happened to the father?" Roarke asked him, and Leonardo shrugged.

"She doesn't talk about it much. Just says that he wasn't involved, or interested. If that's the way it is, he doesn't deserve her or the baby." Leonardo's wide face went tight and hard. "Mavis and I have so much, we want to help her as much as we can."

Eve's cynic antennae hummed. "Financially?"

"No. I don't think she'd take money, even if she needed it. She seems okay there. I meant support, friendship." He seemed to pale a little. "I'm going to be part of her coaching team. It'll, ah, it'll be like a dress rehearsal for Mavis."

"Scared shitless, aren't you?"

He glanced in the direction of the restrooms, then back at Eve. "I'm terrified. I could pass out. What if I pass out?"

"Make sure you don't land on me," Roarke told him.

"Mavis isn't nervous. Not even a little bit. And the closer we get, the more my insides . . ." He lifted his big hands, shook them. "I don't know what I'd do if the two of you weren't going to be there. Backing me up."

Oh, hell, Eve thought, and exchanged a glance with Roarke. "Where else would we be?" She signaled the waiter for another glass of wine.

Two hours later, after dropping Leonardo and Mavis home, Roarke drove south and east toward Tandy's apartment building.

"Really, I can take the tube. Subway. It's too much trouble, and only a few blocks."

"If it's only a few blocks," Roarke said, "it's hardly any trouble."

10

"How can I argue?" Tandy let out a laugh. "And it's so nice to sit in a warm car. It's so bloody cold out there tonight." She settled back with a sigh. "I feel pampered, and fat as a whale. Mavis and Leonardo, they're the best. You can't be around either of them for five minutes and not feel happy. And I see they're lucky in their friends. Oops."

Eve's head spun around so fast it might have flown off her shoulders. "No oops. No oopsing."

"He's just bumping around in there a bit. Not to worry. Oh, you know, Mavis is just giddy about the baby shower you're hosting for her next week. She bubbles over it."

"Baby shower. Right. Next week."

"Here we are. Just down the middle of this block. Thank you both so much." Tandy adjusted her scarf, hauled up a purse the size of a suitcase. "For the lovely food and company, and the luxurious ride. I'll see you both on Saturday, at the baby shower."

"Need any help, ah . . ."

"No, no." Tandy waved Eve off. "Even a whale must fend for itself. And even if I can't see my feet these days, I remember where they are. Good night now, and thanks again."

Roarke waited, engine idling, until Tandy had keyed herself into the building. "Seems a nice woman. Stable and sensible."

"Not like Mavis. Except for the whale factor. Gotta be tough, being knocked up, on your own, and not even in your own country. She seems to be dealing. You know, Roarke, how come just because you're pals you have to go to coaching classes, witness births, *and* give baby showers?"

"I don't have the answer to that question."

She heaved out a breath. "Neither do I."

Eve was dreaming of fang-toothed, many-armed babies bouncing out of Mavis to tear around the room, sending the midwife into screaming retreat while Mavis cooed: *Aren't they mag? Aren't they the ult?*

The signal of the bedside 'link had her popping out of the dream. She shuddered once.

"Block video," she ordered. "Lights on ten percent. Dallas."

Dispatch, Dallas, Lieutenant Eve. See the officers at 51 Jane Street, apartment 3B. Possible homicide.

"Acknowledged. Contact Peabody, Detective Delia. I'm on my way."

Acknowledged. Dispatch out.

Eve glanced over, saw Roarke's laser blue eyes were open and on hers. "Sorry," she said.

"I'm not the one being pulled out of a warm bed at four in the morning."

"You're right about that. People ought to have the courtesy to off each other at reasonable hours."

She rolled out of bed and into the bathroom for a lightning-quick shower. When she rolled back out, naked and warm from the drying tube, he was sipping a cup of coffee.

"Why are you up?"

"I'm awake," he said simply. "And look what I'd've missed if I'd turned over and gone back to sleep." He handed her the second cup of coffee he'd programmed.

"Thanks." She took it with her to the closet where she pulled out clothes. Had to be freaking freezing out there, she mused. And detoured to her dresser to yank out a V neck to go over the shirt, under the jacket.

Twice they'd put off tentative plans to take a couple of days in the tropics. Mavis, plus baby, equalled a pregnant woman wigging out at the thought of part of her coaching team dancing off to sand and surf this close to delivery time.

What could you do?

"Babies don't come out with teeth, do they?"

"No. I don't see how . . ." Roarke lowered his cup, gave her a baffled look. "Why do you put thoughts like that in my head?"

"They're in mine, pal, they're in yours."

"See if I make you coffee again."

She dressed quickly. "Maybe this murder is the work of a criminal mastermind that will take me off planet. You're nice to me, I could take you along."

"Don't toy with me."

She laughed, strapped on her weapon. "See you when I see you." She crossed to him, and because — hell, he was so damn pretty even at four in the morning — gave him a peck on both cheeks, then a long warm one mouth-to-mouth.

"Stay safe, Lieutenant."

"Plan on it."

She jogged down the stairs, where her coat was draped over the newel post. She tossed it there habitually because it was handy — and because she knew it irritated Summerset, Roarke's majordomo and the blight of her world.

She swung it on, discovered a miracle had happened and her gloves were actually in the pocket. Because it was there, she tossed on the cashmere scarf. And still the cold was a shock to the system when she stepped outside.

Hard to complain though, she decided, when you got yourself married to a man who thought to remote your vehicle to the front of the house with the heater already running.

She strode through the cold, climbed into warm.

She glanced in the rearview as she drove toward the gates. The house that Roarke built filled the mirror, stone and glass, juts and turrets — and the light glowing in their bedroom window.

He'd have a second cup of coffee, she thought, while reviewing stock reports, early media bulletins, business news, on the bedroom screen. Probably make some overseas or off-planet transmissions. Starting the day before dawn wasn't a biggie to Roarke, she knew.

Lucky her again, to have ended up with a man who fell so easily into the crazed cop rhythm she often ran by.

She drove through the gates that closed quietly behind her.

This sector of prime and pricey real estate was quiet — the rich, privileged, or fortunate snuggled under the covers in their atmosphere-regulated homes, condos, apartments. But within a few blocks, the city burst into jittery, jumping life.

Heat gushed up in steam from the grates as the underground world of the city moved and shook under the streets and sidewalks. Overhead ad blimps were already touting their bargain of the day. Who the hell cared about Valentine's Day sales at the Sky Mall at this hour? Eve wondered. What sane person would push themselves into the insanity of a mall crowd to save a few bucks on a candy heart?

She passed an animated billboard running a loop of impossibly perfect people frolicking over white-sugar sand into blue surf. That, at least, was more like it.

The yellow streaks of Rapid Cabs were already darting. Runs to transpo centers, mostly, she mused. Early flights to somewhere. A couple of maxibuses belched along, likely carrying the poor suckers on early shifts, or the luckier ones heading home to bed after a graveyard tour.

She detoured around the endless party on Broadway. Day or night, blistering or freezing, tourists and the street thieves who loved them thronged to that mecca of noise, light, movement.

A few of the after-hours joints were still open down Ninth. She spotted a huddle of street toughs in their over-filled rip jackets and jump boots loitering — and most likely ingesting illegal substances. But if they were looking for trouble, they'd have a hard time finding it before 5a.m. with the temps hovering around twelve degrees.

She skirted through a working-class section of Chelsea, then into the more arty flavor of the Village.

The black-and-white was nosed to the curb in front of a rehabbed townhouse on Jane. She took a loading zone a half block down, flipped her On Duty light, then stepped back out into the cold. By the time she retrieved her field kit and set her locks, she spotted Peabody hoofing it from the corner.

Her partner looked like an Arctic explorer wrapped in a thick, puffy coat the color of rusted metal with a mile of red scarf wrapped around her neck and a matching cap tugged down over her dark hair. Her breath puffed out like engine steam.

"Why can't people kill each other after the sun comes up?" Peabody gasped out.

"You look like an ad blimp in that coat."

"Yeah, I know, but it's wicked warm and it makes me feel thin when I take it off."

Together they walked to the townhouse, and Eve turned her recorder on. "No security cams," Eve observed. "No palm plate. Door lock's been tampered with."

There were riot bars on the lower windows, she noted. And the paint on the door and window trim was graying, peeling. Whoever owned the building wasn't big on maintenance and security.

The uniform on the door gave them a nod as she opened it. "Lieutenant, Detective. Bitching cold," she said. "Nine-one-one came in at oh three forty-two.

Vic's sister made it. My partner's got her upstairs. We responded, arrived 'bout three forty-six. Observed the entrance door to the building'd been compromised. Vic's on the third floor, bedroom. Hallway door lock's compromised, too. Put up a fight from the looks of it. Hands and feet bound with your old reliable duct tape. Worked her over some before doing her. Looks like she was strangled with the tie of her robe, since she's still wearing it around her neck."

"Where was the sister while this was going on?" Eve asked.

"Said she just got in. Travels for work. Uses her sister's place as a flop when she comes into New York. Name's Palma Copperfield. Shuttle attendant for World Wide Air. She mucked up the scene some — sicked up on the floor in there, touched the body before she ran outside again to place the nine-one-one."

The officer glanced toward the elevator. "She was sitting on the steps out there, bawling, when we pulled up. Pretty much been bawling since."

"That's always fun. Send in Crime Scene when they get here."

Thinking of the shoddy maintenance, Eve turned to the stairs, unpeeling her cold-weather gear as they climbed.

One unit per level, she noted. Decent space, privacy.

On the third floor she saw that the unit boasted what looked to be a spanking new security peep and cop-lock system. Both were broken in a way that indicated amateur — and effective.

She stepped inside, into a living area where a second female officer stood over a woman who was bundled under a blanket, trembling.

Early twenties, by Eve's gauge, with a long blond tail of hair sleeked back from a face where tears had washed through the makeup. She held a clear glass of what Eve assumed to be water in a two-handed grip.

She choked out a sob.

"Ms. Copperfield, I'm Lieutenant Dallas. My partner, Detective Peabody."

"The Homicide police. The Homicide police," she babbled in a flattened-vowel accent that told Eve Midwest.

"That's right."

"Somebody killed Nat. Someone killed my sister. She's dead. Natalie's dead."

"I'm sorry. Can you tell us what happened?"

"I — I came in. She knew I was coming. I called her this morning to remind her. We got in late, and I had a wind-down drink with Mae, the other attendant. The door, downstairs . . . the door was broken or something. I didn't need my key. I have a key. And I came up, and the lock — she had a new lock, and she gave me the code for it this morning, when — when I called? But it looked broken. The door wasn't even locked. I thought, 'Something's wrong, something has to be wrong,' because Nat wouldn't go to bed without locking up. So I thought I should check, just look in on her before I went to bed. And I saw . . . Oh, God, oh, God, she was on the floor and everything was broken and she was on the floor, and her face. Her face."

Palma started to cry again, the tears running fat and steady down her cheeks. "It was all bruised and red and her eyes . . . I ran over and I called her name. I think I called her name and I tried to wake her up. Pull her up. She wasn't sleeping. I knew she wasn't sleeping, but I had to try to wake her up. My sister. Someone hurt my sister."

"We're going to take care of her now." Eve thought of the time it would take for her, then the sweepers, to process the scene. "I'm going to need to talk to you again, in a little while, so I'm going to have you taken down to Central. You can wait there."

"I don't think I should leave Nat. I don't know what to do, but I should stay with Nat."

"You need to trust us with her now. Peabody."

"I'll take care of it."

Eve glanced at the uniform who nodded toward a doorway.

Eve walked away from the weeping. Then, sealing up, walked into death.

CHAPTER TWO

It was a good-sized bedroom with a cozy little sitting area on the street side. She imagined Natalie had sat there to watch the world go by.

The bed looked female and fussy. Lots of pillows scattered around the room — some of them bloody now — that had likely been piled on the lacy pink-and-white spread, as some women loved to do.

There was a small wall screen angled to be seen from either bed or sitting area, framed pictures of flowers, a long dresser. There were bottles and whatnots on the floor — several broken — that had probably sat in some girlie arrangement on the dresser.

A couple of fluffy rugs graced the floor. Natalie was sprawled over one of them, legs twisted and bound at the ankles, her hands bound in front and clenched together as if in desperate prayer.

She wore pajamas, blue-and-white checked. They were spotted and streaked with blood. A robe, also blue, was tossed in a corner. The matching tie was wrapped around the woman's throat.

Blood stained both fluffy rugs, and a splotch of vomit pooled near the door. The room reeked of both, and of urine.

Eve moved to the body, crouched to do the standard ID test and gauge for time of death.

"Victim is Caucasian female, age twenty-six, identified as Copperfield, Natalie, residing this location. Facial bruising indicates trauma perimortem. Nose looks broken. Two fingers of the right hand also appear broken. There are burns visible on the shoulder where the pajama top is torn. More burns on the bottoms of both feet. Skin has a blue-gray cast consistent with strangulation. Eyes are bloodshot and bulging. Wit touched the body upon discovery, some scene contamination. TOD, 1.45a.m., approximately two hours before discovery."

She shifted as Peabody started in. "Watch the puke," she warned.

"Thanks. I've got two uniforms and a departmental counselor picking up the sister."

"Good. Vic's still wearing her pj's. Sexual assault isn't likely. Look here, around the mouth. See, was gagged at one time. Got some of the tape adhesive on her face. See the right pinky and ring fingers?"

"Ouch. Snapped them."

"Broke her fingers, broke her nose. Burned her. Lot of damage to her things that could have been caused in a fight, or by the killer to make a point."

Peabody crossed to a doorway. "Bath through here. No 'link in place by the bed, and one on the floor here."

"What does that tell you?"

"It looks like the vic grabbed the 'link, made a run for the bathroom. Maybe hoping to lock herself in, call for help. She didn't make it."

"Looks like. Wakes up, hears somebody in the apartment. Probably figures it's the sister. Maybe she calls out, or just starts to roll back over. Door opens. Not the sister. Grabs for the 'link, tries to run. Could be. New lock on the door — a good one, with a security peep. Maybe somebody's been bothering her. Run her, see if she's made any complaints in the last couple months."

She rose, walked to the hall door. "Killer comes in this way, she'd see him from the bed. Smart to grab the 'link, sprint off in the opposite direction toward a room with a lock. Pretty smart — quick thinking, too, if you've just woken from a sound sleep."

She moved back to the bed, walked around it, judging the distance toward the bath, and saw something glint just under the bed. She crouched down, then lifted a kitchen knife with her sealed fingers. "Now why would she have a carving knife in the bedroom?"

"Big-ass knife," Peabody returned. "Killer's?"

"Then why not use it? I bet it's from her kitchen. New locks," Eve continued, "and a knife by the bed. She was worried about someone."

"No complaints on file. If she was worried, she didn't report it."

Eve searched the bed, under the mattress, shook the pillows.

Then walked into the bath. Small, tidy, girlie again. Nothing to indicate the killer had been in it. But Eve pursed her lips when she went through the cabinet and found men's deodorant, Beard-B-Gone, and men's cologne.

"She had a guy," Eve said, moving back in to riffle through the nightstand drawers. "Condoms here, edible body oil."

"Bad breakup, maybe. New lock's a given if you'd given an ex access prior to. Could be he didn't like being dumped."

"Could be," Eve repeated. "That sort of deal usually includes sexual assault. Check her 'link for the incomings and outgoings last couple of days. I want to see the rest of the place."

She stepped out, reexamined the living area. Bad breakup, she'd expect the ex to bang on the door awhile. *Come on, Nat, goddamn it! Let me in. We gotta talk.* Guy's pissed enough, and the door's flimsy enough, most likely kick it down. But you never knew. She went into the kitchen. Good-sized, and from the looks of it, a place the vic had used. A knife block, with one missing, sat on the spotless white counter.

She worked her way into the second bedroom, set up as a home office. Lifted her brows. The place had been thoroughly tossed. The data-and-communication center Eve imagined had sat on the glossy steel desk was missing.

"No d-and-c unit in the office," she told Peabody.

"What kind of office is that?"

"Exactly. Not a single disc in there, either. As other electronics, just as easily lifted and hocked, are still on-scene, the comp was the target. The comp and the vic. So what did Natalie have that someone else wanted?"

"Not only enough to kill her, but to make sure she hurt first." Pity edged Peabody's voice as she glanced back toward the body. "Nothing on this 'link but the call from the sister, ten this morning, and a call out, at 7.30a.m., to Sloan, Myers, and Kraus. She called in sick. It's an accounting firm, offices on Hudson. Entries prior to this — actually yesterday morning — were deleted. EDD can dig them out. You want to listen to what there is?"

"Yeah, but let's take them in. I want a run at the sister again."

On the way to Central, Peabody read off background data on the victim from her PPC. "Born, Cleveland, Ohio. Parents — both teachers — still married. One sib — the sister, three years younger. No criminal. Accountant with Sloan, Myers, and Kraus the past four years. No marriages, no cohabs on record. Resided the Jane Street address past eighteen months. Previously on Sixteenth in Chelsea. Previous to that was Cleveland, parents' addy. She worked for an accounting firm there, part-time. Looks like a kind of internship while she was in college."

"Numbers cruncher, moves to New York. What's the lowdown on the firm here?"

"Hold on. Okay, big-deal firm," Peabody began, reading the data from her PPC. "High-dollar clients, several corporations. Three floors at the Hudson Street addy, employing about two hundred. Been around for over forty years. Oh, the vic was a senior account exec."

24

Eve chewed on it as she angled into the underground parking at Cop Central. "Guess she could get the skinny on some of those high-dollar clients. If somebody was running a second book, laundering. Tax evasion. Mobbed up. Another employee skimming. Blackmail, extortion, embezzlement."

"Firm's got a good rep."

"Doesn't mean all their clients or employees do. It's an angle."

They parked, headed toward the elevators. "We need the name of the boyfriend — past or present. Do the knock-on-doors at her building. See what she may have mentioned to her sister about work, or persona troubles. Way it looks, the vic was expecting or prepared for a problem — and one she didn't want to report, or hadn't decided to report. To the cops, anyway."

"Maybe to a coworker, though, or a superior, if it was work-related."

"Or a pal."

The higher they rose in the elevator, the more people jammed on. Eve could smell minty soap from someone coming on tour, and old sweat from someone going off a long one. She muscled her way off on her level.

"Let's set up an interview room," Eve began. "I don't want to talk to her in the lounge. Too many distractions. She needs the grief counselor, she can have him with her."

Eve swung through the bull pen, and on into her office first. Ditched her coat, then did a check on the witness's alibi. Palma Copperfield had worked the shuttle in from Las Vegas, and had been touching down in the downtown flight center just about the time her sister was strangled.

"Dallas."

Eve glanced over at Baxter, one of the detectives in her squad. "I haven't had coffee in two hours," she warned. "Or maybe three."

"I heard you had a Palma Copperfield up in the crib."

"Yeah, witness. Sister was strangled early this morning."

"Ah, shit." He scooped a hand back through his hair. "I was hoping I got it wrong."

"You know them?"

"Palma, a little. Not the vic. Met Palma a few months back — friend of a friend of a friend — at a party. We went out a couple times."

"She's twenty-three."

He scowled. "I'm not filing for frigging retirement any time soon. Anyway, it was nothing major. Nice woman. A real nice woman. Was she hurt?"

"No. Found her sister dead in the sister's apartment."

"Rough. Damn it. They were tight, I think. Palma said how she stayed with her sister when she came to New York. I dropped her off at the building — Jane Street — after we had dinner once."

"You still involved?"

"No — we weren't. Went out a couple of times, that's all." As if he didn't know quite what to do with them, Baxter slid his hands into his pockets. "Listen, if a familiar face would help, I can talk to her."

"Maybe. Yeah, maybe. Peabody's setting up an interview room. Lounge is too public for this. She was in bad shape when I took her initial statement. She mention if her sister was involved with anyone?"

"Ah, yeah. Had a guy — money manager, broker, something like that. Serious, I think, maybe engaged. Can't say that I paid much attention to that. I wasn't after the sister, you know?"

"You catch the wit, Baxter?"

"Nah." He smiled a little. "Like I said, she's a nice woman."

Which translated to they hadn't slept together, and made it less sticky to have him in on the interview. "Okay, let me get Peabody working the 'link. We'll take the wit."

Eve let Baxter walk into Interview ahead of her, studied Palma's tear-splotched face when the woman looked over. She blinked a few times as if trying to process new information, then a series of emotions streaked over her face. Recognition, relief, dismay, and finally the grief settled on it again.

"Bax. Oh, God." She held out both her hands, so when he crossed to the table, he took them in his.

"Palma, I'm so sorry."

"I don't know what to do. Nat. My sister, somebody killed her. I don't know what to do."

"We're going to help you."

"She never hurt anybody. Bax, she never hurt anybody in her whole life. Her face . . ."

"This is hard. The hardest thing. But you can help us help her."

"Okay. Okay, but you can stay, right? He can stay?" she asked Eve.

"Sure. What I'm going to do is turn the recorder on, and ask you some questions."

"You don't think that I . . . You don't think that I hurt her?"

"Nobody thinks that, Palma." Baxter gave her hand a quick squeeze. "We have to ask questions. The more we know, the faster we can find the person who did this."

"You're going to find them." She said it slowly, as if that, too, had to process. Then she closed her eyes for a moment. "You'll find them. I'll tell you everything I can."

Eve engaged the recorder, read in the necessary data. "You landed in New York early this morning, is that correct?"

"Yes, on the Vegas run. We got in around two, clocked out, I don't know, about twenty minutes later maybe. That's about right. Then Mae — she had the run with me — we stopped at the bar in the airport for a glass of wine. Unwind a little. We shared a cab into the city. I dropped her first. She keeps a place with a couple other attendants, over on the East Side. Then I went on to Nat's."

She stopped, took a breath, then a sip from the plastic cup of water on the table. "I paid off the cab, and started in. Had my key out, and I know Nat's code. But the lock was broken. It happens sometimes, so I didn't think that much about it. Not then. But when I got to her apartment, her lock — she told me she'd put in a new lock — that was broken, too. I had this little jump in my belly. But I thought, I don't know, I told myself she hadn't gotten the lock installed right."

"Did you notice anything off when you went inside — the living area's first," Eve said.

"I didn't really pay attention. I put the security chain on — she'd have left that off for me. And I left my overnight bag there by the door because I thought I'd just peek in, make sure everything was okay. But it wasn't."

Tears trembled, spilled again, but she kept going. "She was on the floor, and there was blood, and the room was — it was like there'd been a fight. Broken glass from her perfume bottles and the little bowls she liked to collect. She was on the floor. The pink rugs. I was with her when she bought them. They were soft, like a cat. She couldn't have pets. The rugs were soft. I'm sorry."

"You're doing fine," Baxter told her. "You're doing just fine."

"I ran. I think — it's all blurry. Did I scream? I think I screamed her name and I ran and I tried to lift her up, to shake her awake, even though I knew . . . I didn't want her to be dead. Her face was bruised and bloody, and her eyes. I knew she was dead. There was tape around her hands."

As if she'd just remembered, she sent Eve a shocked look. "Oh, God, her hands, her ankles. They were taped." Palma pressed a trembling hand to her mouth. "I needed to call for help, but I got sick before I could get out, get my 'link out of my bag, I got sick. Then I ran out. I couldn't stay in there, so I ran out and called nine-one-one, and I sat down on the steps. I should've gone back in, stayed with her. I shouldn't have left her alone like that."

"You did exactly the right thing." Baxter picked up the water cup, handed it to her again. "Exactly the right thing."

"Did she tell you anyone was bothering her?" Eve asked.

"No, but something was bothering her. I could tell. She looked upset when I talked to her earlier, but when I asked what was wrong, she said it was nothing to worry about. She just had a lot on her mind."

"She was seeing someone? A man?"

"Bick! Oh, my God, Bick. I didn't even think of him." Eyes flooded again; she pressed both hands to her mouth. "They're engaged. They're going to be married next May. Oh, my God, I have to tell him."

"What's his full name?"

"Bick, Bick Byson. They work together — well, for the same company. Different departments. Nat's a senior account executive at Sloan, Myers, and Kraus — accounting. Bick's a money manager there. They've been together almost two years now. How can I tell him?"

"It'd be better if we did that."

"And my parents." She began to rock, back and forth, back and forth. "I have to tell them. I don't want to do it over the 'link. Do I have to stay here? I need to go home, to Cleveland, and tell them Nat's gone. Nat."

"We can talk about that after we're done here," Eve told her. "Were your sister and her fiancé having any problems?"

30

"No. I don't know of any. They're crazy about each other. I guess I thought maybe they'd had a fight and that's why she was upset earlier. All the wedding plans, you get stressed out. But they're really happy together. They're great together."

"Did she have an engagement ring?"

"No." Palma took another long breath. "They decided against one — saving their money. Bick's great, but he's pretty frugal. Nat didn't mind. Well, Nat's the same way, you know? Save it for a rainy day."

"He didn't live with her? Save money paying rent."

"She wouldn't let him." For the first time Palma smiled again, and Eve could see how Baxter had been attracted. "She said they were going to wait for that until they were married. We're pretty old-fashioned in my family. I think my parents like to believe Nat wasn't even having sex with Bick. They loved each other," she murmured. "They were good together."

"Were there any problems at work?"

"She never said. I haven't seen her for about three weeks. I had a chance to take the New L.A. to Hawaii run for ten days, then I took a vacation out there with a couple of girlfriends. I'd just gotten back on the Vegas to New York run. I talked to her a couple of times, but . . . We were going to catch up, go shopping, go over wedding plans. She never said anything about a problem, work or otherwise, but I *know* something was wrong. I just wasn't paying enough attention."

Eve stepped out with Baxter. "You know anything about this fiancé of the vic's?"

"No." He rubbed the back of his neck. "Palma said something about her sister getting engaged. She was lit up about it, which is why . . . I backed off. Those things can be catching."

"Your commitment issues don't enter in, so set them aside. It helped you being in there with her, familiar face leveled her out some. Why don't you get her to a shuttle — stay on the clock. See she gets off to her parents."

"Appreciate that, Lieutenant. I can take lost time to do it."

"Stay on the clock," she repeated. "Make sure she understands I need her available. I want to know where she is, when she comes back. The usual routine."

"No problem. Feel so damn sorry for her. You're going to look at the boyfriend."

"Next stop."

"Byson didn't show at the office." Peabody hoofed it onto a glide behind Eve. "Which, according to his assistant, isn't the norm. Hardly ever misses, and always checks in if he's going to take off or be late. She tried him at home, and on his pocket 'link, being concerned, and couldn't reach him."

"Got his home addy?"

"Yeah, he's on Broome in Tribeca. According to his chatty assistant, he and the vic just bought the loft, and he's staying there while they're having some reno done before the wedding."

"We'll try him there."

"Could have rabbited," Peabody said as she hustled off one glide and hotfooted to the garage elevator. "Fights with fiancé, goes off on her, runs home. Runs away."

"It wasn't personal."

Peabody's eyebrows knitted as they clipped off the elevator and across the garage. "Those kind of facial injuries, and face-to-face strangulation often are."

"We find any tools on the crime scene?"

"Tools?"

"Screwdriver, hammer, laser scope?"

"No. What does . . . Oh." Nodding now, Peabody slid into the passenger seat. "The duct tape. If she didn't have any basic tools, why would she have duct tape? Killer brought it with him, which lessens the possibility of crime of passion."

"No sexual assault added to that. Broken locks. When the vic's sister talked to her hours before the murder, she got no indication of trouble in paradise. It wasn't personal," Eve repeated. "It was business."

The loft was in an old, well-preserved building in a neighborhood where people painted their stoops and sat out on them on warm summer evenings. The windows facing the street were wide, to afford the tenants a view of the traffic, and the shops ran from the mom-and-pop bakery/deli to the snazzy little boutiques where a pair of shoes cost the equivalent of a quick trip to Paris and would turn your feet into a study in misery.

Some of the units sported the luxury of balconies where, Eve imagined, people stuck plants and chairs in the good weather so they could sit and sip something cold while they watched their world go by.

From the looks of the exterior, it was a major step up from the Jane Street address, and one suited to the combined incomes of a couple of young, urban professionals on the rise.

Byson didn't respond to the buzzer, but before Eve could use her master, a woman's voice piped through the speaker. "You looking for Mr. Byson?"

"That's right." There was a security screen, and Eve held up her badge. "Police. You want to buzz us in?"

"Hold on."

The door buzzed; the locks clicked. They stepped into a tiny communal lobby where someone had gone to the trouble to set a leafy green plant in a colorful pot. Because she heard the elevator clanging its way down, Eve waited.

The woman who stepped off was dressed in a red sweater and gray pants, with her brown hair pulled back in a stubby tail from a pretty face. She had a baby of indeterminant age and sex perched on her hip.

"I buzzed you in," she said. "I'm Mr. Byson's neighbor. What's the problem?"

"That's something we need to discuss with him."

"I don't know if he's home." She jiggled the baby as she spoke. The kid stared owlishly at Eve, then plugged its thumb in its mouth and sucked as if it contained opium. "He should be at work this time of day."

"He's not."

"It's weird, because I usually hear him leave. We're on the same floor, and I hear the elevator. Didn't catch it today. And he had the plumber scheduled, turns out. When they're having one of the crews in — they're rehabbing — he stops by, asks me if I can let them in, you know? He didn't do that today, so I didn't. You can't be sure. Might be somebody with a pipe wrench just going in to rob the place."

"So you've got the key to his place?"

"Yeah, key and code. Something's wrong, isn't it? You want me to let you in? You've got to give me some idea. I wouldn't feel right letting you in if I don't know something's up."

"Something's up." Eve held up her badge again. "Mr. Byson's fiancée was killed."

"Oh, no." She shook her head slowly from side to side. "No. Come on. Not Nat."

Her voice rose and cracked. In response, the baby unplugged its mouth and wailed.

"You knew her." Eve took a subtle side step away from the baby.

"Sure. She was here a lot. They're getting married in a few months." The woman's eyes filled as she shifted to hold her baby closer. "I liked her a lot. We're all looking forward to being neighbors. Bick and Nat, me and my husband. We . . . I can't believe it. What happened? What happened to Nat?"

"We need to talk to Mr. Byson."

"God. God. Okay, okay." Obviously shaken, she turned to call for the elevator. "It's going to kill him. Ssh, Crissy, ssh." She bounced and jiggled and patted the baby as they jammed into the elevator. "They were nuts about each other — but not sickening about it, if you get me. I liked her so much. Maybe there's a mistake."

"I'm sorry," was all Eve said. "Did she mention any problems? Anything, anyone bothering her?"

"No, not really. Some wedding jitters, just typical stuff. They were getting married up in Cleveland, where she's from. Hunt and I were going — our first trip since Crissy came. Hunt's my husband. Look, I'll go get the key," she added when the doors opened into a hallway. "That's his place, there. We share the floor."

"Just the two units up here?"

"Yeah. Nice space. Good light. Hunt and I bought our apartment when I got pregnant. It's a nice neighborhood, and we've got three bedrooms."

She unlocked her own door, tirelessly jiggling the baby who now had the slack-jawed, glaze-eyed look of a satisfied junkie. Holding the door open with one hip, she snatched a set of keys from a bowl on a table by the door.

"We didn't get your name," Eve told her.

"Oh, sorry. Gracie, Gracie York." She turned the key in the lock, typed a code in on a minipad over it. "Maybe Bick had errands to run or something. I didn't hear him go out before, so he must've left early. Crissy's been fussy so I slept in a little this morning. She's teething." Gracie started to open the door, but Eve held up a hand to block her.

"Just a minute." Eve knocked. "Mr. Byson," she called out. "This is the police. Open the door, please."

"I really don't think he's home," Gracie began.

"Even so, we'll wait a minute before going in." Eve knocked again. "Mr. Byson, this is Lieutenant Dallas, NYPSD. We're coming in."

The minute she opened the door, Eve knew Byson was home, and that his neighbor's earlier words had been right on the mark. Natalie Copperfield's murder had killed him. Or, Eve was banking, her murderer certainly had.

"Ohmygodohmygodohmygod!" Gracie babbled the words so that they came out in a single high-pitched hysterical stream as she pressed her baby's face to her shoulder and stumbled back from the doorway.

"Ms. York, go back inside your apartment," Eve ordered. "Go back in, lock your door. Either my partner or I will be over in just a minute."

"It's Bick. Is it Bick? Right across the hall. We're right across the hall."

At a wordless signal from Eve, Peabody took the woman's arm. "Take Crissy back home," Peabody said gently. "Take her on in. Nothing's going to happen to her. Just go inside and wait."

"I don't understand. He must be dead. Right across the hall."

Peabody got the neighbor inside, turned back to Eve with a resigned look on her face. "I guess you want me to take her."

"You're damn right. Call it in first, Peabody, then go in, get a formal statement from the neighbor. I'll get the field kits and start on the scene."

CHAPTER
THREE

Once she'd retrieved the kits, Eve sealed her hands, sprayed sealant on her boots. With her recorder engaged, she entered the crime scene.

Side window, she noted, facing the neighboring building, and with a narrow balcony. "South-facing window is open," she said for the record, and moved around the outer edge of the room for a closer look. "Appears to have been forced open from the outside. Emergency evac here, probably used to gain access. Possibly exited by the same route."

Safer that way, Eve thought. No chance of the next-door neighbors catching you coming or going.

She turned from where she believed the killer had entered. "The body's face up, hands and feet bound with duct tape, as previous vic. Second vic is mix-race male, late-twenties, wearing only a pair of white boxers. Woke up, didn't you, Bick, heard somebody out here. Gave him some trouble. Signs of struggle apparent. Overturned table, broken lamp. Not all of this blood's going to be the victim's, so there's a break for our side. Victim's face and body show bruises and lacerations."

She worked her way in, then crouched by the body. "Some burn marks here, too, but these look like contact burns from a stunner mid-chest. They fight, killer incapacitates Byson with a stun, binds him, beats him. Questions him? Blue plastic cord of some kind used for strangulation."

Hunkered where she was, she scanned the room again. "There are some building materials in the north corner of the room, tied with blue plastic cord, like that around the vic's neck."

She took the prints for confirmation of ID, bagged his hands.

"Time of death," she said as she read her gauge, "2.45a.m. Came here after doing Copperfield." She bent closer. "Traces of adhesive around the mouth, as per previous victim. Why yank it off? Needed you to tell him something? Wanted to hear you choke as he strangled you? Maybe some of both."

She straightened to move from the body into the room off the living area. Bachelor's bunking area, she deduced. Probably not the master, but where he was sleeping during the rehab. Mattress on a pallet, and the mate of the broken lamp on one of the two tables by the bed. Clothes strewn around, but in a way that said messy guy rather than search.

"Woke up. Grabbed one of the lamps for a weapon. The woman, she grabs for her 'link and tries to run, but the guy's got a different instinct. Protect the cave. Goes out, tangles with the killer. Surprises him maybe. Fight. Bruising on vic's knuckles indicate he got a couple hits in anyway. Full-contact stun, and he goes down."

She walked back out, studied the positioning again. "Killer tapes hands and feet, gags him. Doesn't kill him straight away, then. Why gag him if he's stunned? Has something to say or do first, then. Questions to ask. Did you tell him what you did to Natalie? Bet you did."

She did a quick preliminary walk-through. The loft had three bedrooms, as the neighbor said hers did. The largest of them was empty but for more building supplies. The last was set up as an office. But there was no comp unit. She could see where there'd been one, probably covered with a protective cloth when construction was on the slate. There was a coat of dust on the folding table standing as a desk, and a clear spot on it where a computer would have stood.

She was back in the living area studying the open window when Peabody came in.

"Neighbor's shook, but she's solid. I let her contact her husband, ask him to come home from work. He left, by the way, about seven this morning. Wit says her husband and the vic here sometimes hit the health club together before work. They obviously didn't hook up this morning."

"His TOD's about an hour after Copperfield's. Same MO. No comp on premises, no discs."

"They had something on someone," Peabody concluded. "Work-related probably. Knew something, heard something, worked on something. That how he got in?" she asked, lifting her chin toward the window.

"It's been forced. Evac's here on this level, but he likely exited that way. Could have sent it back up from the ground. We'll want the sweepers to dust the controls. Won't be prints, but it keeps them busy."

40

She ran through the scene, and her take of it, for her partner.

"Maybe some DNA on the pieces of the lamp, some on the vic's fists." Peabody looked down at the body. "Guy was in good shape. Looks like he gave his attacker some trouble."

"Not enough."

They left the crime scene in the hands of the sweepers and headed for the accounting firm.

"You know, seeing the kid back there reminded me. How'd the coaching class go last night?"

"It's not to be discussed," Eve said. "Ever."

"Aw, come on."

"Ever."

To hide a smirk, Peabody glanced out the side window and looked longingly at a corner glide-cart. "Baby shower's coming right up. You set?"

"Yeah, yeah, yeah." Or she hoped she was.

"I made her this sweet baby blanket while I was in the weaving mode over the holidays. It's all rainbow colors. I'm doing these cute little booties and a hat, too. What'd you get her?"

"I don't know."

"You haven't gotten her shower gift yet? Cutting it close."

"I got a few days." Considering, Eve glanced over. "You could go buy something to cover it. I'll pay you."

"Uh-uh. It's not right." Peabody folded her arms. "She's your oldest friend, your best pal, having her first baby. You have to buy it yourself."

"Damn it. Damn it, damn it."

"I'll go with you, though. We can swing by this baby place she's been haunting after we hit the offices. Grab some lunch, too, maybe."

Eve imagined the process of shopping in a baby boutique, and had to fight off a shudder. "I'll give you a hundred dollars to go on your own."

"That's hitting below the belt," Peabody replied. "But I'm too strong to be bribed. You have to do the thing, Dallas. It's Mavis."

"Coaching classes, baby showers, now shopping. Is there no end to the price of friendship?"

Eve put it aside — buried it — and made her way to the main reception area of Sloan, Myers, and Kraus.

In keeping with their service of high-end clients, the area was plush, glass-walled, and full of green, leafy plants. The wide stone-gray counter served as a work area for three receptionists, all of whom wore headsets and worked busily on keyboards. A trio of waiting areas fanned out like sunbeams, boasting deep chairs, media screens, and a selection of entertainment discs.

Eve laid her badge on the counter in front of a three-piece-suited man with streaked blond hair worn in short, tight curls. "I want to see someone in charge."

He gave her a cheerful smile. "That certainly wouldn't be me. In charge of a specific department, or altogether in charge?"

"Let's start small. I want Natalie Copperfield's and Bick Byson's supervisors."

"Let's see. Copperfield's Senior Account Exec, Corporate, Foreign and International. That's this floor. You'll want Cara Greene. And ah, Byson, Byson.

Byson, Bick," he all but sang as he read his screen. "Vice President, Personal Finance, Domestic. That's up a level, and it would be Myra Lovitz."

"We'll take Greene first."

"She's in a meeting."

Eve tapped her badge. "Not anymore, she's not."

"Okay by me. I'll call through. You want to have a seat?"

"No, just Greene."

Swank place, Eve thought as she waited. A lot of money came through these doors. And nothing tempted murder so much as lots of money.

Cara Greene wore a dark red suit, and though it buttoned to the throat, it was cut in such a way that showed she had a nice, perky rack. She also had an impatient expression on a smooth, caramel-toned face, and clipped out into reception on ice-pick heels.

"You're the police?" she demanded and shot an accusing finger at Eve.

"Lieutenant Dallas, Detective Peabody. You're Greene?"

"That's right, and you've just pulled me out of an important meeting. If my son's hooked school again, I'll deal with him. I don't appreciate the cops coming to my office."

"We're not here about your son. We're here about Natalie Copperfield, and if you'd prefer, you can come to my office. Now."

The irritation shifted immediately to wariness. "What about Natalie? You're not going to tell me she's in any trouble. She'd never break the law."

"Can we take this into your office, Ms. Greene?"

The expression changed again, and this time there were hints of fear in bottle-green eyes. "Something happened to her? Was there an accident? Is she all right?"

"Your office would be best."

"Come with me." Moving fast, Cara skirted around the reception desk, through a pair of glass doors that swished open on her approach. She kept up the brisk pace, past a jungle of cubes where the drones slaved away, past offices where accountants crunched their numbers, to the corner office that suited her position.

She shut the door behind them, turned to Eve. "Tell me fast. Please."

"Ms. Copperfield was murdered early this morning."

Her breath hitched, a quick in and out before she held up a hand. She moved, not so briskly now, to a refreshment station along one wall, pulled out a bottle of chilled water. And sank to a chair without opening it.

"How? How? I don't understand. I should have known something was wrong when she called in sick yesterday and didn't make this meeting this morning. I should have known. I was so mad at her. This meeting . . ." She held up her hand again. "I'm sorry. I'm sorry. It's such a shock."

Before Eve could speak, she lurched to her feet. "Oh, God, Bick. Her fiancé. Does he know? She's engaged to one of the vp's in personal finance. He should be upstairs. Oh, God. They're getting married in May."

"She worked for you directly?"

"She's one of my senior account execs and on a fast track. She's good. I mean . . . Oh, God, oh, God, she *was* good. Excellent. Personable, smart, hard-working. I planned to promote her, offer her a vp slot."

"You were friends," Peabody put in.

"Yes. Not best pals. I have to keep some distance being her boss, but yes." Closing her eyes, she pressed the chilled bottle to her forehead. "We were very friendly. I can't believe this is happening."

"Why don't you tell us where you were between midnight and four this morning."

"You don't think . . ." Cara sat again, and this time she opened the water bottle and drank. "I was home, with my husband and our twelve-year-old son. My husband and I went to bed just after midnight. God, how was she killed?"

"We're not releasing the details of that at this time. Since you were friendly, and you were in a position of authority, did she say anything to you about being worried or bothered? Threatened?"

"No. No. No. I'd say she seemed a little off the past couple of weeks, but I put that down to distraction. Wedding plans. She'd have told Bick if someone was bothering her. She told him everything."

Yeah, Eve thought, most likely she did. And that's why he was dead.

"What was she working on?"

"She had several accounts, heads quite a number and is on teams that hold others."

"We're going to need a list of all her accounts, and we'll need to see her files."

"I can't do that. I can't. We have to protect our clients' privacy. We'd be sued up the butt if I turned confidential files over to the police."

"We'll get a warrant."

"Please do. I mean that, sincerely. Please get a warrant and I'll personally see that you have any and all data the law demands. I need to contact Mr. Kraus," she continued as she got back to her feet. "I need to tell him what's going on. What's happened. And Bick. You'll need to talk to Bick."

"Bick Byson was also murdered early this morning."

She lost all of her color, every drop of it. "I — I can't think. I don't know what to say. This is horrible."

"I'm sorry. I understand it's a shock. We need to speak with Mr. Byson's supervisor."

"Um, that's — oh, God, I can't think. Myra. Myra Lovitz. I can contact her for you."

"I'd prefer you didn't talk to her until we have. Who else would have worked on accounts with Ms. Copperfield?"

"I'll get you a list of names. Sorry." She clipped to her desk, yanked open a drawer, pulled out a tissue. "Sorry, it's starting to sink in. I can call upstairs, have Myra's admin tell her you're coming. Would that help?"

"That'd be good. Thanks for your cooperation. We'll be back, with a warrant, for the files."

Upstairs, they were met by the admin and escorted straight back into an office similar to Cara's.

Myra Lovitz sat behind a desk covered with files, discs, notes. She was into her early sixties, Eve judged, and had let her hair go stone gray in a way that suited her tough, sharp-angled face. She wore a suit — blue

46

pinstriped and all business. She smiled sourly as Eve and Peabody came in.

"Okay, what is this, a raid?"

"We're here concerning Bick Byson."

Even the sour smile faded. "Something happen to the boy? We've been trying to reach him all morning."

"He's dead. He was murdered last night."

Her lips folded in, her hands fisted on the desk. "Goddamn city. Goddamn it. Mugged?"

"No."

Eve let Peabody take point on this one, ask the questions, get the statements. It was nearly a replay of the first interview, but with Myra's more acerbic style.

"He's a damn good kid. Smart, reliable. Knows how to schmooze the clients when they need it, how to be all biz when they want that. Good reader of people, you know? He and that sweet kid from accounts downstairs? Both of them? God, what a world."

"What were they working on?" Peabody asked her.

"They? Bick and Natalie didn't work on the same accounts. He did individuals, domestic, she did corporate, primarily foreign."

"How did he seem to you the last couple of weeks?"

"A little jumpy, now that you mention it. Wedding coming up, and they just bought a place in Tribeca. Having it rehabbed, doing decorating, furniture shopping. Man's bound to be jumpy."

"He didn't mention any concerns to you?"

"No." Her eyes sharpened. "This wasn't just some random killing, was it? Are you telling me someone deliberately murdered those two kids?"

"No, ma'am," Eve interrupted. "We're not telling you anything just now."

After starting the ball rolling on the warrant, Eve wanted only one thing. To get back to Central, and from there do both her written and oral reports, write up her timeline, start her murder board.

But Peabody would not be denied.

"You put it off, you'll be sorry, and you'll have to shop by yourself for baby stuff."

"I'm not shopping, with or without you. I'm just going to buy something. And it better not take over ten minutes."

"Then we can get food, right?"

"It's always something with you. There probably won't be anywhere to park. I should just get something online. You can just tell me what I should get and I'll get it. Isn't that enough?"

"No."

"Bitch."

"You'll thank me when Mavis gets all soft and gooey."

"I don't like soft and gooey unless it comes in chocolate."

"Speaking of chocolate, what kind of cake are we having for the shower?"

"I don't know."

Sincerely shocked, Peabody jerked around in her seat. "You didn't get *cake*?"

"I don't know. Probably." Because the idea of the shower, what she had to do, hadn't done, should do, made her stomach jitter, Eve squirmed. "Look, I called the caterer, okay? I did it myself. I didn't dump it on Roarke, I didn't ask — God forbid — Summerset to handle it."

"Well, what did you ask for? What's the theme?"

The jitters escalated into a roiling. "What do you mean, theme?"

"You don't have a *theme*? How can you have a baby shower without a theme?"

"Jesus Christ, I need a theme? I don't even know what that means. I called the caterer. I did my job. I told her it was a baby shower. I told her how many people, more or less. I told her when and where. She started asking me all kinds of questions, which gives me a fucking headache, and I told her not to ask me all kinds of questions or she was fired. Just to do whatever needed doing. Why isn't that enough?"

Peabody's sigh was long and heartfelt. "Give me the caterer's info, and I'll check in with her. Does she do the decorations, too?"

"Oh, my God. I need decorations?"

"I'm going to help you, Dallas. I'm going to run interference with the caterer. I'm going to come over early on the day and help get it set up."

Eve narrowed her eyes and tried to ignore the joy and relief bubbling in her breast. "And what's this going to cost me?"

"Nothing. I like baby showers."

"You're a sick, sick woman."

"Look, look! That car's going to pull out. Get the space! Get the space! It's first level, almost at the door. It's a sign from the goddess of fertility or something."

"Damn Free-Ager," Eve mumbled, but beat out a Minibug for the parking slot.

She thought she'd hate shopping in a baby boutique. And Eve was a woman who knew herself well.

There were gargantuan stuffed animals and mind-numbing music. There were tiny little chairs, strange mesh cages, other animals, or poofy stars hanging from the walls and ceiling. Racks were full of odd miniature outfits. There were shoes no bigger than her thumb. Thumb-sized shoes, she thought, were unnatural. Nothing that small should be able to walk on two legs, so why did it require shoes?

Things rocked and swayed and played more tinkling music if you looked at them crooked.

And there were a number of gestating women, and others who carried the fruit of their wombs in colorful slings or strange padded seats that hooked over their shoulders. One of those fruits was wailing in a thin, alien cry.

And there were others, bigger ones, who sat in pushcarts or wandered around free to pummel the animals or climb on everything in sight.

"Courage," Peabody soothed, and clamped a hand on Eve's arm before Eve tried to bolt.

"Just point at something and I'll buy it. Whatever it is. Cost is no object."

"It doesn't work like that. We go to one of the screens, see? She registered. So we find out what she wants, and what people already bought for her. They have great stuff here."

"Why does something that can't walk, talk, or feed itself need so much stuff?"

"For exactly those reasons. And babies need stimulation, and comfort. Here we go." Peabody engaged a screen. A fresh-faced young woman popped on, smiling cheerfully.

"Welcome to the White Stork! How can we help you?"

"Registration list for Mavis Freestone, please."

"Right away! Would you like to see the entire list of Ms. Freestone's choices, or what is left to be fulfilled?"

"What's left," Eve said quickly. "Just what's left."

"Just one moment!"

"Why does she talk like that?" Eve questioned Peabody. "Like I'm brain dead."

"She's not —"

"Dallas?"

Such was the state of Eve's nerves she nearly jumped at the sound of her name. Turning, she saw Tandy Willowby waddling toward her. "Oh, and it's Peabody, right? We met at Mavis's once."

"Sure, I remember. How you doing?"

"Really good." Tandy patted her belly. "Nearly coming to countdown. Are you here for Mavis?"

"Just tell me what to buy." Eve was ready to beg. "I'm on the clock."

"No problem. Actually, I've got just the thing. Cancel registration search," she ordered. "It may be more than you want to spend —"

"I don't care about that. Just wrap it up."

"It's a little too big. You know, I've had to waylay Mavis a dozen times, convince her not to buy the place out, to wait until after the shower. She's got her heart set on this rocker system."

Tandy moved through the aisles, leading the way through forests and meadows of baby merchandise with her long tail of sunny hair swinging. "I talked my boss into ordering one in, in Mavis's colors. I knew if she didn't get it as a gift, she'd snag it after the shower. I'll show you our display model, then you can look at the one we ordered on screen. It's in the warehouse."

"It'll be fine. Great. I'll just pay for it. Hey!" Eve snapped when Peabody elbowed her.

"At least look at it."

"Oh, you've got to see it," Tandy agreed, her baby blue eyes wide and guileless. "It's absolutely mag."

What Eve saw when Tandy gestured was a minty green cushy deal sort of shaped like a long S, that for some reason made Peabody coo.

"It reclines, rocks, sways, vibrates, and plays music. There are twenty tunes in the default, and you can record and playback or download others. Or just the sound of the mother's voice, the father's voice, whatever you like." Tandy ran a gentle hand over the top curve. "The material is stain and water resistant, and so soft. Just feel."

Because it was obviously a requirement, Eve patted the chair. "Nice. Soft. Cushy. I'll take it."

"You *have* to sit in it," Tandy insisted.

"I don't —"

"Go on, Dallas." Peabody gave Eve a nudge. "Try it out. You have to."

"Jesus, all right, all right." Feeling idiotic, Eve lowered to the chair, and felt it shift, just a bit, like a live thing. "It moved."

"The gel cushions mold to your shape." Tandy beamed. "It'll adjust to you, or you can program a preferred setting — manually, or by voice recognition. Positions, movements, all can be adjusted manually or by voice — controls are under both arm pads — for right- or left-hand use. Just flip it open with a finger."

Tandy demonstrated, revealing the board. "And there's a new feature on the Delux model Mavis is loopy for. Baby sleeping, Mum's tired?" Tandy tapped three buttons, and the chair hummed gently as its side opened and a small padded box lifted out and up.

"You just shift, lay the baby in the chair-side cradle, and both of you can take a little nap."

"That is so completely uptown." Peabody cooed again, like a mourning dove.

"It's safe for up to twenty pounds, will also rock independent of the chair. There's also a small storage compartment on the other side, to hold burp cloths, nursing pads, extra receiving blankets. I swear, it'll do everything but feed and change the baby for you."

"Okay." With some relief, Eve pulled herself out of the chair.

"It got top ratings from *Baby Style, Parenting,* and *Today's Family* magazines. The Mommy Channel had it as their top pick last year."

"Sold."

"Really?" A happy flush pinked Tandy's cheeks. "Oh, that's brilliant. That's mag."

"You can get it to the house, right, for the shower?"

"Absolutely. And since I have some pull around here, I'll arrange for the second delivery to Mavis's apartment to be included. No extra charge."

"Appreciate it." As an afterthought, Eve studied the chair again. "How much is this thing?"

When Tandy named the price, Peabody gulped audibly. Eve just stared and said, "Holy crap."

"I know, it's awfully dear, but it's really worth the price. And I can offer you a ten percent discount on anything purchased today if you open a White Stork account."

"No, no thanks." That, Eve thought as she rubbed her hands over her face, might just be tempting fate. "I'll pay the full shot. The one in the colors Mavis likes."

"It's a fully awesome gift, Dallas," Peabody told her.

"It is. It really is." Tandy's eyes actually went damp. "She's so lucky to have a friend like you."

"Damn right."

It's only money, Eve reminded herself as she completed the transaction. Only a whole shitload of money. While she reeled from sticker shock, Peabody and Tandy bubbled on about babies, the shower, baby gadgets. When they segued into breast-feeding, Eve drew her line.

"We gotta go. Crime and stuff."

"I'm so glad you stopped in, and not just because of the sale. I just can't wait until the shower on Saturday.

My social life's a little thin these days," she added with an easy laugh. "Mavis's baby shower is the highlight on my calendar. Except for this one's birthday." She patted her belly. "The rocker system will be delivered the day before, by noon. Any problems, any at all, just contact me here."

"Will do. Thanks, Tandy."

"See you soon!"

It was with gratitude that Eve stepped out of the warm, scented, musical air and into the cold, windy noise of the city. "What time is it, Peabody?"

"Ah, about thirteen-thirty."

"I want to go lie down in a dark room."

"Well . . ."

"On duty, no rest for the traumatized. Soy fries will have to substitute for the comfort of oblivion."

"We eat?" Peabody nearly did a dance. "We should go shopping more often."

"Bite your tongue."

CHAPTER
FOUR

Eve wasn't sure what it said about her that she was more comfortable in the morgue than in a baby boutique. And she didn't actually care. The cold white walls, the scent of death under the piney odors of cleansers were the familiar.

She pushed through the thick door into Autopsy as Morris, the chief medical examiner, transferred Bick Byson's brain from his skull to a scale.

"A two-for-one sale, I see." Morris — his spiffy suit of the day protected with a clear plastic cape — paused to enter data. Then he set the brain in a tray.

He wasn't tall, but he was built in a way the chocolate brown suit and dull gold T-shirt exploited. He was oddly sexy with those dark, slightly slanted eyes and the ink black hair scooped back in a tight, intricate braid.

"That's how I see it," Eve agreed. "You concur. Same method, same killer?"

"Physical force and trauma. In technical terms, he whaled away on them. Binding, ankles, wrists. I'd be very surprised if the CSIs don't find the tape came from the same roll for both your vics. Death by strangulation on each. Male vic was stunned — full contact just above the sternum. He also has, as you noted in your on-scene, bruises and lacerations on his knuckles. He fought back. I removed a few bits of ceramic from his back and buttocks."

"Broken lamp. Looks like he grabbed it from the bedroom, came out into the living area, tried to use it as a weapon on the intruder."

"No postmortem trauma on either. When your killer was done, he was done. No sexual assault on either. Your female vic . . ."

Morris wiped his sealed hands, then skirted around to where Natalie lay, cleaned, naked, and tagged.

"That's not your Y-cut," Eve observed with a frown as she studied the body.

"Quite an eye you have there, Dallas." And his own twinkled with amusement. "No, I supervised a new ME. Our motto around here is Die To Learn. The female was tortured before death. Broken fingers. The angle and position of the breaks indicate a backward thrust."

Morris held up his own hand, gripped his pinky with the other, and pulled it back and down. "Effective, and painful."

Eve remembered the breathless, shocking pain when her father had snapped the bone in her arm. "Yeah. Yeah, it is."

"Burning — shoulder, belly, bottoms of the feet. Looks like contact burns with a laser pointer or something very similar. See the circular shape? It had to be pressed down very hard, very firm to not only burn the skin, but to leave that defined a burn."

To get a better look, she slid on a pair of microgoggles. "No blurring, or very little on these. Her feet were bound tight at the ankles, but she'd jerk and struggle when he burned her. Had to clamp onto her foot with his hand, hold it still. Very serious about his work."

She pulled off the goggles. "Her nose is broken."

"Yes, but when we use the micros, you can see the detail bruising, both sides of the nostrils." He picked up the pair Eve had laid aside, then offered them to Peabody when Eve jerked a thumb at her partner.

Putting them on, Peabody leaned down. "I just see a big mess of bruising." She focused, frowning, as Morris shined a pinpoint light over the side of Natalie's nose.

"Okay, yeah. I get it. I don't think I'd have seen it, but I get it now. He had her mouth taped, then he clamped her nose closed — hard, with his thumb and finger. Cut off her air."

"With the broken nose she'd have had considerable trouble breathing. He made it harder."

"Interrogating her," Eve said to Morris. "If it was a straight torture killing, he'd have done more. Cut her up some, broken more bones, burned her more severely and over more of her body. There'd most likely be some sexual abuse, or trauma to the breasts and genitals."

"Agreed. He just wanted to hurt her. On the male, he skipped the interrogation portion of the program. Went from beating to strangling."

"Because the woman told him what he needed to know, gave him what he needed to have," Peabody concluded.

"And the second vic had to die because the first told the killer her boyfriend knew what she knew, or had seen what she'd seen. The motive's in her," Eve murmured.

At Central, Eve sat at her desk downing coffee and adding data and notes to her initial reports. She put in another call to the PA's office to check on the warrant, got the runaround.

Lawyers, she thought. The accounting firm's lawyers had knee-jerked a motion to block the warrant. Not unexpected, Eve mused, but they'd get it — not likely before the end of the business day, however.

She knee-jerked herself and called to harass the lab. The evidence had been gathered, was being processed. They weren't miracle workers. Blah, blah.

What she had was two DBs — a couple — killed in their separate homes a few blocks apart, about an hour apart. Female first. Same employer, different departments. Violent deaths, missing comp units and data discs.

No known enemies.

The killer had to have personal transportation, she mused. Can't go hauling d-and-c units from murder scene to murder scene.

Frowning, she checked her incoming to see if Peabody had determined the types of units the victims owned. And found her efficient partner had copied her the list of units registered to both. Two desk units, two PPCs.

And that didn't include the memo books — no required registration with CompuGuard — they must have owned, which, like the comps, hadn't been on either scene.

Good equipment and fairly compact, she thought as she took a look at the models, but she couldn't see the killer hauling Copperfield's machines up Byson's emergency evac.

No, he'd had a vehicle to transport them, to lock them safely away while he finished his night's work.

Where did he park? Did he live close to either scene? Did he work alone?

Brought the binding tape with him, and probably the stunner, the laser pointer or whatever tool he'd used for the burns — preparation. Used weapons on hand for the killings. Opportunistic.

Knew female vic's building lacked security cams, alarms. And that the second scene had better security. Scoped them out first, preparation again. And/or had personal knowledge of the scenes.

Had he been inside before the murders?

Prior personal contact with the victims?

She rose, set up her board, then sat again, angling her chair so she could study the faces of her dead.

"What did you know, Natalie? What did you have? What did you figure out? Had you worried, whatever it was."

Called in sick the morning of the murder. Put on an extra lock, security peep, in a place you were moving out of in a few months. Yeah, you were worried.

But not enough to tell the sister, or the boss she was allegedly friendly with.

But Bick went into work that morning. Maybe not as worried, maybe to keep an ear to the ground.

And not worried, not scared enough to have the boyfriend come over, stay the night.

Not scared for your life, Eve concluded, despite the knife in the bedroom. Shook, upset, nervous — careful. But not scared for your life. Probably felt stupid, even a little embarrassed when you brought that knife into the bedroom with you. But you're not scared enough to call the cops, even move in with the fiancé for a few days.

Maybe working on something. Liked your space, your quiet. But it gets dark, you're a little wiggy.

To refresh herself, she called up the replay from Palma's pocket 'link, reviewed the transmission to her sister.

Hey, Nat!

Tmid:Palm. Where are you?

Somewhere over Montana. Vegas/New York runs, remember. We're loaded with them today. Back and forth, full shuttles. I'm getting into New York late. Still okay if I crash with you, right?

Sure. I really want to see you. I've missed you.

Me, too. Hey, something wrong?

No. No. Just a lot on my mind.

You had a fight with Bick.

No. We're fine. I'm just . . . there's a lot going on. It's . . . listen, you're off tomorrow, right?

After a shift like this, you bet. Want to ditch work and have a girl day?

I really do. We could do some shopping.

Wedding plans.

Yeah. And I could clear my head, maybe run something by you.

You're not changing your colors?

What? No, no. It's nothing to do with that. It's about —

Damn, Five A's beeping me again.

You go. We'll talk about it tomorrow morning. Oh, you've got the new key, the code I sent you this morning?

Right here. Sweetie, you look so tired. What — oh, for God's sake. Beep, beep, beep. Sorry, Nat.

It's okay. You go. I'll see you soon. Palma, I'm really glad we'll have some time.

Me, too. Pancakes for breakfast?

You bet.

Bye!

Stress level up on the vic, Eve thought. No need to run a voice analysis. She could hear it plainly and see it in the vic's eyes. Not fear, but tension and fatigue.

She was going to tell her sister, whatever it was. Lay it out for her as she'd laid it out, Eve was sure, for her fiancé. Lucky for Palma, she'd been out of the loop at the time of the murders.

Looking for advice, someone to share the burden. I know this thing, found this thing, suspect this thing. I'm not sure what I should do.

62

Closing her eyes, Eve brought Natalie's apartment back into her mind. Female, tidy, matching this and matching that. The clothes Eve had pawed through had been the same. Definite style. Hardworking accountant. Practical and organized. New lock. Careful and cautious.

Whatever she'd known or had that had killed her, she hadn't known or had it long. Eve judged Natalie Copperfield as a woman who knew her mind.

Shared the information with someone else besides the boyfriend, maybe. If so, it had been the wrong person.

Taking the list provided, Eve began a standard run on the victim's coworkers, superiors, and the heads of the firm. Then she tagged Peabody on the interdepartment 'link. "Do a search and run on the other tenants in Copperfield's building. Maybe she saw something at home, or in the neighborhood."

"I was heading there. Just went over the statement from the neighbors, both scenes. Nothing on the surface on either."

"So we go under. I got the click on a search of their financials. I'll look there."

"They weren't blackmailers. There's no vibe."

"We look anyway."

No vibe, Eve agreed, but brought up Natalie's data. What she found was, she supposed, what should be expected for a number cruncher. Organized, frugal, balanced accounts. The occasional spree, and a big, fat chunk laid out three months before at White Wedding for a dress, veil, undergarments.

There hadn't been any fancy wedding dress in the apartment. Eve relayed the same to Peabody.

"It would have to be fitted," she was informed. "They'd probably keep it at the shop, and schedule fittings up to a week or so before the big day."

"Oh. Right. Let's check anyway, be sure."

"Got a couple minor possessions — illegal substance — on the first-floor tenant, first scene. Pauli, Michael. Last one three years back. A D-and-D, and a shoplifting charge on tenant on second scene. Neither recent."

"I've been running the office. I'm going to shoot that data to you — you keep at it — and head up to EDD. See if they've dug anything off her pocket 'link."

"I can go to EDD."

"I'm not sending you up there to play grab-ass with McNab."

"Aw."

"Run the names, Peabody. Anything pops, tag me. Otherwise, send the results back to my unit here, and at home. Clock out when you're done. You can go home and play grab-ass."

"He doesn't have much to grab, but what there is —"

To save herself, Eve cut the transmission. She saved herself again by taking the glides rather than the elevator to EDD. At change of tour, the elevators were a box of bodies and odors. The glides were bad enough, jammed with cops coming on, going off, bringing in subjects for questioning, hauling others down to Booking.

Eve squirmed her way off and took the stairs to the last level. She came out into the corridor of the EDD unit and was all but blinded by the wild squiggly pattern of blue lightning bolts on violent pink that only Ian McNab would call a shirt.

"I want to know where you shop," she demanded.

"Huh? Hey, Dallas."

"Because I never want to make the lethal mistake of going there." She dug out credits. "Get me a tube of Pepsi from that sarcastic, sadistic thing people call a vending machine."

"Sure." He caught the credits she tossed him.

Peabody was right, at least about the fact he didn't have much ass. He was built like a reed, dressed like a circus star, and had the soul of an e-geek.

His hair was slicked back in a blond tail leaving his thin, pretty face unframed. There were countless silver hoops in his left ear. She wondered why he didn't list to that side when he walked.

"I caught your case," he told her, and tossed her the tube. "Just on my way back from making a pit stop. About to tag you."

"You got something for me?"

"Got the first vic's trans, seven days back. Can get you more. See, even when you clear the 'link, the trans are on the hard drive for —"

"I don't want a nerd lesson, just the results."

"Come on back."

If Homicide was business casual, EDD was haute couture. On Venus. McNab's lightning bolts sizzled among a storm of clashing colors, shiny materials, gel-boots, and pounds of body adornments. Where Homicide hummed, EDD sang. Shrieked, actually, Eve thought, with beeps and buzzes, voices, music, and electronic whistles.

She'd go mad in an hour under these conditions and often wondered how her old partner, Feeney, captain of the division, survived. In fact, she corrected, *thrived* among the peacocks and passion flowers.

McNab grabbed a disc from his workstation. "We'll take a booth."

He wound his way through the jungle. Most of EDD danced around, talking on headphones. It gave her the jitters. She followed McNab through glass doors where a dozen clear booths were lined up like soldiers. More than half of them were occupied.

McNab snagged one, then slid the disc into a slot on a sleek little comp unit. "Most of the trans are to the second vic. Some to her mother, her sister, the office. Others to shops and stuff — she was getting married, right?"

"That was the plan."

"Yeah, doing checks on flowers, the dress, that kind of stuff."

"Can we skip those?"

"Figured as much so I made two files. This one just has the trans to the boyfriend. You can review the other if you need it. Replay," he ordered.

The computer recited the date of the transmission, the time, the codes used. Byson came on screen, as he would have on Natalie's pocket unit.

He'd been a good-looking guy, Eve mused, before he'd had his face smashed in.

Hey, Nat.

Bick. Are you alone?

Yeah, I'm about to head into a meeting. What's up?

I need to talk to you — about . . . what I've been looking into. Can you take lunch?

I can't. I've got one scheduled. What is it?

I don't think we should talk about it on the 'link. After work — we'll go to my place. I need to show you. Come down when you're finished for the day, okay? I think this is really important.

Okay, see you later.

The computer announced end of transmission, time elapsed.

"A little stressed, a little jumpy, but excited, too," Eve mused. "Like, *Look what I found.*"

The next was a day later, an incoming.

Hey, babe. I'm trying to move this dinner meeting along, but it's dragging. Do you want me to come by after?

No, no, that's okay. I'm working. Bick, I'm finding more. I think a lot more. I'll fill you in tomorrow. Meet me for breakfast maybe? Our spot.

I'll be there. Seven-thirty good?

Perfect. God, Bick. I just can't believe all this. We have to find it all. It has to be stopped.

We could go to the cops.

Not yet. We have to be absolutely sure. We don't know who's involved, not on this end. Not for certain. We have to be careful. I'll tell you about it in the morning.

Don't work too late. Love you.

Love you right back.

There were a handful of others, increasingly tense, equally cryptic, ending with one near midnight, only a couple of hours before the first murder.

Just wanted to talk to you. See your face.

Nat, listen, I'll just come over.

It's late, and you had such a long day. I'm fine, really. Just edgy, I guess. And Palma will be here later. I always feel so odd having you sleep here when she's staying over.

You puritan.

Guess I am.

But she laughed a little.

I'm going to tell her, Bick, talk it through with her.

I don't like the way you were approached. Nat, they tried to bribe you.

And as far as they know I'm thinking about it.

It was more ultimatum than bribe. They might try to hurt you.

I asked for forty-eight hours to think about it. I've got time. There's no reason for them to try anything before I give them my answer. I've got the new lock, the security peep, Palma's coming. I'm in this now, Bick. I want to finish it. I just want to put it all together, talk to Palm. Tomorrow, we'll take everything to the authorities.

I'll come over in the morning. We'll go together.

Don't bring your file copies. Let's just . . . like insurance, you know. If cops don't work, we'll go to the media. This has to be exposed.

One way or the other, Nat. We'll fry their asses.

And get back to our lives. I can't wait to marry you.

Crazy about you. Sleep tight, babe. This'll be over tomorrow.

I can't wait for that either. Love you. Night.

"Civilians," Eve said with a churning mix of pity and anger. "Playing detective. They'd gone to the cops, they'd be alive."

"Had something hot," McNab agreed. "Bribes and threats, ending in bloody murder. I'll push back further, maybe she dropped more detail earlier in the game. Seems pretty clear it was something she came across at her work."

"Still waiting for the fucking warrant for her files. Lawyers. Damn it. Somebody wants to, they've had plenty of time to pull incriminating, do some major covering up."

"Everything leaves a trail. EDD bloodhounds will sniff it out." He pulled out the disc, passed it to Eve. "Damn shame about them. You could see they had the real thing going."

"They'd stuck with numbers, left the bad guys to us, they'd still have it going."

But she was heavy with that pity as she pushed out of the booth.

"Go back," she said to McNab. "Keep going back. Seems to me if someone had contacted her via 'link on this thing, she'd have kept a record of the transmission. She thought she was setting up a case. Accountants, they're all about columns and balancing things out, keeping records. If there was electronic contact, she's got it somewhere."

Or had it, Eve thought as she gratefully headed out of Club EDD. She'd have told her killer anything he wanted to know before he was done with her.

Eve hit the lab on her way home. Her goal was to pin down Dick Berenski, chief lab tech, into passing on whatever they had to this point. But as she moved through the tunnels and glass-walled labs and cubes, she spotted Harvo, a tech she'd worked with before.

Harvo's short, spiked red hair was covered with a protective cap painted, Eve noted, with naked men. "Nice hat."

"Fun where you find it." Harvo snapped gum the color of healthy lungs. "You looking for Dickhead, he's gone. Got leave, a few days south — probably half-juiced by now and hitting on some unfortunate woman who just wants to drink her piña colada in peace."

"Who's running the asylum?"

"Yon's got this tour, but he's in the field. Pulled up a floater from the East River. Being that's his favorite variety, he went out to the scene. You want, I can run you through what we've got on your double murder."

"Appreciate it."

"Live to serve."

Instead of taking Eve to Berenski's domain, Harvo wound her way through the maze to her own workstation. "You looking to do field work, Harvo?"

"Nah. I like my hive." She boosted onto her stool, hooked her thick-soled, high-topped black and green sneakers on the rung. "And the whole dead body thing isn't big on my list of appeals. I just cruise on the evidence, you know?" Wiggling her butt on the stool, she played her long, varnished nails over a keyboard.

"I didn't process your tape. Tech who did just left for the day. Prob'ly shot you the report before, but since you're here . . ."

"Since I'm here."

"Tape on both murders came from the same roll. See here? You got your end from female vic's ankles, dead match with the end from the male vic's hands. Took hours to straighten those suckers out, but you got your match. Garden variety duct tape."

"Don't suppose we got a miracle and found prints."

"Not a one. Some DNA though. None on the female DB, nothing under her nails. Prints on the scene — murder one — vic's, second vic, sister of first vic. Blood spatter, all vic's. She didn't do any damage. But your male DB got some licks in."

"You got DNA from scene two."

"Not all the blood at the second scene was your vic's. Got nice samples off the second vic's knuckles. He popped the bastard. You get him, we can match him. Prints up the waz, second scene."

"Doing reno there."

"Yeah, we got that. You got plenty there to clear. We'll run them for you, give you names and locations. Nothing on the body, as per your first. But what we got on your male vic was blood and saliva — not his. Cord used to strangle second vic was cut from binding on scene."

"Took his fun where he found it, too."

"You could say. Here's a little something. Outside locks on female's building were complete shit. Broke 'em in with a smooth, round object. Little hammer maybe. Whack, whack, you're in. Better locks upstairs. Used locksmith tools on those."

She'd seen that for herself, but Eve nodded. "Came prepared. Knew about the fresh lock."

"So, anyways, we'll get your ID on the prints, second scene, so you can run 'em."

"Appreciate it."

Kept an eye on her, Eve thought as she battled her way home through the cranky wall of traffic. Bribed her first — probably going to kill her anyway. Copperfield thought the bribe bought her time, but it bought her killer time, too. Planning and prep time.

Something hot enough to kill for twice was too hot to take chances with a payoff.

Back to the accounting firm — just had to be. She needed those damn files. Using the dash 'link, she contacted Assistant Prosecuting Attorney Cher Reo.

"I'm on my way out," Reo said. "I have an actual date. Don't screw with me."

"I have two bodies in the morgue. I want my warrant. Don't screw with me."

"Do you know how much paper a lawyer can generate in a few hours?"

"Is that one of those questions like how many angels can dance on the head of a pin?"

Reno smiled sourly. "Runs down the same channel."

"Why would angels dance on a pin? Wouldn't they rather boogie in the clouds?"

"I would." Reo's lips curved slyly. "But I'm not an angel."

"Me either. Now, enough of this philosophizing. About those lawyers, about my warrant."

"I'm going to get it, Dallas, but I'm not going to get it before morning. We're not just talking lawyers, we're talking really rich lawyers with big, fat retainers and hordes of legal drones who can find a precedent in a haystack."

"A haystack? What does that mean?"

"Never mind." Reo sighed, long and deep. "It's been a day, that's the best I can say about it. I've got a judge reviewing their last block right now. If he's not too big on having, say, an actual meal or a life, he may rule on it within a couple hours. I hear, you hear."

"The minute," Eve said, then cut off.

Too much time, she thought. Too much time screwing around the system. Whoever killed Natalie and Bick — or ordered them killed — had probably started deleting or adjusting the files immediately.

She hoped McNab was right about the EDD hounds digging up the scent she had a feeling was being covered up even as the lawyers dug through their haystack.

But if EDD let her down, she had a very sleek, very smart hound of her own.

So thinking, she drove through the gates of home.

CHAPTER
FIVE

Because her mind was on other things, Summerset caught Eve off guard as she came in the door.

"Do you require change-of-address forms?"

"Huh? What?" She yanked herself back to the moment, then immediately regretted it. He was in her moment, the bony, black-suited pain in her ass. "Can't you find another place to haunt? I hear there's one available down on East Twelfth."

His lips thinned — if, she thought, it was possible for what passed as his lips to compress in an even tighter line. "I assumed as you no longer appear to live here, you'd need the proper forms."

She pulled off her coat, tossed it on the newel post. "Yeah, get those forms, I'll fill them out." She started up the stairs. "How many Ms in Summerset anyway?"

She left him behind in the grand foyer. Roarke was probably home, she decided, but she'd wait until she was out of the hearing of those demon ears before she checked on one of the house scanners.

She was tempted to go straight into the bedroom, fall flat on the bed for twenty minutes. But with the case weighing on her, she continued up to her office.

He was there, pouring wine.

"Long day for you, Lieutenant. Thought you could use this."

"Couldn't hurt." Either the man was psychic or she was pretty damn predictable. "Been home long?"

"A couple of hours."

She frowned, checked the time. "It's later than I thought. Sorry. I should have done the call home thing, probably."

"Couldn't have hurt." But he moved to her, handed her the glass.

Then he took her chin in his free hand, studied her face before he touched his lips to hers. "Long, hard day."

"I've had shorter and easier."

"And from the look of you, you're going to make it longer. Red meat?"

"Why is everyone speaking in code around here?"

He smiled, ran his fingertip along the dent in her chin. "You could use a steak. Yes, pizza would be easier to eat at your desk," he continued, anticipating her. "Consider having a meal that requires utensils payment for not checking in."

"I guess that's fair."

"We'll have it up in the conservatory." To avoid protest, he simply took her arm and led her to the elevator. "It'll clear your head."

He was probably right, and in Roarke's world it was a simple matter to order real meat and all the trimmings, have a meal with wine, even candles, in a lush setting where the lights of the city twinkled and gleamed beyond black glass, and a cheerful fire crackled away.

There were times she wondered that she didn't get whiplash from the culture shock.

"Nice," she said and tried to adjust her mind, her mood.

"Tell me about the victim."

"Victims. It can wait."

"They're in your head. We'll both do better if you talk it through."

"So, you don't want to chat about politics, the weather, the latest celebrity gossip over dinner?"

He smiled, sat back, gestured with his glass.

She told him, going step by step through both murders, the timing, the method, the background.

"Listening to them talk to each other? It just hit. They had something. It went beyond the surface, you get me? Beyond that gooey first stage of attraction."

"The potential they had . . . It's not just one or even two people being snuffed out, but the potential of what they might have made together."

"Yeah, I guess that's it." She stared through that black glass to the lights of a city that offered the very best, and the very worst. "Pisses me off."

"You're rarely anything but pissed at murderers."

"That's a given. I mean they piss me off, the vics. What the hell were they thinking?" Frustration rippled through her, into her eyes, her voice. "Why didn't they go to the cops? They're dead not only because somebody wanted them dead, but because they were playing at something they couldn't possibly win."

"Many of us don't automatically run to the police."

"Some of you run from them," she said dryly. "She had that new lock installed just two days before. Tells me she's got some concerns. She takes a knife into the bedroom with her — or I have to assume she did from my read of the scene. Tells me she was scared. But . . ." She stabbed viciously at a bite of steak. "At the same time she says nothing to her defenseless sister who's coming to spend the night. She doesn't, at the very least, hole up with her boyfriend."

And you're suffering some, Roarke thought, because it could have been prevented if she'd come to someone like you. "She had a sense of independence, then, and an underlying certainty she was handling and could handle the situation."

Eve shook her head. "It's that 'It can't really happen to me' attitude. The same one that gets people to stroll around in bad neighborhoods or flip off the expense of decent security. Violence happens to the other guy. And you know what else?" she added, waving her fork. "They were into it. Wow, look what we've uncovered. We're going to blow it open — and do interviews, be important."

"Ordinary people, ordinary lives, and then something that pulls them out of that. The accounting firm has an excellent reputation."

"But you don't use them. I checked. Mostly because I thought what a big, complicated mess if you did."

"I considered them once upon a time. I found Sloan too stuffy and rigid."

"Isn't that the definition of accountants?"

"Shame on you," he said with a laugh. "Such a cliche. There are people, darling Eve, who enjoy and are skilled with numbers and finance who are neither stuffy nor rigid."

"And here I figured you were the exception to the rule. No, I'm just being pissy," she admitted. "Feel pissy. The firm's had their lawyers tangling up the warrant all damn day. They've got two employees murdered and they're blocking me from doing my job."

"By doing theirs," he pointed out. "Sorry, Lieutenant, but if they didn't use their muscle, and the law, to do whatever possible to protect their clients' privacy, they wouldn't have the reputation they hold."

"Somebody in there knows what Copperfield and Byson knew. They were cogs, moving into the center of the wheel, but still cogs. Somebody closer in knows."

He cut another slice of steak. "It wouldn't be impossible for someone with superior hacking skills to access the files on Copperfield's office unit."

She said nothing for a moment because she'd thought the same. She'd considered this streamlined approach. "Can't do it."

"Didn't think you could. And the why is the same as why the firm is paying their lawyers to paper the PA. It's the job. At this point, you aren't aware of other lives on the line. You can't justify the shortcut."

"No, I can't."

"You would be, I imagine, working your way into the wheel. Copperfield's immediate supervisor."

"Interviewed her, ran her. I'm not crossing her off, but if she wasn't genuinely shocked and distressed about Copperfield's death she's missed her calling. Doesn't mean she isn't aware of, potentially, part of what Copperfield discovered. Why wouldn't Copperfield go to her supervisor, with whom she had — allegedly — a friendly relationship? Had to assume Greene, the supervisor, knew the secret. Or was afraid of that."

"You're so sure it was something discovered at the firm?"

"It all points there. Money laundering, tax evasion, fraud, skimming? Some legit front for something not legit." She shrugged. "Could be all manner of things. You probably know people who use the firm."

"I'm sure I do."

"Something for the back pocket," she added. "Not just a little skimming or whatever," she continued. "Not with the level of nerves and excitement it generated, not with the violence of the murders. A big deal. Something that drew an offer of a bribe, and ended with two deaths."

He considered topping off their wine, but it would be wasted. His dedicated cop wouldn't indulge herself in a second glass if she was going back to work. "Are you looking at professional hits?"

"Doesn't feel like it, doesn't look like it. And why cover that up, if so, and not go further? Make it look like burglary. Rape, personal vendetta. But it wasn't sloppy either. When I get him, I'm going to be surprised if these were his first kills."

Down in her office again, she set up a board as she had at Central. With the cat ribboning between his legs, Roarke stood and watched. And studied.

"Hot-tempered and cowardly."

She stopped, turned. "Why do you say that?"

"Her face, for one. It took several blows to do that to her face. That wouldn't have been necessary. Would it?"

"No. Keep going."

Roarke lifted a shoulder. "Binding her hands and feet tightly enough to leave those bruises. That's anger, I'd think. The burns, bottoms of her feet. There's a meanness there. And it's cowardly to strangle her when she was bound — same with the male victim. And the use of the stunner. It just strikes me."

"Struck me the same. But you missed one. He got some kick out of it. No point seeing their faces when he killed them otherwise. Makes it intimate. Not sexual, but intimate. And he pulled the tape off their mouths before he killed them. Took that extra step. It's powerful to watch the life go out, to see it and hear it while you cause it. Could've done it a lot of other ways, but this method?"

Her eyes flattened as she looked at the pictures she'd tacked up. "You feel it, your muscles, your hands. You hear the chokes, the gasps the tape would've muffled. Yeah, there's temper here, but the power's bigger."

She settled into work, unsurprised when the cat padded out after Roarke — who would no doubt be more attentive than she would for the next couple of hours.

She studied the data Peabody had sent to her unit. Copperfield's neighbors were low on the list, in her opinion. Why bother with a new lock when your potential problem could just make a grab at you in the hallway, in the elevator?

As for Byson's, they didn't fit for her either. The source was Copperfield, not her fiancé.

International accounts, Eve thought. That had been Copperfield's bailiwick. Smuggling was always popular. A glossy client fronting illegals, arms, people smuggling?

She replayed the conversations between the two victims, watched faces, tuned in to voices. Upset, she concluded, some shock, excitement, but not horror or real fear.

Wouldn't there have been if what they'd found had involved loss of life?

It said white-collar crime to her. High-dollar, white-collar, and at least to their knowledge, nonviolent.

A thought occurred that had her getting up, walking to the door between her office and Roarke's. But his was empty. Even as she frowned, he spoke from behind her.

"Looking for me?"

"Jesus, you make less noise than the damn cat."

"Tubs of lard aren't particularly stealthy. Come to bed."

"I just wanted to —"

"Twenty hours is enough." Once again, he took her arm. "Did your warrant come through?"

"About a half hour ago. I'm just going to —"

"Get back to it in the morning."

"Okay, okay." She agreed because if he could drag her off without her blocking the move, fatigue was slowing her reaction time. "I was just wondering, as a

82

mogul and all, how many layers does one of your minions have to go through to get to you?"

"It would depend on the minion and the reason he or she wanted to get through to me."

"But whatever, whoever, there'd be the Caro layer, right?" she asked, referring to his admin.

"Yes, in all probability."

"Even if the minion made up a bullshit reason, Caro would know there was an appointment, a meeting."

"Certainly."

"And each one of those top guys at the firm would have a Caro."

"There's only one Caro, and she's mine. But again, yes, they'd have an admin, and I'd assume an efficient one."

In the bedroom, she pulled off her boots, then began to undress in a haze that told her whatever she'd had left had dropped out when she'd walked away from the work.

"Going there bright and early," she mumbled. "Get my hands on those damn files. Asshole lawyers cost me a damn day. Like to kick their asses."

"That's right, darling."

"I heard that smirk."

She slid into bed, let him draw her in so they were close and warm. "Bought the baby shower present thing today."

"Good."

She had a little smirk of her own in the dark. "If Mavis goes into labor during the deal here, you have to drive her to the birth center."

There was utter silence for a solid ten seconds. "You're trying to give me nightmares. Very small of you."

"Somebody told me today you take your fun where you find it."

"Is that so? Well then." His hand slid slickly under her nightshirt and cupped her breast. "Look what I found."

"Sleeping here."

"I don't think so." His thumb stroked over her nipple as his teeth nipped into the nape of her neck. "But go on to sleep if you must. I'll just have my fun and ward off nightmares. Multitasking."

As his mouth and hands were all very busy, she could state without question the man knew how to multitask. And the slow, steady simmer of arousal burned away at fatigue until she arched from the pleasure of it.

Her mind went quiet; her blood went hot.

She turned to him, reached for him, her mouth seeking his.

The taste of it, of her, seeped into him until he was drenched in her. With the long line of her pressed against him, her hands gliding, the feel of her seduced the seducer.

He wanted her skin, the rapid beat of the pulse in her throat, the firm curve of her breast. Soft and strong and warm. Her breath caught, released on a low sound of approval; her hips rose in both invitation and demand.

As she moved with him, trembled for him, the need inside him that was never quite tamed leaped free.

Yes, now, she thought. *Right now.*

It was flash and burn when he plunged inside her, the glorious shock of being taken. She could see his eyes, watching her, even as she flew over the crest. Over it and into a storm of speed and heat.

"With me," she managed. "Come with me."

When his lips crushed down on hers, and the storm reached its peak, she felt him fly with her.

Breathless, with her system starting its long slide back, she blinked up at the dark sky window over the bed. He lay over her, his weight pressing hers into the mattress, his heart drumming with hers.

She felt wonderfully sleepy again, as she imagined Galahad might if he came across an unexpected bowl of cream and gorged himself.

"Guess you never know where you'll find the fun."

His lips brushed her hair, then he shifted, drawing her back against him again. "I do."

Snuggled against him, she fell asleep with a smile on her face.

When she woke, Roarke was in the sitting area of the bedroom, scanning the morning reports as was his habit. She smelled coffee, but headed in to shower first.

When she stepped out of the shower, the scent struck her again. Sniffing like a hound she turned and saw a thick mug of it sitting on the counter by the sink.

It made her smile, and go a little soft inside just as she had as she'd drifted into sleep. She took the first glorious hit of coffee naked and dripping, then left it to use the drying tube and pull on a robe.

Carrying the mug with her, she came out, went directly to him. Bending down, she gave him a kiss nearly as strong as the coffee.

"Thanks."

"You're welcome. I did consider joining you and getting your blood moving in a different manner, but I'm already dressed." Still looking at Eve, Roarke shot out a finger to his left, and warned Galahad as the cat tried to belly his way toward a bowl of berries. "You look fairly well rested."

"Sleepy sex then six solid. Not shabby."

"Said with a smug smile, just to finish off your alliteration."

"Hah. You're a sharp, sexy son of a bitch. See, I finish my own alliterations."

He had to laugh. "Now that you have, sit and have some breakfast, and I'll tell you what I learned of your top accountants from a business associate."

"What associate?" She lowered the coffee she'd started to drink. "When?"

"You wouldn't know him, and shortly ago."

"Tell me while I get dressed."

"Eat."

She heaved a sigh, but dropped down and scooped some of the berries into a smaller bowl. "Spill."

"Jacob Sloan founded the firm with Carl Myers, the father of the current Carl Myers on the letterhead. Sloan has a very small handful of accounts he continues to oversee personally. He does, however, according to my source, take a very active part in the running of the firm."

"His ball, he wants to watch where it bounces."

"I'd say so, yes. Myers handles domestic, corporate, and individual — as did his father — more of the very top individual accounts. Robert Kraus — who was made partner about a decade ago — heads up the legal department, and oversees some of the cream of the foreign and international."

Roarke nudged a bowl of what looked suspiciously like flakes of tree bark toward her.

"Does he, your associate, know how active any or all of them are in the day-to-day?"

"He tells me very. While they are a layered and multifaceted firm with various departments, department heads, and so forth, they hold a weekly partners' meeting — that would be only the three of them — a daily briefing, and there are quarterly account reports and employee evals, which each partner is copied on. Very hands on."

"And if so, difficult for one to slip something shaky by the other two."

"It would seem, but difficult isn't impossible or even improbable."

"Sloan's the top dog," Eve muttered. "Probably the hardest for an account exec to get to, one-on-one. And the one who'd make the most sense to try to seek out if you hit on something that seemed off. At least if you believed he wasn't in on it."

"And if you did, or weren't sure, a reason to try to gather as many facts and as much evidence as possible before you went to the authorities."

"Yeah, yeah." She ate some of the tree bark without thinking about it. "Bio data I got on Sloan is that self-made stuff. Worked his way up, took risks, beat his own drum, built his firm and rep brick by brick. One marriage — and she has some family dough and prestige — one male offspring, conservative bent. Got a second home in the Caymans."

"Makes excellent sense, tax-wise," Roarke said. "And a good way to shelter income. He'd know all the ins and outs there."

"Copperfield handled foreign accounts. Might be she stumbled on something he was into. Guy founds a firm that takes on a big shine over the years, puts all that time and effort into it, he'd have a lot of pride in it — and a lot at stake."

She pushed up. "Well, I'm going to go see what I think of him." Leaning over, she kissed him. "If I need help interpreting some of the numbers, are you up for it?"

"I could be."

"Good to know. Later."

She had Peabody and McNab meet her in the lobby of the building that housed the accounting firm. As ordered, four uniforms with banker's boxes for transporting items were already in place.

McNab wore a coat that looked as if it had been used as a canvas for fingerpainting by a hyperactive toddler.

"Couldn't you just try to look like a cop?"

He only grinned. "We get up there, I'll wear a really stern expression."

"Yeah, that'll make a difference."

She strode across the lobby, flashed her badge and the warrant at Security. He was already wearing a stern expression, and kept it in place as he scanned IDs and paperwork.

"My orders are to have you escorted up."

"See these?" Eve tapped both badge and warrant. "These override your orders. You want to hitch onto the elevator with us, no problem. But we're going up now."

He signaled quickly to another guard, then fell in step behind Eve as she crossed to the elevators. They rode up in silence. When the doors opened there were two suits, one of each gender, waiting.

"Identification and authority, please." The woman spoke snippily, then studied the three badges and the warrant. "These appear to be in order. My associate and I will accompany you to Ms. Copperfield's office."

"Suit yourself."

"Mr. Kraus is on his way. If you'll just wait —"

"Did you just read this?" Eve lifted the warrant again. "It doesn't require me to wait."

"Simply courtesy —"

"You should have thought about courtesy before you held my investigation hostage for more than twenty-four hours." Eve headed off in the direction she and Peabody had taken the day before.

"Privacy matters," the woman began as she quickened her pace to match Eve's stride.

"Yeah, so does murder. You bogged me up. Kraus wants to talk to me, he can talk while we're getting the files and electronics." She swung into Natalie's office.

"This warrant authorizes me to confiscate any and all data, disc, and hard copy, any and all files, notes, communications, personal property — hell, let's cut it down. I'm authorized to take everything inside this room. Let's load it up," she said to Peabody and McNab.

"Our client files are highly sensitive."

In a flash, Eve rounded on her. "You know what else is sensitive? The human body. You want to see what was done to Natalie Copperfield's?" Eve made a move to reach into her file bag.

"No, I don't. And we're very distressed about what happened to Ms. Copperfield and Mr. Byson. We're very sympathetic to their families."

"Yeah, I slapped up against your distress and sympathy a few times yesterday." Eve pulled open a desk drawer.

"Lieutenant Dallas."

The man who entered was well turned-out, middle fifties in a stone-gray suit and blinding white shirt. He had a prominent nose and dark eyes in a strong face with an olive complexion. His hair was ink black, brushed back in waves that made wings out of the silver he'd either let come into his temples or had put there for effect.

She recognized him from the ID shot she'd accessed as Robert Kraus.

"Mr. Kraus."

"I wonder if I could impose on you for a short time. If your associates could continue to deal with this business, my partners and I would like to speak with you in our conference room."

"We've got Byson's office to do next."

He looked just a little pained, but nodded. "Understood. We'll try not to keep you long."

Eve turned to Peabody. "Everything. Boxed and labeled. Uniforms to transport if I'm not back before you're done. I'll find you."

"First let me apologize for the delay," Kraus began as he gestured Eve into the corridor. "Ethically and legally we're obliged to protect our clients."

"Ethically and legally I'm obliged to protect the rights of the victims."

"Understood." He walked past the bank of office elevators to a private car. "I knew both Natalie and Bick, and they had both my professional and personal respect. Kraus to sixty-five," he said into the speaker.

"Did either of them speak with you about a potential problem, personal or professional?"

"No. But it would have been highly unusual for either of them to do so, certainly if it was personal. If there was a problem or question with one of their accounts, they would have gone to their department head, who — if necessary — would have reported to me or one of the other partners. Certainly, the partners would expect a report or memo on such a circumstance, even if it was resolved."

"And did you receive such a report or memo?"

"No, I did not. I'm puzzled why you believe or suspect that what happened to them has anything to do with Sloan, Myers, and Kraus."

"I haven't told you what I believe or suspect," Eve said evenly. "Investigating all areas of their lives, their movements, their communications, is standard and routine."

"Of course."

The car stopped, and once again he gestured Eve ahead of him.

Here was the power center, she realized. As was so often the case, power — like heat — rose to the top.

A wall of glass with a pale gold sheen let in the city with a gilded light that made statements of industry and wealth. Plush carpeting of deep red was bordered with dark, thick wood. There was no reception area here, no waiting alcove. Eve imagined any client worthy of this floor would never be expected to check in or cool heels.

Instead there was a seating area of lush sofas, thick tables, obviously arranged for informal or personal chats. It boasted a small, stylish bar where she assumed the tony clients could request their drink of choice.

Space and silence were the watchwords here. Office doors were few and distant, and all were dominated by an inner wall of that golden glass. Kraus escorted her over to the wall, subtly waving a hand in front of a small security eye. Glass whisked open to reveal the large conference room behind it.

With the city rising behind them, the other two partners sat at a mile-long table.

The younger, Carl Myers, rose. His black suit was softened by a thin silver chalk stripe. There was a black mourning band around the left sleeve. His hair was a wavy, medium brown brushed high off his forehead. His eyes, a soft hazel, met Eve's directly as he came around the table and extended his hand.

"Lieutenant Dallas, I'm Carl Myers. We're sorry to meet you under such tragic circumstances."

"I meet most people under tragic circumstances."

"Of course." He never missed a beat. Handsome, fit, he gestured toward the head of the table where Jacob Sloan sat. "Please, have a seat. Is there anything we can get for you?"

"No, thanks."

"Jacob Sloan, Lieutenant Dallas."

"Roarke's cop."

It was a term she was used to now, even when it was said with a hint of derision. Still, she tapped the badge she'd hooked on her belt. "This makes me the NYPSD's cop."

He acknowledged that with a faint lift of silver eyebrows. He struck her as honed, face and body, as though he whittled himself down to sheer power. His eyes were stone gray, his suit stark black. Like his face, his body, his hands were thin but with a look of steely strength.

He didn't offer one to Eve.

"You, as a representative of the police department, are infringing on the rights of our clients."

"Somebody really infringed the hell out of the rights of Natalie Copperfield and Bick Byson."

His mouth tightened, but his eyes never wavered. "This firm takes both of those difficult circumstances very seriously. The death of two of our employees —"

"Murder," Eve corrected.

"As you say," he agreed with a nod. "The murder of two of our employees is shocking and tragic, and we will cooperate with your investigation to the letter of the law."

"Not much choice there, Mr. Sloan. How about the spirit of it?"

"Please, let me get you some coffee," Myers began.

"I don't want any coffee."

"The spirit of the law is subjective, isn't it?" Sloan continued. "Your concept of it may very well veer from mine, and certainly is bound to veer from our clients' — who expect, who demand, that we protect their privacy. The circumstances of this terrible thing will reverberate throughout this firm. The concern that sensitive financial data will be viewed by eyes not cleared by this firm to do so will distress our clients. I'm sure as the wife of a powerful, influential, and wealthy man, you understand that."

"First, I'm not here as anyone's wife but as the primary investigator of a double murder. Second, the distress of your clients, whoever they may be, isn't a priority for me."

"You're a sarcastic, difficult woman."

"Having a couple of dead bodies on my hands that were beaten, tortured, and strangled just doesn't bring out my sunny side."

"Lieutenant." Myers spread his hands. "We understand completely that you have a responsibility to fulfill. As we do. And believe me, everyone here wants those responsible for what happened to Natalie and Bick caught and punished. Our concerns on a secondary front are for our clients who trust and depend on us. There are people — competitors, if you will — business adversaries, ex-spouses, the media, who would go to considerable lengths to learn the contents of the files you're confiscating today."

"Are you insinuating I'd be open to a bribe by one of these parties to pass on that information?"

"No, no, not at all. But others who lack your integrity may be tempted."

"Any and all who'll have access to the information in those files will be hand-picked by me or my commander. You want reassurance that the data will remain secure, you have it. On my word. Unless such information is determined to be the motive behind or connected to the murders of Copperfield and Byson. That's the best you get."

She waited a beat. "Since we're all here, let's clear up some business. I'll need your whereabouts for the night of the murders. Midnight to 4a.m."

Sloan laid his hands on the table in front of him. "You consider us suspects?"

"I'm a cynical so-and-so. Your whereabouts, Mr. Sloan."

He drew breath through his nose, expelled it. "Until approximately twelve-thirty, my wife and I were entertaining our grandson and his friend. At that time, they left our home and my wife and I retired. I remained home with my wife until the following morning when I left for the office. At seven-thirty."

"Names, please? Grandson and his friend."

"His name is mine. He was named for me. His friend is Rochelle DeLay."

"Thank you. Mr. Myers?"

"I was entertaining out-of-town clients — Mr. and Mrs. Helbringer from Frankfurt, their son and daughter-in-law — until sometime after 1a.m. We were at the Rainbow Room." He smiled wanly. "And, naturally, I have the receipts. My wife and I returned home, went to bed just before two, I believe. I left for work the next day about eight-thirty."

"And how can I contact your clients?"

"Oh, God." He pushed a hand through his hair. "I suppose you must. They're staying at the Palace. Your husband's, I believe."

"Small world. And Mr. Kraus."

"Also entertaining clients with my wife, in my home. Madeline Bullock, and her son Winfield Chase, of the Bullock Foundation. They were our guests for a couple of days while they were in New York. We had dinner and played cards. Until about midnight, I believe."

"I'll need to contact them."

"They're traveling. I believe they're making a stop or two on their way back to London, where the Foundation is based."

So, she'd track them down.

"Mr. Kraus has stated that neither of the victims approached him with any questions or any problems pertaining to their jobs, or their personal lives. Did they approach either of you?"

"No." Sloan said it flatly.

"I spoke with Bick a few days before this happened," Myers began. "Regarding the execution of a trust fund for a client's new grandchild. He never mentioned a problem."

"Thank you. It may be necessary for me to speak with all of you again, and will certainly be necessary for me to interview the supervisors and associates of the victims in this matter."

"Gentlemen, would you excuse us." Sloan lifted a hand. "I'd like a word with Lieutenant Dallas in private."

"Jacob," Kraus began.

"I don't need legal counsel, for God's sake, Robert. Leave us alone."

When they were, Sloan pushed away from the table, walked to the wall of glass. "I liked that girl."

"Excuse me?"

"Natalie. I liked her. Fresh, bright, had a spark in her. She was friendly with my grandson. Friendly," Sloan repeated as he turned. "They worked in the same department. Her department head was about to put her up for promotion. She would have gotten it. I spoke with her parents this morning. You think there's no compassion here? No sympathy? There's more."

Those thin hands fisted. "There's rage. This firm is a home to me. I built it. Someone came into my home and killed two of my people. I want you to find the bastard. But if, in the course of your investigation, confidential data regarding clients of this firm leaks, I'll have your job."

"Then we understand each other, Mr. Sloan. As long as you understand that if, during the course of my investigation, I learn that you had any part — directly, indirectly — in those murders, I'll have you in a cage."

He crossed to her, and this time, held out his hand. "Then we have a perfect understanding.'

CHAPTER
SIX

Eve found Peabody and the rest of the team finishing up in Byson's office.

"McNab, I want you to go with the officers to transport all these items to Central. I want you with the boxes and their contents every step of the way. You personally log them in. And lock them up — conference room five. I've cleared that with the commander. Take the electronics directly to Feeney."

"Yes, sir."

"Those electronics are to be logged a second time into EDD, with your code and with Feeney's."

He lifted his brows. "We got national security in here?"

"We've got our asses in there, so if you don't want yours in a sling, log and document every step. Peabody, you and I are going to get some statements from associates. You take this department, and Byson's people. Do another round with his supervisor. I'll take Copperfield's."

She started out. "Every step of the way, McNab," she repeated, then took the elevator to Natalie's department. She knew just where she wanted to start.

"I need to speak with Jacob Sloan, the grandson."

This time around the receptionist didn't hesitate, but simply beeped an interoffice 'link. "Jake? A Lieutenant Dallas would like to speak with you. Of course."

"Third door, left," Eve was told. "Excuse me? Would you — do you know anything about a memorial?"

"No. Sorry. I'm sure the family will make an announcement."

She followed the direction and found Jake Sloan waiting just outside his office door. He was built like his grandfather, but youth made him lanky. His hair was a dark blond, pulled back in a fat little tail at the nape of his neck. His eyes were a bleak sea foam.

"You're the one who's in charge of Natalie and Bick's murders. Investigating their murders, I mean. I'm Jake Sloan."

"I'd like to speak to you. Privately."

"Yeah, come on in. You want something?" he asked as he closed the door behind her.

"No, thanks."

"I can't settle." He paced around a small office with posters in geometric shapes and primary colors on the walls. There were toys on his desk — or what she thought of as toys, in any case. A bright red squeeze ball mocked up like a devil with horns, a cartoon dog on a fat spring, a curly tube that rocked on a string and changed colors with the movements.

He walked to a tiny refreshment area and pulled a bottle of water from a minifriggie.

"I almost didn't come in today," he told Eve. "But I couldn't stand the idea of staying home. Staying alone."

"You and Natalie knew each other well."

"We were pals." His smile was shaky and brief. "Had lunch together a couple days a week maybe, with Bick if he could make it. Gossip in the break room, hang out. We'd go out together a couple of times a month, usually. Nat and Bick, me and whatever girl I was seeing. One girl the last six months."

He dropped down in his chair. "I'm rambling. You don't care about any of that."

"Actually, I do. Do you know anyone who'd want to hurt Natalie?"

"No." She saw the gleam of tears before he turned his head to stare hard at the image of a blue circle inside a red triangle framed on the wall. "People liked Nat. I don't understand how this could happen. Her and Bick. Both of them. I keep thinking it's going to be some awful mistake and she'll poke her head in the door and say, 'Skinny latte?' "

He turned back, tried that smile again. "We'd get lattes in the break room."

"Were you and Natalie ever involved romantically, sexually?"

"Oh, jeez, no. It wasn't like that." Spots of color rode on his cheeks now. "Sorry, it's kind of like thinking about nailing my sister, you know? We just hit it off, day one. Friends, like we'd known each other already. And I don't guess either of us were what the other was looking for that way. Nat, she was looking for Bick. They were, like, fated, you know? You could just see it. God."

He propped his elbows on the desk, lowered his head to his hands. "It just makes me sick to think what happened to them."

"Did she say anything to you about any concerns, any problems? Since you were close, would she have told you if something was bothering her?"

"I'd have thought she would, but she didn't. And something was."

Eve zeroed in. "How do you know?"

"Because I knew her. I could see it. But she wouldn't talk about it. Said she was handling it, not to worry. I teased her that she was getting wedding jitters, going to do a runaway bride, and she played along. But you know, that wasn't it." He shook his head. "She was anxious about the details of the wedding, but not getting married, if you get what I mean."

"So what was it?"

"I think it was an account. I think she was having trouble with one of her accounts."

"Why?"

"Worked with her door locked a lot the last couple weeks. That wasn't Nat."

"Any idea which account?"

He shook his head again. "I didn't push. All of us have at least a couple of accounts that we can't discuss with other people in the department. I guess I thought she was losing a big client and trying to put out the fire. Happens."

He looked away again, back to the blue circle inside the red triangle. "We were all supposed to go out this

Saturday. The four of us. I don't know how they could be dead."

There was a knock, then the door opened. "Jake. Oh, I'm sorry. I didn't mean to interrupt."

"Dad." Jake pushed to his feet. "Ah, this is Lieutenant Dallas, with the police. My father, Randall Sloan."

"Lieutenant." Randall took her hand, held it firm. "You're here about Natalie and Bick. We're all in . . . I guess we're in a daze."

"You knew them."

"Yes, very well. It's such a shock, such a loss. I'll come back later, Jake. I just wanted to see how you were."

"It's all right," Eve told him. "I'm about done." She flipped through her memory of the pecking order. "You're a vice president of the firm."

"That's right."

But not a partner, Eve thought, despite his expensive suit, his glossy looks. "As such, did you have much contact with either victim?"

"Not much, not at the office. Of course, Nat and Bick were friends of my son's, so I knew them better outside the office than most of our account execs." Randall moved to his son, laid a hand on Jake's shoulder. "They were a lovely couple."

"Did either of them express any concerns to you, inside or outside the office?"

"Why, no." Randall's brow furrowed. "They were both excellent at their work, and happy — as far as I know — in their personal lives."

"I need to ask — it's routine — about your whereabouts on the night of the murders."

"I was entertaining clients. Sasha Zinka and Lola Warfield. We had cocktails and dinner at Enchantment downtown, then went on to Club One to hear some jazz."

"What time did you pack it in for the night?"

"It must have been close to two when we left the club. We shared a cab uptown, I dropped them off. I can't be sure, but I think it was nearly three when I got home."

"Thanks."

"My girlfriend and I were at Pop's — my grandfather's," Jake said when Eve looked at him. "I guess we left there around midnight, twelve-thirty. Went to my place from there. She stayed over."

"Appreciate the time." Eve got to her feet. "If I have any more questions, I'll be in touch."

Eve went from office to office, interrupting meetings and 'link calls, wading through tears and anxiety. Everyone liked Nat and Bick, nobody knew of any problems. She got a little more out of the account assistant Natalie had shared with two other execs.

She found Sarajane Bloomdale in the break room, sniffling over a cup of tea that smelled like wet moss. She was a tiny woman with a short black balloon of hair that cut across her eyebrows in thick, ruler-straight bangs. Her eyes were rimmed with red, her nose pink.

"Been out for a couple days," Sarajane told Eve. "Caught a head cold. Sucks, you know? Mostly, I was sleeping it off, and then yesterday Maize — she's one of the other assistants — she called me. Hysterical, crying. She told me. I didn't believe her. I kept saying, 'That's just bullshit, Maize.' I kept saying that, and she kept saying how it's true, they're dead. And I'd say —"

"I get it. How long did you work with Natalie?"

"About two years. She was great. Didn't expect me to run around doing all the grunt work like *some*. They'll run your feet off around here. But Natalie was great. Organized, you know? You didn't have to forever find where she forgot she put something. And she'd remember stuff like your birthday, or just bring in pastries now and then. And when I broke up with my boyfriend a couple months ago, she took me out to lunch."

"Was she working on anything specific the last couple weeks? Did she make any unusual requests?"

"Nothing out of the usual. She was working on something, locked her door a lot lately." Sarajane glanced around Eve, checking the doorway. "I sort of figured she was doing wedding stuff," Sarajane whispered. "We're not supposed to do personal business on company time, but, you know, your wedding and all."

"How about transmissions made through you, correspondence she asked you to send?"

"Just the routine stuff. But you know, she logged back in after hours a couple times lately. I happened to notice when I checked her daily calendar on her office unit. Just noticed the log-in. I guess I said something to her about it. Like I said, 'Gee, Natalie, your nose is going to fall off if you keep it to the grindstone.' And she looked kinda funny about it and asked if I wouldn't mention it to anybody. She was just catching up on some work."

"Did you mention it to anyone?"

"I might've. Just in passing."

"To?"

"I dunno. Maybe to Maize, or to Ricko down in Legal. We're kind of going out, me and Ricko. I might've said how she was working too hard and it was too bad, 'cause it was making her tired. I could tell. And she should relax more with her guy. And watch out for that piranha who worked with him."

"Which piranha would that be?"

"Lilah Grove. Quinn — she's an assistant down there — she says Ms. Grove's flirting with Mr. Byson every chance, asking him to come into her office and help her out, *discuss* clients over coffee or lunch."

Sarajane managed an expression between a scowl and a sneer. "Got her sights on him, you know? Guys can fall for that crap. I even told Natalie about it. She was my boss, right? So I told her, but she just laughed it off."

"Okay. Do you know if Natalie made any appointments to talk to one of the brass around here? If she intended to have a meeting with any of them?"

"Didn't ask me to set anything up. Um, you cops have mostly taken all my work stuff. I don't know what I'm supposed to do."

"Couldn't tell you."

Eve finished up with Cara Greene, stepping to the office doorway just as the woman was popping a tiny blue pill.

"Blocker," she said. "Vicious headache. It's a completely horrible day."

"Do you know why Natalie logged back into the office unit after working hours?"

"No." Cara frowned. "We all work late, and this time of year we've revved up into tax season. But . . . I've certainly known Natalie to work late, to stay at her desk for a couple of hours after end of business. And we won't even talk about the four weeks before April fifteen when most of us just live here. But it wasn't her usual routine to go then come back.

"Do you want to sit? I need to sit. I'm not feeling very well." She lowered to a chair. "Fielding frantic or angry calls from clients about their accounts being pawed over by the police is very unpleasant. Trying to play mother to the staff here when they come by to cry on my shoulder about Natalie, or allay their fears that something might happen to them. And trying to think, to think if you're right and this horrible thing has anything to do with her work, what I missed. What I should know."

"And nothing comes to mind."

"Nothing does. I have to think it was some sort of personal business. Someone who wanted to hurt them, was jealous or angry. I don't know."

"Was there jealousy here in the office?"

"A sense of competition, certainly. And certainly not everyone is best friends. But I honestly can't think of anyone who held a grudge or genuinely bad thoughts about Natalie."

"Do you know Lilah Grove?"

"The Femme Fatale of Individual Accounts." Cara's lips curved in a little smile. "And, yes, I've heard the gossip that she was overly friendly with Bick. It didn't worry Natalie, and I never heard anything about Lilah and Natalie arguing or even having strong words."

Maybe they saved them for end of business, Eve thought as she went down to meet Peabody.

"Did you get a statement from a Lilah Grove?"

"What is this, a sixth sense thing?" Peabody demanded. "She was the first I was going to brief you on."

"Department's sex queen. Hit on Byson. What's your take on her?"

"A little hard, with a very sharp edge. Vain, ambitious. Likes to flaunt both. Claimed the flirtation was mutual and harmless and expressed disgust and annoyance — both seemed false — that anyone in her department of the firm would gossip about her that way. Watered up a few times when talking about the vics, but never smeared her enhancements — which appear to be expertly applied and really pricey. She wears Do Me."

"What?"

"It's perfume. The real thing, not the off-brand or the cheaper eau de whatever. I like to go in and get sprayed with it when I troll the higher-end department stores."

"You're the one?"

"The one what?"

"The one person in the known universe who likes to get sprayed by those spritz guerrillas."

Peabody stiffened her shoulders, lifted her head high. "We are more than one. We are a small, yet sweet-smelling army."

"Yeah, I bet Do Me smells like a sweet, sunny meadow. I'm going to do a quick follow-up with Grove before we head back."

"Second office, right."

"I'll do it solo. Check in with McNab."

"Yes, sir. And, Dallas?" Peabody's smile was sly. "When I wear Do me, he does." She strolled off, whistling.

"Asked for that one," Eve mumbled.

The door to the office was open. Eve saw a blonde with long, sleek waves, tipped back in a caramel-colored leather chair, examining her manicure as she talked on a headset.

There were flowers in the office, and a chrome coat rack held a long red coat and white scarf. The coffee mug on the desk was also red with a flashy white L scripted on it.

The blonde wore a blue suit with a frill of lace in the V in lieu of a blouse. The eyes that flicked to Eve were a bold cat green. "Hang on. Can I help you?"

Eve held up her badge, and Lilah cast her eyes to the ceiling. "I'm very sorry, but I'm going to have to get back to you. I'll have that information for you before two o'clock. Absolutely. Bye."

She pulled off the headset, laid it on the desk. "I've already talked to one of you."

"Now you can talk to me. Lieutenant Dallas."

"At least I'm going up the ladder. Look, I'm sorry about Bick and Natalie. It's an awful shock for everyone who knew them. But I've got work."

"Funny, so do I. You and Bick have something going on the side?"

"Well, you're certainly more direct than the other detective I spoke with. Just a little office flirtation. Harmless."

"And out of the office?"

She shrugged, a careless and fluid gesture. "Didn't get that far. Maybe with a little more time."

"No problem poaching, then."

Smiling, Lilah took another look at her nails. "He wasn't married yet."

"What's the problem, Lilah? Can't get a man of your own?"

Eve saw it, a flash of temper — hot and sharp. "Anyone I want."

"Except Bick."

"You're a bitchy one, aren't you?"

"You bet. Why Bick?"

"He was great to look at, going places, terrific body. Looked to me like he'd be good in the sack. We might've made a good team, in and out of it."

"Must have pissed you off he wasn't biting."

"He didn't want to bang me, that was his problem, and his loss. If you think I killed him and his little sweetheart because of that, you should check with your detective. I've got two alibis. Twins. Six-two, two-twenty, and dumb as posts. I wore both of them out, but it took me until after three in the morning."

"What was Bick's top account?"

"Wendall James, LLC," she said without a second's hesitation.

"And who gets that account now that he's dead?"

Lilah angled her head. "Officially? It hasn't been decided. Unofficially? I'll make sure I do. I don't have to kill for accounts, honey. I just have to be good at what I do."

"I bet you are," Eve said, and leaving it at that went back to join Peabody downstairs.

"She's what my granny calls a tough cookie."

"I don't get that." Eve whipped away from the curb and headed back to Central. "If a cookie's tough, you throw it away. She's the type that knows how to stick."

"It just means . . . never mind. You think she's in it?"

"Could be. But that kind doesn't have to kill to get what she wants. She'd use her brains, her sex, cheat, maybe steal. She could seduce someone else into doing her dirty work, but what's the point here? Byson's out of the picture, maybe she cops some of his accounts, gets promoted quicker. But why Copperfield? And she was primary target. What did you get on the alibis?"

"Okay, on Jake Sloan it's DeLay, Rochelle. Twenty-five, single, works in Catering at the Palace."

"She's one of Roarke's?"

"Well, sort of. Her father's DeLay, hot-shot head chef at the Palace. She's been employed there for about two years. No criminal."

Eve hung a left. "We'll drop by, confirm the alibi face-to-face. Next?"

"On Randall Sloan. Sasha Zinka and Lola Warfield. Forty-eight and forty-two respectively. Married for twelve years. Big money — generational money on Zinka. They're Femme."

"Which is?"

"Extreme high-end enhancements. The company was founded by Zinka's great-grandfather, and remains one of the few independent companies of its size and scope. They own designer spas, where their products are used and sold. Few little brushes here and there on Zinka. Assault, property damage. Punched a cop."

"Really?"

"No time served. Lots of big fines, a number of civil suits. Nothing in the last decade on her."

"Youthful hijinks. Got a temper."

"More big money on Kraus's alibis, Madeline Bullock and Winfield Chase. Mother and son. Bullock, Sam, was her second husband — no offspring from there. Bullock, Sam, died at the age of one-twelve. They'd been married five years. She was forty-six."

"Isn't that romantic?"

"Heart-tugging. First husband was younger, a callow seventy-three to her twenty-two."

"Wealthy?"

"Was — not Sam Bullock wealthy, but well-stocked. Got eaten by a shark."

"Step off."

"Seriously. Scuba diving out in the Great Barrier Reef. He was eighty-eight. And this shark cruises along and *chomp, chomp*."

She gave Eve a thoughtful look. "Ending as shark snacks is in my top-ten list of ways I don't want to go out. How about you?"

"It may rank as number one, now that I've considered it a possibility. Any hint of foul play?"

"They weren't able to interview the shark, but it was put down as death by misadventure."

"Okay."

"While Bullock, the company, is varied, it started out primarily with pharmaceuticals. The Foundation, which the widow heads since her husband's death eight years ago, is a whopper, and annually disburses multiple millions to charities. Children's health care is priority. Nothing criminal on the widow, sealed juvie on the son, who is now thirty-eight. No marriage or cohabs on record."

"London-based, right?"

"Yep. They do have other homes, but none in the States. Mother and son share the same address. He's VP of the Foundation."

"Ought to be able to afford his own place."

"Last from this: For Myers we have Karl and Elise Helbringer, Germany. Married thirty-five years, three offspring. Karl went into business with Elise when they were both in their twenties. Making boots, which led to shoes and skids and bags and all sorts of things. Including romance, apparently, as they married shortly afterward. Hit big in the fashion and the outdoorsy-type worlds and built a nice little German empire. So, as bootmakers, I wouldn't say they're rolling in it, but stomping in it."

"Boots."

"Their foundation, and the original Helbringer is still their top seller. You're wearing a pair right now."

"Of boots."

"Helbringer boots. Very distinctive in their simplicity. Anyway, nothing on them or their offspring."

"We'll check for corroboration when we get back to Central."

Eve pulled up in front of the grand front entrance of Roarke's Palace. The doorman started over immediately. Eve saw recognition and then resignation flicker into his eyes as she climbed out of the car.

"Good morning, Lieutenant. Would you like me to have your vehicle parked?"

"What do you think?"

"I think you want it to stay exactly where it is."

"There you go." She jogged up the steps and into the glossy marble, the elaborate and enormous flowers, the sparkling fountains.

She wound her way under the waterfall of crystal chandeliers to the desk. When she saw another flicker of recognition on the face of one of the sleek, nattily uniformed desk clerks, she decided Roarke had called a staff meeting with her picture.

Regardless, she took out her badge. "I need to speak with Rochelle DeLay."

"Certainly, Lieutenant. I'll contact her immediately. If you'd care to have a seat."

At the gesture, Eve considered. Since everyone was being so cooperative, she could take the same page. "Sure."

Eve took one of the high-backed velvet chairs arranged in the elegant jungle of flowers.

"If my granny — the tough-cookie granny — ever gets out here, I'm going to take her to tea at the Palace." Peabody drew deep of the floral-scented air as she sat. "I think she'd get a charge out of it. Anyway, so while we're waiting it's a good time to talk about Mavis's shower."

"It couldn't possibly be."

"Come on, Dallas. We're on serious countdown now. Anyway, I got the theme. Thinking it's Mavis, and then with that chair you bought, I went with rainbow. I hit this party store on the way home last night and got all kinds of mag stuff."

"Great. Go you."

"Then there's the flowers. I figured on bopping by this place I know. But the thing is, um . . . I can't really afford to you know, pay."

Though she'd been trying to tune Peabody out, the last hit a chord. "Well, Jesus, Peabody, you don't have to pay. You're not supposed to pay."

"I want to help and everything, but —"

"Not with the dough." Eve forced herself to focus and deal with it. "Listen, you're right. There should be stuff. The more stuff, the more of the large charge Mavis gets. You're willing to get the stuff, I'll pay for it."

"That's good, that's great. Um, I never asked about, like, a budget."

Eve just sighed. "I guess the sky's the freaking limit."

"Yay. It's just completely ult. I mean, it's a total event."

"Put the squealy girl away," Eve said as she got to her feet. "Be a cop."

Eve spotted the pretty young thing headed toward them. Willowy build in a streamlined, almost military-style suit. The leafy green shade suited the coffee-and-cream complexion, and the hair — worn in a sleek updo — was dense brown.

Her lips curved in a polite, restrained welcome, but even that small smile didn't reach the melting chocolate eyes.

"Lieutenant Dallas, and . . ."

"Peabody. Detective," Peabody told her.

"I'm Rochelle DeLay. You must be here about Natalie. Is it all right if we sit out here? My office is a little box of a thing, and currently loaded with supplies for a party."

"This is fine."

"I just talked to Jake. I wish he'd go home. I don't think he's ready to be there, see everyone, not where he saw and talked to Nat almost every day."

"You were friends."

"We were. We got to be good friends when Jake and I started seeing each other. But Nat and Jake?" She looked away a moment, as people did when their composure wavered. "They were like family to each other."

"It didn't bother you that the guy you're dating was so tight with another woman?"

"It might have if there'd ever been anything romantic between them, or maybe it would have if it had been anyone but Nat. She was so into Bick, and I liked her so much. We had a lot of fun together, the four of us. We just clicked. I don't know what to do for Jake."

"Ms. DeLay," Peabody said, "sometimes women tell their women friends things they don't tell a man, no matter how close they are. Did Natalie say anything to you about being worried, concerned?"

"I can't think of anything. But . . . we were supposed to have lunch the day before she . . . the day before. She called and told me she wasn't feeling very well, was staying home from work, just going to stay in, catch up with things. Chill. I was busy. I was busy," Rochelle repeated in a voice that broke. "So I was kind of relieved. And now, when I think back, she sounded, I don't know, a little shaky, maybe nervous. I didn't think about it at the time. I could've gone over, taken her something to eat. It's what I do, but I didn't because I was busy. If there was something wrong, she might have told me. I keep thinking that."

"Hindsight's a choke chain," Eve told her. "You need to let that go. Tell me where you were the night she and Bick died."

"We had dinner at his grandparents'. We played bridge afterward. Well, they played," she said with a weak smile. "They're teaching me, and I blow at it. It was after midnight when we left, and we went back to Jake's. We're sort of cohabbing — unofficially. Sliding into it, I guess you could say. I was in the East Ballroom."

"I'm sorry?"

"The next morning. I was in the East Ballroom helping to set up for a luncheon. Jake came in, came to find me. He was crying. I'd never seen him cry before. And he told me. We sat on the floor, right on the floor in the ballroom."

CHAPTER
SEVEN

Eve took one look at the boxes covering the table in the conference room she'd ordered and felt a headache coming on.

"Okay, here comes the monkey work. We're going to go through the discs and hard copies, memo, memo books, appointment books, everything, going back — for now — two weeks. From the wit statements it was two weeks, ten days, when people started noticing something off with Copperfield, and just under two weeks when the transmission went from Copperfield to Byson that she had something she needed to show him."

"We'll get through the names, the notes — eventually," Peabody said. "But the accounts? We could probably use a numbers guy on this."

"Probably could," Eve agreed. "But for now, it's you and me. We'll look for repetition, a file or account she went back to repeatedly during the time frame. Any of them copied to her home unit, or any data she copied to Byson."

Eve glanced unhappily at the conference room's AutoChef, knowing it wasn't loaded with her personal stash of coffee.

"Any mention of meetings or appointments with the higher-ups," she continued. "Appointments with reps of accounts."

"Going to be awhile," Peabody commented. "Maybe I should order in some sandwiches."

"Whatever. Her assistant said she logged in after hours a couple times recently. Let's find what she accessed after business hours."

She turned as the door opened.

"Anything?" Baxter asked her.

"It's looking like she found something off at work, was pursuing it on her own, and shared her concerns with her fiancé. We're digging there."

"Want another shovel?"

Eve dipped her hands into her pockets. "What's on your desk?"

"A few things, mostly leg and 'link work. Nothing the boy can't handle," he added, referring to his trainee, Trueheart. "Look, the kid'll let me know if he needs me on anything active. I've got some personal time coming. I can take it to work this."

"You work it, you work it on the clock. Anything of your own heats up, you're on that."

"No problem."

When her communicator beeped, she glanced at the readout. "Peabody, fill Baxter in. It's Whitney's office. I need to update him."

She was ordered up, and found Commander Whitney behind his desk. She thought he looked tired, maybe burdened was the better word. His big shoulders carried considerable weight.

Gray was sprinkled generously through the dark hair that was closely cut around his wide, coffee-colored face. He watched her, saying nothing, as she ran through the movements and details of the investigation.

"The data you confiscated is secured?"

"Yes, sir. Detectives Peabody and Baxter are starting the search. Captain Feeney is supervising the e-work, using Detective McNab."

"Other avenues?"

"Sir?"

"Exploration of this being personal business. Jealous ex?"

"I haven't eliminated the possibility, Commander, but nothing points to that. While everything points to this being a double murder motivated by something the female vic discovered at her place of employment."

He nodded. "You understand the sensitivity of the data now in the possession of this department?"

"Yes, sir."

His eyes stayed on hers. "Have you considered the sensitivity of you, personally, having access to that data?"

"Personally, Commander?"

"You're married to a powerful businessman who has interests in many areas of industry and finance — interests that most certainly will be in competition or conflict with some of the parties whose data you now have in your possession."

Something hot formed a tiny ball in Eve's belly. "I have potential evidence in my possession."

"Don't be naive, Dallas."

"I never was. I'm the primary investigator on two murders looking for evidence of motive and culpability. I'm not looking, and have no interest in, inside information on my husband's business competition."

"There's concern that, should this data come into his hands, it might be used to his advantage against those competitors."

The hot little ball expanded. "He doesn't need my help to compete in business. And he wouldn't walk over two dead bodies to make some extra bucks. Respectfully, sir" — though her tone had taken on an edge that had nothing to do with respect — "to imply otherwise is an insult to me and to him."

"It's not a matter of a few extra dollars, but the potential of millions. Perhaps more than millions. And yes, it's insulting. It's also necessary to be understood. If the information now at your disposal should be used in any way unrelated to your investigation, you, this office, this department, will be responsible."

"My understanding of my responsibility to the victim, to the people of New York, and to this department is and always has been crystal." It wasn't a ball in her belly now, but a flood. Like lava. "If you have any doubts of my understanding of that responsibility or my ability to fulfill it, you're not only obliged to remove me from this investigation, but you should be asking for my badge."

"You want to be pissed, be pissed. Now, Lieutenant, go back to work."

She turned on her heel, struggling to keep that fury down, hold it in. But she didn't quite block all of it. She looked back as she yanked open the door. "I'm not Roarke's goddamn stooge," she snapped, and shut the door behind her.

She hauled the temper with her back down to Homicide and into the conference room. One look at Eve's face made whatever bright comment Peabody was about to utter wither and die.

"Sir," she said instead, "Baxter's taking Byson's data. So far we've found nothing transferred to his data records from Copperfield's."

"We keep looking."

"On the e-front, McNab reports that files have been deleted from Copperfield's office unit."

"Is Detective McNab now reporting to you? Was there a change in command during the last twenty minutes?"

Knowing that tone, Peabody kept her own very even. "Detective McNab believed we were together, sir, either here or in the field. As I understood you were with the commander, I took his report, and am now reporting same."

"I'm in EDD."

Baxter and Peabody exchanged eye rolls behind her back. And fortunately for their welfare, had instincts quick enough to have those eyes focused on the work when she spun around.

"Nobody enters this room or approaches these files without my authority. Clear?"

"Yes, sir!"

When the door was slammed, Peabody let out a long, whistling breath. "Whitney put a really nasty bug up her butt."

Eve stormed into EDD and through to the comp lab to find McNab. He was hunkered over Copperfield's office unit. A handful of other detectives or techs worked on various comps in the same area.

"You're to use a privacy cube at all times when working on this case."

"Huh? What?" He dragged off a headset.

"This case is now flagged Blue. Privacy cube, verbal reports. Need-to-know basis."

"Ooooo-kay." He stepped back, just a little, as if he felt the heat pumping off her and was afraid he'd get burned. "I've got some deletions. They were —"

"Privacy cube," she snapped. "Now."

"Yes, sir. It's going to take me a few minutes to set it up."

"Then get started." She stormed out, veered off, and swung into Feeney's office. He was sitting at his desk, machine-gunning on his keyboard while he hummed a tune.

Every so often he'd mutter, "Almost got you, you little bastard."

"Your detectives have trouble understanding direct orders, or the chain of command?" she demanded.

He cursed, glanced up. He saw what Peabody had seen on her face. Easing back, he jerked his chin at the door. "Wanna shut that?"

She slammed it. "When I'm primary, the men assigned to the team, whether they're EDD or Homicide, report to me."

"You got a complaint about one of my boys?" They were all his boys to Feeney, regardless of their chromosomes.

It caught her just before she spewed. What was she doing? Playing tattletale over *nothing* just because she was pissed. "I've got a sensitive case," she began.

"Yeah, I know about it. My boys report to me, and I logged in the electronics as you requested. So?"

"Big money sensitive. You figure Roarke would climb over my two vics, use that big money sensitive data to edge out a competitor? You figure he'd use my investigation or any information I might share with him therein for personal gain?"

"What the fuck you talking about? McNab make some idiot comment?"

"No. Whitney made a direct statement."

Feeney pursed his lips, then blew out a breath. Then dragged his fingers through his wiry tangle of ginger and gray hair. "I got some of that coffee left you gave me for Christmas. Want a hit?"

"No. No," she repeated and walked to his window. "Goddamn it, Feeney. He wants to slap at me for something I did or didn't do on the job, something one of my squad did or didn't, that's okay. But to imply Roarke would use me, that I'd permit it, that's over the line."

"Have some almonds."

She only shook her head.

Feeney dipped his fingers into the bowl of candied nuts on his desk. "Want my take?"

"I guess I do. I come pushing in here when you're busy, I must need your take."

"Then I'll give it to you. I expect some of those honchos — and the lawyers who love them — have

125

been stomping their feet, flapping their jaws. Complaining to the mayor, the chief. Mayor and chief give Whitney the word. He's got to take the departmental line, give you the warning. Want my take on his personal line?"

"I guess I do."

"I've known him a long time. If he had any genuine concerns in this area, he'd take you off the case. Period. By doing that, he'd cover his ass. Instead, he gave you the word, and he's leaving his ass hanging out there."

"Maybe."

"Dallas?" He waited until she'd turned around. "You got any worries about Roarke on this?"

"No. Goddamn no."

"You think I do, or that any member of the team currently working the case has any worries?"

The tightness in her chest eased a little. "No. But I've got to go to Roarke with this — even if I don't share a single byte of data with him, I have to go to him with this. If you think I was pissed when I came in here, let me tell you, that was a sunny day at the beach."

He shoved the bowl of nuts in her direction, and for a moment there was a touch of amusement on his hangdog face. "Marriage is a freaking minefield."

"Fucking A." But she relaxed a little, enough to sit on the corner of his desk and pluck up a few nuts. "Sorry."

"Forget it. We go back a ways, too."

"I don't know how much you've got on your plate, but if you've got room for more I could sure use you on this."

"I can probably clear a space. Me, I like a full plate."

"Thanks. All around."

With her temper defused, Eve headed back down to the conference room, where she found Peabody and Baxter deep into search mode and a mountainous pile of sandwiches. When she entered, Baxter kept his eyes on his screen, but Peabody risked a glance up. Obviously encouraged by what she saw on her partner's face, she nodded toward the pile of food.

"Figured some hoagies would keep us going through this."

"Fine." Though her pissed level was down, so was her appetite. Eve culled out a pile of discs and took a comp unit. Moments later a mug of coffee appeared beside her elbow.

"Ah, also figured you'd want your own brew while we're at this."

"Thanks. I imagine you figured I'd share that brew and loaded the AC on that assumption."

"Would that be an incorrect assumption?" Peabody smiled winningly.

"My assumption would be you're already slurping it down."

"Baxter slurps. I, however, sip delicately."

Eve took a breath. "Listen. The commander wanted more than an update. He had some concerns — or some jerk has concerns — about Roarke being privy to some of this data, through me. Then using same to outswing competitors."

"No wonder you were ready to kick the first available ass," Peabody commented.

"Well." Baxter paused long enough to scratch his cheek. "I'd guess Whitney said what he had to say, even knowing it was flammable bullshit. Must suck being brass."

The last of Eve's temper simply dwindled away. "Must. Let's dig down into this fucking morass and find some goddamn gold."

They dug for hours. Natalie Copperfield's data files were organized and efficient, and gave them nothing.

"McNab said there were deletions." Eve pushed back. "I've got what could be interpreted as lost time, or deletions in files. Little holes, if you look at them that way. You got a serious worker bee here."

"Makes me feel like a slacker," Peabody agreed, then pokered up. "Which, of course, I'm not. Being a detective, and a dedicated member of the NYPSD trained by the best in the department."

"Ass kisser," Baxter said with a grin.

"I have three gold stars for ass kissing."

"That's all really fascinating," Eve said dryly. "But my point is, Copperfield kept superior records of her work, of her time. And I'm seeing gaps. A pattern of gaps going back about five, six months."

"I've got some of that," Peabody agreed. "Could be just wedding planning. A little personal business leaked into the workplace. Happens to the best of us."

"Maybe. And maybe it's an account that was passed to her at that point. Those gaps start widening ten days before her death. About the time we believe she found something questionable."

"If her killer deleted those client files altogether," Baxter began, "he or she had access to her work unit, her data files. Doesn't strike me that a client would be able to access."

"Could hack in by remote, or pay someone with the necessary skills to do so," Eve replied. "Or it could be someone on the inside. Could be both. What we're not finding in her files is evidence there was something her killer didn't want found there."

"Her supervisor would know all her accounts," Peabody put in.

"Yeah. I'm going to go by, have another talk with her before I take this home. Peabody, I need all this data secured. Baxter, if you want to do a little leg work, you can check with the vic's sister. See if Copperfield mentioned getting a new account within the last six months. It should be a big one."

"Got that."

"Check on Trueheart and your actives. If you need to put in extra time, run it through me. I'll clear it."

"Appreciate it."

"Peabody, if McNab has anything, I want a tag. Whenever, wherever. I'm in the field."

The ferocity of the traffic reminded Eve of the time. The accounting firm would be closed for the day. She called up Cara Greene's home address from her memo book, then tried her on the 'link. At the transfer to voice mail, she left a message to be contacted ASAP. On the off chance Greene was putting in some overtime, Eve tried the office 'link, and left the same message.

No point in going by to bang on the door of an empty apartment, she decided. She'd wait for the callback, or hunt Greene down in the morning.

Now she had to figure out the best approach with Roarke.

Keeping her mouth shut just wasn't an option. Even if she wanted to play that game, he'd sense something. The guy had senses like a frigging hawk. And evading would lead, unquestionably, to lying. Lying would put her in the wrong.

Goddamn if she wanted to take the heat for this.

Straight out was probably the best way, she decided. Let him blow, let him spew, and seethe over the insult. He was entitled.

The problem was he was going to blow, spew, and seethe all over her. So she'd take the high road, she'd be the good wife and take the lumps. Then he'd have to apologize, maybe even grovel a little.

How bad could that be?

She was feeling fairly steady about the entire matter when she drove through the gates of home.

Considering various openings, she jogged through the bitter cold and into the warmth. The gilded light, the lightly spiced scent of the air were spoiled momentarily by the looming figure in black that was Summerset.

"I didn't realize you were taking a few days off," he began as the cat left its squat at his side to prance toward Eve.

"What are you talking about?"

"As you've returned home unbloodied, without any of your clothing torn, I assume you've spent the day in some leisurely pursuit."

"Day's not over yet." She tossed her coat over the newel post. "I could end it pursuing your bony ass, but you'd be the one bloodied and torn."

She picked up the pudgy cat and hauled him with her up the stairs. He purred like a jet copter as she idly scratched his ears, then dumping him on the sofa in the bedroom, she checked Roarke's whereabouts on the house scanner.

"Where is Roarke?"

Roarke has not yet returned to the house this evening.

Bought some time, she decided, and stripped off her clothes to change into workout gear. The best way to clear her mind and tune up, she thought, was a good sweaty session in the gym.

To avoid Summerset, she took the elevator down, then programmed a hill climb on the cardio machine. She did a hard twenty minutes until her quads felt the burn, then switched to a flat-out sprint.

She was well into a series of upper-body reps on the weight machine when Roarke strolled in.

"Long day?" she managed, puffing out air.

"A bit." He bent over, touched his lips to hers. "Getting started or finishing up?"

"Finishing. I've got enough in me for a spar if you're looking for a workout."

"I had mine this morning. I'm looking for a very large glass of wine and a meal."

She studied his face. "Was a long day, then. Problems?"

"Irritations, mostly, and mostly eliminated. But now that I'm thinking of it, I wouldn't mind a swim before that wine. If I had some company."

"Sure." She picked up a towel, scrubbed it over her face. Get it over or put it off until he mellowed out? Tough to know, she thought, but it seemed wrong to let him mellow then hit him with a sucker punch.

"Ah, there's this thing." To give herself another moment, she walked over, got a bottle of water from the minifriggie. "The double murder I'm investigating. The accounting firm element."

"You got your warrant?"

"Yeah. That's part of the thing."

"The thing being?"

She braced inside, as she might before diving into a very cold pool. "There's a concern at some levels regarding the sensitivity of the data on the files now in the possession of the NYPSD, and the primary — being me, who's married to you."

"There's a question, on some levels, about your ability to handle sensitive data?" His voice was perfectly pleasant, even amiable. And had her antennae quivering.

"There's a question, on some levels, about the ethics, I guess, of you having some close proximity to private financial information belonging to current or future business competitors. I want you to know that I —"

"So the assumption," he interrupted smoothly, "is that I would use my wife, and her investigations into a double torture murder, to not only learn the financial situation of competitors — current or future — but would then use that information to my own gain? Do I have that right?"

"Nutshelling. Listen, Roarke —"

"I haven't finished." He whipped the words out, one quick lash. "Did it occur to any of these *levels* that I don't need to use my wife or her investigation to beat bloody hell out of a competitor, in a business sense, should I choose to do so. And that I somehow managed to compete and succeed on my own before I met the primary on this case?"

She *hated* when he used *my wife* in that tone. Like she was one of his fancy wrist units. Temper bubbled into her throat and was a very hard swallow down. "I can't speak to what occurs or occurred there, but —"

"Goddamn it, Eve. Do you think I'd use you for fucking money?"

"Not for a single second. Look at me. Not for one single second."

"Crawl over the bloody bodies, risk your reputation and my own, come to that, for an edge in some shagging deal?"

"I just said I didn't —"

"I heard what you said," he snapped back and his eyes were lethal. "But I see for some it's 'once a thief.' I've worked side-by-side with the NYPSD, given it considerable time, taken considerable physical risks, and now they question my integrity over this? Over this? Well, fuck them. If they can't and won't trust you after all you've given them, or me, fuck them to hell and back. I want you to pass the case."

"You want — whoa, wait."

"I want you to pass it," he repeated. "I'll not have one byte of that bloody *sensitive* data in my home, or in my wife's head, or anywhere I can be suspected of using it. Damned, *goddamned* if I'll be accused somewhere down the line of using something like this over some deal I close over someone else. I bloody well won't have it."

"Okay, let's just calm down a minute." She had to take a breath, then another, before her head stopped whirling. "You can't ask me to hand over the investigation."

"That's precisely what I'm asking. And if memory serves, I've asked for very little when it comes to your work. You aren't the only qualified investigator. Pass it," he demanded. "And do it now. I won't be insulted this way. And bugger me if I'm going to tolerate having my wife be the one who has to bring the insult to me because your superiors don't have the balls to do it themselves."

She stood stunned and speechless as he turned on his heel and strode out.

CHAPTER
EIGHT

His anger had teeth and was gnawing at his own throat as he stormed up to his office, closed the doors. And he knew if he hadn't walked away that anger would have taken more than a bite of Eve.

Her goddamn job, he thought. Bloody, buggering cops. Why in hell had he ever deluded himself into believing they could accept who and what he was?

He was no innocent and never claimed to be one.

Had he stolen? Frequently. Had he cheated? Most certainly. Had he used wit, wiles, and whatever came to hand to fight and claw his way out of the alley to where he was now? Goddamn bloody well right he had, and would do it all again, without remorse or regret.

He didn't ask to be considered pure and saintly. He'd been a Dublin street rat with certain skills and specific ambitions, and had used one to achieve the other. And why not?

He'd come from a man who'd murdered in cold blood, and yes, he'd done some of the same.

But he'd made himself into more, into better. Into other, in any case. And when he'd fallen in love with a cop, with a woman he'd respected on every possible level, he'd given up a great deal. Every one of his businesses was legitimate now. He could be considered a shark in the business world, but he was a bloody law-abiding one.

More, he'd actually worked with the cops, the very element that had once been the enemy. He'd offered his resources to the department countless times. The fact that doing so amused, intrigued, and satisfied him didn't change the principle of the thing.

Infuriating, insulting, unacceptable.

With his hands jammed in his pockets, he stood at the window, glowering out at the sparkling lights of the city he'd made his home.

He'd made himself, he thought again. He'd carved out this life, and he loved this woman above everything else. To have anyone, anyone suspect he would use her — that she would allow herself to be used — was enraging.

Well, they could have someone else work themselves to the bone, labor into exhaustion to find their bloody murderer. And if they thought somewhere down the road they could tap him again to play expert consultant, civilian, they could shag a monkey.

He heard the door open between his office and Eve's, but didn't turn.

"I said all I have to say on this," he told her. "It's done."

"Fine, you can just listen then. I don't blame you for being upset."

"Upset?"

"I don't blame you for being murderously pissed off. I felt the same way."

136

"Fine. We're in tune."

"I don't guess we are. Roarke —"

"If you think this is a tantrum or something I can be sweetened out of, you're wrong. It's a line. We've reached my line in this, Eve. I expect you to respect my stand on this matter." He turned now. "I expect you to put me first, and that's all."

"You get both of those. But you've got to hear me out. Line or no line, you can't just go around flinging orders at me."

"It was a statement."

"Screw this, Roarke. Just screw this." Her own anger was rising, but there was a layer of sick fear over it. "I'm pissed, you're pissed, and if this keeps up, we're going to be seriously pissed at each other, maybe enough to cross some other line we can't come back over easily, when we're the ones getting slapped by outside parties."

"When has the department been an outside party to you?"

"I have to prove something to you now?" And there was hurt, churning through the anger, and the sick fear. "To you? What needs to be proven here? My loyalty? The pecking order of that loyalty?"

"Maybe it does." He angled his head, spoke coolly. "I wonder where I'll come in that order."

"Yeah, seriously pissed." But she took a deep breath before she lost what was left of her temper. Or worse, lost the fight to hold back the tears that were stinging the back of her eyes. "I've got things to say, goddamn it, and I'm saying them. If when I'm done, you want me to pass the investigation, it's passed."

Something inside him clenched and released, but he only shrugged. "Have your say, then."

"You don't believe me," she said slowly. "I can see it. You think, or wonder at least, if I'm just snowing you so I win on this. And that's insulting, and I've had enough insults for the day, damn it. So you listen. When someone kicks at you, they kick at me. That's the way it is. And not just because I'm your *wife,* because I'm not some stupid bimbo who takes orders from her *husband*."

"I don't believe the word *bimbo* came out of my mouth."

"It sounds like bimbo, occasionally, when you say 'wife.'"

"Oh, bollocks to that."

"And right back at you, ace. They slap at you, they slap at me because we're a unit. Because I may not get all this being married crap right, but I've damn well got that one nailed. So, believe me when I tell you the department knows just how I feel about this business."

"Fine, then —"

"*I'm* not finished," she spat out. "Sweeten you up, what a crock. But you want some oil on the water? When I spewed this business out on Feeney, then out on Baxter and Peabody, they had the same take. That it was insulting bullshit. And I'm damned, Roarke, if I want to put my tail between my legs and pass this ball. Not just for the victims — and they matter, they matter a hell of a lot to me now. But for my own pride, and for yours. Screw that, for *ours*. I'm not going to back off because the mayor or the chief or the commander — whoever — needs to cover their chicken-shit asses because some jerks are whining because you're just better and smarter and slicker then they are in the first damn place.

"And I'm *pissed!*" She kicked his desk. "Pissed, pissed, pissed about being disrespected. Like I'm some idiot *female* who'd compromise an investigation for her man's gain. Or that my man is some callous cheat who can't bury his competitors without breaking a sweat. They're not getting away with it. We're not going to let them shove us back from this. We're not going to let them put two innocent people who died because they were trying to do something right, however *stupidly*, in the backseat over fucking politics."

She kicked his desk again, and felt calmer for it. "You've done more than stand by me on the job. And you deserve better from the department. So I'll do more than stand by you, and if stepping back from this is what you need, that's what I'll do."

She caught her breath. "That's what I'll do, because if you don't know you come first, you're just stupid. But it's not the way to stick it to the ones who deserve to have it stuck to them. Staying on it is, putting you on in an official capacity as consultant is. Finding the person or persons who killed those two people is. I want to close this case, and I want you with me when I do. But on this one, you get to decide."

She tunneled her fingers through her hair and realized she was exhausted. "Your call."

He said nothing for a long, humming moment. "You'd do this, pass this case, because I asked you?"

"No. I'd do this, pass this case, because in these circumstances I figure you've got the right to ask me. I don't lift off when you say jump, ace, any more than you do for me. But when it matters, it matters. Is that what you want me to do?"

"It was, before you came in here." He crossed to her now, and took her face in his hands. "It was, I'm forced to admit, when I was near certain you'd refuse, and given me a handy outlet where I could blame you for the whole mess of it. Then I could have worked off some of this mad with a good, bloody row with you." He kissed her brow, her nose, her lips. "You didn't, so I guess that good, bloody row is out of the question."

"I'm always up for one."

Now he smiled. "Hard to work up the energy for one when I'm also forced to admit you're right. Actually, thinking about it, that's a considerable irritation. Everything you just said bull's-eyed the entire ugly situation. The victims deserve you, and I'm damned if the department gets the satisfaction of having you toss this one back because of me. And damned again if I'll have fingers pointed at me as a cheat who'd use his wife. I've done plenty in my time to deserve finger-pointing, but not this."

"Are we square?"

He gave her shoulders a light rub before he stepped back. "It seems we are. But the term *wife* is not synonymous with *bimbo*. I love my wife very much.

140

I've only slept with bimbos — occasionally. In the past."

He was still seething mad though, she noted. However cool and collected he might seem, she knew him, and saw the black temper bubbling under the surface. She couldn't blame him. But there were other ways to work off a rage than a sweaty session in the gym, or a good, bloody row.

"I still need that shower." She headed for the door, glancing over her shoulder on the way out. "Wouldn't mind some company."

She ordered the jets on full, at a temperature of 101, and let the heat punch its way into her bones. With her eyes closed and the water pulsing over her head, the worst of the headache she'd been carrying eased off.

When arms came around her, the tension inside her body shifted to a different arena.

"Sorry," she said with her eyes still closed. "You'll have to get in line. I've already got a guy scheduled for shower sex."

Hands slid up to cover her breasts; teeth nipped lightly into her shoulder.

"Well, maybe I can squeeze you in."

She started to turn, but those hands held her in place while his mouth roamed over her neck and shoulders. Little bites while the steam began to rise.

With an arm hooked around her waist, he flipped open the compartment in the glass block and let a river of fragrant soap pool into his hand. He slicked it over her breasts, torso, belly. Slow circles while the water pumped and pulsed.

Everything inside her tightened into delicious knots that released only to snap taut again. The wet heat, the smooth hands teased all of her senses to the edge of nerves, drenching her in sensations.

She lifted her arms, taking them back to wind around his neck, to open herself. Those lazy circles traveled down her again, slid slippery between her legs. Her body bowed, her breath escaping in a moan as he tipped her over the edge.

She shuddered for him, shuddered and bucked against his busy hands, fueling his needs even as he sated hers. His own system began to churn, greed and want and lust and love so twisted together they created one mass of heat that spread from heat to heart to loins.

A unit, he thought. Two lost souls, steeped in shadows, that had found each other. He shouldn't have forgotten, even in temper, the miracle of that.

When he pulled her around to face him, her eyes were heavy, her face flushed — and her lips slowly curved.

"Oh, it's you. I thought there was something familiar, but I wasn't sure." She reached down, took the hot, hard length of him in her hands. "Yeah, I recognize this."

She kept those sleepy eyes open and on his when he pushed her back against the wet wall. While the jetting water thundered he took her mouth, took her taste and quivered with the thrill when her lips met his with equal passion.

Then, gripping her hips, he plunged into her, swallowing her cries, her gasps, her moans, as he drove them both.

Her fingers slid down him, dug in for purchase as shock and excitement ripped through her. There was nothing but the heat, the wet, the glorious hard body against her, in her. The pleasure shot her up so high she had to fight for breath to even moan his name.

Then it wrung her out, made her weak, made her woozy. She felt him let go, felt him give himself to her as she went limp.

"*Ta cion agam ort.*" With his body warm and pressed to hers he murmured it.

I love you, Eve thought, in Gaelic. Knowing he used it when it mattered most to him, she smiled.

Feeling relaxed and accommodating, she let him pick the meal and ended up eating some sort of lightly grilled fish with a side of spicy rice mixed with crispy vegetables. She might have preferred a burger and fries drenched in salt, but she couldn't complain.

And the chilly glass of Italian white made it all go down smooth as silk.

"Before we go any further," he began, "I want to say more than feeling kicked, I felt I'd been sucker punched by this. And it bruised."

"I'm sorry."

"Hardly your fault. The fact is, I was equally furious with myself. I should have seen it coming."

"Why? *How?*"

"A prominent accounting firm, with prominent clients." He moved his shoulders. "There had to be some question that I'd have access to the financial data of some competitors. And the ensuing uproar over it."

"Hey." She stabbed out with her fork. "You're not going to take their side on this one. That'll just piss me off all over again."

"I'm not, no. I think it was poorly handled. Still, I should have expected something along those lines, and been better prepared to deal with it."

"They bitch-slapped both of us. I'm not going to forget it."

"Nor will I. Why don't you tell me about the progress of the investigation. If nothing else, it'll make me feel we've given them a good poke in the eye."

"Sure."

He listened while she brought him up to date.

"So somebody accessed her files and deleted whatever it was she was looking into. A clean job, according to McNab. They're going to keep digging."

"Smarter if they'd taken the units, as they did on the crime scenes."

"Yeah, in hindsight. I'm guessing the killer couldn't be sure we'd pin it to an account and start looking there. And until I talk to her supervisor, I don't know that we will pin it to a specific account. When you take a scan of her office unit, even a hard look, you just see her tidy, organized files and data. The missing pieces only show up if you're looking for them — those specific times and dates."

"Foreign accounts," he mused. "It would be, most likely, a company — or individuals attached to it — that has interests here as well. Most likely directly here in New York. EDD hasn't yet determined if the access was remote or on site?"

"Not yet. My gut tells me on site. The killer hauled off their home units. If he had solid hacker skills, why not just delete the files from them? Or better, do that by remote before or after the killing? He hauled them away so he could get rid of them, ditch the data and dispose of the units. Not so easy to walk off with office equipment."

"Good security?"

"Damn good. I don't think anyone could have wandered in after hours without it showing up on discs. And nothing has. He deleted the files during working hours. Maybe got the passcodes and deleted from another station inside the building, maybe got into her office while her assistant was busy elsewhere. With the delay getting the warrant to confiscate, there was time. The killer or an accessory is inside the firm."

He sipped a little wine. "Did your first victim gain any new accounts in the last few weeks?"

"Thought of that, and no. Nothing new in the last couple that I can see, so there's no way to narrow it down from that route. If she flagged anything hinky, that's gone. Maybe one of the accounts suddenly didn't jibe, and she took a closer look. Could be the client recently started doing the shadowy stuff. Or she just happened to stumble across something because they'd gotten sloppy. Happens. But she didn't discuss a problem with an account to any of the higher-ups or with her assistant. Not that any of them is copping to, at any rate."

"Just the fiancé." Roarke nodded. "Because she trusted him completely."

"I get that. But I don't believe she didn't at least mention something to one of the partners or her supervisor, her department head. She was meticulous. You'll see what I mean when you look at her files."

"I'll take your word on that for now."

Eve set down her glass. "I thought we'd squared this, and you'd step onto the team — at least when you had time for it."

"For now," he repeated, "I'd rather wait to look at the files. By meticulous, you mean she kept everything in excellent order."

Eve struggled back her annoyance. "That, yeah, but she was meticulous in the way she kept her office space, her apartment, her closet. She never had a single work eval that wasn't glowing. She had a good relationship with her department head, and apparently with everyone she worked with. She was tight pals with the grandson of one of the partners."

"Romantic link?"

"No. It comes off as pals. Good, platonic pals. Grandson has a girlfriend, and the four of them hung. But she doesn't mention there's this problem to her pal."

"Blood's thicker?"

"Maybe, maybe." She pushed away from the little table where they'd eaten. "It's inconsistent with her

146

type, her pathology. She was a team player, and she was a rule keeper. She took this to one of them, Roarke, and the one she took it to was the wrong choice."

"She must have dealt with some clients directly."

"In the office, or in theirs — New York-based. Some travel, too, sure. But nothing out of the ordinary I've found. No last-minute appointments worked in, according to her assistant. No last-minute travel to meet with a client or their representatives. If you look at her office, on the surface, it's straight business as usual. Taking the home units without making it look like a bungled burglary was a mistake."

"I don't know." He considered it. "Simpler, as you said, to take the units than to stay there and fiddle with them. Especially since the killer had a second job to do. It could simply be confidence. Go ahead and look at her office files, I've taken care of that. Covered the tracks."

"Nobody ever covers them all the way. Okay, okay, present company excepted," she added when he lifted an eyebrow. "If he was as good as you, and as — let's say — meticulous — he'd have found a better way to do Copperfield and Byson."

"Such as?"

"Arrange a meet, take them out together outside their apartments. You make it look like a mugging or a thrill kill. Rape the woman, or him, or both. Send the investigators mixed signals. I figure I'm looking for someone focused on the task — eliminate the threat, remove the evidence. That's straight-line thinking, leaving out the flourishes."

"Perhaps the only way he could take lives was to block out all but the target. Reach the goal, don't consider the enormity of the action to get there."

"I don't think so, or not completely. Yeah, okay, reaching the goal. But if he'd needed to distance himself emotionally from the action, he wouldn't use strangulation. It's intimate. And it was face-to-face."

Narrowing her eyes, she brought the crime scenes, the bodies, back into her mind. "He experienced the killings. You don't want an active part in it? You got the tape right there. You slap it over their mouths, over their nose, and you walk away. You don't have to see them suffer and die. But he looked right into their eyes as they did.

"And this isn't what I need you for," she snapped. "I can get into his head. Or I can get a profile from Mira, talk it through with her. I need a numbers man. I need a business man. Big business, big risks, big benefits. I need you to look at the data, analyze it in a way I can't."

"And I will. But tonight I'd prefer the generalities. I can take a look at her client list, give you a take on what I know that might not show on records or bios."

"Why tonight?"

He considered again. Easier to evade, but she'd been straight with him and deserved the same. "I'm going to have my lawyers draft a contract of sorts which will prohibit me from using any of the data I may be privy to during the course of this investigation."

"No."

"It covers our respective asses. It will also prohibit you, or any member of the team, from revealing the name of the organization, corporation or company whose data I analyze. I can, quite easily, work with the figures only."

Frustration nearly blew out of the top of her head. "This is a crock. Your word's good enough."

"For you, and thank you for it. But it's simple enough to do, and it's logical. It's very likely I'm in competition, or certainly will be at some point, with some or all of the clients on your victims' list. And at some point, while I can promise you I wouldn't use the data you've put in my hands —"

"I don't want your damn promise!" she exploded.

Her fury over it was like a warm, comforting kiss. "Then none of that between us. But, let's be practical. It could appear, or be argued that I have or will use it. It still could, come to that, but this shows good intent at least."

"It's insulting to you."

"Not if I offer it — more, insist on it. Which is exactly what I'm doing." He knew how to calculate the odds, he thought. How to manipulate them. And how to win. "I won't look at any of the data unless you agree to this provision. We can argue about it if you like, but that's my line. I'll have it taken care of, then we'll move forward."

"Fine. Fine. If that's the way you want it." She had to fight back the urge to kick something again.

"It is. I'm happy to look at the client list."

She moved to her desk, pulled out a hard copy from her file bag. "Look it over, think it over. I've got some runs to do meanwhile."

And some sulking, he imagined. "I'll be in my office, then."

She did sulk, but she worked while she was at it.

She did probabilities and was satisfied that the computer agreed — at 93.4 percent — that someone inside the firm was connected to the double murder.

She studied her notes, Peabody's reports, the lab's, the ME's, the crime-scene records. And put up a second murder board.

New lock on the door, she reminded herself. Kitchen knife in the bedroom. But Natalie hadn't been afraid enough to bunk with her boyfriend, or hole up in a hotel. Not afraid enough to tell her sister not to come and stay with her.

"Knew the killer," Eve said aloud. "Or the go-between. Nervous, excited, cautious, but not seriously afraid for her life. Knife in the bedroom. Girl thing."

She paced in front of the board as she thought. Any serious attacker could probably have disarmed a woman of Copperfield's build. But she's alone, starts wigging just a little. Takes the knife like she could use it if she had to.

"Not a stupid woman, but seriously naive," Eve added. "Gonna handle this deal herself, with her guy. A little excitement in their lives. But who else did she tell?"

When her 'link beeped, she turned, answered it absently. "Dallas."

"Hey, I know it's late but I got this brainstorm." Peabody's brows drew together on the display screen. "Are you still working?"

"Who did she tell?"

"Who, what?"

Obviously, Eve thought as she pulled her mind away from the murder board, Peabody wasn't still working. "What brainstorm?"

"About the shower?"

"Oh, Christ on a plastic crutch."

"Look, it's the day after tomorrow."

"No, it's not. It's on Saturday."

"And tomorrow being Friday, Saturday follows. At least in my pretty little world."

"Damn it, damn it, damn it."

"So anyway, I've got the theme going, and picked up some stuff on my way home. I thought if I came by there tomorrow night, stayed over, we could put it all together in the morning."

"What does that mean, putting it all together?"

"Well, the decorations, and these flower things I ordered, and, well . . . stuff. Plus I got this idea about the rocker system you bought her and how we can use it as a focal point, but disguise it like a throne until —"

"Please, in the name of God, don't tell me any more."

"So it chills with you if me and McNab bunk there tomorrow night?"

"Sure, bring the family, all your friends, strangers you find on the street. All are welcome here."

"Uptown! Catch you in the morning."

She clicked off, then sat on the edge of her desk staring at nothing in particular. Baby showers and double murders. Was she the only one who could see they didn't mix? She wasn't equipped for the first. It wasn't in her makeup.

But she'd tried, hadn't she? She'd called the caterer, and she'd let Mavis invite a horde of people — many of whom would be stranger than alien mutants. And still, it wasn't enough.

"Why do I have to decorate?" she demanded when Roarke stepped to the doorway.

"You don't. In fact, I sincerely wish you wouldn't. I like our home as it is."

"See? Me, too." She threw out her arms. "Why does it have to get tricked out for a baby shower?"

"Oh. That. Well . . . I have no idea. I really choose to remain ignorant in this particular area of societal customs."

"Peabody said we have to have a theme."

He looked momentarily baffled. "A song?"

"I don't know." Confused, Eve covered her eyes with her hands. "And there's going to be a throne."

"For the baby?"

"I don't know." Now she pulled at her hair. "I can't think about it. It throws me off. I was thinking about murder, and I was fine. Now I'm thinking about themes and thrones, and I feel a little sick."

Eve took a huge breath. "Who did she tell?"

"Peabody? I thought she just told you."

"No, God, not Peabody. Natalie Copperfield. Who did she trust or respect or feel obliged to report to if she found something off? Which of her clients did she believe, while they might do something illegal, unethical, might offer a bribe, wouldn't cause her real physical harm? Because there's no way she'd have let her sister come over, talked about pancake breakfasts, if she believed there might be actual danger."

"First, I'd say who she told would depend on the level of the illegality she uncovered. It's not impossible she went directly to the client or their representative. But more likely that she showed the data to a superior."

"Back where I started, running rings. No way to pin down who she might have told other than the boyfriend."

"As for her client list, there are some high-end companies here. Any or all of them has very likely had some slippery moments. You can't operate large companies without some slippage. Then you pay lawyers to slide you out of it, or you pay fines, settle suits out of court. But I don't know of any major scandal involving those on her lists. And I haven't heard anything murmuring on the wind about illegal practices. I can tune myself to that wind a little closer for you."

"That'd be good."

She frowned at the board again. "Wait. What if the client isn't the problem? What if someone inside the firm did something like Whitney suggested you could do."

Roarke cocked his head, nodded. "Fed one client private data on another. Interesting."

"You could demand a percentage, a kickback, even a monthly retainer for information given. One client's got a deal coming up. You just access the files on any competitors your firm might also represent. Pass along some inside data for a fee. Maybe she sees something, like one client consistently nipping out another, or others in competitive areas. She questions the percentages of that, pokes around."

"It would explain her reason for not telling a superior — if she didn't do so."

"Can't tell someone over her head if she's not sure who's part of the unethical practice. I can do an analysis of comparative operations over the last twelve months, check out the clients who most consistently pump out above the rest of the field."

"I can do that for you."

"Yeah?" That seriously brightened Eve's day. "You'd probably see it faster if there's anything to see. I can take a closer look at the financials — incomes, outlays of the partners."

"They'd know how to hide income. They're accountants."

"Gotta start somewhere."

CHAPTER
NINE

In the morning with a sky that looked like soured milk, Eve sat bleary-eyed over her second cup of coffee. It wasn't the hours, she thought. It was the figures.

Roarke plopped an omelette down in front of her. "You need it."

She glanced at it, then looked over at him as he sat. "Are my eyes bleeding? They feel like they're bleeding."

"Not so far."

"I don't know how you do it, day after day." She made the mistake of looking toward the wall screen where he had the morning stock reports running. And slapped a hand over her aching eyes. "Have mercy."

He chuckled, but switched to the morning media. "Had enough of numbers, darling?"

"I saw them in my sleep. Dancing. Some were singing. I think some might have had teeth. I'd rather lie bare-assed naked on the sidewalk and be trampled by tourists from South Dakota than be an accountant. And you." She stabbed her fork in his direction. "You love them. The fives and twenties and the profit margins, overheads, the trading fees and tax-free fuckwhats."

"I love little more than a tax-free fuckwhat."

"How does anybody keep track of money anyway, when it's zinging around all over the place? This guy puts it here for five minutes into pork asses, then *whap!* he kicks the asses and slaps it into gizmos, then shuffles some of that into peanut brittle."

"It's never wise to put all your eggs into one pork's ass."

"Whatever." She had to struggle back a yawn. "Those accountant guys rake it in and spread it around."

"Money's a bit like manure. You can't get anything to grow if you don't spread it around."

"I couldn't find anything off, but then I think my brain fried in hour two. Lifestyles jibe with the incomes, incomes jibe with the business fees and profits, investments and blah-de-blah. If any of them are pulling some in on the side, they've got it buried."

"I'll see if I can scrape off any of the dirt there. Meanwhile, I've got a couple of clients that have shown fairly consistent upswings and profits over the last two years. Could be good management," he added as he ate. "Good luck. Or good information."

"With New York branches?"

"Yes."

"Excellent. Gives me someone to harass and intimidate. Makes up for the long night with numbers." She ate with more enthusiasm. "Roarke. Say you were doing something off the books, under the table, or in the gray area of law and ethics."

"Me?" He gave a good imitation of insulted shock. "What a thing to imply."

"Yeah, right. But if you were, and one of your employees tapped in. How would you handle it?"

"Denial. Complete and utter denial, and while I was denying, I'd be busy covering up anything potentially damaging, crunching numbers, altering data. Depending on how matters shook out, I'd give the employee a raise or transfer them."

"In other words, there are lots of ways around this, if it's a money deal. Killing two people is extreme, brings more heat. Now you've got cops digging."

"A strong and foolish reaction, yes. Someone took it personally, when it's simply business."

"Yeah, that's what I'm thinking."

Since it was something she wanted to run past Mira, Eve copied the files to the profiler's office unit, and contacted Mira's obsessively protective admin for an appointment.

On the way downtown, an ad blimp cruised overhead blasting the news of an INVENTORY BLOWOUT! and a RED DOT EXTRAVAGANZA! at Aladdin's Cave at Union Square.

She wondered about people who got juiced up about blowouts and extravaganzas at places called Aladdin's Cave. What were they after, cut-rate lamps with genies? Overstocked flying carpets?

It was too early for bargain hunters or for any but the most determined tourists. New Yorkers clipped along the sidewalks, heading to or from work, to breakfast meetings. By-the-day domestics huddled in the chill waiting for their buses to rumble up to take them to the apartments or townhouses they'd spend their days cleaning.

More, she knew, would be jammed under the streets, zoning while the subway thundered along the rails.

On corners, glide-cart operators were set up to hawk their hideous excuse for coffee and tooth-chipping bagels to the early commuters. Steam poured off the grills to accommodate those hungry enough or just crazy enough to eat the fake egg pouches the carts fried up.

A few enterprising street hawkers were spreading their designer rip-offs and gray market wares on tables and blankets. Scarves and hats and gloves would be the hot sellers, she thought, on a day with the bitter wind cutting at the bone, and the sky just waiting to dump snow.

Which it did, along with nasty little bits of ice, minutes before she turned into the garage at Central.

In her office, she got another cup of coffee, put her feet up on her desk, and stared at the murder board.

Personal, she thought again.

Jake Sloan had personal relationships with both vics.

Lilah Grove attempted to develop one with the male vic.

Cara Greene, first vic's department head, purportedly had friendly personal relationship with both vics.

All three generations of Sloans had a personal interest in Copperfield.

And all of the above had considerable investment in the firm, its success, and its reputation.

Eve angled her head, shifted her thoughts. So what connection within the firm do or did any or all of those people have?

She plugged in the data Roarke had given her and began to look for one.

While she was working, Roarke was walking into Commander Whitney's office. Whitney rose, offered a hand.

"I appreciate you seeing me on such short notice," Roarke began.

"It's not a problem. Can I offer you coffee?"

"No. I won't keep you long." Roarke opened his briefcase, took out a file. He'd kept his lawyers busy through the night. "I understand there's some concern regarding the Copperfield/Byson investigation, and the ethics of my relationship with the primary."

"Why don't you sit down?"

"All right. What you have there," Roarke continued in the same cool tones, "is a document my attorneys have drafted that binds me from utilizing any of the data I may come across through the primary in the course of her investigation."

Whitney flicked a glance down at the file, then shifted his eyes back to Roarke's. "I see."

"It also stipulates that should I be given access to any of that data, I'll be given it blind. Figures only, without names or organizations. The document is quite detailed, and the penalties, should I break any of the stipulations therein, are quite stiff. Naturally, you'll want your legal department to vet it, and should there be any changes or additions requested, those changes and/or additions can be discussed with my legal reps until the document suits all parties."

"I'll see that it's done."

"All right, then." Roarke got to his feet. "Of course, legalities and documents don't take into account the fact I may lie and cheat my way around the stipulations, and use my wife and two brutally murdered people for my own financial gain. But I would hope this department, and this office, understands — clearly understands — the primary in this investigation would never allow it."

Roarke waited a beat. "I'd like to hear you say you don't question the lieutenant's integrity. In fact, I bloody well insist on it."

"Lieutenant Dallas's integrity is not at issue for me. And is not in question."

"Just mine, then?"

"Officially, this department and this office must insure the privacy of the citizens of New York — that information generated or uncovered during the course of an investigation is not utilized for harm, for personal gain, or in any illegal capacity."

"I thought you knew me better than that," Roarke shot back, barely able to hold on to the slippery edge of his fury. "At least well enough to be sure I'd do nothing to reflect poorly on my wife, to put her reputation or her career on the line."

"I do." Whitney nodded. "I know you well enough to be absolutely sure of that. So, unofficially, all this is bullshit." Whitney flicked his fingers at the file sharply enough to scoot it over the surface of his desk. "Bureaucratic, political, ass-kissing bullshit that infuriates me nearly as much as you. I can offer you my personal apology for it."

160

"You should have offered her one."

Now Whitney raised his brows. "Lieutenant Dallas isn't a civilian, and is under my command. She knows the departmental line. I don't apologize for informing a subordinate of a potential problem within an investigation. Nor would she, I expect, in my place."

"She intends to bring me in, officially as expert consultant, civilian."

"She would, wouldn't she?" Whitney sat back, frowned. "Thumb her nose at anyone who'd question her integrity or yours. Still . . ." Now he tapped his fingers, thinking it through. "That would also put you under the department's aegis throughout the investigation, which goes some way of covering us. And your document, which I'd assume is as complicated as it is detailed, should take care of the rest.

"Some media spinning if we need it."

"That can be handled," Roarke told him.

"I've no doubt about it. I'll have this vetted by Legal, and run it through with Chief Tibble."

"Then I'll let you get to it."

Whitney rose. "When you speak to the lieutenant, tell her I have every confidence this case will be closed in a timely fashion."

And that, Roarke thought, was as close to an apology as Eve would get. "I'll do that."

When Peabody poked her head into Eve's office, Eve was pinning names to the back side of her board. "Baxter and I have been through the lot," she told Eve.

"Nothing pops out of line, and Copperfield and Byson didn't share any clients."

"You gotta go under it," Eve said half to herself. "Forget the numbers for now, look at names. Look at people. Numbers make you crazy anyway."

"I kind of like them." Peabody moved in, squeezing around the desk to view the back of the board.

"You got your big three," Eve began, and tapped names. "Sloan, Myers, Kraus. Under Sloan you've got the son, then the grandson. Connect Copperfield to Jake Sloan, putting them both under Cara Greene. Under Copperfield, you've got the assistant, Sarajane Bloomdale. Rochelle DeLay connects to Jake Sloan, to Copperfield, and also to Byson, who comes over here, under the big three, and under Myra Lovitz, with another connect to Lilah Grove."

"You need a bigger board."

"Maybe. Then you've got your alibis. Myers and Kraus with clients."

"And all checked out," Peabody added.

"Jacob Sloan's got his grandkid and the girlfriend, his wife. Doubling that back as Sloan alibiing the grandson. Handy."

"Yet feasible."

"Randall Sloan has clients covering his ass for the time in question."

"Also checked. And none of the alibis were Copperfield's clients."

"Nope. However, the Bullock Foundation is represented in the legal world by Stuben, Robbins, Cavendish, and Mull, who were Copperfield's. And one

162

of the accounts — according to Greene when I contacted her this morning — Copperfield copped within the last year."

"Aha!" Peabody hunched her shoulders at Eve's beady stare. "I just wanted to say it."

"The British law firm has a New York branch, which is also handy. Byson connects there, as he represented the number crunching for Lordes Cavendish McDermott —"

"Sounds like an opera singer."

"Socialite and widow of Miles McDermott, really rich dude. Meanwhile, other under-the-surface connections. Randall Sloan is alibied by Sasha Zinka and Lola Warfield. Zinka has a sister living in Prague, who, along with two partners, owns and runs a five-diamond hotel. And whose number crunching is done by . . ."

"Sloan, Myers, and Kraus. I did Copperfield's. I don't remember a Zinka. It would've clicked."

"Sister's name is Kerlinko, Anna. And the hotel group was Copperfield's. Also copped within this last year."

"Either a lot of coincidence or a lot of connections."

"I like connections. Pull the data on these companies, and the New York-based staff for now. I've got a quick consult with Mira, then we're in the field."

Heading out, Eve stopped to scowl at a vending machine. She and Vending currently had a cold war in progress. But she wanted a damn Pepsi. In fact, if she took a tube with her to Mira's, the doctor wouldn't insist on pushing into her hands that flower tea she always brewed.

Eve jingled the loose credits in her pockets. She wasn't going to just key in her code. That wasn't just asking for trouble, it was begging for it.

She took out the credits she needed, was about to risk the annoyance and disappointment by plugging them in herself, when a couple of uniforms came her way, quick-stepping a skinny guy in restraints between them.

The skinny guy was squawking like a parrot on Zeus about harassment, constitutional rights, and someone named Shirley.

"Hey." She held up a hand, then held out the credits. With her free hand she stabbed a finger at the parrot. "You. Zip it."

Even with the illegals in his system whirling his eyes around in his head, the mope must have caught the tone of her voice. He went down to whimpers.

"Use this, gimme Pepsi."

"Sure, Lieutenant."

Because the uniform didn't blink at the request, Eve assumed her cold war was known throughout the department.

"What he do?" she asked with a nod toward the now sniveling parrot.

"Pushed a woman down a couple flights of stairs at his flop. She didn't bounce."

"Slipped. She slipped. I wasn't even there. I hardly knew her. Cops tossed me down on the street. I'm gonna sue."

"Three eyewits," the uniform said dryly as he handed Eve her tube. "Fled the scene. Took a little spill during pursuit."

"Who's got it?"

"Carmichael's primary."

Satisfied Eve nodded. "Thanks."

The squawking renewed as she walked off to take the glides to Mira's sector.

She supposed Mira's area would be considered more civilized than hers. You weren't likely to see junked-up suspects being hauled around. Here there was quiet, easy colors, and a lot of closed doors.

Mira's was open, and the admin guarding the perimeter looked relaxed, so Eve decided she wasn't going to have to do a dance to gain admission.

Mira spotted her from her desk. "Eve. Come right in. I'm just finishing up some paperwork."

"Appreciate the time."

"I have a little to spare today."

As always, Mira looked perfectly put together without being obvious about it. She was letting her sable-colored hair grow some so that it waved softly to the nape of her neck. Her suit was a monochromatic three-piece in a rich, plummy tone worn with sparkling silver chains and little glittery hoops in her ears.

She smiled easily, a lovely face with soft blue eyes Eve knew could see right through the skull into whatever secrets the brain might hold.

"Did you get a chance to look at the reports?"

"I did. Have a seat. It's a shame, isn't it, all that youth and optimism cut off so abruptly." She sat back. "Their lives were just beginning, really."

"Now they're over," Eve said flatly. "Why?"

"Why is rarely straightforward, is it? On the profile," she said in brisk, professional tones, "I agree, as you'd expect, with your conclusions and the ME's, that you're looking for one killer. Most likely male, between thirty-five and sixty-five. He isn't impulsive, and wasn't looking for thrills. He didn't rape either victim because it wasn't part of the business at hand. And, very likely, he doesn't equate sex with power and control. He may be in a sexual relationship where he is accustomed to being subservient."

"Rape takes time," Eve added. "He had a schedule to keep, and priorities."

"Agreed. But rape, or the threat of it, is often used in torture killings, as is mutilation. No sexual assault, no mutilation, no serious vandalism. He came prepared, and with a purpose. He fulfilled it, using brute force and physical — very likely emotional — torture."

Mira spread the crime scene photos out on her desk.

"Binding the victims put them under his control, kept them helpless. Removing the tape from both victims' mouths tells me he wanted, or needed, to see their faces. The whole of their faces as he strangled them."

"Pride in his work."

"Yes. A job fulfilled, and the acknowledgment of his power and his control. As he was able to overcome a man of Byson's years and physical build, he's likely in good physical condition himself. Utilizing weapons on scene — the robe tie, the binding cord — shows presence of mind and clear thinking. The lack of any DNA on the first scene indicates he took precautions. The fact that there was DNA on the second tells me he lost that control long enough to lead with temper."

"Because he got clocked."

"Exactly," Mira said with a ghost of a smile. "Byson hurt him, and he reacted poorly to the pain. Copperfield was the primary target.

"And I'm not telling you anything you don't know."

"No, but it solidifies it."

"This was a desperate act committed without desperation. He certainly feared them, or what they could do, but there's no indication of panic on the bodies or on the scenes. He was in control, and illustrated that control to them, to himself, by the face-to-face strangulations."

"Watch me kill you while I watch you die."

"Yes. And while he may have — almost certainly — experienced some sort of thrill through that, he remained controlled enough to move quickly to the secondary target and finish his job."

"But not a pro. It's too messy for a professional."

"I agree. But his focus was very tight, his preparations well thought out."

"A good sense of self-preservation can do that."

"It can. Following that train, he may have been protecting himself, his own interests, or someone close to him. He was very careful."

"But didn't know enough about forensics to know that we'd be able to get his DNA off the scrapes on Byson's knuckles."

"Perhaps not, but I'd judge him as educated, organized, and thorough. I'd be very surprised if he hasn't destroyed or disposed of anything he took from the scenes, anything he used to gain entry. I expect if you interview him during the course of your investigation, he'll be cooperative. If he knew the victims, he'll attend their memorial with every sign of sorrow for their loss. He'll have thought all of that through as well."

"As well as an alibi for the time in question."

"I'd be surprised if he didn't have one. Some in these circumstances might deliberately avoid having an alibi to add to the thrill and excitement during the investigation. The game of it. I don't think that's your type here. He'd have dotted all his i's beforehand."

Eve nodded. "Okay. Thanks."

"I'm looking forward to tomorrow," Mira said as Eve rose.

"What's — oh. Oh, yeah."

With a laugh, Mira swiveled in her chair. "I've never known any sort of an event at your home to be less than entertaining. Mavis must be thrilled."

"I guess. Truth? I'm kind of ducking her. We had to do the class thing — the coach class? Which was a nightmare beyond the speaking of it. I'm afraid she's going to tag me and do, like, a quiz to make sure I was paying attention!"

"And were you?"

"You couldn't look away. It was like watching a horror movie. Freaky," she muttered, and had to struggle not to shudder. "Tomorrow, I'm going to be surrounded by those women who're brewing babies. What if one of them decides to pop?"

"Unlikely, but you will have a couple of doctors on hand. I'll be there, so will Louise."

"Right." The idea relieved her. "I forgot. Okay, that's a load off. Maybe you could be sure to hang around until all of them leave. Just in case."

"Eleven years and counting on the force, and you've never delivered a baby?"

"That's right, and I'm going to keep that record intact."

Eve's first thought when she entered Sasha Zinka's office was that it rivaled Roarke's for space, for plush, for taste. The clean lines and surprising slashes of bold color against the muted made it female without being fussy.

She thought the same of Sasha herself.

The woman could have easily passed for a decade younger than her age on her official records. Honeycomb hair was swooped back and up from a heart-shaped face dominated by clear blue eyes. She wore a suit of rusty red as restrained and subtle as the jewelry she'd matched to it.

She crossed the thick silver carpet in an easy glide in skinny heels as she held out a hand.

"Lieutenant Dallas. We met in passing at some gala or other last spring."

"I remember."

"Lousy way to meet again. You're Detective Peabody. We spoke by 'link."

Peabody accepted the hand held out to her. "Thanks for seeing us."

"Please, have a seat. Tell me what I can do. You wanted to see Lola as well. She's on her way. Would you like anything while we wait for her?"

"We're fine, thanks." Eve sat in a chair of amber leather so buttery she was surprised her butt didn't just melt through it. "You knew Natalie Copperfield?"

"A little. Knew of her more." She took a seat of her own. "It's terrible, what happened to her and the young man. But I'm not sure where Lola and I come into it."

"You've stated that you and Ms. Warfield had dinner with Randall Sloan on the night of the murders."

"That's right. Business primarily, but Lola and I enjoy Ran's company. We were out until after two in the morning, as I told the detective when she contacted me. You don't seriously consider Ran —"

She broke off as the door opened. Lola Warfield rushed in looking flushed and scattered with her wild brunette curls flying. Her eyes, nearly the same color as the chair where Eve sat, were full of laughing apology.

"Sorry, sorry. I got hung up. Dallas, right? I took my life in my hands and snatched your gorgeous husband for a dance at the Marquis event last spring. If he were mine I'd beat any woman who looked at him with a stick, even if she plays for the other team."

"Then the city'd be hip-deep in bodies."

"That'd be a problem. I'm sorry." She flashed a brilliant smile at Peabody. "I can't remember your name."

"Detective Peabody."

"Nice to meet you. Well, not nice, I guess. It's awful, but a little exciting, too."

"Lola glues herself to the screen for the crime reports," Sasha explained.

170

"And here we are in the middle of one. Or right on the sidelines. And I'm being horrible. I met Natalie a couple of times. She was very sweet, it seemed to me."

As she spoke, she moved to the long bar at one end of the office, took a bottle of water from a cold box. "Anyone?"

"No, thanks." Eve waited a beat while Lola moved to perch on the arm of Sasha's chair. "When was the business dinner set up with Randall Sloan?"

"Mmm." Lola glanced down at Sasha. "Couple of days before, wasn't it? We generally meet with him every quarter."

"That's right," Sasha confirmed. "We'd had to postpone an earlier meeting because we were out of the country for a few days right after the first of the year."

"Who set it up?"

"Hmm." Lola furrowed her brow. "I guess Ran did. It's usual for him to get in touch, set up a meeting, or an evening out."

"In the course of your business or conversations with Mr. Sloan, did he mention any difficulties with Natalie Copperfield or Bick Byson?"

"No." Sasha took the ball. "Their names never came up. We work directly with Ran. We did meet her, and her fiancé, as I said. At Jacob Sloan's home. She — Natalie — was friendly with his grandson."

"Ms. Copperfield handles your sister's financials."

"That's right. When Anna and her friends went into business, I recommended the firm, and spoke with Ran personally on who he thought would be best for them.

171

He assigned Natalie. She and Anna hit it off well — so I'm told — when Natalie flew out to meet with her."

"Your sister was satisfied with Ms. Copperfield's work."

"I didn't hear any complaints. And I would have."

"Would you ever," Lola confirmed. "Anna doesn't suffer in silence. Are you looking inside the firm for a suspect? I assumed it was something personal and — well — passionate. Like a jealous ex or unrequited love."

"We're looking everywhere," Eve told her, and rose. "If you remember anything or think of something, you can contact me at Central."

"That's all?" Lola's lips moved into a pout of disappointment. "I was hoping we'd get grilled."

"Maybe next time. Thanks for your time," Eve added.

She waited until they were outside, hiking back to their vehicle. "Impressions?"

"Straightforward, confident, calm. Business as usual on the date for the dinner with Sloan, and they don't strike me as the type to cover for an employee — even if they are on friendly terms. There's Zinka's sister's connection to the first vic, but if I go with the gut, I can't see either or both of them committing double murders, or attaching themselves to same to keep the sister out of a jam. And they're way rich. If this is about money, they don't need to cheat to make more."

"It's not about need, it's about greed and power," Eve corrected. "But I didn't get any vibe there. If it was the sister's account that sent up the red flag for Copperfield, and either of them knew about it, they're damn cool. What do we have on Anna Kerlinko's whereabouts on the night?"

Peabody took out her memo book as she slid into the car. "Figuring the time difference, she was having breakfast with her current lover when Copperfield was murdered, and in her office by nine, her time. Got wits. She couldn't have zipped here, done them, zipped back."

"We move on."

Using geography as much as her own checklist, she maneuvered the six blocks east to take the New York branch of the law firm representing the Bullock Foundation. They'd been assigned to Copperfield within the last few months, Eve mused, and had yet another connection with Byson representing one of the partner's nieces.

The firm had its offices in an elegant old brownstone with the outer office as quiet as a church and manned by a woman who sat bathed in the colored light that seeped through the stained glass of the streetside window.

She was a sharp looker with her red hair in a long, swooping curve. Eve badged her and got several surprised blinks in response.

"I don't understand."

"Badge," Eve said helpfully. "Cops. Now you buzz your boss and tell him we need to speak with him."

"Golly. I mean, I'm sorry, but Mr. Cavendish is in a meeting. I'd be happy to check his schedule with his assistant and set up an appointment."

"No, no, you're getting it wrong. Let me repeat. Badge. Cops." Eve glanced around, saw the straight angle of polished wood stairs. "Offices up that way?"

"Oh, but — but — but —"

Eve left the redhead sputtering and moved with Peabody to the stairs.

The second level changed Eve's opinion from church to museum. The carpets were old, worn, and expensive. The wainscotting the real deal, and very likely original. Paintings of country landscapes adorned the walls.

A door swung open on the left. The woman who stepped out was older than the girl at the downstairs desk, and twice as sharp.

She wore her jet hair in a no-nonsense twist that complimented a striking, angular face. The pinstriped suit might have been no-nonsense as well, but it had been tailored to mold a very fine body.

"I believe you were told Mr. Cavendish is in a meeting and unavailable at this time. What can I do for you?"

"You can get him out of his meeting and see that he's available," Eve returned. "That would be helpful."

She felt an entertaining little buzz up the back of her spine at the woman's silent, burning stare. "Got a name, sister?"

"Ms. Ellyn Bruberry. I'm Mr. Cavendish's administrative assistant. And a paralegal."

"Good for you. We need to talk to Mr. Cavendish in connection with an investigation."

"Mr. Cavendish is, as you've now been told twice, unavailable. And as you must know, is under no obligation to speak with you without notice."

"Got me there," Eve said cheerfully. "We'll be happy to give Mr. Cavendish, and you, and every one in these

174

offices notice of your obligation to come into Cop Central for formal interviews, which — being a paralegal — you must know could take a few hours to, oh, next Christmas. Or gee, we could just talk to him now, in the comfort of his own office. And probably be out of your hair in under twenty minutes."

She paused. "Pick a door."

Eve actually heard the woman suck air through her nose.

"You'll have to tell me what this is about."

"No, I really don't. You may want to ask your boss if he'd rather speak to me now, or come into Central in the immediate future and spend considerable time being interviewed formally. Or you can make that decision for him. Up to you."

"But . . ." Peabody tapped her wrist unit. "Time's a-wasting."

"Wait here."

Eve waited until Bruberry had clicked off on her sharply heeled boots. "Time's a-wasting?"

"It just worked for me. Kind of pissy, wasn't she? And she knows why we're here."

"Oh, yeah, she does. Interesting." Idly, Eve turned to study one of the countryscapes. "How come people live and work in urban areas, then put up pictures of rural areas on the wall? Can't they make up their minds where they want to be?"

"A lot of people find rural landscapes relaxing."

"Sure, until you start wondering what's creeping behind those trees, or slithering along in the grass."

Peabody shifted uncomfortably. "Some people think bounding instead of creeping, as in pretty little fawns, and frolicking as opposed to slithering, like cute little bunnies."

"Some people are fools. Let's entertain ourselves, Peabody, and start a run on Bruberry. And one on Cavendish."

"It could be fawns and bunnies," Peabody muttered, and took out her PPC to do the runs.

Moments later, Bruberry stepped out of another door. Her back was poker straight, her tone cool and aloof. "Mr. Cavendish will see you now. Ten minutes."

CHAPTER
TEN

From church to museum, Eve thought, then through the door into the men's club.

Walter Cavendish presided over an office with wide-armed, port-colored leather chairs and sofas, and dark, heavy woods. The carpets were thickly padded Orientals, likely the real deal, in rich tones and complex patterns. Amber liquid swam in thick crystal decanters that would have doubled as very effective murder weapons.

A trim black data and communication center stood alongside leather and brass accessories that were arranged just so on the antique desk where Cavendish sat looking prosperous, tailored — and to Eve's gauge — nervy.

He was in his early fifties, with a good head of the hair people called sandy in men, mousey in women. His face was ruddy, his eyes a light blue that skipped over Eve's face, then over her shoulder. His suit was a muted brown with just a hint of a gold stripe to show he liked a little pizzazz.

He rose, and his not-quite-handsome face set in solemn lines. "I'd like to see some identification." He spoke, to Eve's mind, in the rounded, fruity tones of a hammy Shakespearean actor.

Both she and Peabody took out badges. "Lieutenant Dallas," Eve said, "and Detective Peabody. Looks like your meeting broke up. Funny, we didn't see anyone leave."

He looked momentarily confused, and those nervous eyes slid to Bruberry even as the admin spoke.

"It was a 'link conference."

"Yes, a 'link conference. With London."

"That's handy." She kept her eyes on Cavendish in a way that told him she knew he was already lying. "Since you've got a few minutes now, we have some questions in connection with an investigation."

"So I'm told." He gestured, started to sit. When he didn't offer a hand, Eve shot hers out deliberately. She wanted the feel of his.

He hesitated, and she saw his gaze dart toward his admin yet again before he took Eve's hand in his.

A little soft, she noted, a little damp.

"What's the nature of your investigation?"

"Homicide. Natalie Copperfield and Bick Byson. Are those names familiar to you?"

"No."

"You don't watch the media reports, I take it. Don't scan the newspapers." She flicked a glance of her own toward a wall screen framed in the dark wood that dominated the room. "These individuals were murdered three nights ago in their respective residences. Both were employed by the accounting firm of Sloan, Myers, and Kraus. And funnily enough, Natalie Copperfield

178

handled the accounts for your home operation. But that name doesn't ring for you?"

"I don't retain the names of everyone I might hear of or read of. I'm a very busy man. As far as accounting, Ellyn — my assistant — deals with that area."

"I'm aware of Ms. Copperfield," Bruberry stated. "What does her death have to do with this firm?"

"At this point, I'll be asking the questions," Eve said coolly. "Where were you, Mr. Cavendish, three nights ago between the hours of midnight and 4a.m.?"

"At home, in bed. With my wife."

Eve lifted her eyebrows. "You can't remember the names of two people who've been all over the media reports, but you know — without a second's hesitation or without checking your book — where you were three nights ago?"

"At home," he said again. "In bed."

"Have you had any contact with Ms. Copperfield or Mr. Byson?"

"No."

"That's odd. Don't you find that odd, Detective, that Mr. Cavendish would have no contact whatsoever with the person who handles his firm's accounts?"

"I have to say I do. Me, I'm on a first-name basis with the guy in Payroll back at Central."

"I may have, at some point, met —"

"I corresponded and met with Ms. Copperfield," Bruberry interrupted. "When necessary. Such matters are, primarily, dealt with through our home office in London."

"And just what do you do here?" Eve asked, speaking directly to Cavendish.

"I represent our firm's New York interests."

"Which means?"

"Exactly that."

"That clarifies it. And you also represent the legal interests of Lordes C. McDermott, who was a client of Bick Byson."

"Ms. McDermott is a family relation, and naturally is represented by our firm. As to her financial manager, I couldn't say."

"Really? Gee, seems like one hand doesn't keep a grip on the other around here. And, second gee, I don't think I said Byson was her financial manager, just that she was a client."

Cavendish fiddled with the knot of his tie. Nervous tell, Eve thought.

"I assumed."

"While we're at it, your whereabouts on the night of the murders, Ms. Bruberry?"

"At home. I was in bed before midnight."

"Alone?"

"I live alone, yes. I'm afraid that's all the time Mr. Cavendish can spare."

Eve got lazily to her feet. "Thanks for your cooperation. Oh," she continued. "Your firm also represents . . ." She took out her memo book as if to check on a name. "The Bullock Foundation."

And there, she noted, just that little ripple over the face. The tightening of the jaw, the flicker in the eyes.

Another brush of the fingers over the knot of his tie. "That's correct."

"Ms. Madeline Bullock and Mr. Winfield Chase were recently in the city. I suppose you met with them while they were here."

"I . . ."

"Ms. Bullock and Mr. Chase had a luncheon meeting here with Mr. Cavendish. That would have been on Monday afternoon. At twelve-thirty," Bruberry added.

"You had your meeting, and your lunch with them here. In the office."

"That's correct," Bruberry snapped before Cavendish could respond. "Would you like me to find my notes on the menu?"

"I'll let you know. This has been just swell. Thanks for the time." Eve turned to go, hesitated at the door. "You know, it's odd that while you're so busy representing your firm's New York interests, you didn't take regular meetings with the senior accountant who looks after their finances."

"I'll see you out," Bruberry said when Cavendish remained silent.

"That's okay. We can manage it."

"Somebody's got a secret," Peabody said when they were back on the street.

"Bet your ass. That guy had guilt and fear plastered all over him. Could be we'll find he's just cheating on his wife or wearing women's underwear."

"Or both if he's cheating with his admin. She's definitely the alpha male in that duet."

"You got that right. Stupid to lie about knowing Copperfield, and he was."

"Puffed up. You know," Peabody continued when Eve lifted a brow. "I'm too important to know the little people. And it's a way of distancing himself from the big stew."

"Big stew being murder." She got behind the wheel, tapped her fingers on it. "They weren't prepared. Never considered the cops would question them, so they went with first instinct. Deny everything. Let's see if we can track down Lordes McDermott, get another angle on this."

Peabody pulled out her PPC to get an address. "Got a place on Riverside Drive."

"'Link number?"

"Right here."

"Try it first. Let's make sure she's home, or where she might be if not."

Lordes McDermott was not only home, but appeared to have no problem having her day interrupted by the police.

They were escorted into her home by a uniformed maid, and through a wide, two-story atrium into a spacious sitting room done in a bold contemporary style with flashing color, glinting metallics, and glittering glass.

Lordes looked comfortably at home in New York black, soft boots, dull gold jewelry. Her hair was short, near the color of a ripe eggplant, and worn with short, spiky bangs over a pair of sapphire eyes.

On the low glass table was a skinny white pot, three oversized white mugs, and a white triangular platter loaded with donuts.

"Don't tell me cops, coffee, and donuts is a cliché."

"It's a cliché for a reason. Lieutenant Dallas, Detective Peabody."

"Have a seat. You must be here about Bick and his Natalie. I'm damn sick about it. He was a lovely guy."

"When did you last see him?"

"December fifteenth."

"Good memory," Eve commented.

"No, not really. I looked it up when I heard about what happened. We had a wrapping-up year-end business meeting right before the holidays. Here in this room, actually. He was a nice guy."

"Did you know Ms. Copperfield?"

"I met her a few times. Bick brought her to a couple of dinner meetings at my request. I like knowing who the people handling my business are involved with. I liked her, too. They had that nice glow on together, anticipation. How would you like your coffee?"

"Black, thanks."

"Light and sweet for me," Peabody added.

"Are you talking to all of Bick's clients?" Lordes asked. She poured the coffee with the gold wedding band on her hand gleaming. "I was surprised when you contacted me."

"We're talking to a lot of people. In fact, we've just come from speaking to Walter Cavendish. He's a relative of yours, isn't he?"

"Second cousin." She wrinkled her nose, just a fraction, just an instant. Another tell, Eve thought. Lordes doesn't much care for Walter.

"My cousin — Walter's father — is one of the partners in the firm, London-based. I think that makes us second cousins," she said with a thoughtful little frown. "Whatever, it's one of those things. Help yourself to those donuts. I'm going to." To prove it, she selected one loaded with colorful jimmies.

"Was it your connection with your uncle that sent you to the accounting firm, and then to Bick?"

"Mmm." Lordes nodded, mouth full. "God, these are obscene. They've handled my financial affairs for years. After Miles died — the idiot — I inherited another bundle. I just let it all lay for a while, huddled in Europe. Then when I came back, I asked for a young, savvy account manager. I got Bick — and he was."

"How did your husband die, if you don't mind me asking?" Peabody tried to be delicate with a cream-filled.

"Playing around in this little plane he'd built. He loved to fly. Crashed and burned. I loved the stupid jerk. Nearly killed me when I lost him. And it's been five years this spring — I'm still pissed at him."

"Can you tell us where you were three nights ago, between midnight and four?"

"That sounds so ominous. I wondered if it would. I looked that up, too, after you got in touch to say you were coming by. I had a little dinner party, just a couple of friends. Female friends. I'm dating again, but it's such *work*, especially when you're not really interested. They left about midnight, and I went on to bed.

184

Watched some screen first. Fell asleep watching some old vid."

"Considering the relationships," Eve continued, "did you ever have meetings, or have occasion to socialize together with Ms. Copperfield, Mr. Byson, and your cousin — second cousin, that is?"

"With Walter?" Lordes let out a hooting laugh. "No. Absolutely not. I try not to socialize with Walter at all. He really is an idiot."

"You don't get along?"

"I can get along with anyone. I just get along better with some if I keep the contact limited."

"Doesn't he represent your legal interests here in New York?"

"Not really. My cousin in London looks out for them, and Walter handles some of the busy work. To be frank, he's not all that bright. He follows directions, files papers, looks good enough in a tux. Anything complex goes through the London office, at least as far as I know."

She angled her head. "You're not thinking Walter had anything to do with the murders? I've known him all my life. I can tell you he's not only not smart enough to have done it, he wouldn't have the stones."

Eve was just sliding behind the wheel when her 'link beeped. "Dallas."

"Lieutenant." Summerset's biting tone fit his stony face. "You failed to notify me that you were expecting a delivery."

"I probably failed to notify you that you get uglier every day, but I've been busy."

"The rocker system from a retail establishment called the White Stork has been delivered. What would you like me to do with it?"

She waited a full beat. "Boy, you must be slipping to open yourself up like that. I'll avoid the obvious answer. Put it in that drawing room place, second level. Where the party's happening."

"Very well. In the future I'd appreciate it if you'd inform me of any deliveries."

"In the future I'd appreciate it if you'd wear a hood over your face before you come on my 'link screen."

She clicked off, satisfied.

"You guys sure are entertaining," Peabody commented. "After shift, I'm going to go home, get all the stuff together, then head uptown to your place. I can't wait to see the rocker and get it decked out for tomorrow."

"Whoopee."

"You know she'll love it."

"Yeah. Yeah, she will."

"She'll be like the Fertility Queen or something. Big kick for her."

"Queen Mavis." Amused, Eve slipped through a yellow light. "She ought to have a . . ." She wiggled her fingers over her head.

"A crown! Sure."

"No, not a crown, too big and formal. The other deal. The whatsit. Tiara."

"Perfect! Man, that's mag. See?" She poked Eve's arm. "You can do this."

"Looks like I'm doing it."

Eve took it all back to Central with her — the statements, impressions, instincts. There, she lined them up, wrote the reports, stewed over them. At her board, she began to tack up keywords beside photos, names, connecting arrows.

"You need a bigger board." Roarke stepped inside, a topcoat slung over his arm.

"I keep hearing that."

"God knows you need a bigger office."

"Works okay for me. What are you doing here?"

"Looking for a ride home. A little business upstairs," he continued when she only frowned at him. And when her frown deepened, he stepped over, flicked a finger down the shallow dent in her chin. "It's done, and everyone's as satisfied as possible."

"It sucks."

"As life so often does. This makes sense to you, I imagine." He tossed his coat idly over the back of her desk chair before circling the board. "Ah, yes. I see. Links within links. For such a big world there are so many interesting and tight little patterns, aren't there?"

"What did Whitney say?"

"Officially or unofficially?" Roarke asked as he continued to study her board.

"I know what he said officially."

"Unofficially then. He said it was all bullshit. That's a direct quote." He shifted his gaze to her face, shook his head. "And that's enough for you, I see. You don't need him to look you in the eye and tell you he trusts and respects you. To apologize on a personal level."

"No."

He moved over, closed the door. "Bullshit it may be, but it's the sort of thing that keeps you in this broomstick of an office instead of in a captain's seat."

"I want to be in the office. Let's not murk this up with that kind of crap. I'm doing exactly what I want to do, and what I'm good at doing."

"Don't tell me you don't want the bars, Eve."

"I thought I did." She pushed a hand through her hair as she shifted her mental gears. "I wouldn't turn them down if they held them out to me — on my terms. Listen, you've got the Irish thing going. Fate, destiny, woo-woo."

His lips twitched. "You're the one who exorcised a ghost recently."

"I cleared a case," she corrected. "And what I mean is sometimes things are just meant. I'm meant to be in the office, doing this work. I believe that."

"All right." The office was so small he had to do little more than reach out to take her arms, to run his hands up and down them. "I'll add that your commander said to relay to you that he had every confidence you'd close this case in a timely manner."

"Okay."

"Should I find myself alternate transportation, or are you heading home soon?"

"I can pick this up there. Give me ten. Hey," she said when he opened the door. "Maybe you should buy me dinner."

He smiled. "Maybe I should."

"But we have to make a stop first. I need a tiara."

"To go with your scepter?"

"Not for me. Jeez. Mavis. Thing tomorrow. It's a theme or something. Is a scepter one of those . . ." She fisted her hand, pumped it up and down in a way that made his eyebrows shoot up as he grinned.

"God, gutter-brain." But she laughed, shifted her arm well out to the side of her body. "You know, like a staff deal?"

"I believe so."

"We should find one of those, too. So maybe you could figure out a costume store or something where we can get them on the way to dinner."

It was remarkably simple to find a rhinestone tiara and plastic scepter, especially when he was shopping with a woman who made a habit of grabbing the first thing that came close to the mark and making an escape.

And since he knew his woman, for the meal he chose Italian in a crowded little trattoria where the atmosphere was simple and the food stupendous. By the time she'd dug into spaghetti and meatballs and hadn't brought up the case, he let it lie.

"You missed lunch."

She spun pasta around her fork. "Probably, but I had a donut in there. And I think I forgot to inform you that Peabody and McNab are bunking at our place tonight."

"Inform me?"

"Summerset. He got pissy because I forgot about a delivery coming in today. Anyway, Peabody wants to decorate for the shower — which I don't get. You're getting a party, presents, food. What more do you need?"

"I suppose we'll find out. That's handy though. I can pluck McNab up tomorrow, and we'll go do something manly."

"Go? Leave?" Absolute panic rushed into her face. "You're not going to stay for the thing?"

He took a bite of manicotti. "There's nothing you could do, say, nothing you could possibly offer — including deviant sexual favors — that would induce me to be within a hundred yards of that baby shower."

"Crap." She forked up a nice chunk of meatball. "Not even if I combined chocolate sauce with the outfit?"

"Not even."

"There could be whipped cream. And choreography."

"An excellent bribe, I grant you, especially for a desperate woman. But no. I've already made arrangements to escape with Leonardo. We'll just add McNab to our happy little troupe."

"But what if something goes wrong?" She grabbed his arm. "Like the caterer goes whacko, because sometimes they do. Or we lose one of the pregnant women in the house."

He merely picked up his wine with his free hand.

"Okay, okay." She rolled her eyes. "I can handle it. But it stinks, if you ask me, really stinks, that you get to go out somewhere drinking beer while I'm stuck at Baby Central. Just because you have a penis."

"We'll think fondly of you over beer, me and my penis."

She ate a little more, then smiled slowly. "You've still got to be in the birthing room when she pushes it out."

"Shut up, Eve."

"Your penis won't save you then, pal."

He picked up a breadstick, broke it in half to offer her a share. "And are you playing games tomorrow? Will there be prizes?"

She winced at his perfect delivery of the perfect stinger. "Okay, I'll shut up. Want to talk about murder?"

"Please."

She brought him up to date as they finished the meal and lingered over cappuccino.

"So Cavendish and his admin struck you wrong."

"Vibes all over the place. Something off there, and the admin pulls his strings."

"I don't know him, though I have met the other players in today's cast."

"I've got the basics on him. Forty-six, trust-fund baby. Likes squash — the game, not necessarily the food. Two marriages, ditched the first wife eight years ago. One child, female, age twelve. Mother has custody, and moved to Paris. Married wife number two as soon as the divorce was final. She's twenty-nine. Former model. My take there is he went from starter wife to trophy wife and fools around with the admin on the side."

She narrowed her eyes as she sipped the frothy coffee. "And she wears leather, high-heeled boots, and makes him bark like a dog when they do it."

"Really?" Amused, Roarke sat back. "And you know this because?"

"Because, of the two of them, she's the one with the balls. He pushes paper, attends events, takes meetings, and does what he's told."

"And did someone tell him to kill Copperfield and Byson?"

"Maybe, and wouldn't that be tidy?" She frowned over it. "But I'm leaning away from that. The killer was too level-headed, too confident. Cavendish broke a sweat just talking to me. But he knows something, and one of the things he knows is who did it."

"So you'll sweat him a bit more."

"I can do that. I can talk to him again, poke at him a little. But I don't have enough to charge him with anything and make him flip. I need more. A direct line. I have to find more because I'm betting he was just where he said he was on the night of the murders. Home in bed, and with the covers over his head because he knew what was going on."

"If the New York branch of the law firm was part of it, used to funnel money or wash funds, I'll find it."

He would, Eve thought, not only because he was good, but because his pride was on the line this time out. "Counting on it," she said. "Maybe we should go get started."

* * *

She knew Peabody and McNab were already there because she could hear the music and the voices coming from what she'd designated as the party room. If it made her a coward, she'd live with it, but Eve made a bee-line for her office.

There she updated her board, then sat down to take a closer look at Ellyn Bruberry.

Forty, she mused as the data scrolled onto her wall screen. No marriages, no offspring. The West Side address listed would give Bruberry a grand view of the park and the price tag to match. Not bad for a paralegal and administrative assistant.

American born, though she'd moved from Pittsburgh to London in her early twenties. To join the firm of Stuben, Robbins, and Cavendish — Mull came later — as a legal secretary. Relocated to New York, and the branch there, as Walter Cavendish's admin six years before.

After the second marriage, Eve mused.

No criminal record.

Eve took a dip into the financials. Hefty salary, she decided, but it wasn't illegal to pay employees well. Major influxes in income jibed with Christmas, Bruberry's birthday, and the time she'd come into the law firm — and would be easily explained as bonuses.

But wasn't it interesting that her personal accounts were handled by Sloan, Myers, and Kraus?

Not Byson's client though, she confirmed after a check of his list. She made a note to find out who at the firm handled Bruberry's financials.

Direct lines, she thought again. What was the most direct line from Copperfield/Byson to Cavendish/Bruberry?

The firm again, but if she spiked out from there it was the Bullock Foundation. Clients of both the law firm and the accounting firm. And Cavendish had been flustered when she'd asked if he'd seen the foundation people during their time in New York.

It was the youngest partner, Robert Kraus, who'd been entertaining Bullock and Chase — and who was alibied by them.

"Hey, Dallas."

She grunted as she called up Kraus's data.

"You're not still working. Come on." Peabody stood beside the desk, hands on her hips. "You need to look at the decorations we've got going. I need to run some stuff by you."

"You just do what you're doing. It's fine."

"Dallas. It's after ten."

"Golly, Mom, did I miss curfew? Am I grounded?"

"See, you're cranky." Peabody pointed an accusing finger. "Take a break, take a look. It's for Mavis."

"Okay, okay. Jesus." But if she was going to be dragged into decorations, she wasn't being dragged alone. Eve marched to Roarke's office. "We're going to look at decorations and see what else needs to be done. I think."

"Have fun."

"Uh-uh. We is you, too."

"I don't want to." But he made the mistake of glancing up, and met the same glowering look on Eve's face she'd seen on Peabody's. "All right, then. But when this whole business is finally over, you and I are taking that postponed holiday, and doing naked handsprings on the sand."

"Right with you, ace."

CHAPTER
ELEVEN

It wasn't numbers that danced in her dreams, but rainbows and strange winged babies. When the flying babies began to buzz like wasps and form into packs, Eve clawed her way out of sleep.

She sat up as if her shoulders were on springs and said, "Whoa."

"Nightmare?" Roarke was already rising from the sofa in the sitting area.

"Flying babies. Evil flying babies with evil wings."

He stepped onto the platform, sat on the side of the bed. "Darling Eve, we need a vacation."

"There were balloons," she said darkly. "And the wings cut through them like razors so they popped. And when they popped, more evil flying babies zoomed out."

He trailed a finger along her thigh. "Maybe you could make an effort to dream about, oh, let's say, sex."

"Somebody had sex, didn't they, to create the evil flying babies?" Suddenly she reached forward, grabbed fistsful of his sweater. Her eyes radiated desperation. "Don't leave me alone with all these women today."

"Sorry. I'm falling back on the penis clause. Which sounds vaguely obscene, when spoken aloud, but I'm using it in any case. No negotiation."

"Bastard," she said, but with more envy than heat as she released him to flop back.

"There, there." He gave her an absent pat.

"Maybe it'll snow. There could be a blizzard, and people won't be able to come because it's a blizzard — a big mother — that brings New York to its trembling knees."

"Forecast is for a high of twenty-two degrees under clear skies."

"I heard that. I heard it." Rearing up again, she jabbed a finger at him. "Not the words, the tone. You think this is funny."

"No. I know it is. And you'll end up having a good time, first because Mavis will be so happy, and next because you'll spend some nonprofessional time with a number of women you like."

"But, Roarke, there have to be games."

"You don't play them."

Her eyes went cop flat. "Why not?"

He couldn't help it if he was amused. She managed to be panicked and suspicious at the same time. "You're the hostess, and it would be wrong for you to participate in the games and win any of the prizes."

"Is that true?"

"It should be, and that's your stand on it."

"Yeah, that's my stand on it." She perked up considerably. "Thanks."

She revved herself up with a workout, a long swim, and a hot shower. Then she snuck into her office to run probabilities on different scenarios.

"You're working again!"

She actually jolted upright, and felt a small twinge of guilt. "What are you," she demanded of Peabody, "the work police?"

"You don't need a cop, you need a keeper. Dallas, the caterer's going to be here any minute."

"Okay, fine, good. Somebody can tell me when they're here." Eve waved a hand. "I'm just checking some things that have to do with pesky details like double murders."

But she shut down the machine when Peabody merely stood, gimlet-eyed, actually tapping her foot. "You're not the work police." It was said with some bitterness. "You're the party gestapo."

"Mavis just called. She didn't try your 'link because she knew you'd be busy with the shower preparations. She's on her way over because she can't wait anymore."

"Man. I turned my machine off, didn't I? I'm leaving the office. See, walking out, shutting the door behind me."

Peabody only smiled. Guilt was the best tool, she knew. She'd learned that one at her mother's knee.

Eve's first surprise was that the caterer didn't want her to do anything. In fact, they wanted Eve and everyone else completely out of the way. Her second was that Summerset had already left the house, and wouldn't be back until the following day.

"You won't find any Y chromosomes on the premises this afternoon," Roarke told her. "Except the cat."

He stood with Eve in the second-level sitting room. It was larger than the downstairs parlor they used most often, and boasted double fireplaces with malachite surrounds. Sofas, chairs, and an abundance of pillows had been arranged in conversation areas, with a long table, covered now with a rainbow hue of cloths and candles, running along the back wall. Over it, rainbow streamers, pink and blue balloons, and some sort of arty flowered vine flowed out of a sparkling circle and formed a kind of canopy over what Peabody had designated as the gift table.

Baby roses, baby iris, baby's breath — and an assortment of other baby-type posies Eve had already forgotten — were spilling out of little silver baskets shaped like cradles.

Buffet tables, also rainbow-hued, were already set up. The caterer had dressed one with china following the color scheme, more miniature candles, more flowers, and an ice sculpture of a stork carrying a little sack in its beak.

Eve had been sure it would be silly, and instead it was sort of charming.

Both fires simmered low, and in the center of it all the rocker was draped in rainbows and decked in flowers.

"I guess it looks pretty good."

"Very sweet." Roarke took her hand. "Very female. Congratulations."

"I didn't do that much."

"That's not true. You dragged your feet every chance you got, but you picked them up and did the job." He brought her hand to his lips, then leaned down to kiss her.

"Oops." Peabody stopped in the doorway and grinned. "Don't mean to interrupt if the stork and all the cradles are giving you guys ideas."

"Don't make me hurt you," Eve warned.

"I've got Mavis out here. I thought maybe you'd want to show her in."

"Has pregnancy affected her eyesight?"

"No, I just — never mind," Peabody said with a laugh. "Okay, Mavis."

She might have been carrying an extra twenty pounds, but Mavis could still bounce. She all but boinged into the room on pink airboots that slicked up to her knees. Her blue and white skirt fluttered like flower petals beneath the basketball bulge of her belly. The sleeves of her dress displayed a geometric pattern of color that came to points over the backs of her hands.

Her hair — a soft, pale blonde today — was scooped back in a long, twisty tail as bouncy as she was.

She stopped short, slapped both hands over her mouth. And burst into tears.

"Oh shit. Oh shit," was all Eve could manage.

"No, no, no." Still sobbing, even as Leonardo rushed in behind her, Mavis waved one of her hands. "I'm so knocked-up. I'm a total victim of the hormones. It's so *pretty*! Oh, oh, it's all rainbows and flowers. It's so mag. It's so mag, Dallas."

She sobbed her way across the room and threw herself into Eve's arms — bulging belly first.

"Okay, good then. Glad you like it."

"I abso *love* it. Peabody!" Mavis flung out a hand, pulling Peabody into a three-way embrace. "Thank you. Thank you."

"Maybe you should sit down."

"No, I'm okay. I just flood off and on. Isn't that right, honey pie?" she said to Leonardo.

"We had baby carrots last night." He was already passing her tissues. "She cried for ten minutes."

Obviously the memory made her laugh, as she grinned and turned to give the bulk of him a squeeze. "I don't know how you put up with me. Three in the morning? I woke up starved. Like shackled-in-the-cellar-for-a-week starved. And my baby bear got up and fixed me scrambled eggs. Oh, oh, check it out!" She bounced again as she looked at the canopied chair. "It's like a throne, right? I get to sit there."

"That's your spot," Eve confirmed.

"Can I give you a hand, your majesty?" Roarke offered his.

"This is TTF. Too Totally Frosty. You're going to run away for the day with my sweetie, aren't you?"

"As soon as humanly possible," he told her, and helped her into the chair.

"Well, okay. I give you leave."

"Give her the stuff," Peabody whispered.

"She might start crying again."

"I get stuff? Already?" Since she was sitting, the best Mavis could do was bounce on her butt. "What? Where? Oh, God, I love stuff."

Uneasy about the results, Eve went to a cabinet, took out the scepter and tiara.

"Oh, boy! Uptown squared."

Relieved because this time Mavis's eyes glittered with laughter instead of tears, Eve passed the tiara to Leonardo.

"You probably know how to get it on right."

"Crown me, moonpie," Mavis told him. "And let the games begin."

Within the hour, the room was so full of estrogen Eve thought she could bottle it and sell it on the black market. Women nibbled, sipped, cooed over other women's protruding bellies and chatted about the things she understood they chatted about when they got together as a species.

Hair. *That's a great look for you, and what a mag color! Where do you go?*

Clothes. *Absolutely fabulous shoes. Are they comfortable?*

Men. *He just doesn't listen to what I need to say.*

And due to the nature of the event, they talked of babies, babies, and more babies.

The new fact she discovered was that women who'd already had children felt compelled to share their childbirth experiences with those about to head to the labor mines.

Sixteen hours, and two and a half of that pushing. But it was worth it.

Titania popped out as soon as my water broke. If I'd been ten minutes later getting to the birthing center, she'd have been born in the cab!

I had to have a C. Wiley just wouldn't turn.

202

They were also full of advice.

You have to get Magdelina's Symphony For Giving Life! I'd have been lost without it. So empowering.

Water births are the only way to go. I had both of mine in a birthing lagoon. It's a religious experience.

Take the drugs.

And that one, Eve thought, was the most sensible statement of the day.

With a frosty bellini in her hand, Nadine Furst — ace reporter and soon-to-be host of her own crime-beat show — wandered over. "You give a good party, Dallas. I don't think I've ever seen Mavis look happier. She's literally radiating."

"Wait, she could start bawling any minute."

"Hormones." Nadine shrugged. She was wearing her streaky blonde hair sleek these days around her sharp face. "Wanted to talk to you."

"Hair looks great, fantastic shoes, and I'm sure whatever man you're currently banging is handsome and wise. Does that cover it?"

"No, but you got three out of three. We're fine-tuning the format for my show, and the producers and I thought it would just top it off if we had a monthly segment with you. An intense hour every four weeks that not only focuses on whatever case you're working, but gives a roundup of what you've handled through the month."

Nadine lifted her glass in a kind of toast before she sipped. "Adds a nice punch to the format, and it's good exposure, good PR for the NYPSD."

"A monthly deal? Let me think about it a minute. No."

Nadine merely sipped her drink, cocked a brow. "Which is exactly what I told my team you'd say. So I have this alternative, which I think would suit us both. A monthly segment with Homicide. Someone in your division comes on every four weeks. All you have to do is assign the detective, give me the heads-up so I can prep. It's good screen, Dallas. And it gives the viewing public a face."

"Maybe." The reality was there had to be some give and take with the media, and the plus was Eve knew she could trust Nadine to give a balanced view. "Something like that I'd have to run by the brass."

"You're still first up." She tapped Eve's shoulder. "The one you're working now would have a kick. Two lovers — young, attractive, and seemingly ordinary — bound, tortured, and killed. How's it going?"

"That's what I like about you, Nadine. You know how to make party conversation."

"Would you rather talk about childbirth and breast-feeding?"

"I'd rather be stabbed in the eye with a burning stick. It's going. You got any dish on a Walter Cavendish? Rich lawyer."

"No, but I can poke around."

"How about the Bullock Foundation?"

"Huge. Donates mucho moolah, funds programs, gives grants. London-based with a worldwide reach and some off-planet interests. Headed now by Bullock's widow and second wife, who enjoys the limelight, and her son, who's rarely far from her side. Just what does the respected and generous Bullock Foundation have to do with two dead accountants?"

"That's the question."

Because she saw Peabody rushing over and knew she was about to be tossed back into Babyland, Eve grabbed a bellini for herself.

"We have to do the games." Peabody had a gleam in her eye that might have come from the bellinis, or the overdose of estrogen.

"Go ahead," Eve told her.

"Nuh-uh! You have to run them. If I do it, I can't play. I wanna play."

"Don't look at me," Nadine said when Eve turned to her.

"Oh, hell. Fine, great. I'm on it."

She'd run ops, she ran a squad of detectives. She could handle a hundred women over a bunch of stupid games.

They were insane, Eve discovered within the first fifteen minutes. The room was packed with women who were psychotic and certifiable. Screaming, shouting, laughing like mental patients over the race to decipher each rubric she held up.

She wasn't entirely sure she wouldn't be forced to subdue a brunette who looked big enough to be carrying triplets.

"Cradle Robber!" The woman screeched out.

"Okay, good. You got it. Settle down." Eve pressed a finger to her eyes, breathed, and prayed she'd make it through the next two rounds without becoming a gibbering idiot.

At last she got a break as the victor insisted on being hauled to her feet to waddle over to inspect the prizes and select her spoils.

"Dallas?" From her throne, Mavis reached up for Eve's hand.

"You need something? You okay?"

"Yeah, I'm better than good. It's just Tandy's not here. I don't know what could've happened. I tried her place, and her pocket 'link, but she's not picking up. Maybe she went into labor, but I tried the birthing center, and she hasn't checked in."

"Maybe she forgot."

"Just couldn't. Last time I talked to her she was all about it. I'm kind of worried."

"Don't be." A worried Mavis could turn on a dime into a blubbering Mavis. "Listen, she was pretty close to popping, right? Maybe she was just too tired or whatever. She turned off her 'links and took a nap. Try her again later."

"Yeah, maybe. Sure, she's fine. Just needed to rest. I hate that she's missing it. It's the ult party. Everything's just frosty, and she was really looking forward to it."

When Mavis started to water up, Eve crouched beside her. "Hey, don't get upset. We'll, um, we'll put some cake away for her. And one of the favor things."

"That'd be good. I'm never going to forget today, Dallas. Not if I live to be a zillion and five."

"Just relax and enjoy. I've got to start the next round."

206

Crazed game-playing females were slightly less scary than an emotionally wound-up, extremely knocked-up Mavis.

She got through the games, and with Peabody happily volunteering to deliver the booty, the party shifted to the present portion of the program.

Hoping to distance herself from the coos and squeals that broke out each time Mavis ripped at wrapping paper, Eve dropped into a chair across the room. Moments later, Mira joined her.

"Quite a celebration."

"How do they stay so charged?" Eve wondered. "I was afraid I'd have to put on my riot gear."

"Babies, particularly when they're so wanted, bring unparalleled joy. And for us, for women — whether or not we choose to have them — we know we're the only ones capable of bringing them into the world. We're the power." She patted Eve's hand. "You've done a lovely thing for your friend."

"I wasn't sure I'd be able to pull it off. Not sure I would have without Peabody cracking the whip. It's been worth it."

"Like sixteen hours of labor?" Mira said with a smile.

"Oh, God, *why*? Why do they revel in talking about all that? It's creepy."

"It's the power, and the love. And each experience is unique, no matter how long the human race has propagated. It's intimate and astonishing, and it binds us as women. One day, when you're ready, you'll know."

"Seeing all this — and that birthing class I had to take — it's pushed the idea — which is actually more of a concept — way, way down on my to-do list."

"When you're ready," Mira repeated. "I like watching them. Women. The different sizes and shapes, the colors. The dynamics that form. Look at Louise and Nadine, sitting over there with their heads together. And Mavis's friend Trina, huddled with those two women. Probably giving them hair and skin-care advice for during pregnancy. And Peabody, hauling gifts in her efficient way, so happy to be useful. Mavis on her throne — a charming concept, by the way — looking so healthy and vital.

"And here we sit, you and I. The observers."

"A lot of it, for me, is like watching aliens. Still, not without its entertainment value," Eve admitted. "Take that blonde over there, in the red dress. Her feet are killing her. But people complimented her shoes, and she claimed they were comfortable. Now she's stuck. And the brunette — short, green skirt? She keeps wandering back to the food table. She takes this little sliver of cake each time. Hit it about a dozen times now. But she can't just go and take a human-sized piece straight off. She tells herself the sliver doesn't count."

When Mira laughed, Eve relaxed into a game she knew how to play. "And Trina? First, let me thank God she's been too busy to corner me about my hair. She's soliciting clients — no point letting an opportunity like this go by. But at the same time, she's rarely more than three feet away from Mavis. Watching out for her.

Brought her a fizzy, some cake. Went with her every time Mavis made one of her countless trips out to pee."

"She told me she had a new product that, quote, 'Kicks the ass out of winter dryness.' She even gave me a sample. Ah, Mavis is about to open Peabody's gift. I can't wait to see it."

"She's nervous. Peabody," Eve added. "Standing there sweating, afraid Mavis won't like it as much as she hoped. Giving gifts is torture."

But when Mavis lifted the lid on the box, there was a stunned look on her face, followed by a collective gasp by those close enough to see the contents.

"Oh, *Peabody!*"

And the awed, almost reverent joy in Mavis's voice told Eve her partner had hit the bull's-eye.

She lifted out, gently, the little booties and hat done in a rainbow of pastels. It seemed to Eve every woman in the room went gooey. And when Mavis took out the blanket, there were exclamations, and fingers reaching out to touch and stroke.

"It's lovely," Mira commented. "Absolutely lovely. She's just given Mavis an heirloom."

Obviously thrilled, Mavis managed to level herself out of the chair to grab Peabody in a giddy hug. Flushed and shiny, Peabody accepted the compliments.

"Um, since you're up," Peabody began. "You got one last gift coming from your hostess. Dallas?"

"Jeez. That's my cue." Eve set her drink aside, crossed the room. Since Peabody had nagged her brainless on just how it had to be done, Eve took one edge of the cover as Peabody took the other.

When they whipped it off the chair, Mavis actually slapped her hands to her heart. "Holy shit! Holy shit! It's the exact one I wanted. Oh, oh, look at the colors! And I've been sitting in it this whole time. Dallas!"

It was Eve's turn for a hard hug. "It's the ult in rocker systems. The absolute! You didn't have to give me a present. The party was enough."

"Now you tell me." It was the exact response needed to make Mavis laugh instead of cry. "Go ahead, take it for a spin."

When it wound down and thinned out, and there'd been no catastrophes, no emergency child-birthing procedures, and happy faces all around, Eve figured she'd scored a winner.

She also figured on dumping herself into a hot jet tub with a double bellini until she was comatose.

"The guys are heading back," Peabody announced. "They're going to load up your haul, Mavis. Leonardo, McNab, and I will get it all up to your apartment."

"I'll give you a hand," Trina told her. The beauty consultant had her hair in a complicated pattern of braids and curls today, and in showy magenta. She turned her eyes on Eve. "You're due for a treatment."

"Don't start on me. I'm riding on alcohol and sugar."

"You did good. You get a break. Sit down, Mav, take a load off."

"I'm too juiced. I can hardly wait till Leonardo gets a load of all this stuff. It was the best of the best, Dallas. And now I've got to ask you for something else."

210

"We forgot something?" She glanced around. "There can't be another baby item left in Manhattan."

"No, it's about Tandy. She's still not answering. It's like hours now, and I keep seeing her in her apartment, in labor. I want to go by. Would you come with me. Please?"

"You've had a really big day," Trina reminded her. "You should go on home and rest."

"I just can't, not until I make sure she's okay. She doesn't really have anybody. And I . . . I've got so much of everything."

Sensing a new jag, Eve stepped in. "Sure, no big. We'll run by there, and I'll take you on home after."

Which meant a long delay in becoming comatose, but it got her out of hauling presents out of the house. Of course, it meant she was now solely responsible for a tired, emotional, churned-up pregnant woman.

"Don't have the baby on my watch, Mavis," Eve warned as she loaded her friend into her vehicle.

"I'm solid, don't worry. Just a little tired. And I know I'm probably being a zero about the Tandy thing, but I can't help it. She's been like my knocked-up buddy for months now, and I talked to her just a couple days ago. It was all 'I can't wait till Saturday,' and how she'd sprung for this new outfit for the shower. She wouldn't have forgotten about it, Dallas."

"Okay, so we'll check on her. If she's not home, we'll talk to a couple of her neighbors. She went into baby mode, one of them probably knows."

"Sure, sure. Could be she went to a different center for some reason. The midwives work at more than one.

211

That's probably it. Wow, she's probably had her baby! Or she's having it now." Mavis began to rub her belly. "I might be up next."

"Just not today, okay?" she slanted Mavis a leery eye. "Absolutely not today."

"No way! I want time to play with all the gifts, and put all the little outfits away, and make it all abso perfect before little Roofus or Apricot come along."

"Roofus? Apricot?"

"Just trying them out."

Eve glanced at her friend. "My advice? Keep trying."

CHAPTER
TWELVE

After she led Eve to Tandy's apartment door, Mavis shifted from foot to foot. "Gotta pee again. My bladder feels about the size of a chickpea lately, and what there is of it keeps getting kicked."

"Just . . . think about something else." Eve knocked. "Don't bounce like that. It can't possibly help, and you might shake something loose."

"She's not answering. I really, seriously, completely need to pee."

Changing tactics, Eve turned and knocked on the door across the hall from Tandy's. Moments later, the door cracked open to the security chain, and a woman peered out the crack suspiciously.

"What?"

"Hey, Ms. Pason! Remember me? I'm Tandy's friend, Mavis."

"Oh, yeah." The eyes warmed fractionally. "You're looking for Tandy?"

"Uh-huh. She missed my baby shower, and didn't answer the 'link, so I was . . . Wow, Ms. Pason, I really have to pee."

"'Course you do. Come on in and use the bathroom." She unhooked the chain. "I don't know you," she said, pointing a finger at Eve.

"This is my friend, Dallas. She gave me the most magolicious baby shower today. I'll be right back."

Ms. Pason folded her arms as Mavis dashed off. "I don't like letting strangers in."

"I don't blame you. I can wait in the hall."

"It's okay, this once, since you're her friend. Tandy and Mavis are nice girls."

"You seen Tandy lately?"

"Couple days ago, I guess. We left for work at the same time."

"That would have been . . ."

"Wednesday, Thursday?" Ms. Pason shrugged. "One morning's the same as the next. And I keep my nose out like I expect people to keep theirs out of mine."

"Good policy."

"Gosh, thanks, Ms. Pason." Mavis beamed a smile when she came back in. "You're a lifesaver. Did you maybe see Tandy today?"

"No. Couple days ago, like I told your friend here."

"A couple days?" Mavis reached out, gripped Eve's arm. "Dallas."

"Stay calm. Anybody come see her since you saw her that morning?" Eve asked Ms. Pason.

"Didn't notice. I keep —"

"Your nose out, yeah."

"Dallas, we need to go inside. We need to go into Tandy's. You could use your master."

214

"Master what?" Ms. Pason demanded. "You can't just go around going into people's homes."

Eve pulled out her badge. "Yeah, I can."

"You're the police? Well, why didn't you say so? You think something happened to that nice girl?"

"No," Eve said quickly. "But since she's not answering her 'links or her door, and you can't remember seeing her today, it may be best to check her apartment. Maybe Mavis can wait here."

"I'm going with you." Mavis clung to Eve's arm. "I want to go in, make sure."

"Fine, fine." And if Tandy objected to having her premises entered without a warrant or probable cause, it was just as well to have Mavis there to run interference.

Eve knocked again, then pulled out her master. "Tandy, if you're in there it's Dallas, and Mavis. We're coming in." She uncoded the locks, eased the door open.

The room was the same size as the one across the hall, which meant it felt claustrophobic. Tandy had it spruced up in soft colors with ruffled curtains at the single window. They were open so that a couple of live plants in white pots could soak up the winter sunlight.

On the table in front of a small sofa was a box wrapped in white paper with purple cows dancing over the surface. It was topped by a huge purple bow.

"See, that's my gift." Mavis pointed. "I told her how cute that paper was when I was in the baby store a few weeks ago. Tandy! Tandy! Are you all right?"

The place was empty — Eve could feel it — but she let Mavis go in.

No sign of struggle, she mused as she scanned the area. No evidence of hurried departure. The place was neat, ordered, and organized.

"I'm going to check the bedroom. She's using it for a nursery, too." Mavis started for a door, but Eve moved past her, checked it herself.

The bed was neatly made, and beside it was a white cradle already dressed with blue sheets. A little stuffed lamb sat in it looking, to Eve's mind, very out of place, and just a little creepy.

Why did people put farm animals in kids' beds?

"She's not here. And that's her go-to-the-hospital bag." Mavis pointed at a little tote standing next to the door.

Saying nothing, Eve moved into the bathroom. There was a white towel hanging over the shower rod. Bone dry.

As was the living room, the bedroom, the bathroom were spotless and organized. *Spare* would have been another word Eve would have chosen for it. Except for the baby gear, it didn't seem as though Tandy was one for collecting things.

She had the basics, and coordinated them in a pleasing way, but there was none of the excess most people — and most women, to Eve's mind — surrounded themselves with.

She moved back into the bedroom where Mavis stood hugging her elbows. "Dallas, I think —"

"Don't think yet. There's no sign of trouble in here, so you take that as a good." She moved to the closet, glanced through Tandy's wardrobe. Spare again. The basics in nice fabrics and colors, and nearly all of them clothes for the very knocked-up. No coat — and there'd been no coat on the chrome rack beside the front door.

There was a purse, a brown one, hanging in the closet. But it was empty. Eve recalled Tandy had carried a huge black one the night they'd met.

"No sign of her coat, her purse. Every appearance that she went out, and just hasn't gotten back yet."

"Then why doesn't she answer her pocket 'link? Why didn't she show at the shower?"

"Okay. Good questions. We're not done yet."

And the fact was there was a little twinge at the base of Eve's spine. Something was off here, but there was no point winding up Mavis any more than she already was.

Eve walked back into the living room where the pretty box sat waiting on the table. She moved to the window and the pair of leafy green plants. When she tested the soil she found them like the towel in the bath. Bone dry.

She turned toward the kitchen, a smaller box off the box of the living room. Counters were clean and uncluttered. There was a white bowl holding three red apples, a smaller bowl, a mug, a small glass, and a spoon left to drain beside the sink.

Breakfast dishes, Eve concluded. Cereal, she decided after a glance in the cupboards, juice and herbal tea or a decaffeinated coffee substitute.

Eve took out a couple of bottles of pills.

"Those are her supplements for the baby. Like vitamins."

"Okay. She's got service for four — plates, flatware. She do much entertaining?"

"No. I don't think. She had Leonardo and me over once, and we had her to our place a couple of times. She isn't seeing anyone. Like a guy, I mean. She's completely focused on the baby."

Mavis shifted her own gaze as she saw Eve studying the wall. "Oh, that's her calendar. Isn't it cute, with the baby dressed up like a tulip?"

While Eve thought the idea of dressing a human, even a new one, like a flower was just plain silly, Mavis bubbled on. "There's a different baby for each month, and . . . She didn't cross off the last two days."

Eve had seen that already. There were red x's in each boxed date, through the past Thursday. Mavis's fingers shook as she curled them around Eve's arm.

"She marked off each day, heading for B-Day. Baby Day. See, see? January thirty-first. She's got it circled in a heart. She crossed them off every morning for the countdown. But not yesterday."

Full of fear, Mavis's eyes latched onto Eve's. "Not today. And she's got today marked with little raindrops and my name. Mavis's shower. Oh." Mavis pressed a hand to her side. "Oh."

"You're not going to do that. You're not doing that now. Breathe or something."

"Baby's kicking, that's all. And I guess I feel a little shaky in the knees. Maybe a little bit sick."

218

Moving as fast as she dared, Eve hooked an arm around Mavis's waist, moved her into the living area and a chair. "Just sit, close your eyes. Breathe. I'd suggest putting your head between your knees, but I think that's physically impossible for you at the moment."

It brought a half-laugh out of Mavis as she obeyed. "I'm okay, really. Just scared and worried. Something happened to Tandy, Dallas. You have to find her."

"That's what I'm going to do. She had 'Max' and 'eight' written on the Friday box. Who's Max?"

"I don't know. She wasn't seeing anybody. She'd have told me."

"Listen." Eve crouched down in front of the chair. "First thing, I'll check the health centers, birthing places. I'll get the name of her boss at the store, give her a call, see if Tandy was at work on Thursday."

"That's good. Maybe she went into labor at work, and they took her to the closest birthing place. That could be."

"Sure. Simple is usually true."

"But if that happened on Thursday, why haven't I heard from her? Oh, God, what if she lost the baby!" Mavis reached out, gripped Eve's hands with fingers that were like little vices. "Or she had an accident, and —"

"Or she had one of those sixteen-hour deals and is too whipped to talk to you, or anyone. Chill it out, Mavis."

"You'll find her."

"I'm going to make the calls, and if that doesn't ring the bell, I'll tag Missing Persons. Just as a precaution."

"No. No. You have to find her." Mavis gripped harder. "You can't give her to someone else. If you look for her, you'll find her. I know you will."

"Mavis, I'm Homicide, and up to my ears in a double murder. Missing Persons is set up to handle this kind of thing. I'll start the legwork, and we're probably going to find her fast and fine. But if I don't find her by tomorrow —"

"Please." Tears shimmered in her eyes, swam in them. The fact that they didn't fall, that she didn't simply collapse into a jag, was more wrenching. "I need you to do this, Dallas. I don't know anybody in Missing Persons. I know you. I know you'll find Tandy. She doesn't have anyone to look out for her. But if she has you, she'll be okay."

"Mavis —"

"I'm scared for her." She pressed their joined hands to her own belly. "And her baby. If I know you're looking for them, I won't be so scared."

"Okay, I'll fix it. But you have to go home now and lie down."

"But I want to help you —"

"That's the deal, Mavis. I'll do this, but you go home. I'm going to contact Leonardo, have him come get you."

"But you'll tell me as soon as you know anything?"

"The minute."

It wasn't just Leonardo who showed, but Roarke, Peabody, and McNab as well.

"We'd just finished loading up the gifts," Peabody explained. "No sign of Tandy?"

220

"Not yet. You go ahead, give Leonardo a hand. I'm just going to make a few inquiries."

"Dallas is going to find her," Mavis said.

"Of course she is." Leonardo's voice was easy and confident as he draped his arm around Mavis, but his eyes, meeting Eve's, were full of concern. "I'm just going to get you home, baby doll. You've had a long day."

"Dallas?" McNab held up a hand. "How about if I go along, give Leonardo a hand with the loot. I can tag you when we're done, and swing on back if you need more hands on this."

"That'll work." As long as they got Mavis home and horizontal. The rosy glow she'd had all day had changed into a strained pallor.

"Find her quick, okay?"

"Sure," Eve said to Mavis. "Don't worry."

"It'll be all right now." She stepped over, wrapped her arms around Eve, sighed. "It'll be all right since you're taking care of it."

"You're tired, sweetie-pie." Leonardo drew her away. "Let Dallas get started. You and the belly need a nice nap."

The minute the door was closed behind them, Eve dragged her hands through her hair. "Shit."

"Want me to do the knock-on-doors or take the 'link?" Peabody asked her.

"Take the 'link, thanks. All health and birthing centers. Contact her boss, find out what went down Thursday, anything out of routine."

"You think something happened to her," Roarke said.

"Yeah, I do. Maybe Mavis's nerves are contagious, but something's wrong here. Look at this place." She spread her arms. "Neat and tidy, everything in its place."

"Nesting," Peabody put in. "Making everything nice for the baby."

"Whatever. She's organized, and I'd say habitual." She told them about the kitchen calendar. "Going by that, the plants, bath towel — all dry — I don't think she's been back here since she left for work Thursday morning."

She took a breath. "I don't know much about it, but if she went and had the baby unexpectedly, why didn't she contact someone — Mavis or her boss — and have them come get her hospital bag?"

"Something could've gone wrong with the baby."

Eve nodded at Peabody. "Let's find out."

"What can I do?" Roarke asked, and Eve blew out a breath.

"Well, since we're already stomping all over Tandy's civil rights by just being in here, you could take a look at her 'links, her comp unit. See if you find anything unusual."

"Do you want me to contact Missing Persons?" Peabody asked.

"Not yet. I have to figure out — if we don't find her in the next few hours — how to convince them to let me handle it. Otherwise, Mavis is going to wig out on me again."

Eve started with Ms. Pason across the hall, but got nothing more there than had already been told.

She worked her way, floor by floor. Most of the tenants who answered knew Tandy by name — which was a small surprise — the rest knew her by sight. None of them recalled seeing her in the last couple of days.

She was on the ground floor about to knock on the last door when a woman gripping the hand of a kid — so bundled in outdoor gear Eve could only see the huge dark eyes — came up behind her.

"You looking for someone?" As she spoke, the woman shifted just a little so the kid was behind her.

"As a matter of fact. You live here?"

"That's my door you're standing in front of. What do you want?"

Eve pulled out her badge, and the woman frowned at it.

"Look, if the disaster that is my ex is in trouble again, it's nothing to me. I haven't seen him in over a year and that's the way I like it."

"It's about Tandy Willowby. Apartment 4B."

"If Tandy's done something to earn a visit from a badge, I'll fly on the first pig that wings by."

"When's the last time you saw her?"

"Look, no offense, but cops've been a pain in my ass. You're looking to hassle Tandy, you won't get anything from me."

"I'm not looking to hassle her, just find her. Apparently nobody's seen her for a couple of days. I'm a friend of a friend of hers."

"Who's the friend you're a friend of?"

"Mavis Freestone."

"You're a friend of Mavis's." The woman narrowed her eyes.

"That's right. Mavis had a baby shower today. Tandy didn't show, and Mavis is worried. We came by to see if she was here. She's not. Looks like she hasn't been since Thursday. Have you seen her since?"

"Well, hell. Come on inside. Me and Max are roasting in these coats."

"Max?" Eve looked down at the dark eyes framed in a puffy red hood.

"Yeah, Max is my son, and the only thing worth spit I got out of the ex. Come on, pal of mine," she said to the boy. "Let's go inside. Zeela," she added to Eve. "I'm Zeela Patrone."

"Dallas. Lieutenant Dallas."

Zeela unlocked the door, led the boy inside. Then she crouched down, grinned into his face. "You in there, Maximum Force? Let's see. Hey, there you are!"

He giggled as she stripped off the coat, unwound the scarf, pulled off mittens. Under it all, he was sturdy and dressed in some sort of overalls with a bright plaid shirt.

"You go play in your room for a few minutes, okay?"

"Can I have juice?"

"Soon as I'm done."

Then he tugged her hand, whispered in her ear. "I don't think so, handsome. Get your trucks, why don't you, and we'll have a race with them when Mommy's done talking to the lady. That's my boy."

When he toddled off, Zeela smiled, rose. "Kid's a fricking miracle. Not a chromosome of his old man's, far as I can tell. Sweet and fun and smart. Somebody decided to cut me one huge break. He asked me if maybe the tall lady could stay for a tea party."

"Appreciate it, but I have to pass. Tandy Willowby."

"Yeah. No, I haven't seen her. That's the thing. She was supposed to baby-sit Max Friday night." Absently, Zeela tunneled her fingers through the hair that had been flattened by her cap. "I was going out on a limb and taking in a vid with this guy I keep running into at the deli down the block. I've been off dating since Max came along, so this was like a maiden voyage. Tandy was supposed to come down, watch Max for the evening."

"She didn't show."

"No. I called up there, then I went up. No answer. I gotta say, I was pretty steamed." As she spoke, she hung up the outdoor gear on little pegs by the door. "Figured she forgot or was too tired. Max was bummed because he likes her a lot. We were both looking forward to Friday night, and she let us down. I decided to be pissed. Now I'm trying to decide if I should be worried."

"How well do you know her?"

"We got to be friendly over the last few months. I've been there, done that — the having a kid on my own deal. Have you checked with her midwife? She could've gone into labor. She's close to due."

"My partner's up in Tandy's apartment, making inquiries about that. Did she tell you anything about the baby's father?"

"Not much. Just he was back in England, and wasn't part of the picture. No rancor, so I figure they'd just split amicably like."

"She ever mention his name?"

"I don't think so. Don't remember anyway. Most she told me was that somebody's bc didn't do the job — happens — and she got pregnant. He wasn't looking for permanent or family, she wasn't sure she was ready to take it on by herself. Then she decided she was — the family thing. She decided to come to New York. Fresh start, new scene. That's about it."

"How about other friends, men she was seeing?"

"She was friendly. Mavis came by off and on. I met one of the women she works with, and sometimes she'd walk out with Ms. Pason from across her hall. They went to work about the same time most days. But as for men, she wasn't into it. Not now."

"Did you get the sense she was worried about anything, anyone?"

"No, just the opposite. She was revved up and ready to be a mother. But now I'm starting to worry. This city can eat you up. I don't like thinking it could've taken a bite out of Tandy."

"Nothing," Peabody reported when Eve returned to Tandy's apartment. "I know she has the same midwife as Mavis, so I contacted her. Randa Tillas. She states she hasn't seen or heard from Tandy since her appointment on Monday. She was fine, right on schedule. Checked with her boss. She had Friday off.

She's slated to work tomorrow, noon to six. They've lightened her hours."

"She show for work Thursday?"

"Right on time. Worked a full eight, last full day for her. She got in at just after nine, left at six. Nothing out of the ordinary during the day. She had three breaks. A full hour for lunch — maternity benny. She took them in their back room, with her feet up. Didn't leave the shop all day, until six. No contact via the store 'link for her. Can't say on her personal."

"How did she get to and from work, as a rule?"

"Boss said she takes the bus. I got the route. The Thursday driver's off today. We can track him down at home, or talk to him tomorrow. He's on."

"We'll take him at home."

"I've contacted the health and birthing centers nearest her work and her residence. Nobody by her name has checked in."

Eve rubbed her eyes. "Okay, we'll spread out from that. And we'll check if any MTs did a run with a pregnant woman matching her description."

She glanced over as Roarke came out of the bedroom. "I've checked her 'links and her comp," he told her. "No outgoing on the 'links since Wednesday evening when she talked to a Zeela Patrone, this building."

"Yeah, I've gotten her statement. Tandy was supposed to run herd on Patrone's kid Friday night. Didn't show, didn't contact her to cancel. Incomings?"

"Nothing Thursday. Friday evening, from the same neighbor's little boy. Came in at about seven in the evening, obviously coached by his mother. 'Are you coming down to play with me' sort of thing. Another transmission from the mother just after eight, faintly irritated. Asking where Tandy was, did she forget. Transmissions from Mavis today, from our house. Nothing else."

"And the comp?"

"Nothing that seemed useful. She surfs baby boards, pregnancy and childhood sites. E-mails Mavis. She has Mavis's e-address in her book, along with the addresses of her midwife, the downstairs neighbor, her work, her coworkers. Precious little, really," he replied. "There's nothing on there, Eve."

"And nothing that indicates she'd rabbit," Eve added. "If there was an accident, they'd have contacted her medical group. A woman this organized would have that data in her bag. Listed in her memo book, on her pocket 'link. Why does someone snatch a woman that close to giving birth?"

"For the baby," Peabody finished.

"Yeah, for the baby." A grim and nasty thought, Eve decided. But there was more grim, more nasty. "Or because they're some sicko who rapes and/or kills pregnant women. We'll do a run through IRCCA, see if we have any like crimes. And I want a full background run on Tandy. Things look this quiet, this normal, this settled, there's often something shaky underneath."

"Does Mavis know who the father is?" Roarke asked.

"No. But we're going to find out."

"I'll contact McNab," Peabody began. "He can meet us at Central."

228

"No. I need to do that, work this out with MPU. We're stepping on toes here."

She stopped a moment, lined up the steps in her mind. "Go back to your place, go ahead and do the search for like crimes. If Mavis is up to it, go there and ask her if she knows anything about what Tandy did back in England, what she might have said about the baby's father, her family, that kind of thing. We'll do the data run on Tandy, but Mavis may know more than she thinks. Keep her calm, you're good at that. Let her know I'm talking to the people I need to talk to."

"We can help Leonardo set up some of the baby stuff. That'll do the trick."

"If you say so. Roarke? With me?"

"Always."

When they were in her vehicle, Roarke turned to her. "You think she was taken."

She thought of the pretty, cheerful blonde, the way she'd talked about looking forward to Mavis's shower. "I see no reason for her to walk. I can't jump to abduction or foul play from there, but yeah, that's the way it feels."

"If you give Mavis a little time to calm down, I think she'd be satisfied if Missing Persons took this over, and you simply stayed in the loop."

"You didn't see her, you didn't hear her." Resigned to it now, Eve shook her head. "And besides that — which is plenty — I told her I'd do it. All I have to do is convince MPU to leave it with me, then convince Whitney I can take this on without it infringing on the investigation I've already got going."

He brushed a hand over her hair. "You might want to convince yourself of that first."

She smiled thinly. "Working on it."

CHAPTER
THIRTEEN

At central, she split off from Roarke, asking him to go straight to Homicide and wait for her in her office while she arrowed off to MPU.

"I may need to offer whoever I deal with on this an incentive," she told him.

He cocked his head and those wonderful lips curved in an easy smile. "You mean a bribe."

"Bribe's such a strong word. Yeah, I may need a bribe. Sports or booze, probably. Those are the usual hot tickets. I'll keep it within reason."

"Bribing cops not to do work is a time-honored tradition."

"Hey."

He laughed. "Do what you need to do, Lieutenant. I'll be in your office."

She didn't know who might have caught weekend duty, or who might be at a desk, but she hoped it was someone she had at least a passing and cordial relationship with.

Otherwise, she'd have to start from scratch with whoever had the weekend command — and if things got sticky, and an *incentive* didn't make the cut, she'd go straight to Whitney. But that was something she hoped to avoid.

She figured she lucked out when she spotted Lieutenant Jaye Smith grabbing what looked like an energy bar at Vending.

"Smith."

"Hey, Dallas. Caught a Saturday tour, too?"

"Not exactly." Eve dug credits out of her pocket. "Grab me a tube of Pepsi, will you?"

"Sure. It's on me."

"Thanks."

"Great coat. Hell for leather, huh?"

"You could say. Thanks," Eve repeated when Smith offered the tube. "You got a minute for me?"

"Sure. Want the lounge or the office?"

"Let's take your office."

"Business, then." With a nod, Smith led the way.

She was near fifty, Eve remembered, and had better than a quarter century on the job. Married with a kid, maybe two. She was on the short side, about five-three with a boxer's kind of build. Tough and muscular. Her hair was many shades of blonde, and worn straight with shaggy ends that swung past her jaw.

She wore her weapon as a sidearm at the hip, low, with a navy sweater over it.

Eve knew her to be a solid cop, so tucked away the idea of waving sports or booze into the mix. With Smith, she could be direct, and put it all straight up.

Lieutenant Smith's office was bigger than Eve's — but most were — and boasted what appeared to be two reasonably comfortable visitor chairs as well as a brushed steel desk that looked new.

On it were the standard d-and-c unit, stacks of files, and a framed picture of a couple of teenagers — one of each kind — who Eve took to be Smith's kids.

From her office AutoChef, Smith got herself a mug of tea so dark it looked like coffee, then gestured to a chair. Instead of taking the desk, Smith settled into the other visitor's seat.

"So, what's up? Lose somebody?"

"Somebody looks to be lost. And I need you to do me a solid on it."

"You want me to shuffle a MP to the top of the pile for you, I can do that." Rising, she opened a desk drawer. She was reaching for a recorder and a note pad when Eve shook her head.

"That's not exactly it either. Let me give you the situation."

Eve ran through it, watched Smith's face, saw she was taking it in. "You're thinking a snatch, and could be. But you got a pregnant woman, no partner, no known family, foreign. That's a big plate heaped with several helpings of emotion. Could have snapped, taken off."

"Could, yeah. Thing is, nobody who knows her sees that."

"But you don't," Smith pointed out, "know her. Really."

"No. But I met her myself, twice, and I got a good gauge of her. I wouldn't peg her to rabbit, or even to take a few days off somewhere. Not without telling anyone, missing an event she was juiced about, leaving all her things behind."

"You said you checked her 'links. No communication in or out that indicated any plans." Smith pursed her lips. "An appointment she didn't keep, a party where she didn't show — with the gift wrapped and waiting. Okay, looks like you've got one to me."

"Time line and circumstance point to something going down after she left work, before she got home."

"I'd agree with that." Sitting back, Smith sipped her dark, strong tea. "But you don't want me to open a file and move on this?"

"This friend of mine? The other pregnant one? She's turned around about this, and she . . ." Eve blew out a breath. "Okay, she put me on a spot with this. So I'm going to ask you to let me handle the case.

"I'm not looking to elbow you out," Eve continued, when Smith frowned over her mug. "And I'd welcome any help or direction you could give me, but Mavis is holding one of those emotion-heaped plates, too, and she's looking to me to take care of it."

"Knows you, doesn't know me or anybody in the unit."

"That's the big of it, yeah. Mavis and I go back a long time. I don't want her any more screwed up over this than she has to be."

"How far along is she?"

"Mavis?" Eve pushed at her hair. "Heading to the final countdown. Couple more weeks, I guess. I told her I'd do this. I'm asking you to let me keep my word."

"This would be Mavis Freestone, music sensation?"

"It would."

"I got an eighteen-year-old daughter who's a major fan."

Eve felt the tension in her shoulders ease. "She might like backstage passes next time Mavis performs in the city. Or anywhere, for that matter, if you wouldn't mind her being transported by a private shuttle."

"I'd be her hero for life, but that sounds suspiciously like a bribe."

Now Eve grinned. "And a damn good one. I had booze or sports lined up if I needed them. I appreciate this, Smith."

"I've got friends, too, and I don't like to let them down. Here's what I'd need. You'd copy me on every report, every statement, every note you make. I'm apprised of every step of your investigation as you make it. I'll keep my own file on her here, and if I feel at any point I need to step in, or assign someone to step in — to work with you, or to take over — I don't want to hear the squawk."

"You won't. I owe you one."

"Find them — the woman and the baby — and we'll call it even." Smith dug up a card. "I don't have anything current that mirrors this one, but I'll do a search, see if there's anything in the city that reflects a like crime."

"Appreciate it. All of it."

"The missing's who matters, not who runs the show from here. My home 'link, pocket 'link numbers are on the back. Day or night."

Eve took the card, offered her hand.

Back in her office she found Roarke at her desk working on her comp. He glanced up at her, lifted his brows in question.

"I'm clear. I got lucky."

"That's good then. I got started on your background checks. Do you want to work here or at home?"

"Neither, not yet. Right now we're going to see a man about a bus."

The bus driver's name was Braunstein, and he was about two hundred pounds of hard fat in a New York Giants football jersey. He was fifty-two, married, and was spending his Saturday evening watching a post-season game on-screen with his brother-in-law and son while his wife, his sister, and niece took in some — in his words — "girlie vids" at a local theater.

His irritation at having his viewing interrupted was obvious, until Eve mentioned Tandy's name.

"London Bridge? That's what I call her. Sure I know her. Rides with me most every night. Always has her fare card ready, lots don't. Got a nice smile. She sits right behind me. Somebody takes that seat, I make 'em get up, give it to her. Her delicate condition and all.

"She gave me a nice tin of cookies for the holidays. Made them herself. She got trouble?"

"I don't know that yet. Did she ride with you Thursday evening?"

"Thursday." He scratched his chin, which badly needed a shave. "Nope. Funny now you mention it, 'cause I remember her saying, 'See you tomorrow, Mr. B,' when she got off at her stop on Wednesday. She calls

236

me 'Mr. B.' I remember because she was carting this box wrapped in funny paper with a big-ass bow on it."

He glanced around as both of his companions erupted with rage at a call on the field. "Offside, my rosy red ass," one of them shouted.

"Goddamn refs," Braunstien muttered. "'Scuze the language. Anyway, I asked her about it — the box — when she got on, and she said how she had a baby shower on the weekend. Listen, that little girl get hurt or something? I told her she ought to take the maternity leave, close as she was. She okay? She and the baby okay?"

"I hope so. On the bus, you ever notice anyone paying too much attention to her? Hanging too close, keeping an eye? Anything like that?"

"No, and I woulda." He scratched his prominent belly. "I kinda looked out for her during the run, you know? Got some regulars, and some of them might strike up a conversation with her the way people do when a woman's carrying a bun. You know, 'How you feeling?' 'When are you due?' 'Pick out any names,' that kind of thing. But nobody bothered her. I wouldn'a let them."

"How about people who got off at her stop?"

"Sure, there'd be some. Regulars and otherwise. Never noticed anybody looking funny, though. Someone hurt that girl? Come on, I feel like her uncle or something. She hurt?"

"I don't know. No one's seen her, as far as we can tell, since Thursday, at around six o'clock."

"Well, Jesus." This time Braunstien showed no reaction to the shouts and curses coming from the living room. "Jesus, that's not right."

"People like her," Eve said as she drove. "Like people liked Copperfield and Byson."

"Bad things happen to likable people," Roarke pointed out.

"Yeah, yeah, they do. I'm going by where she worked. Walk from there to her bus stop. Get a feel."

Outside the White Stork, Eve watched traffic zing uptown on Madison. It was later than it would have been when Tandy left work, and a Saturday rather than a weekday. But it would've been going dark at six, and, as she recalled, that day was gloomy.

Streetlights on, she mused, headlights cutting through the dank light.

"Cold," she said aloud. "People bundled up, like they are now. Walking brisk, most of them walking brisk. Want to get home, or get where they're going. Early dinner, after-work drinks, errands to do on the way home. She comes out. Has to walk over to Fifth to catch her bus. Two blocks down, one block over."

Eve started to walk it with Roarke beside her. "She's going to move with the lights. If she hits the walk, she'll go on down the second block, then over. If she doesn't, she'll do the cross-town block first. You want to keep moving."

"No way to know which way she did it."

"No." But since they caught the light, Eve continued through the intersection. "Least likely place to snatch her — if it was a snatch — is the corner. More people, closer together. You want to come up behind her."

She demonstrated when they were near the middle of the block, falling back a few steps, then coming in quick, banding an arm around Roarke's waist.

"Using a weapon?" he speculated. "Otherwise she'd react — call out, struggle. Even the most jaded would stop when an obviously pregnant woman is in trouble."

"A weapon," Eve agreed. "Or it was someone she knew. Hey, Tandy!" Eve shifted her arm, firmed it tight around Roarke. "How's it going? Boy, you sure are carrying a load there. How about a lift home? Got my car right down there."

"Possibly." He turned west as she did to walk to Fifth. "Who does she know?"

"Customers, neighbors, someone through the birthing class or center. Someone from back in England. Baby's father. Had to be force or familiarity. Maybe both. Had to be quick and quiet, because, yeah, somebody's going to notice a pregnant woman struggling with someone. We'll show her picture around this area, in case someone did."

Once they hit Fifth, she turned north to walk back on the alternate route.

"Probably took her on the cross street," Eve said. "Always less foot traffic than the avenues. Had to have a vehicle, or possibly . . ." She scanned up, frowning at the apartments overhead. "Possibly a place close by.

But then you've got to get her inside without anybody making note of it. I don't like that one, but it could be."

"And why wouldn't she resist once she was in a vehicle?"

"Force? She could have been sedated, or she was afraid. Maybe there was more than one abductor. Familiar, she could have been pleased to see someone she knew, and to be off her feet, catch a ride home."

She scanned the area as they crossed back to Madison. Most people moving quickly, most with their heads or at least their eyes down. Thinking their thoughts, bubbled inside their own worlds.

"Somebody willing to take a risk, moving quick and smooth. Sure, you could pluck a woman right off the sidewalk. It happens. One of the cross streets," she repeated. "Makes the most sense, but you can't be sure which one she'll use. Wouldn't park the vehicle, if you're using one, on the street. Not if you're doing the snatch alone. And if you were lucky enough to find a spot anyway. Closest parking lot to her work, that's what you'd use."

"Logical," Roarke agreed, and took out his PPC. He tapped a few buttons, nodded. "There's a lot on Fifty-eighth, between Madison and Fifth."

"That'd be handy, wouldn't it? You'd only have to walk her a couple of southbound blocks. Let's go have a look at it."

She wanted to walk it, again taking the most logical route. It was an automated lot with no attendant, human or droid, and on this Saturday evening, at capacity.

It boasted a security cam, but even if it worked, she knew the disc would have been dumped every twenty-four hours. She noted down the number posted for contact. "Maybe we'll get lucky on the security disc," she told Roarke. "They should have records, in any case, of payments. We'll want ID on any vehicles leaving the lot between eighteen and nineteen hundred on Thursday."

She dipped her hands in her pockets. "Or he could've had a partner circling the blocks, and we're screwed on this angle."

Or they paid in cash, Roarke thought. Used a stolen vehicle. Eve would be considering those possibilities as well, he knew, so didn't bother to comment. "If she was taken the way you're theorizing, it was planned out, timed. Do you think she was stalked?"

"I'd say the probability of it being a random snatch is low, but I'm going to run it. Somebody knew her routine, her schedule, her routes. Somebody wanted her and/or the baby she's carrying specifically."

"Leans toward the father, then, doesn't it?"

"High on the list. All I have to do is identify him."

"I'd like to think that would mean he'd be less likely to hurt her or the child, but that's probably not true." He thought of his own mother, and what she'd suffered at the hands of his father, and tried to shake that off. "I've seen too much of what happens in these circumstances with the women at Duchas."

"Primary COD in pregnant women is violence at the hands of the father."

"That's a bloody sad state of affairs." He looked out over the street, over the people who rushed by in the cold, blowing air. But for a moment he saw the alleyways of Dublin, and the hulking figure of Patrick Roarke. "A bloody sad commentary on the human condition."

Because she thought she understood where his thoughts had gone, she took his hand. "If he took her, we'll find him. And her."

"Before he does for her — or them." He looked at her now, and she saw the past haunting his eyes. "That's the key, isn't it."

"Yeah. That's the key." Eve shook her head as they continued to walk. "She told somebody who he was. Maybe not once she moved to New York, but back in England. Somebody knows who he is."

"She might have moved to New York to get away from him."

"Yeah, I'm circling that. So, let's go home and try to arrow in."

"Tandy Willowby, age twenty-eight."

Eve sat at her desk in her home office, reading the data Roarke had already run. "Born London. Parents Willowby, Annalee and Nigel. No sibs. Mother deceased, 2044. Tandy would've been twelve. Father remarried, 2049, to Marrow, Candide — divorced with one offspring from first marriage. Briar Rose, female, born 2035."

She continued scrolling. "Willowby, Nigel, deceased 2051. Bad luck. But that leaves her with a stepmother

242

and stepsister still alive and kicking. Computer, contact information for Willowby, Candide, or Marrow, Candide, and Marrow, Briar Rose, London. Use birth dates and identification numbers in file already running."

Working . . .

"Eve, if you're thinking of contacting them now, I'll remind you it's after one in the morning in England."

She scowled, glanced at her wrist unit. "That's such a pisser. Okay, we take that in the morning."

The computer told her Candide now lived in Sussex while Briar Rose retained a London residence.

"Okay, back to Tandy. See here, she was employed over six years at this dress shop in London. Carnaby Street. Position, manager. Kept the same apartment there —"

"That would be 'flat,'" Roarke interrupted.

"Why would it be flat? How can you live — oh." She rubbed the back of her neck as she cued in. "Right, she'd call it a flat, which makes no sense to me. But she kept it, just like she kept the same employer, for more than six years. She settles in, she roots, she's habitual. We'll want to talk to the owner of the shop."

Now she leaned back, stared up at the ceiling. "If she had a guy, I bet she kept him a good chunk of time, too. She doesn't bounce around. But she relocates not just to another part of England, even of Europe, but goes three thousand miles. Gives up her longtime home, longtime job. That's not a whim, not for someone like

Tandy. That's a big step, and one she would have thought about a lot, one she had to have a strong reason for taking."

"The baby."

"Yeah, I'd say it comes back to that. She put an ocean between someone or something and the kid. Strong reason, or she'd be nesting in her flat in London."

"A creature of habit," Roarke put in. "As were your other two victims."

"Let's hope Tandy makes out better than they did. I'm going to set up a board for her, and do a timeline."

"All right. Unless there's something specific I can do for you here, you might send me some of those blind accounts on the Copperfield/Byson case. I'll start looking at numbers."

The fact was, he wanted to step away — at least for the time being — from the thought of a woman so completely vulnerable at the mercy of someone who wished her harm. Someone, he thought, she might have loved once.

Eve stopped for a moment, turned to him. "If I'd been in your place on that one, I'd've told Whitney to kiss my ass."

"What?" He pulled himself back, into the now. "Ah, well, all in all, I'd rather have your lips in that vicinity than his."

"Find me something useful, they might find their way there."

"And my incentive keeps rising."

She swiveled away from the screen, looked him in the eyes. "Are you all right on this? The Tandy thing."

Foolish, he admitted, to believe she didn't see, didn't know. More foolish, he supposed, for him to try to block it from her, or from himself. "I'm not, actually, not completely. It resonates a little too deep for me. I don't know if it's anger or grief I'm feeling. It must be both."

"Roarke, we don't know Tandy's in the same kind of situation as your mother was."

"We don't know she isn't." Idly, he picked up the little statue of the goddess Eve kept on her desk. A symbol of the female. "He waited until after I was born to murder her, my mother. But she was trying to protect me, do what she thought best for me. As I expect Tandy is doing, whoever has her now."

He set the statue down. "I just want my mind off it for a while."

He so rarely hurt, she thought. So rarely let himself, she corrected. "I can take this one back to Central. Keep it out of here."

"No." He moved to her then, taking her face in his hands. "That won't do, not for either of us. What once was made us who we are, one way or another. But it can't stop us from doing what we do. They'll have won then, won't they?"

She put her hands over his. "They can't win. They can only screw with us."

"And so they do." He leaned down, pressed his lips to the top of her head. "Don't worry about me. I'll

245

steep myself in numbers for a while. They always clear my head."

"God knows how. I'm going to make coffee. All around?"

"If I had some cake to go with it. I got shafted on that end of the deal."

"Cake?" Her mind circled around. "Oh, right. Mavis. I think there was some left. Those women were like vultures when something had icing on it. Maybe the Dark Shadow stocked some of the leftovers in the AutoChef. I could probably choke down a piece myself."

And thinking that sugar and caffeine kept the blood moving, she made it a large piece along with strong, black coffee. He'd be all right, she told herself, because he wouldn't let himself be otherwise. But she'd keep a finger on the pulse, and if she didn't like the beat, she'd move the Tandy investigation out of the house.

For convenience, she set Tandy's board next to the one she'd already started on her other case. And on the side with a slick white surface began to handwrite a time line.

She made lists of names. People she'd already spoken with on one side, those she would contact in the morning on the other. She tacked up Tandy's ID photo.

Her first step was to call the contact number of the parking lot. As she expected, she was transferred to an endless menu of choices, and quickly selected operator before the droning litany could bore her into a coma.

"Courtesy Messaging Service." The voice was nasal as a trombone and dense with Queens.

"This is Lieutenant Dallas, NYPSD," Eve began and gave her badge number. "I need information on the Park and Go, Fifty-eighth Street."

"For information, please call Customer Service between the hours of 8a.m. and —"

"I need information now, and I don't want to talk to some hand patter at Customer Service."

"Well, jeez. This is a messaging service, you know, for, like, twenty businesses in Manhattan alone. I don't have information about a parking lot."

"Put me through to the owner."

"I'm not supposed to bother the client with —"

"Maybe you should give me your name and location. I'll send a couple of uniforms to pick you up, and you can tell me how you're not supposed to bother the client when you get down to Cop Central."

"Well, *jeez*. You gotta wait a minute."

Eve was put on wait mode while music sweeter than the icing on her cake tinkled in her ear.

During the ten minutes it played — with periodic computer-generated bulletins assuring her that her call was important — she began a series of probability runs.

By the time an actual human came back on, she was drinking her second cup of coffee and studying the results.

"Lieutenant, is it?" The man looked slick and sounded same.

"That's right. And you are?"

"Matt Goodwin. You're inquiring about the Park and Go on Fifty-eighth?"

"That's right. Do you own it?"

"I represent the corporation that does. What seems to be the problem?"

"I'm investigating a possible crime in which this lot may be involved. I need the security discs as well as the logs for Thursday last, between eighteen and nineteen hundred hours."

"What possible crime?"

"It's a Missing Persons matter. I need the discs and the logs as soon as possible."

"I believe those discs are dumped every twenty-four, Lieutenant. As for the logs, I assume you have a warrant?"

"I can get one."

"Well, when you do —"

"And when I do, I'll see it includes logs for an entire week, as well as a search into the lot's — and the corporation that owns it — standards and practices. I'll have to bring you and your client into Central for questioning. Or, you can get me the logs for that single hour of that single day."

"Of course my client would want to cooperate with the authorities."

"Good for your client."

"I'll have to contact my client, and with their permission, arrange to have the logs you specified copied and made available to you."

"You do that. Relay to me at this number where the logs can be picked up. By 9a.m. tomorrow morning."

"Lieutenant, it is the weekend."

"I've heard that. 9a.m., or I get that warrant."

She clicked off, went back to studying her probability results. Even with the sparse data at her disposal, it was running in the mid-nineties that Tandy Willowby had been target specific.

Tandy had no criminal record on either side of the Atlantic, no known association with criminal elements. She had a small, tidy nest egg that jibed with someone who lived carefully on the salary she'd pulled in since the onset of employment. Her parents were dead, and from the basic data Eve could access without a warrant, her stepmother and stepsister had no wealth. Middle-income salaries.

There were no suspicious deposits or withdrawals in Tandy's accounts that indicated blackmail on either side.

On the surface it appeared the only thing of true value Tandy owned was what she carried in her womb.

Playing a hunch, she contacted the owner of the White Stork.

"Lieutenant Dallas. You've found Tandy."

"No."

"I just don't understand this." Liane Brosh was a youthful sixty, with a face strained with concern. "She must have just taken a weekend away. Maybe a quick trip to a spa to rev up before the baby comes."

"Did she talk about doing that?"

"No, not really. I suggested it a couple times, but she always said she was already revved." Liane smiled weakly. "We had a little shower for her here at the store, and I gave her a gift certificate to a day spa in the city. She said she was saving it until after the baby. But I'm sure she's fine. Maybe she just wanted to get out of the city for the weekend."

"Does that strike you as something she'd do?"

"No, it doesn't." Liane sighed. "It doesn't sound like her at all. I'm so worried."

"Can you tell me if anyone came into the store to see her specifically, to speak with her?"

"Tandy worked with several expectant parents. All the staff is available for personal shopping, for helping with registries, decor, layettes."

"How about someone she might've worked with, or who might have frequented your shop whose expectations weren't realized. Miscarriage, for instance."

"It does happen. I can't think of anyone offhand, but I can certainly check the records, ask the other girls."

"I appreciate that. Did she ever speak about the baby's father?"

"In general, and vaguely. No specifics, and since she didn't want to talk about it, I didn't press."

"If you think of anything, even if it doesn't seem important, I want you to contact me. Twenty-four/seven."

"I will. We love Tandy. All of us will do anything we can to help."

Eve tried another hunch and contacted Tandy's midwife.

"This is Randa."

"Randa Tillas, Lieutenant Dallas."

"Tandy."

"Nothing yet."

"Well, damn it." She was a striking black woman with the faintest hint of the islands in her voice. Her rich brown eyes filled with concern. "I contacted members of her birthing circle, in case she was spending a couple of days with one of them. But no one's heard from her since Wednesday."

"Any member of that circle have a problem pregnancy?"

"I've got one with high blood pressure and another on bed rest, but nothing major, no."

"Maybe a birthing coach who's had trouble conceiving, or carrying to full term."

"I don't have full medical on coaches, but that sort of thing usually comes up during the class. I'd try to discourage coaching by anyone who might be in a dark place. It wouldn't be good for them, or the mother."

"Did she ever talk to you about the baby's father?"

"Some, yes. It's important for me to know as much as the mother is comfortable telling me. For a single mother, more so. Especially one, like Tandy, without family support."

"Can you tell me what she told you about him?"

"I'm treading a line here, but I'm worried enough I'm stepping over it. He was someone she dated for about a year back in London. I think she was very much in love with him. The pregnancy was unplanned, and wasn't something he wanted or was looking for. She decided it was something she wanted, so she broke things off and moved to the U.S."

"Long way to go."

"I thought so, but she said she'd wanted everything fresh, and it seemed reasonable. I'd say she's very resolved to have this baby and to raise it on her own, with no murky feelings toward the father. She was very spare on the details about him, but she did slip once or twice and call him by name. Aaron."

"That helps. Thanks. Anything else, contact me."

"I'm going to go through my file on her, and ask the other members of the team if she spoke to them about anything that seems important. We all want her and the baby back, safe and healthy.'

CHAPTER
FOURTEEN

She went over the data Peabody sent to her computer on like crimes. IRCCA had popped a few for her. Abductions, abduction/murders, rapes, rape/murders. Abductions where the baby had been delivered then stolen, and the mother left behind.

Alive or dead.

In the majority of the abductions, the woman had known her kidnapper, or had had previous contact.

Eve separated them into known or unknown, into family strife, cases where the abductor had been mentally ill, and those done for profit.

She culled out the rapes into a separate file.

Then she worked them geographically.

There had been cases in New York with similar elements, and those involving family members of the victim she separated out again. She set aside those cases where the perpetrator was doing time, earmarking those to check other family members, and any possible contact with Tandy.

She outlined Missing Person cases where the investigator found the woman had gone into a shelter to escape an abusive relationship, or simply walked out.

And others where neither mother nor child had ever been found.

Because Tandy had come from London, Eve moved there next. A smattering of like cases again, but none that had any outward link to hers.

So she branched out to Europe.

The most interesting was a case, still open, in Rome where the missing woman had walked out of her regular OB exam in her thirty-sixth week, and poofed. Like Tandy, earlier in the pregnancy she had relocated to another city, moving from Florence three months before she went missing. She was single, had no family in that area. She'd been healthy, and lived alone. Unlike Tandy, this woman had applied for and received paid maternity leave during her second trimester.

A struggling artist, she had been in the process of finishing a mural of a fairyland on the walls of the nursery she'd outfitted in her apartment.

Or was it "flat" in Italy, too? Eve wondered.

Sophia Belego had been missing for nearly two years. Gone without a trace.

After making a note of the investigator's name, Eve stewed over the time difference. Italy was another place she couldn't contact yet.

"Lieutenant."

"What? Huh?"

"It's now after two in the morning. New York time."

"What is it in London?"

"Too early." Roarke laid his hands on his wife's shoulders, dug at the rocks that had taken up residence there. "And time for both of us to recharge."

254

"I've got more in me."

"You'll have more yet after a few hours of sleep."

"I'm working something from the data Peabody got from IRCCA."

"And how much further can you take it tonight?"

Nowhere really, she thought. But still. "I haven't written it all down. I need to put it into a report for the file, and copy MPU."

"Which can wait until morning."

"If she got snatched, she's going on better than fifty hours missing. I need the damn data from the parking lot. And I'm not going to get that until morning," she argued when he only looked at her. "Okay, a couple hours down."

Because she was looking glassy-eyed, he moved to the elevator with her.

"You got anything for me?" she asked him.

"Nothing concrete. It's going to take longer without names. With them, I could do more thorough excavating." And he thought, make use of his unregistered equipment and avoid CompuGuard's beady eye if he went down a bit deeper than was technically allowed. "I've left a couple of programs running. We'll see what we get in the morning."

"I have to do some digging myself on that." She pushed her tired brain from possible abduction into murder. "Cavendish to Bullock to Robert Kraus to Jacob Sloan — maybe three generations of Sloans — and from there to my vics. Something there. I think if I squeeze Cavendish right, he'll spurt."

As her mind shifted between two investigations, she undressed. "Why does a firm with that kind of — what is it — panache — use a guy like Cavendish to head up its New York branch? Nepotism, maybe, because he's not as smart as he could be. Bruberry, his admin, she's smart. But she's not blood, so you put his name on the letterhead, and let her run it behind the scenes? That's how it feels."

Eve slid into bed. "Copperfield said she was offered a bribe. If I can show contact around the time of the murder between her and Cavendish's office, I could squeeze from that angle. Or —"

"Too much coffee for you." He drew her close. "Turn off that head of yours and go to sleep."

And how the hell was she supposed to do that? Because he was right, as usual. She'd poured too much coffee into her system. Her brain was running sloppy loops inside her head, from Copperfield to Byson to Tandy and back again.

"Might have to go to London," she murmured. "Huh. Wouldn't it be a kick in the head if I really did have to be out of the country hunting a criminal mastermind when Mavis goes into labor?"

"I, my ass. That goes to *we* or I'll hurt you."

"Yeah, big talk."

Since her brain was up, and her body insisted on following suit, she didn't see why she shouldn't put both to good use.

She trailed her fingers up his spine, then down while she angled her head and found his lips with hers in the dark.

"Are you trying to take advantage of my weakened state?"

"Damn right."

"Just checking." His lips curved against hers. "Go ahead then. I can't stop you."

"Guess you'll have to lie there and take it." She nipped at his jaw, slicked her tongue down his neck. "You could call for help."

"My pride prevents me."

Chuckling, she slid a hand down, found him already hard. "Yeah, you're just full of pride."

He tasted so good, all warm and ripe, and as her body pressed to his, rubbed bare flesh to bare flesh, she felt his heartbeat kick. She shifted, stretched herself over him so she could press her lips where that heart beat for her.

More than desire, she thought lazily. Here was knowledge and comfort, and a kind of communion. *Turn to me, and I'll be there.* That was the simple answer they could always find together no matter what shadows hung over them. Through the past, through the present, they could always find the answer, and each other.

She felt his hands on her now, stroking to soothe or to arouse, and succeeding in doing both. For another moment, she stayed as she was, eyes closed, absorbing the sheer and simple pleasure of knowing where she belonged. Then, in the deep dark, in the deep quiet, she slid up him again until their lips met.

Movement and heat, he drifted into both as she did and rode on the warm current of sensation. The shape of her, the scents and the sounds, were so familiar, and

257

so alluring. She, as no other ever could, reached every corner of his heart. His woman with her long, lean body, her courageous spirit and questing mind. His joy, and his salvation.

Here it was so clear, so easy, with only the two of them in a dance either could lead, both could follow.

And the need for her sang through him like a favorite melody.

She straddled him, laying her hands over his as he took her breast in his mouth. Letting her head fall back as she immersed herself in the next thrill, letting her mind empty of everything but what they gave to each other.

She took him in, slow, slow.

He quivered for her, he murmured to her, and at last he filled her. Her body bowed back, a slim white curve in the shadows. Then forward to rock them both breathless in the dark.

They wrapped around each other, sliding languidly down from that peak, her leg tossed intimately over his hip. She rested her brow lightly against his jaw until sanity returned.

"Better than cake," she said, and made him laugh.

"So it was. And it was damned good cake."

"Mmmm. What time is it anyway?"

"Ah . . . somewhere after three."

She did the calculation in her head. "Good enough." She tipped her head up, pressed her lips firmly to his. Then rolled away and sat up.

"And what are you about, Lieutenant?"

"I'm about waking up some people in Europe. Light on, five percent. Going to grab a shower first," she said when the lights glowed dimly. "Wash the rest of the cobwebs out."

He folded his arm behind his head. "So I served as a way to use up a bit of time till you determined it was reasonable to wake some poor sod up on a Sunday morning."

"Yeah."

"I feel so used. Thanks."

"Welcome." She felt clearheaded now, a good second wind. "I'm just going to get some things rolling, then I'll catch a couple hours down."

"Too right you will." Then he sat up. "A bit longer then."

"You don't have to stay up."

"You weren't singing that tune a few minutes ago." When she grinned, he walked by her, giving her a quick pat on the ass. "Let's have that shower, and maybe both of us will be back in bed before dawn."

Eve tried Candide Marrow first, and was bumped to voice mail. She left a message, then moved down the list to the stepsister.

A hoarse, muffled voice said, "Bugger off."

"Briar Rose Marrow?"

"Do you know what bloody time it is?"

"Where you are or where I am? This is Lieutenant Eve Dallas, from the New York City Police and Security Department. Are you Briar Rose Marrow?"

The lump in the bed had a mad thatch of black hair streaked with gold, and muttered, "What the fuck is it to you?"

Since Eve figured she might've had the same attitude under the circumstances, she held onto her patience. "Are you Briar Rose Marrow, and do you have a stepsister by the name of Tandy Willowby?"

"So fucking what?"

"When did you last have contact with your stepsister, Ms. Marrow?"

"Well, Christ." The lump moved, shoved at the mad thatch and revealed a pale face with sleepy and improbable purple eyes heavily lined with black, and full lips where the lip dye had faded to splotches of crimson. "How the bleeding hell should I know when it's eight bleeding o'clock in the bloody morning? Who the hell are you again?"

"Lieutenant Dallas, in New York."

"Cops? What do the cops want with Tandy? New York? I haven't had my sodding coffee." Briar Rose scrubbed at her face with her hand, then pressed it over the sheet in the vicinity of her belly. "Oh, fuck me, how many orgasms did I have last night?"

"That would be your personal business."

The woman snorted. "The drinks, more's the pity. Why are you waking me up on a Sunday morning about Tandy?"

"Are you aware she's been living in New York for the past several months?"

"New York? Well, fuck me. You serious? Handy Tandy in New sodding York."

"I take it you haven't spoken to her recently."

"Not since . . ." She scratched her fingers in her hair, and crawled across the bed to a little table where she shoved around at debris and came up with some sort of cigarette. "I'm trying to think. June maybe. Why? You're not going to tell me she's done something illegal. Not our girl."

"She's missing."

"Missing what?" She fumbled with a lighter, then lowered it before it sparked. "*Missing?* What do you mean, missing?"

"She hasn't been seen since Thursday."

"Maybe she had herself a massive piss-up."

"Which would be?"

"You know, a bender? A drinking binge. Though that isn't much like Tandy."

"I doubt it, particularly given her condition."

"Condition of what?"

"Are you aware Tandy's pregnant? Due to give birth in a matter of days?"

"What? What the fuck? Up the duff? Tandy? Oh, bollocks to that." But the sleepiness cleared out of her eyes. "Just a bloody minute." She rolled out of bed, and to Eve's mild relief was at least wearing underwear. She grabbed some sort of baggy red shirt out of a pile of clothes and dragged it over her head. "You're telling me Tandy's knocked up, and nobody knows where she is?"

"That's exactly what I'm telling you. You said you hadn't spoken to her since June. Is that usual? That long a gap?"

Briar Rose walked back to sit on the side of the bed. This time she lit the cigarette. "Listen, we were steps less than a couple of years, really. Her widower father married my stone bitch of a mother when I was about fourteen. He was all right, too, nice sort. Then he ups and gets killed in a pile-up on the M4."

She paused a moment, let out a long breath and a cloud of smoke. "Tandy was finishing up at University, and already had a job. My mother dragged me off to Sussex for Christ's sake. Tandy made some tries at keeping up a kind of relationship, but the stone bitch wasn't interested. I moved back to London first chance, but I was in a phase, you know? Mostly interested in piss-ups and getting laid. I didn't want the big sister deal, especially with one who was bog standard while I was busy shagging wankers and gits. Cocking up right and left. I'd see her now and again, if she cornered me."

She drew deep on the cigarette. "Even when I got myself a decent job and eased back some, we just didn't have much in common. I saw her last spring, it was. She rang me up, said she needed to talk to me."

"And you talked about?"

"We didn't, not really. I knew she was wound up about something, and thought she'd probably got herself engaged, or got a bloody promotion, again. I acted a pillock because the bloke I'd been seeing turned into a berk and dumped me for some bit of fluff. And bollocks to him. I just met her for coffee and had a right go at her and buggered off. Bloody hell."

It was a challenge, but Eve thought she'd picked her way through the foreign slang and idioms to the meat of it. "No contact after?"

"Well, I felt a right arse, didn't I? A couple weeks later, I did penance and went by her flat, but she'd moved. All they said was she'd moved, maybe to Paris.

It pissed me off that she didn't let me know where she'd gone but there was bugger all I could do about it. She's having a baby?"

"That's right. Do you know Aaron?"

"Met him a couple of times. They were all but shacked up. Is he there in New York with her?"

"Not to my knowledge. Do you have his full name, a contact number or address?"

"Aaron Applebee, in Chelsea, I think. He's a writer for *The Times*. You telling me that git got her up the duff, then turned her out?"

"I'll have to speak to him about that. Was she seeing anyone else?"

"Tandy? Not our girl. One at a time for her, and they'd been tight for months and months. Bastard. Maybe she's come back home, come back to confront him. I'll ring up a few people. A girl wants to be home, doesn't she, when she's about to be a mum."

"I appreciate the information. If you think of anything else, or find out anything about her whereabouts, contact me."

Eve did a search for Aaron Applebee and got his number and address.

When she hit his voice mail, she did a standard run on him instead.

Applebee, Aaron, the computer recited, DOB June 5, 2030, Devonshire, England.

It listed his parents, and a complicated series of half-sibs through each side. He was employed, as Briar

Rose had said, as a staff writer for the London *Times*, and had been employed there for eight years. No marriage on record, no criminal. Several pings for traffic violations. He'd resided at the same address, in Chelsea, for five years.

His ID photo showed an attractive blond man with a long jaw. A height of five feet ten inches, a weight of one-sixty.

On the surface, he looked steady, ordinary. A regular *bloke*, she mused.

"Want to talk to you, Aaron."

She tried his home 'link again, bounced to voice mail and clicked off. After looking up the name of the investigator on the like crime in Rome, she began to wind her way through the maze of the Italian cops until she found one in his unit who not only spoke perfect English but agreed to contact Inspector Triveti, and ask him to get in touch.

She updated her notes, then rose to add the printout of Aaron Applebee's ID photo. When she turned toward the kitchen, Roarke stepped out of his office.

"No more coffee," he said, definitively.

"Just one more hit. I'm waiting for a callback from Rome."

"Then order a cappuccino — decaf — and make it two."

She very nearly pouted. "Decaf's got no punch."

"The depth of the shadows under your eyes makes it look like you've already been punched. What's in Rome?"

"A like crime, and a cop who I hope speaks English." Since Roarke followed her into the kitchen, she couldn't sneak real coffee. "I talked to Tandy's stepsister."

She relayed the gist of the conversation as the AutoChef served up two frothy coffees. "How are you on Brit slang?"

"Reasonably fluent."

"I could've used you as an interpreter. What's 'bog standard'?"

"Boring, basically."

"I wasn't far off. She had this Aaron's full name — it's Applebee. He works for the London *Times*, lives in Chelsea. Both parents married or cohabbed multiple times, but not currently with each other. Got a brood of half- and stepsibs."

"Which might put a man off the idea of marriage or family."

"Might. Reporters have a lot of sources. If he'd wanted to find Tandy, it seems he could and would have. Maybe he decided he wanted the kid, and they're just off playing kissy-face. Or maybe he found out she was having it when he thought she wasn't, and he came over pissed. Or he's just at home, sleeping off a Saturday Night Special and not answering his 'link."

"Or, it's still possible she just walked away. She'd done it before, leaving London."

"Yeah, there's that." And the probability run she'd done on that angle had given her a near fifty-fifty. "But I'm betting when she left London, she packed her things, all nice and neat. She gave her landlord and her employer notice. I already know she did none of those things here. No, she didn't work all day, leave the shop, and decide somewhere between Madison and Fifth to just keep walking."

"No." Roarke laid a hand on Eve's shoulder and rubbed. "She didn't."

"So." She struggled with a yawn. "You getting anywhere with the numbers?"

"A couple of interesting things. I want to come at them from another angle, then I'll put it together for you."

"Sounds like a plan. Look, why don't you pack it in for now, go on to bed? I'll just wait for the Italian, then head in, too."

"Not a chance. If I leave you on your own, I'll come back in a few hours and find you facedown at your desk, snoring."

"I don't snore."

"Wake the dead."

"I do not." Did she?

He only smiled, then wandered off to study the Willowby side of the board. "You've gathered quite a bit in a short amount of time."

"Nothing that points to where she is and why. In the Italian case, they never found the woman, or the kid."

"They didn't have you." Nor had his mother, he thought. She'd had no one, and there was nothing that could change it. He turned to Eve. "Look at you. You're running on empty, and pushing at two fronts."

"It may already be too late for her." She nodded at Tandy's photo. "Pushing's all I can do."

When her 'link signaled, she spun around to answer. "Dallas."

"Triveti. I am returning to you."

His accent was thick and exotic, his face lean and handsome. "Thank you for getting back to me so quickly, Inspector."

"I am pleased. My English, *scuzi*, it is small."

"My Italian's smaller." She glanced toward Roarke. "I have someone with me who can help if we get in a bind. You investigated a Missing Persons case a couple years ago. A pregnant woman."

"Sophia Belego. You have the same."

"Tandy Willowby," she told him, and gave him the bones of the case, with Roarke refining some of the details in Italian when the Inspector expressed confusion.

"Like yours, my Sophia, she had no close family, no ties to the city where she disappeared in. She left her — *momento* — her, ah banking account. It had not been used, or her credit cards, since the time of her disappearing. Her clothes, her possessions remained in her apartment. In this place, her neighbor speaks to her that morning when she is leaving. The statement says that Sophia was — what is *lieto*?"

"Happy," Roarke translated.

"*Si*, she is happy and full of excite. She is going to see her *dottore*."

"Doctor," Roarke translated.

"And she will shop for the baby. She sees the *dottore*, and is well. Healthy. Her spirits are good, and she makes the *appuntamento*?"

"Appointment."

"Appointment," Triveti repeated, "in one week. She is very great with child, you see?"

"Yes," Eve told him.

"But she does not shop for the baby, not in Rome. I am talking to everyone in these places. Some, they know her from other times, but not from that day. She is not seen after she leaves the *dottore*. There is none of her at transportation — bus, train, shuttle. There is no use of her passport, and I find it in her apartment. There are no messages, no communications that take me to leads."

"Nothing in the hospitals, the birthing centers, the morgues?"

"Nothing. I look for the father of the child, but no one knows. Not in Rome, not in Florence. In all our efforts, she is not found."

Using Roarke, Eve took Triveti through the steps again, squeezed out a few more details. She requested a copy of his file, and agreed to reciprocate with hers.

After, she sat frowning at the notes she'd taken. "I need to write all this up."

"Sleep first."

"I told the LT in MPU that I'd copy her all reports and notes. I need to —"

"You think she's sitting by her comp waiting for your report at . . ." he glanced at his wrist unit, ". . . four forty-eight on bloody Sunday morning."

"No, but —"

"Don't make me haul your ass up and drag you to bed. I'm tired, and I might rap your head against the wall on the way. I'd hate to damage the paint."

"Ha-ha. Okay, okay. Just let me try Applebee one more time. Listen, listen, if she's gone off to see him, I can go to bed with a clear head."

"You know damn well she hasn't. One more, and that's the end of it."

"You get bitchy when you're tired."

"I get bitchier yet when I watch you run yourself into the ground."

She tried Aaron again, and again got voice mail. "Damn it."

"Bed. Sleep. Or being in a bitchy frame of mind, I might hold you down and pour a tranq into you."

"You and what army?" She got to her feet, and the ensuing head rush told her he was right. She needed to put the circuits on pause for a few hours.

Two hours, she thought, three tops. And she glanced back at Tandy's picture on her board as she walked out with Roarke.

"It's harder than homicides," she stated.

"Is it?"

"They're already gone. You're there to find who took their life, to find out why if you can, to build a case that will give the dead justice. But this, you just don't know. Is she alive, dead, hurt, trapped, or did she just say screw it and walk? If she's alive and in trouble, you can't know how much time you have to find her. And if you don't, not in time, she may end up being yours again, as a homicide."

"We're going to find her."

Eve glanced at the bedroom clock. Seventy-one hours missing, she thought.

CHAPTER
FIFTEEN

Eve came out of the blank black of exhausted sleep into a bright flash of white. There were babies crying, women screaming, and though they seemed to be all around her, she was alone in the white box. She pushed at the walls, but they were strong as steel, and all she managed was to smear bloody handprints against the white.

Looking down, she saw that her hands were covered with fresh blood.

Whose blood? she wondered, and reached for her weapon. But in her harness was only a small knife, already gorey. She recognized it — of course she did. She'd used that very knife to hack her father to death once upon a time.

If it was good enough for him, it would be good enough now.

Shifting it to a combat grip, she began to walk along the white wall.

Did they ever stop crying? she wondered. She supposed she couldn't blame them. Babies were squeezed and pushed out of the nice, warm dark and dumped into the cold hard light of reality. With pain, she thought, and with blood. With their mothers screaming through it.

It was a tough start.

The wall angled, and she followed it as the box narrowed into a tunnel. Not unlike the morgue, she noted. Birth and death, the beginning and the end of the human journey.

Angling again, she saw Mavis stretched out on the floor.

"Hey! Hey!" But as she rushed forward, Mavis smiled, waved at her.

"I'm good, I'm fine. Next to magolicious. Just cooking the bun 'till it's done. You better go help the others."

"What others? Where are they?"

"That's the big problem, right? You gotta fix it so you can get back before I pop. You remember all the stuff from the class?"

"I got an A."

"Knew I could count on you. B-day's coming, Dallas. Don't be late. Tandy's counting on you, too."

A white stork flew overhead, a white sack swinging from its beak. Eve ducked and cursed.

"There goes another one!" Mavis laughed. "Maybe it's Tandy's. Better go after it, better hurry. Could be a COD!"

Eve started off at a jog, glanced back. Mavis was standing on her head, her feet propped on the white wall. "I'm keeping it in the oven until you finish."

"That can't be right," Eve muttered, but chased after the stork.

In a cube built into the wall, Natalie Copperfield was tied to a desk. Her eyes were blackened and bloody and running with tears. There was a blue robe belt wrapped tight around her throat.

"It won't add up," she sobbed. "It won't come out right. I have to make it right. That's my job. They killed me for it," she said to Eve, "but it still has to add up."

"You have to give me more than that."

"It's all right there, all right there in the numbers that won't add up. Haven't you found her yet? Haven't you found her?"

There was a door. Eve yanked at it, then kicked it in when it refused to give way. Inside was a white room, and Tandy, strapped to a labor/delivery chair like the one used as a demo in the birthing class.

Blood stained the sheets, her face was shiny with sweat. Her engorged belly rippled obscenely.

"The baby's coming," she panted out. "I can't stop it."

"Where's the doctor? Where's the midwife?"

"I can't stop it," she repeated. "Hurry, hurry."

Even as Eve ran forward, Tandy vanished.

The floor opened under her feet. As she fell, the babies were crying, the women screaming.

She landed hard, heard and felt the bone snap in her arm. The room was cold, so cold, and washed with a dirty red light.

"No." Shuddering, she pushed to her hands and knees. "No."

He was lying in a pool of his own blood, the same blood that dripped from her hands, from the blade of the little knife she still gripped.

And as she watched, her father turned his head, and those dead eyes smiled at her. "It always comes back to the beginning, little girl."

She came out of it on a muffled cry to find herself wrapped in Roarke's arms.

"Dreaming, that's all. You're all right. I'm here."

"It's okay." She drew in his scent to steady herself. "I'm okay. It wasn't bad."

"You're shaking." He ordered the lights on low, and the fire on so the room glowed softly, and the flames burst into life in the hearth.

"It was just mostly weird. Weird and creepy."

"Dancing numbers?" He kept his voice light, but held her close and tight. "Flying babies?"

"Not this time." She ordered herself to relax, just relax against him. "Tangling up my cases," she said after she told him of the dream. "And ended with the big finish. Bastard always manages to get in there."

"Lie back down now. Let it go."

She let him draw her back, let herself curl in. But she knew she wouldn't be able to sleep, or to let it go. "There was this sense of urgency. I had to find Tandy, but even when I did, I couldn't get to her. And there was Natalie Copperfield, and all I could think was that she deserved better from me. She's trapped there, with those damn numbers, until I can fix it. Add it up. Make it come out right."

"No point in telling you you're spread too thin."

"No, no point. Sorry."

"Then let me remind you that you're not alone in that white room, that white tunnel, or even in that goddamned room in Dallas. Not anymore."

She tilted her head so she could see his face, lifted her hand so she could touch it. "Thank God."

He kissed her forehead. "Well now, you managed a rousing three hours of sleep. Back on the clock, are we?"

She didn't argue about eating a decent breakfast first. Instead she programmed a couple of whoppers herself while he dressed.

"And here's my lovely wife, serving me breakfast on a Sunday morning."

"You earned it." She gave the cat a baleful stare as he meandered over from the spot of sunlight where he'd been curled. "You haven't." But Galahad sent her such a mournful look, she rolled her eyes, went back to the AutoChef and ordered him up some breakfast kibble and a small side of tuna.

"Played you," Roarke said as he dug into his eggs.

"Maybe, but it'll keep him from begging and sneaking while we eat. I'm thinking," she began.

"As ever."

"The Italian case, too close to mine for comfort. If they connect, it most likely puts this Applebee in the clear. And it points to someone who targets women in this situation."

"Pregnant, no family to speak of, new city — toward the end of their term."

"Right. And while I don't pop out others that match just so, who's to say there haven't been others — women who weren't reported missing. Or others that came through IRCCA that didn't play out exactly the same way as these two. And if so, it could lean several ways."

274

Considering, he cut into the short stack of pancakes he'd drizzled with syrup. "A long way from Rome to New York if you're talking about someone who stalks women in this situation, abducts them. And Sophia Belego has never been found, leading to the assumption that the abductor then disposes of them."

"Or disposes of the woman. Babies are a commodity."

"Black market sales, slavery, illegal adoptions. Yes, a commodity they are."

She forked up some pancakes, and though they were already swimming in syrup, dunked them in more. Across from her, Roarke actually winced.

"It should make your teeth hurt," he commented.

"What? Oh, no it's good." She popped them into her mouth. "I like the sugar rush. Anyway, could be a psycho, who likes to travel, likes variety. Could be with enough digging I'll find some strange connection between Tandy and Belego. Could be a business. Both had to be planned out. Women snatched off the street — in Belego's case, in broad daylight. But there's another connection. Both women started their terms in Europe."

He watched, somewhat fascinated as she swished a slice of bacon through the pool of syrup. His steely-minded cop had the appetite of a five-year-old. "You think the root of it may be there rather than here."

"It's a thought. I'm going to let it circle around some while I write it up for Smith in MPU. Maybe she'll have some thoughts on it. It's more her area than mine."

"Let me know when you're done, and I'll bring you up to date on my little project."

"Run it by me now."

"There's one of the files that appears to add up, but doesn't. Not when you peel it apart, shake it out. An outlay and an income that double back on each other, and a separate expense that pulls out of that same income again and gets funneled through yet another account — a nontaxable one, where it shouldn't be. Not as far as I can tell, blindfolded as I am."

"Your call."

"So it was. There are repetitions of that, and subtle variations on it. Could be someone trying to tuck away a bit of the ready, someone hoping to avoid a bit of tax, or a little laundry."

"How little?"

"I'm not sure yet. Thanks," he added when she topped off his coffee, then her own. "It's cleverly done, and I'll need to peek under a few more covers. But it's considerable."

"Ballpark?"

"So far, mid-seven figures, for the time frame I'm working with."

"Millions then?"

"So it seems." He brushed a hand over her hair. "Motive enough, I'd think, for two murders."

"A handful of credits dropped in the gutter's enough motive for some. But yeah, for this type of thing, motive enough. Why don't you let me have a look so I can match it with the client?"

"Why don't you let me finish first?"

276

"You're working blind, so I work blind, too?"

"Now, would I be that small and petty?" He considered a moment. "I might be, but in this case, I'd just rather put it all together first. Not as if you've nothing to do in the meanwhile."

True enough, she thought. "I'm calling some more hands and eyes."

"We work on Sunday, so everyone does?"

"Would I be that small and petty?"

He grinned, and this time patted her hand. "Peas and pods. If you're pulling in troops, Lieutenant, I could make use of McNab."

"You'll have him," she said, and sitting back laid a hand on her stomach. "I think I feel a little sick."

"Small wonder after you sucked down a liter of maple syrup."

"Couldn't have been that much." But she thought she could almost hear it swish inside her as she turned to her 'link.

She had a message from the garage manager on Fifty-eighth. The discs were wiped — that was a dead end.

She'd barely finished waking up cops and moving into her office when Mavis walked in with Leonardo.

"I knew you'd be working." With shadows dogging her eyes, Mavis gripped Leonardo's hand. "See, I told you she'd be working. Have you found anything?"

"I'm talking to people. I told you I'd let you know as soon as something broke."

"I know. But . . ."

"She barely slept all night," Leonardo put in. "She wouldn't eat this morning."

"I'm standing right here," Mavis said irritably. "Don't talk like I'm stupid." She pulled away from him. "I can't think about anything else. How could I? I should be able to help. There has to be something I can do."

"You can go home and let me do my job."

"Don't you talk to me that way either," Mavis snapped. "Like I'm defective or whatever just because I'm pregnant. Tandy's my friend, and she's in trouble. I'm not going to sit home and do nothing."

"Why don't you sit here then," Roarke began, and she rounded on him.

"I don't *need* to sit. Do you see these?" She pointed down at purple gel-sole boots. "They call them feet, and I can stand on them. The next person, the *next* who says I should sit down, or lie down, or eat is going to get bloody."

There was absolute silence as three people eyed Mavis as if she were a homemade boomer with a questionable fuse.

"I'm strong and I'm healthy." She took an audible breath. "And I'm not sitting home on my fat, knocked-up ass while Tandy's missing. Look at you." She jabbed her finger at Eve now. "You think I can't look at you and see you haven't slept either? You think I don't know I asked you for a major? If you were in my place, you wouldn't be brushed off either."

"I can't be in your place as I don't have a fat, knocked-up ass to sit on. Yeah, you asked me for a major, and if you want me to come through on it, you'll sit down, shut up, and let me work. Bitch."

There was a second moment of humming silence as color flooded into Mavis's face. Then she jerked up her chin. "That's über bitch to you." Now she sat, and the room seemed to sigh in relief. "I'm sorry." Mavis pressed the heels of her hands to her eyes. "I'm sorry. Multiple apologies all around. Don't make me go home. Please." She dropped her hands. "Please give me something to do."

"You can write up the time line from my notes for my report. And you can make coffee."

"Okay. Okay."

"I could make the coffee." Leonardo glanced at Mavis. "I'd like something to do, too."

Mavis reached for his hand, then pressed it to her cheek. "Maybe you could make me one of your special breakfast frappés." When he leaned down to kiss her, she took his wide face in her hands. "You're the best thing that ever was, and I'm so sorry."

"Now that we've all kissed and made up . . ." Eve began.

"I haven't kissed you yet. Or you," Mavis added with a flirty smile for Roarke.

He responded by crossing to her and brushing his lips over hers.

"Maybe we could all get something done," Eve finished. "Roarke, I'll pass McNab on to you as soon as they get here. Leonardo, make the coffee strong and black." Eve rose as the men moved in opposite directions, then rolled her auxiliary computer to where Mavis sat.

"Thanks for calling me a bitch. I needed it."

"Anytime."

"Dallas, would you tell me what you know?"

Eve ran through it briefly while she set up the comp so Mavis could work.

"You found out so much already, so much I didn't know. I guess Tandy and I were always talking about now, and tomorrow. She didn't go into yesterday. Do you think . . . maybe do you think she and the baby's father got together? Maybe they're just taking a couple days alone?"

"I'm going to try to contact him again. We'll find out."

"Dallas? Whatever happens with this, I want you to know I'm really grateful. And I love you."

Eve laid a hand briefly on Mavis's shoulder. "No mushy stuff while I'm doing cop work. Timeline."

"I'm all over it."

Eve went back to her desk to try Aaron Applebee again. With a glance toward Mavis, she put the transmission on privacy mode.

And this time he answered.

"Applebee here."

"Lieutenant Dallas, New York Police and Security. You've been tough to track down, Mr. Applebee."

"I've been on assignment in Glasgow. Just got in." He rubbed a hand over a face that was shadowed by several days' worth of light brown beard. "Who did you say you were?"

"Dallas, Lieutenant Eve. NYPSD."

"Well, good morning, and I'm baffled. What can I do for you?"

"You can tell me the last time you had contact with Tandy Willowby."

"Tandy?" His face changed in a fingersnap. Eve would have said what came into it was a burst of hope. "You've seen Tandy. Is she there? In New York? I never would have thought . . . She's had the baby. She's all right? They're all right? Oh, God, I can get a shuttle and be there in a few hours."

"Mr. Applebee, you're the father of the child Ms. Willowby's carrying?"

"Yes, yes. Of course. Carrying? You said carrying?" Another flash of hope lit his face even as his voice trembled. "I'm not too late."

"You claim you didn't know she was living in New York."

"No, she — we — It's complicated. What do you mean 'was'?"

"Ms. Willowby's been missing since Thursday evening."

"Missing? I don't understand what you mean by missing. Wait, wait a bloody minute."

She could see him shift, sit down, struggle to orient himself. "How do you know she's been missing since Thursday?"

"She left work at 6p.m. on that evening. She did not return to her residence. She didn't keep appointments. She hasn't contacted her midwife, her employer, or her friends. I'm investigating."

"She's pregnant. She's due any time now. Have you checked the birthing centers? Of course, you have," he said before Eve could answer. "All right, let's just keep calm. Let's not lose our heads." But he gripped the back of his neck with his hand as if to hold his own head in place. "Maybe she came home. She came home and I wasn't here."

"There's no record of her boarding any transportation out of New York. Mr. Applebee, what was your relationship with Ms. Willowby when she left London?"

"Strained, maybe shattered. Stupid, stupid. I was such a bloody berk about it all. I was just panicked, or God knows. We hadn't planned . . . it just happened. The pregnancy, and I bungled it. I buggered it up, that's what I did. I suggested she terminate, and she got upset. Of course, she got upset."

He pressed his fingers to his eyes now. "God. God. What an idiot I am. We quarreled, and she said she'd have the baby, and give it up for adoption. That I wouldn't have to be bothered. She went to an agency, I think. She was barely speaking to me and I was so bloody righteous."

"What agency?"

"I don't know. We weren't talking so much as sniping at each other. But she changed her mind. At least she left me a message that she had, and that she was going away. She quit her job, and left her flat. I was sure she'd get in touch with me, that she'd come back. I've been trying to find her, but I never thought to try the States. She didn't take a shuttle from here, or from Paris.

That's where, after I'd begged and groveled, one of her coworkers said she'd gone, at least for a bit."

"Let's just get this out of the way. Give me your whereabouts on Thursday."

"I was here, at my office through Thursday until about eight. I left for Glasgow that night, straight from there. I work for *The Times*, the London *Times*. I'll give you my editor's name and number, and the hotel where I stayed in Glasgow, so you can verify. Whatever you need. I can make some calls from here — friends of hers, coworkers, the OB she saw when she found out she was pregnant. Maybe someone knows . . . she might have contacted someone."

"Why don't you give me a list of names and contact numbers?"

"Yes, all right. Better from you than the git who mucked the whole business up. I'm coming to New York. I'll be there this afternoon. I'll give you my pocket 'link number, in case . . ."

By the time Eve had taken all the data, she had a cup of coffee on her desk along with her time line, in hard copy and disc.

"We can make calls," Leonardo began. "Mavis and I can contact the birthing centers and the hospitals again, on the chance Tandy checked in this morning."

"Call the midwife," Eve told him. "Have her do it. They'll talk to her quicker than either of you. Mavis, did Tandy ever mention she'd considered putting the baby up for adoption?"

"She did." At her station, Mavis sat very still, her hands crossed over her belly. "She told me once she'd considered all the options. And she'd even gone to an agency, taken the first steps toward that one. But she'd changed her mind."

Reading Eve's expression, Mavis shook her head. "You think she changed it again, and went into a shelter or agency. She didn't. She wouldn't have. She was committed, Dallas, to making a family."

"It's worth looking into. Do you remember the name of the agency?"

"I think maybe she said the name." Mavis pressed her fingers to her temples as if to push the name out of her head. "God, I can't remember. It was just one of those nights we were sitting around, talking about stuff."

"If you remember, tell me." Eve looked over as Peabody and McNab came in. "McNab, you're with Roarke next door. E-work on the Copperfield/Byson case. Peabody, I've got a list of names and contacts in London regarding Tandy Willowby. You take those. Mavis, you and Leonardo can do a search on adoption agencies with London offices. Go through and see if one rings for you. Peabody's going to need that unit, so you'll have to take it into another room."

"We'll start right now." Mavis levered herself up. "I feel better doing something. I feel like it's going to be okay now."

Peabody waited until Leonardo led Mavis out. "And now that you've got her out of the way?"

"Look over the file I got from Italy. Like crime. Woman poofed at thirty-six weeks. No trace of her or the baby. He's got names from Florence, where she lived before she moved to Rome and vanished. Do followups."

"I don't speak Italian. Except for, like, manicotti, linguini, and the occasional *caio*."

"Me, either. Improvise. Try this new angle, see if anyone knows if she explored other options. Termination or adoption."

For herself, Eve went back to Peabody's IRCCA data and took a harder look at the other cases. Possible, she thought, possible one or more of the other open cases was a bungled abduction, resulting in death. Cover up the mistake with rape or assault or theft. Ditch the body.

She picked through the details, pored over the autopsy reports. Then narrowed her eyes at the data on a twenty-one-year-old victim in Middlesex. The mutilated body and fetus had been found in the woods, which the local police had determined was a dump site rather than the murder scene. Mutilation postmortem. COD: head trauma.

Following through, Eve contacted the primary investigator. Fifteen minutes later, she sat back, frowned over at her murder board.

There were differences, she mused. This victim had been married — but only weeks before her death. She had family in Middlesex, had lived there most of her life.

Except for a brief period when she'd gone to London. Gone there, according to the statements taken by the investigator, specifically to look into placing the baby with an agency.

She held up a hand when Peabody crossed the room.

"Just getting coffee," Peabody told her.

"Twenty-one-year-old vic, England. Pregnant with casual boyfriend, opts to have the baby. Family is upset, don't like boyfriend much. He's been in trouble a couple times, doesn't have regular employment. After some hand-wringing, vic goes to London to look into adoption options. Stays at a hostel for a few days, then moves to a midpriced hotel. Remains in London six weeks before returning to Middlesex. Boyfriend gets steady job, love conquers, and plans are made to marry and keep the baby."

"But?"

"A couple weeks before her due date, she goes missing. Turns up two days later in the woods near the house she and new husband have rented. It's a dump site. Murder occurred elsewhere, never determined."

"They look at the new husband?"

"With a laserscope. Alibied tight. COD was head trauma, most likely from a fall. DB also showed signs of restraints, hands and feet, and minor perimortem bruising on the arms. The body was mutilated after death. Hacked up, and the fetus removed. Nonviable."

"Nasty." Peabody glanced toward the door to make sure Mavis wasn't within earshot. "But there are essential differences to Tandy."

"And similarities. If you theorize that whoever took these women wanted the babies, and when this vic died, the abductor attempted to retrieve the baby. Too late for that, so he or she covers it up by mutilating the body, then dumping both of them."

286

Eve rose to add the new picture and name to her board. "What have we got? Three young, healthy pregnant women. None of whom were legally attached to the father at the time they conceived. At least two of them sought information on adoption."

"Make it three for three," Peabody put in. "Italian vic's cousin confirms Belego researched that option, and made an appointment with a counselor regarding same."

"Got a name?"

"No. But the cousin's going to ask around, see if Belego mentioned it to anyone."

"Three for three speaks to me. Let's try this. Search for agencies that have offices in London, and Florence and/or Rome. I've got the name of Tandy's obstetrician in London. We'll tag him, too. But first, let's see if the doctor's associated with any adoption agencies or counselors."

A quick search revealed that Tandy's OB volunteered three days a week at a women's clinic. The same clinic, she noted, that the woman from Middlesex had used while in London.

Worth a conversation, she decided, and spent the next fifteen minutes tracking down the doctor.

After she'd spoken to him, she added his name and the clinic to her board. "He confirms that he gave Tandy the name of some agencies, and counseling services. He can't confirm whether she visited any as she canceled her followup appointment with him, and requested copies of her medical records. He'll check his book, get back to me with the date she called to cancel, and he's sending a list of the agencies and services they routinely give to patients."

"All that's in Europe," Peabody pointed out. "If Tandy was taken, it was here."

"It's a small world," Eve answered and turned as Roarke stepped in.

"I think you'll be interested in our findings, Lieutenant," he said, and handed Eve a disc.

CHAPTER
SIXTEEN

Eve shifted Tandy aside while Roarke in put data into her unit, and ordered it on-screen. It seemed like a lot of numbers to her, in a lot of columns in a complicated and overly detailed spread sheet.

He, apparently, saw a great deal more.

"Two accounts were questionable for me," he began. "The first, McNab and I agree, has gaps, little voids. A precise, methodical accountant such as Copperfield wouldn't have these voids in one of her files."

"Tampered with?"

"Again, McNab and I agree."

"Yeah." McNab nodded. "I might not get the financial mumbo, but I know when a file's been diddled with. At least some of that diddling corresponds with the dates you gave me when Copperfield first talked to Byson about finding something, when her assistant claimed she'd logged on after hours. Some of it goes back farther."

"Someone very carefully removed and/or doctored her work," Roarke continued. "Someone, in my opinion, with a good working knowledge of accounting."

"Inside job. What's the file number?"

When he gave it to her, Eve looked up the corresponding file name. "Well, well, well, it's our old friends Stubens, Robbins, Cavendish, and Mull."

"Interesting."

"You said it was a law firm." Grinning, McNab pointed at Roarke. "Blinders on, but you slammed it."

"Billable hours." Roarke used a laser pointer to highlight columns from his blind copy still displayed on-screen. "Retainers, partners' percentages. Odds were."

"But do we have them on anything?" Eve asked. "Illegal practices; finances, taxes?"

Roarke shook his head. "You have the gaps, and when they're filled in you may. But the numbers jibe, and nothing on the surface appears off."

"But it is," Eve complained. "It is off."

"On the second account I've brought up, something certainly is." He switched displays. "The bottom lines add up precisely," he continued. "And the account would, I believe, hold up under most standard audits. But what I found, and what I suspect your victim found, were areas of income and outlay that were carefully manipulated in order to add up. On their own, they simply don't. There are fees — here."

He used the laser pointer to highlight a section. "These fees repeat — not in amounts, but in precise percentages of coordinating areas of income — and simply don't jibe. Always forty-five percent of the take, if you will, and with the corresponding amounts, that same percentage appears first under an area of nonprofit contributions, making it exempt from taxes. Which, in the way this is manipulated, makes that fee exempt."

"Tax fraud," Eve said.

"Certainly, but that's only one piece of the pie. The income itself is split into parts, juggled into subaccounts, with expenses attached to, and deducted from it. The income, minus this, is then tumbled back into the main. It's then disbursed — the sum of it — in a way that, since I have to guess, I assume is through some sort of charitable trust. The client received a hefty write-off, straight from the top, which you see here. Annually.

"The amounts vary, year to year, but the setup remains constant."

"How much are they washing?"

"Between six and eight million a year, for the time frame I've been working with. But it's more than that. There are simpler ways to evade tax, and to launder money. I'd have to say this particular client has income that is perhaps not strictly legal. It's an operation," he told Eve. "Slickly run and profitable, and with these fees and expenses, I'd say a number of people have a piece of it."

"Copperfield would have found this?"

"If she was looking. Or if she had a question and dug back to find the answer to it before she took over the account. Once you start to peel at the layers, they lift off systematically, simply because the setup is very systematic."

"I don't get it." She shook her head. "I don't mean the numbers, it's a given I don't get them. But I don't get why. If this is an operation like you say, why didn't they just keep a second set of books?"

"Greed's a powerful incentive. There are hefty tax breaks under this system not only for the questionable income, but for all of it. But you have to report the income, the outlay, to get them."

She nodded. "What's the blind number on this file?"

"024–93."

She went back to her desk, called it up. "Sisters Three. A restaurant chain. London, Paris, Rome, New York, Chicago."

"A restaurant?" Roarke frowned. "No, that's not right. These aren't the accounts of a restaurant."

She rechecked. "That's how it comes out."

"That may be, but these aren't the files and accounts for a restaurant."

"Roarke, I'm looking at the file, the file Copperfield marked 'Sisters Three' . . . And none of the names in the account are listed anywhere but on the label."

"She switched files."

"Labels. Discs. Now why would she do that? And who did she switch it with?"

Eve began to scroll down the file, scanning her computer screen. "Madeline Bullock. Son of a bitch. These are the accounting files for the Bullock Foundation. They weren't her client."

"Cavendish, etc., was," Roarke recalled. "And they represent the Bullock Foundation."

"She accessed the foundation's files," Eve murmured. "Labeled it under another account. Nobody would bother going into that file on her unit if they were looking for what she had on the law firm, and through them the foundation. Kraus, Robert Kraus. He headed this account, and was — allegedly — entertaining Bullock and her son the night Copperfield and Byson were killed. If you need an alibi, why not pick the client whose books you're cooking?"

She paced around her desk. "Copperfield sees something in the law firm's accounts that doesn't balance for her. Something that connects to the Bullock Foundation — both clients of her firm. Wouldn't she go to one of the big bosses on this *and* the foundation's accountant? She goes to Kraus, expresses some concern, asks some questions. Maybe he brushes her off, or says he'll look into it. But she's curious and she's precise. Something doesn't add up so she wants to fix it. She takes a look on her own. Sees what you see," she said to Roarke.

"Makes a copy." He nodded. "She couldn't be sure she could go back to Kraus, because she'd asked herself why he hadn't seen what she'd seen. Who can she talk to about this?"

"Her fiancé. But since she's come in with questions, Kraus is careful. And he's going to see she's accessed, made copies. Time to panic a little. So you threaten, you bribe."

"And set up a double murder, alibied by two people with a vested interest. Two people who are the face of one of the most prestigious and philanthropic charitable foundations in the world."

"And who are now accessories to murder, times two. I think I want to have a chat with Bob. Peabody, with me."

"Ah, Dallas, always happy to be with you, but I think in this case, you should take your number cruncher. No way I can talk the talk."

Eve pursed her lips, studied Roarke. "She's got a point. You up for it?"

"Should be fun."

"And a big sigh of relief from the math-impaired," Peabody stated. "McNab and I can work the Tandy Willowby case while you're talking to Kraus."

"Good. You're on Mavis duty. Let's move," she said to Roarke.

They didn't find Kraus at home, but his wife interrupted her Sunday bridge game to tell them he was playing golf at The Inner Circle in Brooklyn.

She was a comfortable-looking woman, spiffed up for the bridge party in baby-blue cashmere.

"This is about that sweet girl and her darling young man, isn't it? It's just horrible. I spent such a lovely little while chatting with her at the company holiday party last December. I hope you find whatever vicious person did this."

"I will. You were here that night, entertaining, I understand."

"Oh, yes. We had Madeline and Win as our guests. Dinner, some cards. And all that while —"

"You played late?"

294

"Until nearly midnight, as I recall. I was ready to drop. Actually thought I was coming down with something, I was that tired. But after a good night's sleep, I was fine. We had a lovely brunch the next morning."

"Give your wife a little something to help her sleep," Eve theorized as they drove to Brooklyn. "Plenty of time to get to Copperfield's, take care of her. Get to Byson's, do him, get home. Catch a few z's, then have a lovely brunch."

"What did he do with the computers and discs?" Roarke asked.

"Yeah, there's that. Hauled them home. Probably has an office there the wife doesn't fool with. Or he rented a place to hold them until he could properly dispose of them. Only one little hitch with that particular theory though."

"Which is?"

"Robert Kraus has never had a driver's license or owned a car. Whoever did this had to have private transportation. So he worked with an accomplice."

"Bullock or Chase?"

"Maybe. Likely. Or someone else in the firm. Cavendish or his keeper. It spreads out, the way I see it. One or more people in the accounting firm had to know what was going on. One or more people in the foundation. One or more in the law firm. You said it was an operation. I'm going with that. Where does the money come from? The funds they're laundering, funneling, juggling? What's the source?"

"It's listed as donations, charitable trusts, privatized income. I couldn't dig deeper without specific names and companies."

"The fees, the percentages. They'd likely be kickbacks, or hush money to the accountant, the lawyer. We'll need to follow that, because it landed somewhere."

The Inner Circle was an indoor golf course and driving range where aficionados of the sport could play a round, practice their putting, and have a friendly drink. For added fees, there were tony locker rooms with sports channels cued into wall screens, efficient attendants, shower facilities, and the services of a masseur or masseuse. The wet area included whirlpools, saunas, a lap pool, steam room.

They found Kraus in a party of four, on the ninth hole.

"A few minutes of your time," Eve told him.

"Now?" His brows drew together under a tweed golf cap. "I'm in the middle of a round, with clients."

"You'll have to catch up later. Or I could walk along with you," Eve said obligingly, "and we can discuss the discrepancies in the Bullock Foundation's account in front of your clients."

"Discrepancies? That's ridiculous." But he glanced at the woman and two men at his tee. "A moment." He moved to them, hands spreading in apology. His face was full of annoyance as he walked back to Eve. "Now what's this about?"

"It's about a multimillion-dollar motive for murder. Natalie Copperfield came to you regarding questionable accounts in the Stuben and Company file."

"Stuben? She did not. You asked me if she discussed anything of the sort regarding a client with me, and I told you she hadn't."

"The questionable accounts relate to the Bullock Foundation, which is your client. And your alibi for the murders."

He flushed, glanced around. "Would you mind keeping your voice down?"

Eve merely shrugged and hooked her thumbs in her coat pockets. "If you have a problem with someone overhearing this conversation, we can take it back to Central."

Looking thoroughly put out, he gestured for them to follow. "We'll take this to the clubhouse." Kraus strode off the ninth green toward an open patio under simulated sunlight, and after swiping a key card in a slot, gestured them to an umbrellaed table.

"I don't know what you think you've come across," he began.

"The laundering of funds through charitable trusts," Roarke began. "The disbursement of funds claimed as tax exempt to subaccounts, which is then funneled back into the trust and redisbursed. It's a clever circle, washing considerable income annually."

"The Bullock Foundation is above reproach, as is our firm. What you're saying is impossible."

"Natalie Copperfield accessed the Bullock accounts."

"I don't understand you, and obviously you don't understand how we run our business. Natalie wasn't cleared for that data."

"But you were. They're yours. Her killer got her home unit, her discs. Got to her office unit and deleted files. But he couldn't delete all of them, certainly not files that were on record as her clients. She changed the label on the file. The Bullock data was still there."

"Why would she do such a thing?"

Eve leaned forward. "We're going to get you cold for money laundering, for tax fraud. You're going to want to talk to me now, if you want any kind of help with two counts, murder one."

"I didn't kill anyone. My God, are you insane?" His hand trembled a little as he pulled off his cap. "I've never doctored an account. It's ludicrous."

"Your wife states you played cards on the night of the murders until after midnight. And she was extremely tired. She went to bed, giving you more than enough time to get to Natalie Copperfield's apartment. To break in, to restrain her, torture her, kill her, and take her data unit."

He wasn't just pale now, he was gray. "No."

"From there, to travel to Bick Byson's loft, struggle with him, stun him, restrain and question him before you killed him and took his data unit. Have you disposed of them already?"

"I've never hurt another human being in my life. I never left the house that night. My God, my God, what is happening?"

"So you let Bullock or Chase do the dirty work?"

"This is absurd. Of course not."

"I'm going to get a warrant for your other files, Mr. Kraus. What you did with one, you did with others."

"You can get a warrant for whatever you like. You'll find nothing because I've done nothing. You're mistaken about the Bullock accounts. Natalie must have been mistaken, because there can't be anything wrong with them. Randall —"

Eve pounced. "What does Randall Sloan have to do with it?"

Kraus rubbed his hands over his face, then signaled to the waiter he'd initially waved away. "Scotch, straight up. A double. My God, my God."

"What does Randall Sloan have to do with the Bullock account?"

"It's his account. It's my name of record, but it's his account."

"Why don't you explain to me how that works?"

"He brought them into the firm, years ago. I had just come on as a junior partner. But his father wouldn't allow him to head the account. There'd been some question of Randall's reliability, his — ah — skills and work ethic. He's better suited in public relations. But he brought the account in, and I was new. He came to me, asked me . . . It wasn't precisely asking."

Kraus took the glass the waiter brought him, downed a quick swallow. "I felt pressured, and to be honest, I thought it was unfair that he wasn't given the account. So I agreed to keep my name on it, and he would do the actual business. I'd check the bottom line, of course, every quarter. And if there was any problem, any question, I'd take over. But the client was satisfied."

"I bet they were," Eve replied.

"She didn't come to me. I swear to you, Natalie didn't come to me about any problems, any questions."

"Who knew that Sloan was doing the books for Bullock?"

"I didn't think anyone did. He told me it was just a matter of pride, and I believed him. But he'd never hurt Natalie. She was almost like a daughter to him. This has to be some horrible mistake."

"Does Madeline Bullock normally stay at your home when she and her son come to New York?"

"No. But Madeline was talking to my wife and mentioned that she loved our home, how welcoming it was, how peaceful. One thing led to another, and they agreed to stay with us. I need to see those records. I'm entitled to see them. I'm sure there's just some misunderstanding."

"Tell me about Randall Sloan's lifestyle."

"Please don't ask me to speak behind the back of an associate. A friend. The son of my partner."

Eve said nothing, just waited.

Kraus drank the rest of his scotch, signaled for another. "He gambles. Or he did. And poorly. There were rumors that some time ago — before I came to the firm — he skimmed a bit from one or two clients, and his father had to replace the funds. But he went into a program, for the gambling. There's been no hint of anything improper for years. His father . . . Jacob's a hard man, integrity is a god. His son smeared that.

Randall will never be a partner. He accepts it. He prefers the work he does, in any case, to the administration, the accounting."

"Yet he pressured you into giving him, under the table, we'll say, a major account."

"He brought them in," Kraus repeated, and Eve nodded.

"Yeah, that's interesting, isn't it?"

"You believe him," Roarke said when they left Kraus sitting under the umbrella in the pseudosunlight with his head in his hands.

"Yeah. You?"

"I do, yes. The outsider, the last man in, so to speak, doing a favor for the big man's son. It's reasonable. And clever of Sloan and the Bullock people not to use each other for alibis."

"You got a dupe, you use the dupe. You drive," she told him, and gave him Randall Sloan's address. "Looks like I'm tagging London again."

She put in a transmission to Madeline Bullock's home in London and got what she thought of as a Summerset clone. Not quite as bony in the face, she decided, but just as dour.

"Ms. Bullock is traveling."

"Where?"

"I couldn't say."

"If Scotland Yard knocked on your door in the next thirty minutes, could you say then?"

He actually sniffed. "I could not."

"Okay. Say the house burns down. How would you reach Ms. Bullock to tell her the bad news?"

"On her private number, on her pocket 'link."

"Why don't you give me that?"

"Lieutenant, I am under no obligation to provide foreign authorities with Ms. Bullock's private business."

"Got me there. But even in the colonies we have our ways of getting information." She clicked off. "Do they go to school for that?" she demanded of Roarke. "Is there a Tight-Ass University? Did Summerset graduate *cum laude?*"

"First in his class. Do you want to drive while I find the number you need?"

"I somehow managed to fumble my way through such pesky chores before I met you." She started the search, then stopped. Sat back. "You know what? I've got a better." She got Feeney at home.

He was wearing a baggy and faded New York Liberties Arena Ball jersey with a ball cap pulled over his explosion of ginger hair. "There's a costume party at your house and I didn't get invited?"

"Game, two o'clock."

"You look ridiculous."

He pokered up. "My grandson gave me this jersey. You tag me on a Sunday to critique my wardrobe?"

"Need a quick one. I'm looking for a pocket 'link number, private, and its current location."

"Game," he repeated, "two o'clock."

"Murder. Twenty-four/seven. It'll be quick. I just need the number and the area. The fricking country. Madeline Bullock. It may be registered to her, or to the

Bullock Foundation. Probably her as it's a personal 'link. London home base."

"Right, right, right," he said. And hung up on her.

"I could have done that for you," Roarke pointed out.

"You're driving." And she contacted Peabody. "Take another look at Randall Sloan. Finances, travel, property, real estate. He's a gambler, so look at it with an eye to that."

"You got a scent?"

"Yeah, I'm following it now. Mavis?"

"She conked. Been out about a half-hour."

"Good. If I can track down Randall Sloan, I'm bringing him in for questioning. I'll let you know."

"Dallas, I've got that list of agencies and counselors from England. All European-based."

She shifted gears, focused on Tandy. "Give them to the investigating officers, Rome and Middlesex. Meanwhile, run them yourself, zero in on any that have offices in both countries. Especially those that have multiple locations in Europe. And shoot them to my PPC while you're at it."

"Got that. Good luck."

Eve rubbed her eyes, blinked them open.

"Why don't you get a little sleep before we get to Sloan's?"

She shook her head, wished she'd thought to bring a vat of coffee with her. "No way of knowing if she's still alive. If it's the baby they want, if they just went in there and took it out. She'd be, what, like a vessel." Eve turned to Roarke. "When she gives up what she's holding, she's expendable."

"You can't do any more than you're doing, Eve."

"Maybe not, but that doesn't mean it's going to be enough. If she's alive, she has to be out of her mind with fear. Not just for herself, but the baby. You're carrying that . . . potential inside you, it's the whole focus of your world, I guess. You're creating it, protecting it, bringing it — you know — forth. Through all the discomfort, inconvenience, pain, and blood and fear, it's vital. Its health, its safety, that's paramount. I see that in Mavis, the way she looks, holds herself, holds it.

"I don't know if I've got that in me to give."

"You have to be joking. Darling Eve, you give all that, and more, to complete strangers."

"It's the job."

"It's you."

"You know how fucked up I am about kids, parents, the whole ball of it."

He took her hand as he drove, brought it to his lips. "I know the two of us have strange, dark places inside us, and we might need some time for a little more light to seep in before we're ready to add to the family we've already made."

"Okay, good. More light. I'm for it."

"Then I think we should have five or six."

"Five or six what? *What?*" She thought . . . for a moment she thought her heart actually stopped. The buzz in her ears was so thick she barely heard his laugh. "That's not funny."

"It certainly was, especially from my point of view. You couldn't see your face."

"You know, one day, perhaps in our lifetime, medical science will find a way to implant an embryo into a man, incubating it there while said man waddles around looking like he swallowed and is unable to digest a pot-bellied pig. Then we'll see what's funny."

"One of the many things I love you for is your delightful imagination."

"Remember that when I put your name on the implant list. Why don't people stay home on Sunday?" she wondered, bitterly, as she cued into the traffic. "What's wrong with home? What kind of transpo did Bullock and her son take out of New York?"

"Another thing I love you for is the many and varied channels of your mind. No doubt private, given the depth of the Bullock wells."

"Foundation shuttle. They came, ostensibly anyway, on foundation business. If they're still traveling, they've probably made use of the same shuttle."

"Where were they when you originally verified Kraus's alibi?"

"I don't know. Peabody did the verify, and she had to contact a foundation number and get a callback. It wasn't pertinent at the time. But I can track that shuttle if I have to. Have to hack my way through international law and relations, and I *hate* that, but I've got enough to hold them for questioning. And I think the British government's going to be very interested in their accounts."

"They may take a hit there," Roarke agreed. "But if they're smart, and their legal representatives will be, they can dump that on Randall Sloan personally, and the firm."

"I can tangle that, seeing as their legal reps fall under the same shadow. I'm going to have to turn this over to Global. After I talk to Randall Sloan."

Randall Sloan lived in a trim and elegant old brownstone on the edge of Tribeca. From the sidewalk, Eve could see that the third floor had been converted into a solarium so that it was topped with curved, pale blue glass.

"He has a current driver's license," Eve said. "And keeps a vehicle four blocks from here in a private garage. Means, motive."

"Opportunity is dicier, isn't it, given that he has an alibi. Or do you think his dinner companions for that evening are covering for him?"

"Didn't feel like it, but we'll go back over that. He may have been a tool. Tools don't always get dirty. If he didn't do the murders himself, he knew about them." She started up the three steps that led to the main entrance. "Alarm's on green," she pointed out.

As she lifted her hand to press the buzzer, she noticed there was more, and engaged her recorder.

"Dallas, Lieutenant Eve, and Roarke, Expert Civilian Consultant, at the residence of Sloan, Randall. Upon arrival I've found the security system disengaged and the front door unlatched."

Automatically, she drew her weapon. She buzzed, and called out, "Randall Sloan, this is Lieutenant

Dallas with the police. I have a civilian consultant with me. Please acknowledge."

She waited, ears cocked for any sound. "Mr. Sloan, I repeat, this is the police. Your residence is unsecured." When there was no response, she circled around the line she had to walk, and eased the door open.

"Nothing in plain sight," she stated. "He could have gone rabbit. I need a warrant."

"Door's open."

"Yeah, and I could go in, check it out. I can argue probable cause, but without authorization I risk giving his lawyers something to whine about. I can get a warrant quick enough."

She started to call in when someone hailed her from behind.

Turning, she saw Jake Sloan and Rochelle DeLay walking toward the house, hand-in-hand, faces rosy from the cold.

"Lieutenant, Jake and Rochelle, remember?"

"Yes. This is Roarke."

"I recognize you." As he came up the first step, Jake shot out a hand. "Good to meet you, and so you know, any time you're looking for a young, hard-working accountant, I'm available."

"I'll keep that in mind."

"This is Rochelle."

"Nice to meet you both."

"You come to see Dad? He keeping you waiting in the cold?" Jake nodded toward the door. "It's open."

"We found it that way," Eve told him.

"Really? That's weird." He moved by them and inside to give a shout. "Hey, Dad! You've got company. Come on in," he said to Eve and Roarke. "We're swinging by to get him for a Sunday deal at Grandpa's." Jake pulled off his watch cap, stuffed it messily in his coat pocket. "You want to have a seat? He must be upstairs."

Eve had slipped her weapon into her pocket when he'd called out to her from the street, and kept her hand on it now. "Mind if I come with you?"

"Well . . ."

"Door was open, Jake, security off. It's the cop in me."

"Sure. Okay. He probably just opened it to look out for us. We're running a little late. He forgot to engage it again. That's all."

But she could see she'd put worry in him as he turned to the stairs. "Dad? Hey, Dad. I'm coming up, and I'm bringing the law." He tried a smile as he said it, but when there was no answer, it faded.

Her senses caught something all too familiar. "You want to stay behind me?" she said it casually, and shifted in front to take the lead. "Which is his bedroom?"

"Second on the right. Listen, Lieutenant —"

Eve eased the bedroom door open with a knuckle.

Randall Sloan wasn't going to make Sunday brunch, she thought, restraining Jake as he tried to rush into the room.

An elaborate chrome chandelier dripped from the vaulted ceiling. Randall Sloan hung from the rope that had been tightly looped around its gleaming post.

CHAPTER
SEVENTEEN

"He's gone." Eve had to hook Jake's arms behind his back, hold him against the wall. "You can't help him."

"Bullshit! Bullshit! That's my father. It's my father."

"I'm sorry." He was young, strong, and desperate, so it took all of Eve's muscle to keep him from shaking her off and running inside. And compromising the crime scene. "Listen to me. Listen, goddamn it! I'm the one who has to help him now, and I can't do it if you go in there and screw up any evidence. I need you to go downstairs."

"I'm not leaving here. I'm not leaving him. Go to hell." And Jake pressed his face to the wall and wept.

"Give him to me." Roarke stepped up beside her. "Downstairs," he said before she could ask about Rochelle. "I convinced her to stay put when we heard the shouting. Let me take him."

"I need a field kit."

"Yes, I know. Here now, Jake, you have to leave him to the lieutenant now. This is what she does. You come with me. Rochelle's frightened, and she's alone. Come downstairs and stay with her."

"It's my dad. My dad's in there."

"I'm very sorry. I'll get him settled," Roarke told Eve, "best I can, then go get your kit out of the car."

"I don't want him to contact anyone yet."

"I'll see to it. Come on, Jake."

"I don't understand. I don't understand this."

"Of course not."

As Roarke pulled Jake away, Eve contacted Central for Crime Scene, then turned back to the room. "Victim is hanging from a rope attached to the master bedroom chandelier," she began for the recorder. "Visual identification is of Sloan, Randall. There's no apparent sign of struggle."

She scanned the room as she spoke. "The bed is made and appears undisturbed. The privacy screens are engaged, curtains open."

The bedside lamps were on, she noted, and a single wine glass with a bit of white left in it sat beside the one on the right. While Sloan was barefoot, there were slippers — leather from the look of them — under the body. He wore a tan sweater, brown pants. A chair was overturned. Behind him in a work area the minicomp was on. She could see its active light blinking.

She brought the front entrance back into her mind. No sign of break-in.

She nodded to Roarke as he came back with her kit. "Thanks."

"Do you want me to contact Peabody?"

"Not yet. She's got enough on her hands. Can you keep them under control down there? I don't want them touching anything, talking to anyone."

"All right." He set somber eyes on Randall. "I suppose he knew you'd follow the trail that led to him."

"Looks like that, doesn't it?" she said as she sealed up.

Roarke shifted his gaze to her, lifted his brows. "But?"

"Doesn't feel like it. He knows his son is coming today. Is this how he wants Jake to find him? He leaves his security off, door unlatched. Why not run instead?"

"Guilt?"

"He's been dirty for a long time. Suddenly, he gets a conscience?"

"Fraud and murder are far apart on the scale."

"Maybe, but he strikes me as a runner, not a suicide."

She stepped inside, got to work.

She took the room first. Slick and stylish, like the man. Pricey clothes, pricey decor, high-end electronics. A man who liked his comforts, she thought, his conveniences, and his symbols of status.

Lifting the wineglass, she sniffed. Left a marker in its place before she sealed the contents, then the glass itself.

She tapped the comp unit with a gloved finger, and the screen engaged. She read the text written on it.

I'm sorry. So sorry. I can't live this way. I see their faces, Natalie and Bick. It was only money, just money. It got out of hand. I must have lost my mind to pay to have them killed. I lost my mind, and now I've lost my soul. Forgive me, because I can't forgive myself. I take this terrible act with me to Hell, for eternity.

She turned from the screen to the body. "Well, one thing on there's pure truth: It got out of hand."

She identified the body for the record by the fingerprints, then examined the hands, bagged them. Her gauge put time of death at twenty-fifteen, Friday evening.

Moving to the adjoining bath, she recorded while she studied. Clean, she noted, with a few men's toiletries on the counter along with a big leafy plant in a glossy black pot. Separate steam shower, drying tube, glossy jet tub with a marble surround. An oversized black towel was draped over a chrome warmer.

She opened the cabinet, scanned the contents.

Lotions, potions — anti-age skin and hair products for the most part. Male birth control tabs, pain blockers, sleep aids. In the counter drawer were more grooming aids, dental hygiene products.

She looked back up at the body.

"You practice tying that noose, Randall?" she wondered. "It sure is perfect. Takes a steady hand and some skill to create a textbook hanging noose."

She stepped out of the room when she heard the buzzer and went down to meet the sweepers and give them the lay of the land.

She found Roarke sitting with Jake and Rochelle in the living area. Jake sat hunched over, his arms dangling between his legs. His eyes were red and swollen as were Rochelle's, who sat beside him in silence.

"I need to see my father," Jake said without looking up. "I need to see him. I need to talk to my grandparents."

"I'm going to arrange for that soon." Since it was handy, Eve sat on the low table in front of him. "Jake, when's the last time you saw or spoke to your father?"

"Friday. We had a memorial service for Nat and Bick at the offices. Their families aren't having one in the city. We wanted to do something. We were all there."

"What time was that?"

"Toward the end of the day. About four. The partners let everyone who wanted to go home leave immediately after. We left together, my father and I, about five. He asked if I wanted to go have a drink, but I just went on home. I should've gone with him. I should've talked to him."

"Did he seem upset, depressed?"

Jake's head snapped up, and his eyes went hot. "It was a memorial service, for Christ's sake."

"Jake," Rochelle murmured, and rubbed a hand over his thigh. "She's trying to help."

"He's dead. How can she help? Why would he kill himself?" Jake demanded. "Why would he do that? He was young and healthy and successful. He — Oh, God, was he healthy? Did he have something wrong with him, and we didn't know?"

"I'm going to ask you again. Did he seem upset or depressed recently?"

"I don't know. Sad. We were all sad, and shocked. I guess he seemed edgy on Friday. Jumpy. He asked me if

313

I wanted to go have a drink, but it was knee-jerk. He didn't want to hang any more than I did."

"Do you know where he did his gambling?"

"That was before. Jesus, that was years ago. He doesn't do that anymore. He stopped."

"All right. Did he mention where he was going when you left him on Friday?"

"No. I don't know. I wasn't paying attention. I was upset. God, I have to tell my mother. They've been divorced forever, but she has to know. My grandparents." He put his head in his hands again. "I don't know how much more they can take."

"Would you say your father was a religious man?"

"Dad. No, not at all. He says you have to get all you can out of life, because once it's done, it's done." His voice cracked. "It's done."

"He do any sailing, Jake?"

"Sailing?" His head came up again, his eyes clouded with grief and confusion. "No, he didn't like the water. Why?"

"Just curious. Was he in a relationship?"

"No. He liked women, but he just cruised."

"He takes care of his house? Cooking, cleaning."

"He's got a droid."

"Okay. I'm going to have a uniform take you and Rochelle to your grandparents."

"I want to see my father. I need to see him."

"I'll make arrangements for you and your family to see him as soon as I can. But not now, not here. Go, be with your family now."

314

Once she'd seen them off, she began to work her way through the first level of the house. "He left a note on the computer," she said to Roarke.

"Handy."

"Yeah. Actually, only a small percentage of self-terminations leave a note. Confessed to hiring the hit on Copperfield and Byson."

"Also handy."

"Yeah, you're following me." She moved through a small media room, a dining room. "They weren't professional hits, number one. So sure, he could've hired some mope. But who's he going to trust with the info that was tortured out of Copperfield?"

"Only someone else directly involved."

"Bingo. He wrote about losing his soul and going to Hell. Upper case H on Hell. That says a religious bent to me, or some sort of belief in the big fire down there. Also, the noose looked like it was tied by a professional executioner. Or a very skilled sailor or Youth Scout. Someone very calm and precise."

She moved to the kitchen, opened the doors on the pantry — well stocked — the utility closet. "Where's the droid?"

"Not down here. Upstairs?"

"I'm going to check. Why don't you play e-man and check his security, the discs and so on?"

"Is this a homicide, Lieutenant?"

"Smells like one to me. We'll see what the ME says. But fingers point. Why is the door open, the security off?"

"Someone wanted the body found easily, and expeditiously."

"There you go. Why does a man contemplating offing himself ask his son out for a drink a couple hours before the act? He just doesn't. Or if he does, he insists. 'I've got to talk to you. I have to get something off my chest.' But he doesn't.

"What you've got here is a man who liked to live well, by whatever means available. No steady relationships, no real vestige of interest in the family business. Hard-line father, up-and-coming son, and you're the black sheep. But you know how to see to your own comfort. You've got a gambling problem."

"Had or have?"

"Well, he's dead as a doornail, whatever a doornail is, so it's 'had.' But I'm betting he had one right up until the last hour. Great way to wash unexplained income is playing with it. I'm not seeing a man with a heavy conscience here. I'm seeing an opportunist, and one who'd have run like the freaking wind if he thought we were sniffing at him. And I'm seeing somebody's patsy."

There was no droid on the premises, and according to her e-man the discs for Friday had been removed and replaced with blanks.

"There's going to be a tranq in his system," Eve said. "Something that can be put down to calming himself before he put the noose over his head. We might find, since we'll be looking, a stunner mark on him."

"Why kill him?"

"Maybe he got greedy, wanted a bigger cut. Maybe he didn't like having his son's friends murdered, or got nervous. One way or the other, he was a liability — and a handy goat. I buy the note, the scene, I pack up my toys and walk away. Putting the finger on this guy also smears the accounting firm. Apologies, sorry about that, but the Bullock Foundation will require a new firm. Too much scandal, bad for the image. Their lawyers demand their files, and there's no record at the firm of any fraud or whisper thereof. All parties involved in Sloan, etc. — as far as we know — are now dead."

"Clean and tidy."

"The killer likes it that way. Two strangulations, one hanging. Same basic method. He takes the droid in case there's any record in the banks of his visiting this residence. Because he's been here before. He knew his way around."

"And came prepared," Roarke prompted.

"Oh, yeah. Comes to the door. Let's have a chat. How about a drink with that? Slips a tranq into the vic's wine. Let me help you upstairs. Gets him up there, lays him on the floor. Stuns him if he has to. Writes the note on the computer. Mistake there, I figure, because he puts too much of himself into it. Lost my soul, going to the big H. Fixes the rope, hauls the woozy or stunned vic onto the chair, gives it a kick, and watches the show.

"He'd watch," she mused. "Like he watched Natalie and Bick. Watch the face, the eyes. Randall kicked, kicked off the slippers, grabbed at the rope. I've got what looks like rope fibers and tissue under the vic's nails. Takes awhile. It's not a quick death unless the neck breaks on the drop. He suffered, but I guess he earned it."

She frowned at the now empty bedroom. "Might've had his own transpo, but that's not an absolute. He could've come on public — subway'd work best, and taken the droid away by the same method if he deactivated all but its mobility."

"So you're looking for a man with a droid."

She smiled a little. "Maybe." She pulled out her 'link when it beeped. "Dallas."

"It's halftime, so I'm making this quick."

She frowned at Feeney. "If you were making it quick, you'd have gotten back to me two hours ago."

"Can't do a locate if the 'link's not in use, can I? I got the number." And he read it off to her. "Put a tracer on that, but it wasn't engaged until a few minutes ago, and then only for fifteen seconds."

"You got a location?"

"Best I can give you is Upper East."

"New York? The 'link's in New York?"

"Yeah, where'd you expect it to be? Listen, Dallas, they got cheerleaders."

"Who has cheerleaders?"

"The Liberties. I'm missing halftime."

"For God's sake, they're young enough to be your kids. Your kids' kids."

"A man don't watch a bunch of half-naked girls doing jumps and high kicks, he might as well be dead. You got what you need?"

318

"Yeah, yeah, and thanks. Keep the trace on, will you? Cheerleaders," she grumbled when Feeney clicked hurriedly off. "Men have simple minds."

"It's not our minds that are simple," Roarke corrected.

She had to laugh. "New York. Son of a bitch. They probably never left the city. Upper East. Hotel maybe, or a private residence. I need to run a check, see if the foundation or either Bullock or her son own or have interest in any properties in that area."

"I can run that for you from home. Home's where we're going. You can write up your report on this just as easily from there," he said, and took her arm before she could argue. "You need food, and so do I. You're running on empty, Eve. I can see it in your eyes."

"However I'm running, I need to move. I'd moved faster on this, Randall Sloan would still be alive and I'd be closing this."

She started for the door with him, then stopped. "Wait. Wait. A guy like Randall. He'd have insurance." She turned a circle. Three-story house, she mused. Twelve rooms, and the solarium. Lots of places to hide insurance.

"He wasn't stupid. The way he got Kraus to keep his name as account exec, but did the work himself. Something goes wrong, he just palms off the trouble on Kraus. Insurance."

"The goat kept a backup goat in Kraus."

"You bet. Randall had trouble, needs to needle his client, he's got a copy of those books somewhere. If he

319

didn't before, he sure as hell copied them when he doctored Natalie's files."

"I imagine they thought of that as well, and got the location out of him."

"Maybe, maybe not. He wasn't tortured, and the place wasn't tossed. Could be they figure they have all the copies, or already got his. But suppose he was smarter than that, more careful than that. This place needs to be gone over, top to bottom."

"Which will take hours," Roarke pointed out. "If you think you have hours left in you, you're mistaken. Compromise," he said, anticipating an argument. "Send Peabody and McNab back to do that. An e-man and a detective. If there's something here, they'll find it."

"I'll let them take first swing at it."

She went out, sealed the door.

"It's possible, if you're right about the copy, he kept it off-site. A bank box."

"Possible, but it seems to me he'd want it easily accessible, especially now. Shit's flying, he needs his shield. What if he wants it after banking hours, or on Sunday? Traveled a lot," she continued as she got into the car. "If he used a vault, it could be anywhere. Guy who travels that much would know how to run, know how to move fast and light if he had to."

And thinking that, she dropped into sleep.

She woke, stretched nearly horizontal as Roarke stopped in front of the house. Rather than refreshing her, the mobile nap left her groggy and disoriented, and fumbling for the controls to bring her seat back up.

Roarke lifted it, as he'd lowered it, from his side of the controls. "You need actual sleep."

"I need actual coffee."

She'd have food to go with it, Roarke determined as he walked with her into the house.

"Red meat," he said to Summerset. "Her office AC. If the others haven't eaten, send up a bloody cow."

"Right away." As they headed up, Summerset lifted the cat that ribboned between his legs. "We'll just put some nice green beans along with that steak. She won't like it, but he'll make her eat them, won't he?"

Mavis didn't exactly pop up when Eve entered the office, but she managed to shove herself out of the chair. "You're back."

"Yeah, sorry, things got complicated. You've got to give me a few minutes to deal with another thing."

"You get the list?" Peabody asked her. "There are a couple that look good to me."

"List of what?"

"The agencies, counselors. You said I should send it to your PPC."

"Right, right." Her brain felt like mush. "I didn't get the chance to review. Something came up. I would give you the world drenched in chocolate for a cup of coffee."

"I'll get it for you." Leonardo eased Mavis back in a chair.

"Chocolate thief," Peabody said, hoping to make Mavis smile. "Anyway, a couple stand out for me. So —"

"I'll look it over in a few minutes. I need to pull you and McNab off this, put you on another assignment. Randall Sloan is dead."

"Well, shit, you've had a busy day."

"Staged suicide, that's my take. I worked the scene, sweepers will be processing."

Peabody opened her mouth, glanced at Mavis, then nodded. "Okay."

"I'll fill you in, then I need you and McNab back at the scene."

"You'll fill them in over a meal," Roarke added.

"As soon as I look over the list."

"It'll wait." It was Leonardo who spoke as he carried in a mug of coffee. "I'm sorry, sweetheart," he said to Mavis, "but she needs to eat, to rest for a little while."

"Jeez." Eve took the coffee as if it contained the staff of life. "What is it with men?"

"He's right." Mavis pushed her hands though her hair. "He's right. You look whipped and kicked. We'll eat. We'll all sit down and eat."

They brought in a table, dragged up chairs. While the coffee helped cut through the fog in her brain, Eve had to admit the protein got her blood moving again.

"A hell of an operation," McNab commented when she'd run through the bulk of it. "What's funding it?"

"That's another question. Illegals, weapons, mob money?" Eve lifted a shoulder. "We'll dig it out. Or Global will. Bullock, Chase, or someone on their payroll murdered three people — that we know of — to protect that operation."

"And they're still in New York." Peabody tried not to hum out loud in pleasure as she swallowed steak. "Why? I mean, after killing Randall Sloan, why not make tracks? It seems they'd want to be long gone before his body was discovered."

"Another question. They still have business here. They feel safe where they are. From their point of view, they're removed from the investigation. They were an alibi for a man who was not involved — and he, in turn, covers them. Another man has confessed to the murders, and being dead, can't recant that confession. But you're right, they'd need a reason to stay here, when they could be anywhere else."

She contemplated as she ate. "They wanted the body discovered, and in good time. No reason to leave the security off and the door unlatched otherwise. The sooner it's found, the sooner they can put this whole untidy business behind them. Must be irritating," she decided, "to be so rich and powerful and have little people picking at your foundation. Like ants."

"I don't think ants pick," Peabody said. "They more dig, probably."

"Whatever. You are what you are, and they're nothing. Tried to buy the nosy accountant off, but she's annoyingly honest. You're not going to see your whole lifestyle, your rep, your wealth put in jeopardy by some number cruncher. That's why the murder was personal. She got in your face, so you got in hers. I can come right into your home, you stupid bitch. What are you going to do about it? And I'm going to hurt you because you had the *nerve* to threaten me and mine.

Then, when I'm satisfied you've told me everything I need to know, I'm going to kill you with my own hands, and watch you die. But not before I tell you that I'm going to do the same thing to your lover. So you die in pain, in fear, and in grief."

She forked up a tiny new potato. "What?" she demanded as the table sat in silence, staring at her. "What?"

"Creepshow." Mavis picked up her water glass, drank deep. "Squared."

"Oh. Sorry."

"How do you know he thought those things, felt those things?" Leonardo stroked Mavis's arm as he goggled at Eve.

"Well, he sure as hell wasn't thinking about the weather." Then she narrowed her eyes. "Randall Sloan kept a car garaged. He didn't use it that night. Both he and his alibis stated they used cabs. Let's see if there's any sort of log in and out of the garage. The killer may have borrowed it for the job. If not, we start checking rental companies. Or car services. The Bullock Foundation may keep a car in the city, or use a specific service when they're here."

When Peabody dug out her memo book to note it down, Eve shook her head. "No, you've already got enough going. I'm going to tag Baxter. He wanted in on this. He can take that assignment." She pushed back from the table. "I'll contact him now, then I want to look at the lists of those agencies you got on Tandy."

Across the table, Mavis closed her eyes, took a long breath. "Thanks. Thanks, Dallas."

Eve waited until she'd talked to Baxter, then asked Mavis to come with her to a sitting room. Closed the door.

"You're going to tell me you think Tandy's dead."

"No, I'm not. Sit down." When she did, Eve sat across from her, leaned in so their eyes were level. "But I am going to tell you that you need to prepare yourself for that possibility. She was taken for a reason, and everything's pointing to the baby being that reason."

"And once she has it . . . It's been since Thursday. She could —"

"A lot of things could," Eve interrupted. "We're going to deal with what is. Look, I know it might seem like I'm not paying much attention to this, not looking hard enough. But I promise you, it's in my head. And Peabody's working it when I'm not."

"It doesn't seem like you're not paying attention." Mavis reached out now, took Eve's hands. "I don't think that. And I know Peabody's doing everything she can, and — and that she's good. But Dallas? She's not you. That's a bitch-weight of pressure, I know, but —"

"Don't water up. Come on, give me a break on the tears."

"I'm so scared for her. And I keep thinking, what if it was me? What if I was locked up somewhere, couldn't protect my baby. It's going to sound Princess of Drama, but I'd rather die than have anyone take my baby, or hurt it. I know Tandy feels the same. She said once that's why she decided to have it, to keep it, even though she'd be on her own. That even though there were good people who wanted babies, who'd give hers a good life, it was hers. And she'd never be absolutely sure they'd love it as much as she did."

"What kind of good people? Did she ever give any details, anything specific?"

"No, it was just . . . wait." Eyes closed again, hands rubbing light circles over her belly, Mavis breathed slowly in and out.

"Oh, shit. *Shit!* Are you —"

"No, no, don't go wig. I'm just trying to focus. We were talking once, me and Tandy, about raising a kid in the city. Pros, cons, la-la. She said how she hoped she was doing the right thing, choosing the urban deal when she could've given her baby a plush life as a country squire. She talked like that sometimes," Mavis added and opened her eyes. "You know, squire. What is a squire?"

"How would I know, I'm a New Yorker. Okay, let's you and me go over Peabody's list. Maybe something else will ring for you."

CHAPTER
EIGHTEEN

Eve set Mavis down with the list, then gestured Leonardo to sit down beside her. "Why don't you be another pair of eyes, another brain on memory mode? You were in on some of the baby talk?"

"Sure. Tandy's having a boy." He laid his big hand gently on Mavis's belly. "Tandy wanted to find out, and I talked to her about the baby, and herself, and her plans. I wanted to get a sense of it, not just because I'm her birthing coach, but because I'm designing a few basic — and a couple of special — outfits as a gift for her."

"Is he the sweetest huggie-bear in the universe and beyond?" Mavis cooed.

"You bet. Look at the list. Remind yourself of conversations you had with her, about her. Individually and together. One of you may prompt something out of the other's memory. I'll be back in a minute."

She moved into Roarke's office where he sat at his desk running her search. She shut the door.

"Problem?" he asked her.

"Our house is full of people, one of whom could go off like a bomb of emotionally charged hormones at any moment. You're doing drone work for me on two cases, one of which started with a huge personal insult to you. I dragged you to Brooklyn on a Sunday, then dumped you into another crime scene, and left you in charge of a hysterical witness. There's probably more in there, but those are the high points."

"Just another day in paradise."

"I love you. I just wanted to give you a heads-up on that."

It came into his eyes, that charge of pleasure and love, and blew right through her. "It's nice to be reminded. You're so tired, Eve."

"You're looking a little worn yourself."

"Am I now?" He rose. "Maybe you should hold onto me a minute then."

"Maybe I should."

She came around the desk, and they held onto each other. She could stand on her own — God knows she'd proven it. But it was an amazing gift to have a man you could lean on without either of you thinking you were weak.

"I postponed that winter holiday deal we were planning a couple of times now."

"Hmm." With his eyes closed, he swayed a little with her, drawing in the scent of her hair, her skin. "Things came up."

"They'll always come up. As soon as Mavis pops that kid out, and we've done our duty, we're going."

"Are we?"

"You got my word." She drew back to look him in the eye. "I need you, the just you and me time. I don't know why I let myself forget that. Besides, I'm thinking after the doing-our-duty deal in the fun house that is the birthing room, we're really going to need to go somewhere where we can stay zoned on alcohol and sex for a few days."

"You just had to bring that up."

"What? Sex?" She lifted her hands, patted both of his cheeks. "It's wormed its way into my brain like a tumor. If I have to think about it, so do you."

"I always think about sex."

"Funny guy." She pressed her lips to his just as his computer signaled his task complete. "That my data?" She pulled away, grabbed up the hard copy that spit out.

"So ends a charming interlude."

Ignoring him, she scanned various properties, holdings, addresses, then zeroed in on one that made her smile spread, sabersharp. "And look here, Madeline has herself a pied-à-terre on East End Avenue, off of Eighty-sixth."

"I take it we're about to pay another Sunday call."

"I can handle it on my own if you want to hang here."

"With the ticking bomb of explosive hormones? No, thank you."

When they stepped back into Eve's office, Leonardo sat alone at the auxiliary unit, brows knit as he studied the screen.

"Mavis?"

"Oh, peeing. Again." He smiled. "She has the cutest little bladder these days."

"Adorable. Tell her I've got to follow up this lead on the homicides while it's hot. I'll be back as soon as I can. If you hit on anything that seems familiar, even like a maybe, earmark it. We'll give it a push when I get back. Peabody and McNab get back first, give it to them."

"We will. Dallas, Roarke, would it be all right if we stayed here tonight? She'll just want to come back tomorrow, or sit down at Central if you're working there. I hate to have her going up- and downtown when she's so worn down."

"You're always welcome," Roarke told him. "Why don't you ask Summerset to fix her a soother? He'd know what was safe for her and the baby."

"You ought to take one yourself," Eve added. Then because she knew he loved her friend, she stepped to Leonardo, gave his wide shoulder a squeeze. "Tell her Tandy's in my head. I do some of my best work there."

"She believes in you. That's getting her through this."

But no pressure, Eve thought wearily as they headed out.

"You drive," she told Roarke. "I'm going to do some of that work in my head."

She tipped back her seat a few inches, closed her eyes, and brought Tandy into focus.

Young, healthy, single, pregnant, no close family ties. Relocated. Why not keep in contact with friends/coworkers back home?

Hiding?

From what? From whom?

Father of the baby? Possible, but unlikely. No bitching to new coworkers or new pregnant pal about the lousy bastard who knocked you up.

Eve thought of Tandy's apartment. A nest, Peabody had said. Not a hidey-hole. Hiding, maybe, but not obsessively. More like the fresh start angle.

The like crime victims had been similar there, too. Relocation — at least initially on the other Brit vic. New job, new place, new life. So maybe it was more getting away than hiding.

Getting away from what? From whom?

One woman dead, two missing. She'd get a doctor — Louise or Mira, or maybe Mavis's midwife — to look over the autopsy report on the Middlesex vic. If the vic was injured, dead or dying, the killer might have tried to carve the baby out.

And God, that was gross.

No attempt to hide the body. Dump it instead near the vic's home base. Away from where she'd been held, Eve thought. Away from the killer's location.

But Belego never surfaced, alive or dead. Take the baby? Dispose of the body? Logical, she mused. Cops are looking for an abductee, pregnant or with infant. Or a runaway. Changed location once, change again.

They're not looking for a nice healthy baby newly placed with some nice couple. In the country maybe, well away from the location of the abduction.

Healthy baby, priority one. Can't put a woman that far along on a shuttle or any air transpo. Mavis said she couldn't travel after her — what had it been — thirtieth week?

"She's still in New York," Eve mumbled. "Unless they drove her outside the city. Not far, though. They wouldn't want to put any more stress on her than necessary. Any stress on her is stress on the fetus. And she's still alive."

"Because?"

"Unless she went into labor on her own, she's still got the package in her. I don't think they'd push that — give her whatever you give to start the whole process up. All these women were taken in the last weeks of their pregnancy. Maybe that's coincidence, or maybe the kidnapper waits until they're near end-of-term."

She let it run through her head. "Maybe he or she is a frustrated midwife or OB. Likes to deliver babies. Then the mother had to be disposed of, somehow. Can't keep the babies. Somebody's going to notice if this guy, this woman keeps adding newborns to the household. Or . . ."

"Maybe he continues to botch it," Roarke said quietly. "Loses both, and keeps trying."

"Yeah. Yeah. That's one we won't mention to Mavis. Could be a moral fanatic. Except one of the vics that coordinates for me got married to the baby's father."

"If you're fanatical enough, she still conceived out of wedlock."

"Can't rule it out." She glanced idly at a corner glide-cart, grill smoking. "But the fact we've got echoing vics in three countries points me to profit. A business. Snatch, grab, deliver, sell. Destroy evidence."

"Cold."

"The coldest," she agreed, then straightened as Roarke parked on East End Avenue. "But I'm thinking this ranks up there on the ice scale, too."

It was a little palace of glass and stone, built on the ashes of the Urban Wars. There were a few like it — in size and style — along New York's rivers, affording lofty views of the waterways. The glass reflected gilded bronze to any who stood outside its walls to admire it. Since the sun had set at the end of the long day, the security lights beamed that same rich color over the blind glass and warm brown stones.

It spired up, with generous terraces on the riverside, and a tall, wide arch at the entrance.

After pressing the buzzer, Eve held her badge up to the security screen. The red beam of the laser scanned it before the door opened.

She made the attractive, uniformed maid as a droid even before it spoke. "May I help you?"

"Lieutenant Dallas, NYPSD, and associate, to see Ms. Bullock and/or Mr. Chase."

"Neither Ms. Bullock nor Mr. Chase is at home to callers. Would you care to leave your card?"

"When I show you this," Eve held the badge up in the droid's face, "it means I'm not here to socialize. Do you think Ms. Bullock and/or Mr. Chase would prefer to call on me at Cop Central?"

"If you'll wait here, I'll inform Ms. Bullock."

Here was a formal foyer with gold and silver tiles for the floor, complex shapes in thin red glass dripping light from the ceiling. There were paintings in sleek

333

gold frames — all flash and color, and to Eve's mind, no substance or sense.

Benches, tables, chairs were all ebony and trimmed in deep, dark red.

She wandered away from the entrance, glancing up a sweep of silver stairs and looking east into a spacious room where the decor colors had been reversed — black and red for the floor, gold and silver for the furnishings.

A fire roared away in the ruby hearth, and beyond the wall of gilded glass was the long, dark river.

Nothing soft, she thought, nothing quiet or feminine or comforting. Just meticulous, somewhat regimented decor — the sort that gave her a mild headache.

No one would dare put their feet up on the gleaming silver table, or curl up for a nap on the gold cushions of the straight-lined sofa.

She heard the click of heels on the tiles and turned to study Madeline Bullock, in the flesh.

The ID photos hadn't done her justice, Eve decided. She was a *presence*. Tall, stately, handsome, with silver-blonde hair sleeked back from a youthful face and rolled smooth at the nape of her neck.

Her eyes were arctic blue, her lips painted red as the hearth. She wore a sweater and full-legged pants that matched her eyes, and diamonds glittered like drops of ice from her ears and her throat.

"Lieutenant Dallas." She crossed the room the way a well-appointed yacht sails a calm sea. Smooth and important. The hand she offered sparkled with both diamonds and rubies. Eve wondered if she'd accessorized to match the room.

"I spoke with your associate a few days ago," Madeline continued, "about that terrible tragedy at Sloan, Myers, and Kraus."

"That's right."

"And you're Roarke." Her smile warmed several degrees. "I don't believe we've ever met. How odd, considering."

"Ms. Bullock."

"Please, please, sit. Tell me what I can do for you both."

"I was under the impression you'd left the country, Ms. Bullock," Eve began.

"And you've caught us out." She laughed lightly, crossed her legs with a whisper of silk. "My son and I decided we wanted a little time, incognito, if you understand."

"I know the term," Eve said dryly, and Madeline's smile didn't falter a fraction.

"We did tell Robert — Robert Kraus — and several others that we were leaving New York. I'm sure you understand that being entertained can be just exhausting. Of course, you're both young. You must enjoy the constant round of dinners and parties and fêtes."

"I live for fêtes. Can't get enough." This time, that smile flickered toward a frown for just an instant. "You couldn't just refuse an invitation? Or explain that you and your son wanted a few quiet evenings?"

"So much is expected of people in our position." On a heavy sigh, Madeline lifted her hands, let them fall gracefully to her lap. "Sometimes those expectations are a burden. Accept this invitation, and refuse that one, feelings are hurt. It was just a little ploy to avoid all that and have those quiet evenings. We do love your city. Ah, here's some refreshment."

The droid wheeled in a cart holding decanters, a teapot, plates of fruit and cheese, and little frosted cookies.

"May I offer you brandy or tea? Perhaps a bit of both."

As he anticipated her refusal, Roarke laid a hand on Eve's knee, squeezed lightly. "Tea would be lovely."

"Wonderful. I'll pour. You're excused," she said to the droid, who slipped silently away. "Cream, lemon?"

"Neither, for either of us. No sugar, thanks." Roarke took the lead. "You have an impressive home. Marvelous view."

"The view was the pull. I could sit and watch the river for hours. All of our homes are near water of some kind. I feel very drawn to it."

"You have this lovely home," Eve put in, "but you stayed in Robert Kraus's this trip."

"We did. His wife — have you met her? Lovely woman. She extended the invitation, and it seemed like fun. We do have a nice time together. We enjoy cards." After passing out the tea, she poured her own. "I'm afraid I don't understand why that would be of interest to you."

"Every detail of a murder investigation is of interest to me."

"Then it's still being investigated? I'd hoped it was all settled by now. Terrible thing. They were both so young. But surely you're not looking at Robert?"

"Just getting the full picture. You knew Randall Sloan."

"Of course. Now there's a social butterfly. Such energy! Nothing stay-at-home about him."

"I don't know. He died there."

"I'm sorry? What did you say?"

"Randall Sloan was found early this afternoon, hanging from the chandelier in the bedroom of his brownstone."

"My God." Madeline pressed a hand to her breasts. "Dear God. Randall? Dead?"

"When did you see or speak to him last?"

"I don't . . . I can't take this in. It's such a shock. I . . . Please." She reached over, tapped open a silver box. Inside was an intercom system. "Brown, please tell Mr. Chase to come down right away."

Madeline sat back, pressed her fingers to her brow. "I'm sorry, this is such a shock. I knew the man nearly a decade. We were friends."

"How close friends were you?"

Hot color streaked Madeline's cheeks as she dropped her hands into her lap. "I realize you must ask questions at such a time, but I find the implication in that question in very poor taste."

"Cops have very poor taste. Were you and he involved on a personal level?"

"Certainly not in the way you mean. We enjoyed each other's company."

"I'm told he persuaded you to bring your business to his father's firm."

"He did. Years ago. I found the firm's reputation, ethics, and service more than satisfactory."

"Robert Kraus was listed as your accountant."

"That's correct."

"Yet Randall Sloan kept your books, the books for the foundation."

"No, you're mistaken. Robert does."

"Randall Sloan oversaw the finances of the Bullock Foundation from day one, until his death."

"I don't know what you're talking about. Oh, God! Win! Sloan is dead."

Winfield Chase stopped short in his stride across the room. He had the look of his mother, the same strong build, same strong face, same glacier eyes. Then he moved quickly to take the hand she'd thrown out toward him.

"Randall? How did this happen? Has there been an accident?"

"His body was found today, hanging from a rope in his bedroom," Eve said.

"He hanged himself? Why would he do such a thing?" Winfield demanded.

"I didn't say he hanged himself."

"You said . . ." Winfield checked himself as he stroked his mother's hand. "You said he was found hanged, I assumed . . ." He widened his eyes. "Are you telling us he was *murdered*?"

She had to give him credit for the fancy British play on the word. It made it sound as if Randall should have been wearing a smoking jacket while he choked to death.

"I didn't say that either. The matter is under investigation. And as the investigator I'll ask you both where you were on Friday between the hours of 6 and 10p.m."

"This is insulting! How dare you question my mother in this manner." His fingers linked with Madeline's now, and her free hand moved to rest on his thigh. "Do you know who she is?"

"Bullock, Madeline. Formerly Chase, born Madeline Catherine Forrester." Their body language had something curling in her gut, but she kept her eyes steady. "And in case you don't know who I am, it's Dallas, Lieutenant Eve. Until the cause of death is determined by the Medical Examiner, this matter is being treated as an unattended, suspicious death. Answer the question."

"Mother, I'm going to ring our solicitor."

"Go ahead," Eve invited. "You'll need one if you're afraid to tell me your whereabouts on Friday."

"Calm down, Win. Calm down. This is all so upsetting. We were home all evening. Win and I discussed plans for our spring gala, a fundraiser the foundation is hosting in April in Madrid. We dined about eight, I believe, then listened to music and played cards. I suppose we retired about eleven. Does that sound right to you, Win?"

He looked down his nose at Eve. "We had lamb cutlets for dinner, preceded by a smoked tomato soup."

"Yummy. Have either of you ever been to Randall Sloan's New York residence?"

"Of course." Madeline kept a firm hold on her son's hand. "He often entertained."

"On this trip?"

"No. As I explained before, we were looking for quiet evenings."

"Right. Do you do any driving in the city, Mr. Chase?"

"In New York." He gave her a look of mild distaste. "Why would I?"

"Couldn't say. Well, thanks for your time." Eve got to her feet. "Oh, your accounts, as overseen by Sloan, Myers, and Kraus will be turned over to the U.S. and British tax authorities — and, I imagine, those same agencies in several other countries."

"That's outrageous!" Winfield might have lunged forward, but his mother surged to her feet and kept the reins on him.

"What's the meaning of this?" she demanded.

"There are a number of questions regarding those accounts. Me, I'm a murder cop. What do I know? I'm sure the proper agencies will find the answers."

"If there are any questions regarding the foundation accounts, they'll be answered by Sloan, Myers, and Kraus. Robert Kraus . . ." Madeline paused, laid her free hand on her breast again. "But, no, you said it was Randall who, in actuality, kept the accounts for us. That alone is an outrageous breach of trust. Has he embezzled? Dear God, we trusted them, trusted him."

She leaned into Chase, and his arm draped around her shoulders. "Was he using us?" Madeline demanded. "Is that why he killed himself?"

"That would be tidy, wouldn't it? Thanks for your time."

And that, Eve thought, would give them plenty to think about.

She was grinning darkly when she slid into the car.

"I don't believe we'll be invited to the spring gala in Madrid," Roarke commented.

"Breaks my heart. You get a load of them? They're like one of those Brit drawing room vids you like — the old-time ones? She thinks on her feet, I'll give her that. She never figured we'd come knocking on the door, but she was ready for us when we did. He, on the other hand, needs direction, and a short leash. Got a temper, he does."

"He killed them."

"Bet your righteous ass he did. Question me, will you? Threaten me? Oh yeah, he did them all, then he came home and told Mommy all about it. Bet they're pissed off to realize three murders haven't covered up the accounts after all."

"They'll push it onto Randall Sloan."

"They'll try. I'll let the Feds and Global worry about that end. Murder in the First, three counts. Conspiracy to commit, accessory before and after. I'm going to roll them up in a ball on this."

"I might ask how?"

"He left his DNA on Byson's fist. So science is going to get him. And my canny investigative skills are putting together enough to get a warrant to compel him to give us a sample of that DNA. Peabody and McNab get lucky, Sloan will have something incriminating on them at his place. I get that one, *Win*, into Interview, I'll piss it out of him. Without his mother holding him back, he'll come at me, and he'll spew. I can see it in him."

"They could take off for England, for anywhere, tonight."

"Could. Won't. Flight makes them look suspicious. She's got too much control for that. What they have to play is shocked and outraged. Their pal, their handily dead pal, deceived and abused them. He used their lauded foundation for his own gain. Shame and horror! She's working that out right now, and she's calling Cavendish — or one of the contacts on that in England — to give him the lowdown, have them start injunctions, restraining orders, anything they can pull out of the hat.

"Gotta get Cavendish in the box, too. I'll sweat it out of him inside thirty minutes. He hasn't got the spine. He'll flip on them. He knows about the murders, and he'll flip for a deal that keeps him out of a cage on accessory."

Roarke stopped at a light, studied her. "Pretty damn wound up, aren't you, Lieutenant?"

"Yeah, I am. It's falling for me, piece by piece. I'm going to get started on that warrant on Chase, and one for Cavendish." She dug out her 'link. "I can have them both in the box by morning."

She interrupted both an APA and her commander's Sunday night, put them on conference on the dash 'link and was still running the case through when Roarke drove through the gates.

"I need the mandatory DNA sample on Chase," Eve argued.

Dressed in something slinky, APA Cher Reo scowled on-screen. "Allegedly questionable accounting practices, allegedly overseen by a man who was *not* the accountant of record, and who has left a suicide note confessing to the murders before hanging himself."

"The ME isn't going to rule self-termination."

"You can't be sure."

"I fucking *am* sure." Eve winced. "Excuse me, Commander."

Whitney only sighed. "If the lieutenant 'fucking' is sure, Reo, we should push for this. If Chase is clean, the worst that happens is he's insulted and complains to his embassy, has his lawyers screw with us."

"I'll find a judge who agrees with you," Reo said. "The same's going to go on Cavendish. It's shaky, Dallas."

"I'll make it solid. I want them both in by eight-hundred tomorrow. Thank you, Commander. I'm sorry to interrupt your evening."

"How about me?" Reo demanded.

"You, too."

"Nice work." Roarke leaned over to kiss her. "I'd give you a warrant."

"Bet you would. They'll lawyer up the gonads, but it's not going to help them. I'm going to nail them,

Roarke. For Natalie, for Bick, and for that asshole Randall Sloan. And by the time I've finished, the Feds and Global will have to pick up the pieces to add time for tax fraud and money laundering and whatever the hell else they want to stick to them."

She hooked an arm around his waist as they climbed the steps to the front door. "Really needed you on this one, ace."

"Pay me."

Her laugh turned to a sneer as she stepped into the house and saw Summerset. "Can't you ever be somewhere that's not here?"

He ignored her, spoke directly to Roarke. "The soother calmed Mavis enough that she's sleeping. I've put her and Leonardo in the blue guest room on the third level. It's quiet, and she needs to rest." Now he aimed those dark eyes toward Eve. "She's been much too active and upset today."

"Yeah, blame me."

"Whoever kidnapped Tandy Willowby is to blame," Roarke said. "And we all want Mavis to get as much rest and care as she needs."

"Of course." Summerset cleared his throat. "I'm concerned." He looked at Eve again with what might have been an apology in those same dark eyes. "I'm concerned."

If a broomstick with legs could have affection for anyone, Eve knew Summerset had it for Mavis. "I can't keep her down unless I tie her down. All I can do is find Tandy Willowby."

"Lieutenant," Summerset said as she started up the steps, "I can make you an energy booster, one that contains no chemicals as you dislike them."

"You could make me a booster, and I'd consume it into my body?" She gave a snort. "Do I look like I've recently lost my mind?"

She kept going, and glanced back at Roarke. "I'm not taking any witch's brew he concocts, so forget it."

"I said nothing."

"You were thinking it. I'm getting coffee, and tagging Peabody. If Mavis is down for the count tonight, I can go over there myself, relieve her and McNab. I have to update Baxter. He'll want in on the interviews tomorrow."

"Eve, Christ Jesus, you need sleep."

"I thought you were saying nothing."

"Bloody goddamn shagging hell."

It was as far as he got when her 'link signaled. "I guess you'd better hold that Irish thought. Dallas."

"Check it out," Peabody sang, and turned her 'link so Eve saw the dark mouth of a safe.

"Hot diggity damn!"

"It's the second we found. Nearly gave up, but my guy here is stubborn." A very tired-eyed Peabody made kissy noises.

"Cut that out."

"Aw, he earned it. First safe was in the library. False front, nothing any burglar with a working brain couldn't have found and popped. Cleaned out. We were very sad, figuring whoever killed Sloan got to it first."

"I bet that's just what he did, too. Figures he cleaned up anything incriminating Sloan had tucked away."

"But McNab said, 'Screw that, She-Body' — speaking to me. How you said the vic has some brains, so why wouldn't he have another hole, and a deeper one. If not here, somewhere else, but we're here, so we'll keep right on looking and looking and —"

"You're babbling."

"Sorry. My brain went to sleep an hour ago. The rest of me hasn't figured it out yet. Anyway, we found this one in the kitchen. It's built into the pantry — where, I might add, the guy had prime consumable goodies. We didn't eat anything. It was hard and painful, but we resisted. And in this nice little safe — which took my Scottish stud thirty-five minutes to crack — we found cash. Two hundred and fifty large — some jewelry. And . . . a shitpot load of discs. They're labeled, Dallas, and some of that shitpot is Bullock Foundation records."

"Motherload. Bag it all, log it all, bring it all."

Eve turned to Roarke with a toothy grin. "Got the bastards." The grin faded when she saw the tall glass of murky green liquid in his hand. "Where'd you get that?"

"From the faeries."

"I don't want faerie juice." She planted her feet, lifted her fists into a boxer's stance. "And if you try to pour that into me, you're going to bleed."

"Oh, dear, I'm terrified. Threatened with bodily harm by a woman who can barely stand upright. Half for me," he said as she snarled. "Half for you."

"Damn it." She couldn't punch him if he was going to be reasonable. "You first."

With his eyes on hers he lifted the glass, drank half of the contents. Then cocked his head, held the glass out.

"Disgusting, isn't it?"

"Absolutely," he agreed. "Your turn."

She made a face he thought a recalcitrant twelve-year-old would have been proud of, but she snatched the glass, squeezed her eyes shut, and gulped the rest down. "There. Happy now?"

"I'll be happier when we're dancing naked under the tropical sun, but this will do."

"Okay." She rubbed her gritty eyes. "Let's start tying this up."

CHAPTER
NINETEEN

When she contacted Baxter, he was nearly at her gates. "Figured I could give you what I got, you give me yours. In person. I got Trueheart with me. Ought to be something the kid can do."

There was always something, Eve thought, and began to cobble together her notes. Trueheart could play drone and write her report. Despite the months working with Baxter, Trueheart was still fresh as daisies in May and eager as a puppy gamboling through them. He wouldn't squawk about drone work.

"More cops," Roarke said. "More coffee, then."

"Dancing naked, tropical sun, near future."

"I don't suppose we could take fifteen minutes in the holo-room to practice." He set coffee at her elbow.

"We've been practicing every chance we get the last couple years. I think we're ready to go pro. Where's the money they're washing coming from?"

"I thought you were going to let the Feds and Global worry about that?"

"Yeah, but it bugs me." She rose to walk to the board, to study the photos of Bullock and Chase. In her mind she saw the way they'd stood together, the way they'd touched each other. "They're not just mother and son."

When Roarke said nothing, she turned to look at him. Nodded. "You saw it, too."

"I suppose you and I may be more attuned to that kind of thing than most. I saw . . . we'll say . . . the intimacy between them."

"That's too clean a word for it, but to my mind, so's incest. It just doesn't get to the base of it. She runs it, runs him." It made something curdle inside her. "She's the spider when she should have been shielding him from the bad stuff. Instead, she uses him and twists him . . . and this isn't about me."

He crossed to her, laid his hands on her shoulders, his lips on her hair. "How can you stop it from resonating with you, just as what may be happening to Tandy does with me?"

Eve reached up until her hand covered his. "He'd have been the one to do the killing. You could see that in him, the violence under the polish. But she'd be the one pushing the buttons. And maybe I'm reading too much into it."

"If you are, I'm reading the same page."

"Well." She drew a breath, lowered her hand. "If we're right, it's something I'll use when I've got them in Interview. But for now . . . What's the source of the money? Illegals, weapons? It just doesn't feel right. Mob money. I don't know. They don't give that off. Lots of other ways," she mused. "Lots of ways to make money off the books, but it seems to me — it feels to me," she corrected, "like it would be something they're into. Or enjoy. Or believe in. They're self-satisfied fuckers."

"A perfect description."

"You get me." She nodded. "Prissy and righteous and full of themselves. I can't see them hooking up with organized crime, because she likes to run the show. Wish I could walk through this with Mira, get a profile."

"It sounds like you have one of your own."

"She wears diamonds around the house. He's wearing a suit on a Sunday night when they're hanging at home. They have this image, even when no one's around to see it. That's what they've created and nurtured, even when they're coupling in the dark. And the sex, that's another level of the unity, the being above the rest. *Do you know who she is?* Smuggling maybe — it's got that thin sheen of class and romance."

"Why thank you, darling."

She rolled her eyes at him. Trust him to remind her that that was how he'd earned a good portion of his fortune in his youth. "Jewelry, art, fine wines. That kind of thing might be it. Maybe some subtle blackmail."

"The discs Peabody and McNab are bringing in should tell you, at least some of it."

"Yeah. Probably encoded. Pain in the ass. A lot of their houses, other property, are in the foundation's name." Restless, she paced in front of the board. "But that's just a way big wheels loop the loopholes in tax laws. And I'm betting a lot of the jewelry, the art, the high-dollar items were bought with cash."

Then she jerked a thumb at the data she had on-screen. "And you look at him. Hitting onto fifty, no marriages, no cohabs, still lives with his mother. Works with his mother. Travels with his mother. They don't feel they have to bother with a cover over what goes on between them. He didn't say: 'Do you know who *we* are,' but who *she* is. She's the power. She's the control."

Eve pushed that avenue aside as she heard cop feet heading toward the office.

It was always a surprise to see Trueheart out of uniform. They walked in looking, to Eve's mind, like the leads in a buddy vid. The slick-looking veteran cop and his young studly apprentice.

"Coffee." Baxter said it like a prayer. "Hook me up, kid. Dallas, Roarke."

"What's the word on the vehicle?" Eve demanded.

"Dump the discs every twenty-four, so the night in question's long gone. No logs."

"You brought me squat?"

"Would I bring you squat?" He took the coffee from Trueheart, sat, stretched out his legs. "Private garage, with monthly rates that cost more than the rent on my apartment and the kid's here combined. Key card and passcode to get in. Place holds a half-dozen vehicles, and let me tell you, they were all flash. Vic's is a sinewy all-terrain. Four-seater. Loaded."

"That's fascinating, Baxter."

"Gets that way. We're looking it over — had to call the manager in, and he's the one gave us squat. But while we're there, this guy whose ride is this classic Sunstorm — Triple X model, jet charger, six on the floor. Black and shiny as the mouth of hell, silvered glass roof. You know the model?" he asked Roarke. "First run in 2035?"

"I do indeed. A very fine machine."

"I nearly wept when he drove it in."

"It was a sweet ride," Trueheart agreed, then flushed a little when Eve flicked him a glance.

"Sounds like you boys had tons of fun playing with the toys. But what does that give me?"

"In the course of the conversation, the Sunstorm's owner — one Derrick Newman — stated that while he'd never actually met Sloan, he had admired his vehicle, and was considering purchasing one like it for hard weather and off-roading."

"Maybe he can get a deal on it seeing as the owner's dead."

"While he'd never met Sloan," Baxter repeated, "he had noticed that the all-terrain was, always and habitually, backed into its slot. It was parked in that manner a week ago Wednesday at approximately 7p.m. when Newman retrieved his own vehicle to pick up his current squeeze and drive to Oyster Bay for a rehearsal dinner for his brother's wedding — which was the following Saturday. He returned his vehicle to the garage at just after three on Thursday morning as the current squeeze did not deign to put out that evening. At which time he noticed, with some curiosity, that the all-terrain was front-in."

Eve pursed her lips. "That may not be squat."

"It ain't. When Newman mentioned Sloan's parking habit, the manager corroborated. Sloan's rented that space for three years, and has never parked front-in. Until a week ago Wednesday night or early Thursday morning."

"I want that vehicle impounded. I want the sweepers going over it molecule by molecule."

"Thought you would. I made the call while we were there. It's on its way in now."

"Good work."

"Feel like I've done something, anyway," Baxter said with a shrug. "I've been talking to Palma every day. She wants to come in, pack up her sister's things as soon as the scene's cleared."

"Working on that." Eve filled him in, nodded toward Peabody and McNab, who came in as she was wrapping up.

"Bagged, tagged, logged, delivered." Peabody yawned as she and McNab dumped evidence bags on Eve's desk. "Money smells pretty. 'Specially lots of it."

"Get her coffee," Eve ordered.

"Have this first." Roarke held out another booster he'd already poured.

"Looks yucky," Peabody said and pouted at it.

"I made it just for you."

"Aww." With stars in her heavy eyes, she gulped it down. "Is yucky."

"Yes, I know. You, too, Ian."

"Energy booster? I kinda like them." He drank his without complaint while Trueheart passed around more coffee.

"Now, if everyone's refreshed." Eve unsealed the evidence bags marked with Peabody's initials that contained the Bullock Foundation discs. "We'll start with last year, work back."

She plugged the first disc into her computer. "Display data, screen one."

Not encoded she thought, and would have done a little happy dance if she'd had the energy. "Roarke? Translation?"

"Monthly accounts," he verified. "I'd say Randall Sloan's personal copy. It's spelled out quite clearly here, unlike the files registered with the firm. You see his monthly fee." Roarke picked up a laser, pointed. "And Madeline Bullock's, Winfield Chase's commissions — as they're listed. Also deductions for legal fees, Cavendish, in New York. The London law firm takes a cut through monthly retainer, and billable hours."

"Which means, in English."

"The way these accounts were done, officially, the funneling and turnovers are more clearly documented here. And very, very illegal. The tax hounds will be wiping drool off their faces for years."

"I'm looking at income here," Eve said, scrolling through. "Primarily through individuals. Fees out of that to other individuals, and some institutions. Hospitals, medicals . . . food, lodging, transpo.

"Samuel and Reece Russo, a quarter million paid."

"That's an installment," Roarke explained. "One of four."

"A million for Sam and Reece, and a like amount from a Maryanna Clover. More of the same — you got, what, four — no, that's five installment payments here from individuals, just in the first quarter of last year. What are they paying for?"

"The expenses attached to that income might tell the tale." Roarke ordered the expenditures on-screen. "The Russos' fee has a ten-thousand-euro payment, per installment, to a Sybil Hopson, a two-thousand-euro payment as monthly retainer to a Leticia Brownburn, M.D., with a lump payment of ten thousand in October of last year. Another, listed as donation to Sunday's Child. Legal fees come to . . . twelve thousand for this transaction — as paid by the foundation."

"So for a million, in what they're finagling as primarily tax-free income, they expend under a hundred thousand. Good return," Eve decided. "What's Sunday's Child?"

"Child placement agency," the half-asleep Peabody muttered. "London-based."

Eve spun around. "What?"

"Huh? What?" Peabody pushed up from her slouch in the chair, blinked rapidly. "Sorry. I must've zoned out."

"Sunday's Child."

"Oh, we switched to the kidnapping. It's one of the agencies on the list. London-based, with offices in Florence, Rome, Oxford, Milan, ah, Berlin. Places. Sorry, I'll need to review my notes."

"This agency is on the list in Tandy's file, and appears as a major beneficiary of the Bullock Foundation?" She looked at Baxter. "Coincidence is hooey, right?"

"Words to live by. Christ, Dallas, are we dovetailing here?"

"Trueheart, run Leticia Brownburn, M.D., London. I want to know if she's associated with Sunday's Child. Roarke, I need you to go through these files as quickly as you can, see if we've got a pattern. If there are other like agencies, birthing centers."

Movement was quick. Since every unit in the two offices was being used, Eve pulled out her PPC. "Data run on Russo, Samuel, and Russo, Reece," she began and read off the identification numbers Sloan had listed on the file.

Working . . . Russo, Samuel, DOB: 5 August, 2018, married to Russo, Reece, nee Bickle, 10 May, 2050. Residence: London, England; Sardinia, Italy; Geneva, Switzerland; Nevis. One child, male, DOB: 15 September, 2059, through private adoption.

"That's enough, hold run. Begin data run on Hopson, Sybil," she ordered and read off the identification number.

Working . . . Hopson, Sybil, DOB: 3 March, 2040. Parents —

"Skip that. Residence and offspring."

Resides Oxford University. Student. No offspring. One registered pregnancy, through term with live birth, male, 15 September, 2059. Placed through private adoption.

"Placement agency used for both Russo and Hopson."

Working . . . Sunday's Child, London.

"It's not illegal, Dallas." Baxter stood beside her. "I don't know the ins and outs of private adoptions or surrogacy in Europe, but they could slide with this here."

"Payments are too high," Eve disagreed. "This girl sold her kid, and selling human beings is illegal, globally."

"You can call the fee educational incentive, expense reimbursement. They'd go through some shit, but they'd probably scrape it off."

"Maybe. But they hid the money, doctored the accounts so they fell well under the acceptable limit, left the bulk of the income unreported. And if this is what it looks like, they are, in essence, running a baby-selling operation at a big, fat profit. They won't look good on the media reports when this hits. More, they killed three people to keep this buried."

"This is what Palma's sister stumbled onto," Baxter murmured.

"I doubt she knew exactly what it entailed, but she dug around and got a strong clue. Baxter, there are other missing women like Tandy, and at least one who was killed, along with the fetus. It's going to come back to this." She nodded toward the screen. "Right back to this."

"Grabbing women off the damn street? Stealing their kids?"

"Something like that. If these women contacted Sunday's Child, maybe even started proceedings. Fees collected by the foundation."

It was more than pieces now. The picture was full and complete in front of her. "Then, say the woman changes her mind, takes off. These women relocated, so maybe they felt threatened, or were afraid they'd be pressured, legally pursued. They're snatched close to term. There's a reason for that."

"Shorter wait time for the product," he said grimly.

"When the product's delivered, the woman's no longer needed, and is disposed of. Keeps those expenses way down. Work with Roarke, find me someone who paid the baby fee where the expenses don't follow the rest of the pack."

"I've got it."

"Trueheart."

"Lieutenant, Brownburn is on the board of Sunday's Child, and the OB in residence."

"Peabody, is there a branch of the agency in New York?"

"Europe only."

"Another agency then, one that pops on the files. They didn't haul her back to England, not this close to term. They want to be sure the product is safe and viable. Maybe New Jersey, Connecticut. Maybe . . ."

On an oath she leaped to the desk 'link. The big house with the blind windows. *You can see out but you can't see in*, she thought as she hurriedly contacted Cher Reo.

Incognito, my ass.

"Jesus, Dallas, just how many times tonight are you going to ruin my evening?" Reo pushed at her tousled blonde hair. "I'm about to get lucky."

"You're going to get luckier. I need a warrant."

"I got your damn warrants, and let me tell you, I worked my well-toned ass off for them."

"I need a search-and-seize for the Bullock residence on East End Avenue. All contents."

"Oh? Is that all?" Reo's faint Southern drawl went sweet as honey.

"I have reason to believe they're holding a woman there against her will. A very pregnant woman whose life will be over if she delivers before we get to her. If she's not being held there, I need authority to search the premises for proof of her whereabouts."

"Dallas, are they killers or kidnappers?"

"One's led to the other. Reo, this woman's been missing since Thursday. I may already be too late. Don't make me later."

"I need more than 'you have reason to believe,' Dallas. I tap-danced my way to your mandatory DNA. I push for a second warrant on a separate matter, the lawyers for the other team are going to scream harassment."

"I don't have time —" Eve cut herself off, breathed. "I'm going to put Peabody on, and she'll give you the song. I'm putting an op together, Reo. With or without a warrant, I'm going in within the hour."

Jabbing a finger toward the 'link, Eve strode into Roarke's office.

"I've got your pattern, Lieutenant," Roarke told her. "A maximum of ten children placed per year, at birth, for fee, a minimum of four. Over the past eight years, sixty-five placements, for a gross profit of sixty-five-million euros."

"I'm getting a warrant for the East End house. I think they could be holding Tandy there. Baxter."

"Got some way uptown e-toys here," he said without looking up from the screen. "I've got six out of that sixty-five where the expenditures were significantly lower than the others, and in one case where the buy fee was reimbursed."

"Jones, Emily, Middlesex and/or London, England."

"That's the name listed on the first and only expenditure to an individual other than the medicals on the reimbursed fee. And, Dallas? Tandy's on here." McNab looked over at her. "One payment to her late last May, recorded as returned in full early June."

"Changed her mind, paid them back. But that didn't do the trick. We're going in."

In her office she outlined the layout, as she knew it, of the house.

"The subject is most likely being held on the second or third floor. Third gets my vote. She may be restrained, and is undoubtedly guarded, certainly by cams. There are at least two suspects and one servant droid on the premises. Given the situation, we have to assume there is a medical as well, droid or human. Both suspects should be considered violent."

She looked at Roarke. "Can you compromise their security by remote?"

"I can, yes."

"Once the security is down, we go in fast. The priority is to locate and secure the safety of the subject. Peabody, you and Trueheart will head that. McNab, I need you and Roarke to take down any electronics, including droids. Baxter, that leaves the suspects to you and me. They resist, they're restrained."

"Any and all means?"

"I want them talking. Walking's optional. Communicators on Channel A throughout. I want to know the minute the subject is located, and her condition. Here's how we move."

She turned back to the wall screen where she'd sketched the bones of the East End mansion.

When she'd finished, she went to the bedroom, strapped on her clutch piece, checked her primary weapon and her restraints. Then, because her eyes felt hot and gritty, she ran ice-cold water in the bathroom sink.

Sucking in her breath, she plunged her face into it.

She came up gasping, then her eyes met Roarke's in the mirror over the sink. "Don't tell me I'm burning low."

"I don't need to state the obvious, the other portion of that being this can't wait until you've recharged."

"You either." Still dripping, she turned, touched his cheek. "You look pale. You hardly ever do."

"The past couple of days remind me that you couldn't pay me twice what I already have to be a cop."

"It's not about the money, it's about the adventure." When he laughed, she grabbed a towel, scrubbed it over her wet face. "I think about that dream I had where all this was tangled together. And son of a bitch, it was. It is. If I'd seen it before —"

"How?"

"I don't know, but if I had, Tandy would be at home in her own bed right now, and Bullock, Chase, and the rest of them would be in cages." She tossed the towel aside. "Jesus, Roarke, Jesus, the way I went in there tonight, got in their face. I put the pressure on them, and if they panic because of that, or push up the schedule . . . She was in there. Goddamn it, Tandy was in there, I *know* it. While we sat there and that bitch poured tea."

"And we wouldn't know that yet if you hadn't followed a hunch and sent Peabody and McNab back to Sloan's to look for records. No one found the others, Eve. No one got close to finding them. Remember that."

"I will, when and if we do find her, and she's still breathing." She checked the time. "I'm not waiting any longer for the warrant. Let's line it up and knock it down."

Sometime in the last hour it had started to snow. Thick, fat, wet flakes. Her team and the electronics Roarke and McNab had selected for the op were loaded into one of Roarke's burly all-terrains.

As they rode, she visualized the interior of the Bullock house. Wide foyer, stairs to the left, living area

362

to the right. Glass doors on east wall to terrace. Possible escape route.

But they wouldn't run, she didn't believe they'd run. They were too steeped in their own importance to run.

Chase wouldn't be served with the mandatory until morning. She bet he and Mommy were both sleeping the sleep of the conscienceless by now. And they were about to get a nasty wake-up call.

Roarke stopped the van a half-block down and across the street from the mansion. "Let's break out the toys, Ian."

"Ahead of you."

McNab sat crosslegged on his seat working the controls of a small keyboard. "Now this is frosty. I already programmed the coordinates. Ready to engage, if you're set."

"Baxter? Why don't you change seats with me." Though he made his way to the back, Roarke let McNab work the controls. "Go ahead."

"Infrared and heat sensors engaged. Image on-screen — this bitch is fast! Okay, looks like we got two warm bodies, second level. Horizontal. Sleepy-by. Same room, same bed. I thought we were looking for mother and son."

"We are," Eve said as something twisted in her belly.

"Oh. Sick. Two warm bodies," he repeated. "Second level, east, second room."

"Only two," Eve demanded and he sent her an apologetic look.

"That's what I'm getting. Showing body heat, heart rate, mass and density, height and weight. This is wild-ass equipment, and it gives me the droid count — three first level, one third — but I'm not seeing any sign of a third human. And neither one of these images shows a baby on board."

"Ian," Roarke murmured, "have a look here." Roarke tapped an area on the third level with a fingertip.

"Blank space where there can't be blank space. Cold room. Jeez, I must be slipping. It's shielded against the sensors."

"Can you get by them?" Eve demanded.

"This'll take a few minutes," Roarke told her.

"I'm not waiting. We're on go —" She broke off when her 'link beeped. "Reo. Tell me you got it."

"I had to sell what's left of my soul and my hot date went cold. You better bring in the goods, Dallas. Warrant coming through now."

"Good work, Reo."

"Tell me about it. You find the woman, you tag me. The minute."

"Done. One more favor."

"You're racking them up."

"Contact Lieutenant Jaye Smith. She's MPU. Fill her in on this. I didn't want to pull her in when the warrant was still hanging."

"Oh, well, sure, happy to be your message droid. Anything else while I'm —"

Eve clicked off. "We're a go."

"I'm not clear here yet."

"Leave it," Eve told Roarke. "Peabody, Trueheart, you're in behind me and Baxter, straight up to the third level. You take that room. Roarke, McNab. You sweep the main level, then work up. Take down the security," she ordered.

Though she could see irritation flicker over his face because he hadn't finished the first task, Roarke picked up a sleek little jammer, climbed out of the car, and strolled down the block.

Eve wasn't sure if he required the proximity to the target, or didn't care to have a load of cops watch his method of shutting down a high-end security system in just under thirty-five seconds.

"Secondary system's activated." His voice was cool and breezy when she joined him. "I need to bypass the automated alarm, if you want the household unaware."

"I do. How long have you got?"

"Another twelve seconds."

She watched the time count down on a grid of the jammer, while a flashing series of others blurred by on another grid. They stopped, the jammer beeped. And the time showed three seconds to spare.

"Secondary coming up. And there we are."

She signaled the others, then jogged across the quiet, snowy street. "Record on," she murmured, then nodded to Roarke.

The recorders might have been activated, but she turned her body just enough to keep his hands out of their range as he crouched to begin work on the locks.

When it was done, she used hand signals to remind the team which direction each unit was to take. To Baxter she said, "I go low."

"Suit yourself."

He went through with her, weapons drawn. Behind them, Roarke and McNab peeled to the right.

"This is the police!" Eve shouted as she charged up the steps with Peabody and Trueheart behind. "We have a warrant to enter these premises, to search same, and to seize any items relating to the terms of the warrant. Go, go," she ordered Peabody, then swung off the steps with Baxter on the second level.

She heard something crash below, and kept going.

Chase burst out of the room on the left, hastily tying the belt of a plaid robe.

"What is the meaning of this? This is outrageous."

Eve held up the warrant. "This is America, and we love the outrageous. You will cooperate with the terms of this warrant, or be restrained and removed from the premises. I'm hoping you're not feeling cooperative."

"I'm ringing our solicitor, immediately." Madeline's robe was bright red, her pale hair loose. And without the carefully applied enhancements, Eve counted a good five years older. She stood, vibrating with rage, in the doorway beside her son.

Her lover.

"Help yourself. Detective Baxter will be happy to accompany you."

"Detective Baxter can go to hell, and so can you. This is my home. This is my bedroom." She gestured dramatically behind her. "No one enters without an invitation."

"Invitation," Eve said, holding up the warrant again. Then she reached behind and jiggled her restraints. "You want a new set of bracelets?"

Fury blotched her cheeks with red. "Win, say nothing. Do nothing. I'll not only have your job before this night is done, Lieutenant, I'll have your hide." The skirts of the robe swirled out as she spun back into the bedroom.

"Got a flair, doesn't she?" Eve said conversationally. "You always do what she says, *Win*? You a good boy and mind your mommy, even when you're diddling her?"

"How dare you, you filthy-minded whore."

"Call them as I see them. Did your mother tell you to torture Natalie Copperfield before you killed her, or was that your idea?"

"I have nothing to say to you."

"Right, Mommy told you to be quiet. It's okay. When we finish searching the house we'll have everything we need. I know Tandy's on the third floor. I've got two cops upstairs right now, getting her out of your cold room."

She saw it in his eyes, so when he yanked the stunner out of his robe pocket she was ready. She kicked out, disarming him, then pivoted when he charged so the fist he struck out with glanced off her shoulder. The elbow she jabbed into his solar plexus doubled him up, but he used his forward motion to ram her like a bull. Adrenaline pumped into her as her back hit the wall, and his hands closed around her throat. When her knee came up, hard, between his legs, the air wheezed out of him so he deflated like a balloon.

"By not cooperating you made my night. Now, Winfield Chase, you're under arrest for assaulting an officer." She bent down to roll him onto his face, yank his arms behind his back, and slap on the restraints. "And believe me when I say that's just the beginning."

She looked up in time to see Madeline run out of the bedroom, her hands curled like claws, her face murderous. Even as Eve sprang up, Baxter leaped out of the doorway and took Madeline down with a flying tackle.

"Sorry, Dallas. She got away from me."

"No problem." She rolled her shoulder, watched Roarke and McNab come up the stairs.

"First level's secure, Lieutenant," McNab told her. "Three droids — one servant, two security. They're down."

"And so are these two. McNab, help Baxter keep them down. Roarke and I are going up."

CHAPTER
TWENTY

On the third level a droid in a pale green lab coat was sprawled on the floor against an overturned chair.

"We had to take it down." Peabody pulled her master out of a lock slot in a door designed to blend into the wall.

Trueheart crouched in front of a small comp unit. "The droid must have deactivated this when it heard us come in." Trueheart shook his head. "I can't reactivate."

"I'll have a go at the lock." Roarke took some tools out of his coat pocket.

"Looks like a medical." Eve gave the droid a light boot with her foot. "Portable birthing equipment, fetal monitor." She lifted her chin toward a roll cart. "Warming tray. Got your towels, your scale, and so on. I saw this stuff at the birthing class. She's in there."

"Must have cams on her," Peabody said. "Droid could sit out here, monitor her on-screen. Suspects?"

"Down. McNab and Baxter have them. Call this in, Peabody. I want the suspects taken in. Put an ambulance and OB team on alert. Roarke?"

"It's coming. Complicated little bastard."

"Peabody, have uniforms pick up a copy of the warrant on Cavendish. I want him brought in now. And contact Reo and Lieutenant Smith, give them the situation. I want a warrant on Bruberry, too. Let's have a big party down at Central."

"I'll pick up the hats and streamers."

"Nearly there," Roarke mumbled. "Aye, you shagging bitch, I've got you now."

A dot of green light flashed along the narrow strip of chrome.

"Might have another guard inside," Eve said, "So —"

"You go low," Roarke finished.

With a nod, she shoved the door open. "Lights on," she called out, swept the room with her weapon, with her eyes. "Tandy Willowby, it's the police. It's Dallas."

Quiet classical music played, and the air smelled subtly floral. The walls were cheerfully warm yellow with paintings of meadows and calm blue seas. Cozy chairs, padded tables, snow falling gently outside the screened windows created a scene of comfort and ease.

In the bed, a pale, hollow-eyed Tandy sat up, gripping something white and sharp in her fist.

"Dallas?" Her voice was thin, rusty, and her body began to shake. "Dallas? They're going to take my baby. They're going to take him. I can't get out."

"It's all right now. You're all right now. We're going to take you out."

"They locked me in. I can't keep the baby. I don't have the right."

"Bullshit. Peabody."

"You don't have to worry about them anymore. Here." Peabody moved slowly toward the bed. "Why don't you give me that now? We'll get you a coat. We'll take you to the hospital."

"No, no, no!" Eyes wild, Tandy cringed back. "No hospital. They'll take the baby."

"They won't." Eve holstered her weapon and walked briskly to the bed. She held out her hand. "Because I won't let them."

Tandy dropped the thin, sharp plastic, then simply collapsed against Eve. "Please, please, please, get us out of here."

"Here now." Roarke took off his coat. "It's cold outside. Put your arms in, there's a girl."

"Stay with me." Tears streaming, Tandy gripped Eve's hand. "Please, stay with me. Don't let them take my baby. Who's that? Who's that?" She wrapped herself around Eve when she spotted Trueheart.

"He's one of mine. He's one of the good guys. Trueheart, go on down, assist Baxter and McNab. I want those people gone."

"Yes, sir."

"You okay to walk, Tandy?"

"Out of here. I can walk out of here. The baby's okay, he's been kicking. I don't want to go to the hospital, please. I don't want to be alone. They might come back. They might —"

"You'd like to see Mavis, wouldn't you?" Roarke kept his voice light and gentle as he helped her out of bed. "She's at our place, and she's been worried about you. Why don't we go see Mavis now?"

Roarke gave Eve a long look as he helped Tandy out of the room.

"A little shocky," Peabody commented. "Mostly just scared. How do you want to handle? I can go with her to your place while you take the suspects."

Oh, how she wished. But she couldn't very well dump two pregnant women on Roarke. "I'll go with Tandy, get a statement out of her when she's settled. Make sure the suspects are booked and caged for the night. They're going to wait until morning for Interview. Let's see how they like being locked up. Then go home, get some sleep."

"I'm so all about that. Look at this room. All the comforts. Bastards."

Eve called in Crime Scene, left Baxter, Trueheart, and McNab to work with them to process the room where Tandy had been imprisoned, to search the house. She hated leaving the scene, leaving the work, but climbed into the back of the vehicle. She had a victim who needed care.

"I was so scared." Bundled in Roarke's coat, covered with a blanket, Tandy sat in the front passenger seat. "I think they were going to kill me. Take the baby, then kill me. They left me in there. He came in once a day, every day. And he looked at me like I was already dead. I couldn't do anything."

"Where'd you get the sticker?" Eve asked her.

"The what?"

"The plastic shiv you were holding."

"Oh. They brought me food. The droid did. Have to keep the baby healthy, that's what she said. Horrible thing, always cheerful. Even when she restrained me for exams. I palmed a couple of the plastic spoons — that's all they brought in for me to eat with. Plastic spoons. And when they turned off the lights at night, I sawed and rubbed them together under the covers. Hours, it seemed like. I was going to hurt one of them. Somehow."

"Wish you'd had the chance. Do you want to tell me what happened, or do you want to wait on that until later?"

"It was Thursday. I left work to walk to the bus stop. And she — her name is Madeline Bullock — she walked up to me. I was so ashamed. Before, in London when I found out I was pregnant, and things didn't seem as if they were going to work out, I went to this agency. I was going to put the baby up for adoption. It seemed like the best thing to do. I —"

"We know about that. They're running an operation, under the cover of the foundation. Selling babies."

"Oh, God. God. I'm such an idiot."

"You're not," Roarke told her. "You trusted them."

"I did. I did. There were counselors, and they were so kind, so understanding. Ms. Bullock came in to meet me herself, and so did he. Her son. They said how I was giving a gift, to a worthy couple, and to my baby. I signed a contract, and they gave me money. For expenses, they said. Proper food, clothing. I had to agree to use their medical people, their facilities, but it was all so nice. I was to have regular care and monitoring, counseling, and the foundation would help me with lodging, and with education should I want to go back to school, or with career counseling. All of it."

"A very sweet pot."

"Yes, very sweet. But I changed my mind." She wrapped her arms around her belly as she hunched in the seat. "I'd always wanted to make a family, to be a mother, and now I was denying myself. I'm smart enough, and strong and healthy. I'm not a child. I could make a good life for the baby. I took the money back. I'd hardly spent any, and I made up the difference with my savings."

She swiped at the tears on her face. "They were very harsh. I'd signed a contract, it was legally binding. They'd take me to court, and the law would force me to fulfill my obligations. What kind of a mother would I be, a liar and a cheat. It was horrible. I left the money. I was so upset, and questioning myself. Were they right? Would I be a terrible mum? Would the courts take my baby? How could I prove I'd given the money back? Stupid, so stupid."

"So you came to New York," Eve prompted.

"I thought, I'm not going to have this. I can't risk it. I . . . I nearly went to see the baby's father a dozen times, but I'd made this choice, so I was going to follow it through. I packed up, quit my job, sold some of my things. I had a friend who was driving to Paris for the weekend, and hitched a ride with her. I even lied, told her I was going to look for work there. I don't know why, exactly, but I was afraid they'd set the cops on me, or something."

Letting her head fall back, Tandy closed her eyes as she traced light circles over her belly. "I was so angry, just so angry at everyone. I took a bus from Paris to Venice, and a shuttle from there to New York. I was lonely at first, I nearly went back. But then I found my job, and it was brilliant. And I signed up with a midwife, and I met Mavis. Everything seemed to be so right. I missed . . . I missed people from home, but I had to think about the baby."

"Then you left work on Thursday."

"I had Friday off, and Saturday was Mavis's shower. I was feeling so good about everything. And there she was. So surprised to see me, so kind and asking how I was doing. I was so ashamed at the way I'd run off, but she just waved all that aside. She said she had a car, and would see me home. And when this lovely limo swooped up to the curb, like magic, I went right along."

Circling, Eve thought. Not parked, leaving no record.

"She sat in the back with me while the driver started on. She gave me a bottle of water, and we chatted about London. And then . . . I felt so strange, and I can't remember. Until I awoke in that room."

"You're out of it now," Eve said when Tandy trembled again. "You're out, and they're the ones locked up."

"I'm out. Yes, we're out, and we're safe. They were there, both of them," she continued in a steadier voice. "And that horrible droid, sitting there, staring at me when I woke up. And they told me how things would be. The baby wasn't mine, I'd signed it away. I was only the means to its birth."

She shifted now, to look behind her and meet Eve's eyes. "They said this to me, all so calm, even when I was screaming and trying to get away, and the droid forced me back on the bed. They said I'd be treated well, have proper nourishment, rest, stimulation, and they expected me to deliver a healthy baby boy within the week.

"I said they were mad, they couldn't force me to give up my child. He said — the son — he said they had wealth, power, position. I had nothing but a fertile womb. They left that music playing day and night. Good for the baby. Everything in the room was bolted down. I couldn't even throw anything. I beat against the windows, but no one could see. I screamed until I hadn't a voice left, but no one could hear me.

"What day is it?"

"It's early Monday morning," Eve told her.

"Only Monday," Tandy said and turned to rest her head again. "It felt longer. So much longer. You saved my baby. You saved me. If I live two hundred years more, I'll never forget it."

The lights were on, gleaming against the windows, flooding the grounds where the snow lay like white mink. Tree branches were heavy with it as it continued to fall in a hushed whisper.

"Oh. It's like a palace." Tandy's voice shook. "Like a winter palace. I feel as though I'm the princess who's been rescued. You're my knights in shining armor," she said, rubbing fresh tears from her cheeks.

Even as they pulled up in front, the door to the house burst open, and Mavis, dwarfed in one of Eve's robes, ran out. Summerset and Leonardo rushed behind her.

"Mavis, you promised you'd wait." Summerset reached for her arm.

"I know, I'm sorry. I can't. Tandy!" She wrenched open the door. "Tandy! Are you all right? The baby?"

"They saved us."

On cue, Eve thought, both women burst into tears and fell into each other's arms.

"Let's get you inside now, out of the cold, sweetheart." Leonardo wrapped his big arms around both of them. "Come inside now, Tandy."

"Take them straight up to the room I prepared," Summerset ordered. "I'll be there in a moment."

As they walked toward the house, sheltered by Leonardo, Mavis looked back at Eve. "I knew you'd find her. I knew you would."

"They're yours now." Eve pointed at Summerset. "I've got work."

"Lieutenant."

She turned, scowled at him. "What?"

"Well done."

"Huh. Thanks." She raised her eyebrows at Roarke as they went inside. "I've got to tag Peabody, make sure the prisoners are secured, check in with Baxter on-scene, and round it out with Reo and Smith."

"Yes, of course. After you've had some sleep."

"Loose ends dangling."

"That can be tied up later. Whatever you got from the booster and your own adrenaline is washed,

Lieutenant. You're pale as the moon, and your words are starting to slur."

"Coffee."

"Not a chance in hell."

He must have been right because when she managed to focus, she was standing — barely — in the bedroom. "One hour horizontal," she said as she took off her weapon harness.

"Four — which gives you enough time to put some fuel in your system in the morning and get downtown to grill your suspects."

"Not just grill." She sat to yank off her boots. "I'm gonna fry 'em. Aren't you gonna carry me to bed?"

"You're still dressed."

"'S' okay. I can sleep in my clothes." She smiled sleepily, held up her arms to him.

He got her up, staggered a little as he carted her to the bed, then dumped both of them onto the duvet. "Best I can do."

"Good enough." She curled into him, he wrapped around her, and they both tumbled into sleep.

He'd been right about the four and the fuel, Eve decided. She was going to have a long and tricky day, and needed to charge up for it.

As expected, Bullock and the rest had called in a fleet of lawyers. Eve was letting them all stew while she and her team gave complete reports to Whitney and Reo.

"The Feds and Global are going to want to take over the fraud, the baby-for-profit op, and whatever else the foundation had its fingers into," Reo told her.

"They can have it."

"And a field day with it. The London law firm is also going to be on the hot seat. You've got yourself an international incident, Dallas."

"I've got three DBs. Those are mine. As for the abduction and held-against-will of Tandy Willowby, that's a share with Lieutenant Smith in MPU."

"How's she doing? Willowby?"

"Good, I'm told. She was sleeping when I left the house." She turned to Whitney. "I want to start with Cavendish on this, sir. He's the weak sister."

"Your call."

Reo got to her feet. "Got them cold on the kidnapping, and the evidence is there for Global. The three homicides, that's the sticker."

"I'll get them."

Reo nodded. "Mind if I watch?"

Cavendish was in Interrogation, looking pale and sweaty and flanked by two sharp-looking suits. The one on the left got immediately to his feet. "My client was held overnight without bond, and kept waiting in this room nearly an hour. We intend to file complaints, and when you've finished this ridiculous charade, demand an internal investigation on you."

"Charade?" Eve said to Peabody.

"It's like that game where you can't talk, but you have to use your hands and body language to get the other person to guess the word or phrase."

"No kidding? That's good, because while Mr. Cavendish is entitled to his representation, and may speak with same, I'm not obliged to speak to lawyers.

Record on. Dallas, Lieutenant Eve, and Peabody, Detective Delia, in formal interview with Cavendish, Walter, and his two representatives. I'll just read off the charges."

When she had, she sat, kicked out her legs. "You've already been read the Revised Miranda, Mr. Cavendish —"

"My client is a citizen of Great Britain —"

"God save the King. Do you understand your rights and obligations in this matter?"

"I understand. I have nothing to say."

"Okay, I'll do the talking. We'll start with accessory to murder, three counts. That's good for three consecutive life sentences in the good old U. S. of A. Now, the Brits may want you, and we may agree to deport you into their custody, which would make me sad. Still, they'd lock you up for the rest of your natural life there, too — and save the taxpayers money."

"You have nothing to link my client to any murder, or any crime."

"I have enough not only to *link* you," Eve said, speaking directly to Cavendish, "but to chain you head to foot and throw you overboard. Randall Sloan kept private records, Cavendish. Chase didn't get them. I did. Your name's on them."

She smiled when a line of sweat beaded over his top lip. Yeah, the weak sister.

"You were aware of the operating practices of the Bullock Foundation, which included the sale of infant human beings for profit and fraudulent tax reporting to boost the profit on that operation. You were also aware that Chase intended to murder Natalie Copperfield and

Bick Byson, who had discovered at least part of those practices. You knew he was going to do this to them."

Eve shoved two crime scene photos across the table.

"My client has no knowledge of any of the circumstances of these crimes."

"You may be bottom of the food chain, Walt, but you knew. Bullock and Chase came to your office to discuss it in private, didn't they? You had a nice little lunch while you discussed how he'd kill two people."

"This is absurd." One of the lawyers got to his feet. "You have nothing but speculation. Groundless speculation. This interview —"

"I've got more, Walter. I've got your girlfriend in the next room."

Eve grinned when his eyes darted toward the door. "Yeah, that's right, and I'd make book she'll push this whole thing into your lap. She worked for you, did what she was told, didn't know. She can play that, and you'll go down for it. Your kind always does. You've got SAP tattooed on your forehead. I don't like her, so I'm talking to you first. I'm offering you the deal I'm going to offer her if you don't make me happy."

"No deal," the suit snapped.

"I bet you work for Stuben, Robbins, Cavendish, and Mull." Eve spoke to the lawyer for the first time. "They're in a big pile of crap, too. Lot of smart lawyers there, right, Walter — smart lawyers who represent Bullock and Chase. I imagine they've got you all picked out as fall guy. Sent you over here, gave you busy work, show you no real respect. Now the heat's on, and who do you think's going to burn?"

"I was home in bed with my wife when these murders occurred." Cavendish tugged on his tie. "I have nothing to do with this."

"You don't want to lie to me. You really don't want to piss me off when I'm the only one here looking out for you. Chase killed Randall Sloan, set him up, took him out. I wonder what he'd do to you. Maybe I should put the two of you in a box together and find out."

"Threats won't be tolerated," one of the lawyers snapped.

"Not a threat, just speculation. Here's how it happened, how it's documented in Randall Sloan's private records. Copperfield came across something that didn't quite add up for her, and she — being a good girl — went to Randall Sloan for advice. She knew him, the father of her friend, the son of the head of the firm — she trusted him. Maybe he tried to put out the fire himself, but she's asking the wrong questions. He contacts Bullock, she contacts you. You're in it now. She sets her son on Copperfield when bribery doesn't work. You knew just what they did — that makes you an accessory."

"More speculation," the lawyer said. "You have nothing concrete against my client, or Ms. Bullock and her son."

"Who do you believe, Walter? The suit from Stuben, or the cop who's got you by the short hairs? It's over for you, and you know it. Your life, your career, the plush office, the expense account. But you can choose how you want to spend what you've got left. Three counts, accessory to murder or — if you cooperate now

— three counts obstruction of justice. You'll do time in a cage, but you'll be eligible for parole. You'll end your life on the outside, instead of in. One-time offer, and you've got thirty seconds."

Eve leaned in close until he had little choice but to meet her eyes. "You know she'll take it when I go next door. She'll throw you to the wolves without a second's thought. Tick-tock, Walter. Twenty seconds left."

"I want it in writing."

"Cavendish —"

"Shut up!" he rounded on the lawyer. "It's not your life on the line, is it? I'm not taking the fall for this. In writing," he repeated. "And I'll tell you everything I know."

"That was easy," Peabody commented after they'd stepped out.

"Didn't even get me warmed up." Eve rolled her shoulders. "Spineless bastard. He'll do a solid dime on the obstruction."

"And there's the fraud. You didn't mention that to him in the offer."

Eve grinned. "Oops. Well, it's not in my authority to offer a deal on international tax fraud or any international crime. Gee, I guess he's going to do considerably more time than the dime."

"Who do you want next?"

"We'll take Bruberry. She's going to be very, very unhappy her boss flipped on her."

"You think she'll crack?"

"Two hours tops."

"Put money on it?"

Eve considered. "Fifty."

"Done."

In one hour and fifty-three minutes, Peabody walked out of Interview. "I'm kind of torn. I'm out fifty, but it was fairly frosty to watch her go down. Didn't just crack, she exploded."

"And knew more of where the secrets are locked than her boss." Eve rubbed her hands together. "Double or nothing on Chase?"

"I figured we'd hit Bullock next."

"Nope, I'm saving her for last."

"No bet," Peabody decided. "You're hitting your stride."

As they turned, they saw Baxter hotfooting it down the hall. "Sweeper report, wanted to hand-deliver it." He slapped a file, with disc, into Eve's hand. "On Sloan's vehicle. They found a single hair, headrest, driver's seat. It's Chase's. EDD report," he added, handing her another. "My new best friend, McNab, found transmissions to and from a Doctor Letitia Brownburn, London. Authorities there have already picked her up, and acted on a warrant to close down Sunday's Child, until further investigation into its practices. There are also transmissions to Cavendish's office — Madeline to Bruberry, and from Madeline to the London office where she conversed for some length with Stuben. They spoke cryptically, of an imminent delivery."

"Cavendish and Bruberry both sang like fat ladies," Eve told him. "We're taking Chase next."

"I'll be in Observation with Reo."

"Baxter, why don't you take this round. I'll observe." Peabody glanced at Eve. "That work for you?"

"Fine."

"I appreciate it. How do you want to handle it?"

"Hard and mean. No deals, no good cop. He's got a temper. Let's piss him off."

"Like your style."

They went in together. Eve slapped the files on the table where Chase sat with three lawyers.

"Record on." She read off the data. "There's one suit in here too many." She shot up a hand before any one of them could speak. "Anything over two reps is at my discretion. One of you get out."

"As Mr. Chase is a British citizen and the absurd charges levied against him so serious, we require special representation for international law, for criminal law, and for tax law."

"I don't much care what you require. One of you get out. Now, or this interview is over, and your client goes back to sit in his cell until you're down to two."

"We expect some courtesy."

"You're not going to get it. Detective." She turned for the door.

"I can handle international and criminal." The lone woman, a brunette of about fifty, spoke in clear, unaccented tones. "I think it's in our client's interest to have this straightened out as soon as possible."

One of the men rose, strode stiffly out of the room.

"Mr. Chase, you've been read the Revised Miranda, is this correct?"

When he sat stonily silent, the woman spoke again. "Mr. Chase acknowledges the reading of his rights."

"I hear that from him, on record, or again, this interview is over."

"I was read my rights," Chase snapped. "And manhandled. I intend to file charges of police brutality."

"You look okay to me. Are you requesting a physical examination to document any injuries you may have incurred during your arrest?"

"You attacked me."

"Beg to differ, and the assault against me was recorded. Now, do you understand your rights and obligations, Mr. Chase? He answers," Eve said again. "On record."

"I understand them, such as they are in this uncivilized city of yours."

"Good. In this uncivilized city we like to put people in cages for their entire natural life for various offenses. Now, where should we start?"

"Lieutenant." The brunette took a sheet of paper from her briefcase. "If we could clear up the matter of one Tandy Willowby residing temporarily in Ms. Bullock and Mr. Chase's New York home?"

"Residing? Is that what you Brits call it when a woman's locked in a room and held against her will?" She shook her head at Baxter. "And they say we speak the same language."

"Didn't look like she was residing to me. Bet you like women locked up and helpless, Chase. Pregnant, too, so they can't fight you off. Fucking pervert."

386

"We will make note of any obscenities," the brunette said primly.

"Wanker." Eve grinned darkly at Chase. "I bet you watched Tandy on that security screen while you slapped the monkey."

"You disgusting bitch."

"Mr. Chase." The brunette laid a hand over his. "Lieutenant, please. I believe we can clear this up quickly, and move on. I have here a statement Ms. Bullock dictated to her representative, and which Mr. Chase has corroborated and signed. I'd like to read it into evidence."

"Help yourself."

"On Thursday, shortly after 6p.m., Ms. Bullock noticed Ms. Willowby on Madison Avenue, where Ms. Bullock had been shopping. In May of last year, Ms. Willowby had enlisted the help of the Bullock Foundation to assist her in placing her child for adoption. However, Ms. Willowby failed to keep subsequent appointments with the counselor, the obstetrician, and the placement agency. Relieved to see her well, Ms. Bullock approached her. At that time, Ms. Willowby became quite distraught and begged Ms. Bullock for help. Concerned, Ms. Bullock helped Ms. Willowby to her car, intending to have her driven home. But Ms. Willowby only became more hysterical, to the point of threatening suicide. She was nearly at term and had realized, she stated, that she could not raise the child, having neither the emotional nor the financial wherewithal. Out of concern, and with a desire to assist, Ms. Bullock took the young woman to her home — with Ms. Willowby's full consent. She lodged Ms. Willowby there, arranged for medical assistance, and began to make arrangements for counseling and for adoption proceedings should Ms. Willowby remain in the same state of mind."

"You can just stop there, because we didn't bring shovels, and that's the biggest load of bullshit we may have ever had dumped in this room. We've got you on Tandy, Chase. Not only her statement, but the statements of five cops and one civilian, who will all testify she was locked in a room against her will."

"Ms. Willowby's state of mind," the lawyer began, and Eve shoved up from her chair, got in her face.

"I wonder what your state of mind would've been if you'd been locked in a room, examined by a medical droid without your consent. You can cram your statement and the rest of this *bullshit*. You can cram it, sister, because when Stuben and company goes down, your ass is very likely going to be hanging naked in the wind."

"If this interview can't be conducted with some measure of decorum —"

"Screw decorum and you with it. You don't like it, there's the door." She shifted to Chase. "EDD is even now mining the medical droid's memory banks. I don't have to waste my time on that, because you're going down for it, *Win*, you and Mommy. Oh, by the way, did you tell your representatives you were sleeping with Mommy when we took you down?"

"Shut up."

"Lieutenant, please." The female lawyer held up a hand, but Eve had seen the blink of shock. "Impugning Ms. Bullock's and Mr. Chase's reputations is unacceptable."

"Here, again in the uncivilized U.S., so is incest. Twenty-five to life for the abduction and held-against-will of Tandy Willowby. And if we find you raped her while she was held —"

"I never touched that filthy slut!"

"Oh?" Eve flipped through one of the files. "Right, right, you don't play that game, because it's all about Mommy."

"Maybe he likes — what do you call them — Nancy boys," Baxter suggested. "Yeah, I bet this one likes to stick it to little boys when he's not doing it with Mom."

"You revolt me. We'll bury both of you before this is done."

"No, he wouldn't play with boys," Eve said. "Mommy wouldn't like it. Didn't rape Tandy either, did you, Win? Never got it up for anyone but your mother. Can't get the wood on for anyone but her, can you?"

At Eve's words, Chase shoved out of the chair, lunged toward her. It took both the lawyers and Baxter to hold him back.

"Lieutenant, this is simply unacceptable. I won't have my client spoken to in this way."

"Write a complaint." She rose, circled around, leaned over the back of Chase's shoulder. He was breathing hard, and she could feel the heat pumping off of him. "You didn't rape Natalie either. Another filthy slut? Not like your mother, who's important and understands you, your needs. You and your mother have so many secrets. Isn't that what she told you when she touched you when you were a boy? A secret, just between the two of you. As long as you're a good boy, do what your mother says, everything's fine.

"Then that bitch Copperfield started poking around where she had no business, and she was going to try to take you down. She had the *nerve* to question your business. Did your mother tell you to do it, Win? I think so. You do what your mother tells you, or there's no sack time with her. Did she tell you to use Randall Sloan's car? Found your hair in it."

"My client and Mr. Randall Sloan were acquainted. He might have ridden in that car at any time."

"Driven it," Eve corrected. "Hair was on the driver's seat. Your hair. Your DNA, just like your DNA was on Bick Byson's knuckles. Popped you before you could use your stunner — you coward. Don't know how to fight like a man, but then you're not a man. Just a boy who sleeps with his mother. Still, it was easy to slap around some woman half your size, bind her up. Break her fingers, beat her face, burn her skin. You enjoyed it, just like you enjoyed watching her eyes when you strangled her. I bet it's the only way you get it up when you're not with your mother."

"This interview is terminated," the brunette began.

"I'd enjoy watching yours," Chase said softly.

"You going to let the girl lawyer say what you do? Just like Mommy. Do this, Win, do that. Good dog."

"Nobody tells me what to do. Shut up!" he shouted at his lawyer. "Stupid git. I've had enough of this. Enough of being questioned by this *person*, of being placated by you. I've done no more than what needed to be done. It was Randall Sloan who hired some thug to kill those people. He confessed before he hanged himself."

"How do you know? Were you there?"

"You told us yourself."

"No, I didn't. I said Randall Sloan was found hanging, period. He didn't self-terminate. You killed him, and staged it. Because you're a spineless coward. You killed Sophia Belego, Rome, and Emily Jones, Middlesex, England. Pregnant women must be an offense to your eye."

"'Cause he can't get it up except with Mommy Dearest," Baxter said.

"It has nothing to do with *sex*! They signed a contract!" He slammed his fist on the table. "They signed a legal document, and we gave our word to properly screened parents. They had no right!"

"Yeah, carting a fetus around for nine months doesn't give you any rights to it. You snatched Sophia Belego, didn't you? Took that kid, got rid of the incubator. Didn't work so well with Emily Jones. Lost the product on that one. How many others, Chase?"

"We provide a service!" he shouted over his lawyers' warnings. "We give our time, our expertise, our *name* to help these women in trouble, through their own doing, their own weaknesses, and give a gift to worthy couples."

"For a nice, fat fee."

"They're paid, aren't they? Given a chance to better themselves while the child is properly raised. How dare you question me?"

He literally shook off the lawyer to his left, and backhanded the one on his right. "I don't need to justify my actions." He surged to his feet.

The brunette wiped at her bloody lip and tried to stand. "This interview is —"

"Shut up! Didn't I tell you to shut the hell up?"

"Natalie Copperfield," Eve said flatly. "Bick Byson, Randall Sloan."

"Sneaking around, sticking their noses into our business. Sloan's fault for being sloppy. Lazy, incompetent."

"So you had to kill them. All of them. It was a matter of pride," Eve continued calmly. "Of business."

"The Bullock Foundation needed to be protected. It's bigger than any of those pathetic people. My mother is the heart of the foundation and has taken it beyond what it was. It was blackmail against us, all of them. What I did was self-defense, to preserve an important charitable institution."

With a handkerchief still pressed to her bleeding lip, the brunette lifted a hand. "We need to consult with our client."

"You're fired." Chase bared his teeth as he swung around violently enough to have both lawyers scrambling back. "Do you think I need you? Idiots. Panderers. Get out. I've had enough of both of you. Out of my sight."

392

"Mr. Chase —"

"Now! I can and will speak for myself," he said as the lawyers emptied out of the room.

Now, Eve thought, *we'll do this thing*. She kept her face blank, her voice even. "Mr. Chase, for the record, you have dismissed your representatives?"

He curled his lip at Eve. "I speak for myself."

"You're waiving your right to counsel at this time?"

"How many times do I have to say it, you ignorant twit."

"That's probably enough. Let the record show Mr. Chase has dismissed his representatives and has agreed to continue this interview without the benefit of legal counsel."

She paused, put a concerned, respectful look on her face. "Blackmail, you said? That puts a different face on it. Why don't you tell us how this started? You were informed by Randall Sloan that Natalie Copperfield was asking questions," Eve began.

And he gave them every last detail.

CHAPTER
TWENTY-ONE

Peabody had a tube of Pepsi waiting when Eve came out. "You usually like your caffeine cold after a hot interrogation." She held one out to Baxter. "Wasn't sure about you."

"I'll take it any way I can get it."

"Yeah, I've heard that from several women," Eve said before she took a deep drink.

For the first time in hours, Baxter laughed. "Thanks for letting me take that scum down with you, Dallas. I'm going to contact Palma, let her know we've got him."

"Dallas, Jacob Sloan came in while you were in Interview. They put him in the lounge."

"Okay, I'll take him. You can have Bullock brought up."

"Sure you don't want a break before her? You've been at this for nearly six hours, pretty much straight."

"I'm tying it up, wrapping it up, writing it up." She rubbed at the stiffness in her neck. "Then I'm going home, and so are you."

"Yay. I'll have her brought up."

Eve carried her drink into the lounge, scrubbed her hands over her face, then walked over to sit at the table across from Jacob Sloan.

He looked older, more frail, and exhausted.

"Mr. Sloan, you should go home, be with your family."

"Did Winfield Chase kill my son? I have sources," he said when Eve lifted her eyebrows. "I know he was arrested, along with his mother. I can't see Madeline doing more than pulling strings, so I'm asking you, did Winfield Chase kill my son?"

"Yes. He's just confessed. He staged the suicide to implicate your son in the murders of Natalie Copperfield and Bick Byson, who he also has confessed to killing."

When he folded his lips tight, nodded, Eve rose. She broke her boycott on Vending and programmed a bottle of water. She sat back down, put it in front of him.

"Thank you." His hand shook a little as he lifted the bottle and drank. "My son was a disappointment to me, in many ways. He was selfish and lazy and gambled away his youth, his marriage, his reputation. But he was my son."

"I'm very sorry for your loss."

He drank more, slowly, then breathed out. "Natalie and Bick, they were bright and they were clean. Their lives together were just beginning. I'll regret . . ." Once again he pressed his lips together. "Have their families been told?"

"It's being done now."

"Then I'll wait until tomorrow before I contact them. Why did he kill them? Can you tell me?"

"I can tell you that Natalie was doing her job, and she found something she tried to fix, tried to make right."

"My son. He was not doing his job." He shook his head when Eve said nothing. "This will be hard, very hard, on my grandson, on my wife."

"Then you should be with them, Mr. Sloan."

"Yes, I should be with them." He got to his feet. "Anything you need from me, my family, my firm to make certain Winfield Chase spends every last second of his life in prison, you have only to ask." He held out his hand. "Thank you."

Eve sat another moment after he'd gone, finished off her drink. Then she went into the washroom, scrubbed cold water over her face.

She went to face down Madeline Bullock.

Word had gone out, Eve imagined, as there were only two lawyers with her.

"Record on," Eve said and started the routine.

"Your son's confessed to five counts of murder," she began, watching Madeline's eyes. "I see you've got wind of that. He's also detailed your involvement in each of these murders, and in the abduction of Tandy Willowby."

"Ms. Bullock is prepared to make a statement," one of the lawyers said.

"Not dictating this load of crap, Madeline? Okay, let's hear it."

"I don't expect you to understand my terror, my grief, my guilt." Madeline pressed a lace-trimmed handkerchief to her lips. "My son . . . how can I not blame myself? He came from me. But something . . . twisted in him. Such violence, such rage. I've lived in fear of him for so long."

396

"Please. You're not afraid of anything but losing your grip on the foundation — its money and prestige and the operation you've been running through it almost since your husband died."

"You can't possibly understand. He's forced me to . . . it's unspeakable."

"Have sex with him? See, it's speakable. And that's more crap. You've been abusing your son sexually most of his life."

"What a horrible thing to say." Madeline seemed to break down, and for a moment buried her face in the handkerchief. "Win is sick, and nothing I could do —"

"He came from you," Eve said, feeling the rage rise up, seeing herself trapped in a cold room with the man she'd come from, the man who'd raped her repeatedly. "And you exploited and abused him. You made him exactly what he is."

"You can't possibly know the horrors I've lived through."

"You don't want to talk to me about horrors. I've got statements from your son, from Walter Cavendish, from Ellyn Bruberry, all naming you as the one in control, the one who made the decisions and gave the orders. You think because you didn't get your hands dirty with murder, you're walking away clean?"

"I did whatever Win told me. He might have killed me otherwise."

Madeline reached across the table to grip Eve's hands, and Eve allowed it though her skin felt tainted. *You're good,* she thought, *you're damn good at this, Madeline.*

"I appeal to you, woman to woman. I beg you to protect me. There's a monster inside my son. I'm so afraid."

"Ms. Bullock has been virtually a prisoner of her son's sickness," one of the lawyers began. "A victim of physical and emotional abuse. He used her — "

"He used you?" Eve interrupted, wrenching her hands free as she looked into Madeline's face, and saw her father's. "That's just crap, Madeline. No one uses you. And I can't think of anything more weak, more pitiful, than a mother who'd roll on her own son to try to save her ass. You're done, you get that? You've got no way out."

I want you to sweat, Eve thought. *I want you to tremble, and suffer and fucking* wail. "We've got the playback from the medical droid's memory. You're on there. The British authorities have picked up your Doctor Brownburn — who has already confessed, already stated that she took her orders straight from you. Nobody's going to buy the weak, frightened little mother act, Madeline. You're the power. More, you're a fucking spider, a bloodsucker, and it shows."

"I have nothing more to say to this *person*," Madeline snapped. "I want to speak with the British consulate. I'll be speaking to your President, who is a personal friend, and the Prime Minister."

"Toss in the King of England, it's fine with me." Eve leaned forward. "They're going to scramble back from you so fast they'll get whiplash. And just wait until Global starts talking to the women whose babies you bought, the people who bought them. We've got the list,

398

Madeline. We've got the names, the locations, and the international media's going to do a tango when this hits."

"That's what you're looking for, isn't it?" Madeline sucked air through her nose. "Media attention. My name, the reputation of the Bullock Foundation, will stand against anything you manufacture against me. You'll be crushed."

"You think so?" Eve looked Madeline dead in the eyes, and she smiled. She kept smiling until she saw the first true glitter of fear. "They'll crucify you while thousands cheer. And when I'm done with you here, you'll have to answer to the Italian authorities for Sophia Belego — Chase told us where they'll find her remains. You were with him, in Rome, when she went missing. You've got a home there, too, and they'll find evidence she was held there."

"My son is mentally ill. He needs professional help."

"If he is, you made him that way, twisting his view of sex, of women, of himself so you could get your jollies."

"Lieutenant." The lawyer spoke up while Madeline simply stared at Eve with those arctic eyes. "Ms. Bullock has already stated that Mr. Chase was the aggressor."

"Ms. Bullock is a liar and a pervert and a coward. You shouldn't discuss plans for murder and kidnapping in front of the servants, Madeline. Even droids, especially droids, as they keep records."

Eve flipped open a file. "Got a voice-print match right here, with you telling Win to kill Natalie Copperfield."

"That's impossible. We were alone when I —"

"When you gave him the orders," Eve finished when Madeline cut herself off. "You know, people like you are oblivious to servants. You probably thought you were alone." She closed the file.

"I've got Randall Sloan's records — your boy messed up there and didn't find the second safe. I've got multiple corroborating statements, and Tandy's firsthand account. I've got 'link transmissions you didn't have time to delete before your arrest that add further weight to the mountain of evidence. Give it up, Madeline. At least your son had enough pride to take credit for what he considered his work. Work you assigned him."

"I have nothing more to say."

"Okay." Eve rose. "I've got you for conspiracy to murder, multiple counts. That's going to put you in an off-planet facility, several life terms. And that's before the Feds, Global, the Brits, the Italians weigh in. How long do you think she'll keep those classy looks in an off-planet cage, Peabody?"

"Six months, outside."

"I'll go with that. You won't be getting bail, and your lawyers will tell you the same — no matter how they try to sweet-talk the judge. You're a prime flight risk. You're going to want to deal after another day or two in The Tombs, but when I walk out of this room, there will be no deal."

She headed for the door.

"Lieutenant." It was one of the lawyers who called out, then leaned in to murmur in Madeline's ear.

"I certainly will not consider it." She tossed her head. "She's bluffing. She doesn't have half what she claims. She's bluffing."

Eve smiled as she opened the door, then spared one last look back. "No, I'm not."

"You didn't want her to deal," Peabody said when they walked away.

"No, I didn't. She's worse than her son could ever be. She created him, she corrupted him and used him. She's worse and I want to imagine her living the next fifty years or so in a concrete cage. Go home, Peabody. You did good."

"I go when you go."

Eve sighed. "Then let's get this damn thing written up, and get the hell out of here."

She might have been walking in the door by six, but Eve was ready to admit she was dragging her ass to do it. She wanted a long soak in the jet tub, and an entire bottle of wine followed by lazy sex with her husband before sleeping for ten hours straight.

She wanted the image of Madeline Bullock stroking the body of her son out of her head.

Because she heard the music coming out of the parlor, and Mavis's voice piping through it, Eve knew she might have to wait just a little longer before soaking, sex, and sleep.

Mavis was sitting back in a chair, her feet on a hassock while Summerset passed her a cup of tea — which explained why he hadn't been looming in the foyer. Leonardo sat beaming at her, while Roarke sipped at wine with an indulgent look in his eye.

"I feel so pampered. Not that you don't take mag care of me, sugar lips," she said to Leonardo. "But today's been like a little vacation or something. Summerset, you should come live with us."

"Take him, he's yours," Eve said as she walked in.

"Dallas! Dallas!"

"Don't get up." Eve waved her back. "It'll take you too long and I'm going to sit anyway." She did, on the arm of Roarke's chair so she could cop his wine.

"Tandy's resting. She's been up and around today, and Summerset said she's doing just fine." Mavis sent him an adoring look. "He treated us both like pregnant princesses."

"You've had a trying few days, both of you. Have one of these canapés." He held out the tray. "They're your favorite."

"I'm not really hungry, but maybe one. Or two. We're taking Tandy home with us when she wakes up, get out of your hair. She's not ready to go home alone yet. Though *that* may not be the situation for long."

"Hmm?" It was the best Eve could do as her mind was already starting to float.

"Aaron's tagged her here a half-dozen times today. Her boyfriend? He's so sweet, so groveling. They've talked and talked. She cried a lot, but she laughed, too. He wanted — begged, actually — to come over to see her today, but she just wasn't ready. But she said he could come by our place tonight. He asked her to marry him."

402

"Nice."

"She didn't say yes yet, but she will. She told me it was all she ever wanted, and that maybe all this happened so they can be a stronger family. I knew you'd find her, Dallas."

"So you said."

"I can't say it enough. I can't tell you what it all means, what you did. You and Roarke, and Peabody, McNab, Baxter, that cutie Trueheart. I hope those terrible people sit in a cell in their own body waste until their faces rot off."

"Teddy bear," Leonardo murmured, and she winced.

"I know. Out with the bad energy, in with the good." Mavis shifted in her chair. "But I can't help it. She told me everything that happened."

"Wrapped up. Confessions all around, except for Bullock. But I didn't push too hard for one there. Didn't need it, and I like watching her try to squirm and writhe."

"Busy little bee," Roarke put in.

"We're going to get out of your hive." Mavis shifted again, winced again.

"Mavis?" Leonardo came half out of his seat.

"Just sitting wrong, that's all. Hard to get comfortable these days. Only ten days to go. Help me up, baby doll, so I can work these kinks out."

As he drew her to her feet, Tandy waddled in. "I'm sorry. Oh, hello, Dallas, Roarke. I want to thank you, so much, and there's so much I want to say. But I'm afraid my water just broke."

"Really?" Mavis squealed it as Eve went pale. "Oh, boy, oh, boy! Tandy." She hurried, as fast as possible, to take her friend's hands. "We're going to have a baby! You want us to call Aaron, don't you?"

"I do." The sunlight switched on in Tandy's face. "I really do."

"Don't you worry about a thing. Leonardo will go by and get your bag at your place, and I'll go with you to the birthing center. And we'll . . . Oh. Uh-oh."

Mavis pressed a hand to the side of her belly, hunching a bit, breathing out. "Wow. Gee. Oops. I kind of think maybe I'm in labor."

Eve pressed her fingers to her eyes as Leonardo bounded across the room like a drunken bull. "That's just perfect."

"Both of them?" Roarke gripped Eve's hand, pushed to his feet, pulling her with him. "Now? Both?"

"Just bloody hell perfect."

Hadn't she just run an op that had taken down two international criminals? And during which, hadn't she personally kicked a killer in the balls?

Hadn't she just faced a personal demon by sitting in Interview with Bullock and seeing her own father's face?

She could handle this. Please God.

But she had two women in labor in her parlor squealing at each other and talking so fast the words were a shiny blur, one expectant father who looked as if he was going to pass out at any moment. And her own husband, who was notoriously cool-headed, had just — literally — shoved her toward the insanity.

404

When she glanced over her shoulder to glare at him, he merely pointed at her and gulped down the rest of his wine.

"Okay, stop! *Stop!* Here's what we're going to do."

The squealing and babbling cut off as if she'd sliced through it with a laser, and all eyes turned to her. Since her first clear thought was to scream wildly for Summerset, she bit down ruthlessly on her own rising hysteria.

"Right. Everybody's going to get in one of the all-terrains, and we're going to go to the birthing center."

"But I need my bag." Tandy rubbed her belly, breathed out in little puffs. "I have to have it. It has my music and my focus —"

"Me, too, me, too." Mavis pressed a hand to the small of her back. "If we don't have our bags —"

"And here's what we're going to do next. I'll get Peabody and McNab to go by both your places, get both bags. But we're going. Now."

"Ladies, you need your coats." Roarke stepped up, laid a bolstering hand on Eve's shoulder. "Sorry, I clutched," he said to her. "Ah, Summerset, just who we need. We need a vehicle brought around right away."

"Are you in labor, Tandy?"

"My water broke, and Mavis is having contractions."

"Isn't that lovely," he said with a calm that made Eve want to punch him even harder than she usually wanted to. "You'll have your babies together. Mavis, how far apart are the contractions?"

"I forgot to time." Ripe panic bubbled out of Leonardo. "I forgot to time."

"It's all right. Did you just start to have contractions?" Summerset asked her.

"I think I've sort of been having them off and on for a couple hours. Maybe three."

"A couple *hours*." Eve heard that same ripe panic come out of her mouth. "Jesus, Mavis."

"It's perfectly fine." Summerset shot Eve a damning look. "Tandy, when was your last contraction?"

"Um. More or less now." She took a slow breath.

"I need to time!" Leonardo threw his long arms in the air. "I need to time."

"No." Eve pointed a finger at Leonardo. "We need to go."

"Has anyone contacted the midwife?" Summerset asked.

"Shit." Eve pulled at her hair. "You call her," she ordered Summerset. "Tell her we're heading in, carrying two. And contact Peabody, have her and McNab pick up the baby bags in Tandy's and Mavis's apartments. Apparently if we don't have them, we're doomed. And you need to contact Aaron Applebee."

"Oh, yes, please." Tandy beamed.

"Tell him where we're going and why."

"Certainly, now, ladies, sit down."

"Sit down! No sitting," Eve snapped. "Going."

"These things take time. You be comfortable while we get your coats and the proper vehicle warmed up for you. Tandy, wouldn't you like to speak to your Aaron yourself?"

"Yes. Yes, thank you, I really would."

Summerset took a 'link out of his pocket, offered it. "I'll just contact the midwife, and I'll be back in a moment with your coats."

Whatever his legion of faults, Summerset was efficient — Eve had to admit it. Within fifteen minutes they were driving through the gates. All of them, including Summerset, at Mavis's and Tandy's insistence.

There was constant chatter — about dilation, contractions, focus points, breast-feeding. Eve thought nostalgically of the last time she'd ridden with a crew on a mission. The chatter of cops, the possibility of death or injury.

It had been a lot less stressful.

Twice on the drive, Leonardo had to put his head between his knees. She couldn't really blame him.

"I'm going to drop them off at the entrance, then park." Roarke slid a glance toward Eve. "I'm not going to keep driving until I get to Mexico. I'll be right along. My word."

"Just remember, if you're not, I'll hunt you down, disarticulate all your limbs, then feed them to small, ugly dogs."

"Noted."

They were greeted inside by two bright-eyed, cheerful nurses, but Eve's relief in passing the burden was short-lived.

"You have to come with us."

"Come with you?" She goggled at Mavis. "Leonardo —"

"He has to check us in." Mavis grabbed Eve's hand and clung. "You have to come. Uh-oh."

Recognizing the signs now, Eve looked at Summerset. "She's having another one."

"Yes, that's how it's done. Go along with her. I'll bring Leonardo and Roarke."

It didn't seem fair, it didn't seem right, that she should have to take any part of this solo. But Mavis's hand was glued to hers, and the nurses were leading them all away.

"You're not going to shoot anything out before the rest of the team's in place, right?"

"I don't think so."

"Plenty of time." Mavis's nurse smiled at Eve. "I'm Dolly, and I'll be taking care of you, Mavis. Randa will be here soon."

"I'm Opal. We'll just get both of you settled in your room and see how far you've progressed. I didn't see your bags."

"Somebody's bringing them." Tandy found Eve's free hand, grabbed it. "We weren't home when we started. My boyfriend — fiancé — the baby's father, he's coming."

"We'll make sure he's sent right up to you. Don't worry, Mommy. It's the first for both of you, isn't it? And you're friends, having babies at the same time. Isn't that fun?"

"A barrel of monkeys," Eve muttered.

CHAPTER
TWENTY-TWO

She hated hospitals, it didn't matter if they put pictures of angelic babies on the pastel walls, arranged small, gardenlike seating areas, and wrapped the staff with rainbows. It was still a hospital — a place where doctors and machines took over your body, and there was usually some sort of pain involved.

It was no doubt due to Mavis's celebrity status that she was taken to a birthing room that was appointed like a high-end hotel suite. Bathed in the spillover glory, Tandy was settled into a plush room across the hall.

Eve's hopes that all she'd be called on to do, for the moment, was get her charges where they were going were quickly dashed. The only way Mavis would release the vicelike grip on her hand was with the promise Eve would go over, check on Tandy, and come right back.

"Leonardo and I were going to be with her. And now we're at countdown, too. She doesn't have anyone until Aaron gets here."

Since Eve was prepared to treat both women as she would a dangerous, wounded animal, she patted Mavis's white-knuckled hand. "Sure, no problem. I'm on it."

She walked over, pushed open the door, and found herself staring at a completely naked, enormously pregnant woman being helped into a short blue gown.

"Jesus." Eve slapped her hand over her eyes. "Sorry. Mavis wanted to be sure you were okay."

"Oh, don't worry about me." Tandy's voice was cheerful and bright. "You need to be with her now."

"No problem. I'm going."

"Oh, oh, Dallas. Do you think you could reach Aaron again? Make sure he's on his way."

"You bet." She turned, went back over, and was flashed with a naked Mavis. "Please, in the name of all that's holy and good, will someone cover these women?"

Mavis giggled as Dolly slipped a gown in mad swirls of blue and pink over her head. "Is Tandy all right? Is Leonardo coming? Is Aaron?"

"She's fine. I'll check."

Desperate to escape, Eve darted into the hall. There she determined that Aaron had finally gotten into a cab, and Leonardo had just completed the check-ins.

"Courage," she reminded herself, and went back into Mavis.

"Hey! I'm wired!" She was sitting up in bed, flushed with excitement. "See, that's the baby's heartbeat, and that one's to measure contractions."

Dolly snapped on a protective glove. "We're just going to do a cervical check."

God have mercy. "I'll be in the hall."

"No, don't leave!" Mavis shot out a hand. Resigned to the idea there was no God, Eve took it as Mavis assumed the position.

410

"Leonardo's on his way up," Eve told her, careful to keep her eyes trained on Mavis's face.

"About three centimeters," Dolly announced. "You've got plenty of time, so be comfortable. Let me know if I can get you anything. And you, Dallas, is that right?"

"Yeah."

"What can I get you?"

"A huge glass of wine."

Dolly laughed. "Now, now, no alcohol until the toast after baby. How about a nice cup of tea?"

Eve started to ask for coffee, then remembered hospital sludge was as bad as cop coffee. "Got Pepsi?"

"Of course."

"Moonpie!" Mavis called out when Leonardo came in, carrying an emormous vase of yellow roses. "Aw, you brought me flowers and I haven't even had the baby yet."

"They're like sunshine, so you can focus on them until the bag gets here." He leaned over, kissed her gently on the forehead. "Are you all right? Should I get you ice chips, the stability ball? Do you want music?"

"I'm mag. Three centimeters and counting. I'm so glad you're here. I'm so glad you're all here. It's just like I pictured it. Summerset, would you be an abso angel and be with Tandy until . . . Oh! Here comes a little one."

Since Leonardo was there to hover, Eve stepped away to stand with Roarke. "I saw them naked, both of them, and now I'm scared for life. The human body isn't meant to stretch like that."

"I'm more concerned about other areas of their body stretching."

"Oh, please."

"That wasn't so bad," Mavis said cheerfully, then she gave Leonardo a gooey look. "Honey bear? You know what you asked me before. Last week, and last month, and the month before that?"

He had both of her hands in his, and pressed them to his heart. "Angel Eyes!"

"Yes."

Eve averted her own eyes as they engaged in the sort of intense liplock that had likely been the precursor to the current situation.

"We're getting married!" Mavis sang out.

"No shit?" Eve responded.

"Absolutely none. We're going to be totally hitched."

"I've been asking her for months." Leonardo's face shone like a copper moon. "And finally! I'm going to design you the most fantastic wedding gown."

"Oh, but no. Honey-pie, we have to do it now. Before the baby comes."

"Now?"

"I just know it's right. The baby's coming, and I want to be your adoring wife when we see him, or her, for the very first time. Up close and personal. Please?"

"But we don't have a license, or any arrangements."

Her bottom lip trembled. "But it has to be now."

"Hold on." Eve held up a hand before the waterworks could start. "I think we can handle this one. Give us a few."

She stepped out with Roarke. "I'm hitting up the mayor," she said as she pulled out her 'link. "If he won't clear a license because I fast-talk him into it, I want you on tap to bribe him."

"I can do that. They'll need someone to officiate. The center must have someone who fits that particular bill. I'll go find out."

Eve nodded, took a breath. "Mr. Mayor, this is Lieutenant Dallas. I have a personal favor to ask of you."

As she ended the call, Peabody and McNab bounded off the elevator. "Relief troops, sir, with supplies." Peabody grinned like a maniac. "What's the status?"

"They're having babies. And as if that wasn't enough, Mavis decided she and Leonardo are getting married. Now."

"Here? Now? Holy crap."

"I talked the mayor into issuing them a special license. Roarke is hunting up somebody to do the deal."

"McNab, go back and start the 'link tree over. We did the contacting," Peabody told Eve. "I had a list. Now you start it again, and give them the update. Wedding *and* baby."

"I'm all over it. Tandy?"

"That way. Mavis this way."

"I'll take hers." Peabody did a little dance. "I'm so glad I put the tiara thing in her bag before we came. She gets to wear it for a bridal headdress."

As Peabody opened the door there were squeals — from her, from Mavis. Eve just pressed her fingers to her eyes. When she dropped them, Roarke was coming down the hall with a very pale man Eve recognized as Aaron Applebee.

"I found a wandering Daddy," Roarke said.

"I've been so turned around, and my mind just won't work. Oh, God, you're Dallas."

Before Eve could defend herself, he'd thrown his arms around her, dropped his head on her shoulder. Her terror only increased when she heard him give a muffled sob. "Thank you. Oh, bless you. Thank you for my Tandy, for our baby."

"Ah. She'll probably want to see you. There."

"Tandy." He lurched away, rushed through the door across the hall. *Tandy!*

"I don't know how much more of this I can take."

"Steady on, Lieutenant." With his hand on Eve's shoulder, Roarke lifted an inquiring brow at Summerset when he came out of Tandy's room. "And?"

"She's progressing very quickly. I'd say we'll have a baby in another two hours, three at the most."

"We're about to have a wedding as well. Mavis and Leonardo."

Summerset's lips curved into a smile, so rare to Eve's mind, she was surprised his face didn't simply cave in from it. "That's lovely. Shouldn't you be with her? As her coaching team?"

"We've been working here." Eve shifted. "Peabody's in there."

"It's you she wants," Summerset reminded her. "I'll just go in for a moment myself."

"I'm not going to feel guilty," Eve stated firmly. "I'm not going to feel guilty. Okay, shit, I feel guilty."

"Once more into the breech?"

"Don't say breech."

The next hour was busy, with Peabody and McNab standing in as runners between the two laboring women. Trina hurried in, and insisted on doing Mavis's hair. The midwife moved between the two rooms and pronounced both women right on schedule, with Tandy well in the lead.

Mavis stalled at six centimeters as Tandy hit ten and was cleared to push.

The suite filled up, thanks to the 'link tree. It was full of voices and bodies. Doctor Mira and her husband, Louise DiMatto and Charles, Feeney, Nadine, the huge bulk of Crack who'd come straight from his club, the Down and Dirty.

"It's like a real wedding. I'm so happy. How do I look?"

Leonardo kissed Mavis's fingers. "You're the most beautiful woman in the world."

"Oh, my sweet puppy. Let's do it! We've got everything, right? Flowers." She clutched the little nosegay of violets Roarke had brought her. "Music, friends. Matron of honor." She sighed at Eve. "Best man." And at Roarke.

"Everything." Then Leonardo's eyes widened. "A ring. I don't have a ring for you."

"Oh." Her bottom lip trembled again, and was heroically firmed. "Oh, well, that's no big, baby doll. Rings, um, they're not always the deal anyway."

Summerset moved forward. From under his stiffly starched shirt he drew a chain. "If you'll accept something borrowed, I'd be pleased if you used this until you have your own. It was my wife's."

Tears trembled on Mavis's lashes. "I'd be so completely honored, thank you. Would you mind giving me away? Would that be okay?"

He took the ring from the chain, passed it to Leonardo. Eve heard him quietly clear his throat. "I'd be so completely honored."

When he shifted back, Eve met his eyes. "Well done," she said.

It was perfect, Eve thought. Perfectly Mavis to make her vows and promises — with a couple of pauses for contractions — in the swanky birthing room surrounded by friends and wearing a silly tiara.

With McNab memorializing it all on his police recorder.

There wasn't a dry eye in the room, including her own, when Leonardo's big hands slipped the borrowed ring on Mavis's dainty finger.

After the applause, the kisses, the champagne Roarke smuggled in — you could always count on him — the midwife swung through the door.

"Congratulations, best wishes, and I'm pleased to announce a new life has begun. Tandy and Aaron have a son. Eight pounds three ounces of perfection. Mavis, I'm to tell you Tandy's sending her energy to you now. And Dallas? She'd like to see you for a moment."

"Me? Why?"

"I'm just the messenger. All right, Mommy, let's see how you're doing."

"You're coming with me," Eve said and gripped Roarke's hand.

"She didn't ask for me."

"I'm not going in there alone." She pulled him with her.

In the other suite, Tandy looked pale, sweaty, and a little glassy-eyed, as did the new father. She held a small bundle wrapped in blue.

"Everything okay in here?"

"Everything's brilliant. Isn't he beautiful?" Tandy turned the baby, so snugly wrapped it put Eve in mind of a blue sausage with a round, alien face.

"Beautiful," she agreed, knowing what was expected. "How are you feeling?"

"Tired, thrilled, madly in love with both my men. But I wanted to introduce you, especially, to Quentin Dallas Applebee."

"Who?"

"The new addition, Lieutenant." Roarke gave her a little nudge forward.

"It's all right, isn't it?" Tandy asked her. "We wanted him to honor your name. He wouldn't be with us if it wasn't for you."

Surprised, touched, Eve pushed her hands into her pockets and smiled. "That's nice. Really nice. That's a lot of name for a little guy."

"We're going to teach him to live up to it." Aaron bent down, kissed mother and child. "And how is Mavis?"

"Slow and steady, the midwife said. It'll be awhile."

"I'll come over when they let me."

"She'll be around. You'd better get some rest."

When she stepped out, Feeney was standing in the hall drinking bad coffee. "Midwife's checking something on her. I'm not staying in there during that."

"What sane person would?" Eve's communicator signaled.

"Don't think you're going anywhere," Roarke said darkly.

"Hey, I signed up, I'm seeing it through. Dallas."

"Lieutenant." Whitney's face filled the screen. "You're to report immediately to Riker's, female facility."

"Commander. I'm currently unable to comply. I'm at the birthing center. Mavis —"

"Now?"

"Yes, sir. Or shortly. Is this a problem with Madeline Bullock?"

"It is. She's dead. Her son broke her neck."

When she had the details, was assured Whitney would call in Baxter to handle the investigation, she sat in one of the pretty garden spots with her head in her hands.

"Why do you blame yourself?" There was impatience in Roarke's voice. "Why must you take this on? She's the one who convinced a guard to let her son have visitation."

"Stupid. Stupid. They should never have been allowed to see or speak to each other. Not at this point. I'll be damned if she *convinced* a guard. She bribed one, and asses will be thoroughly kicked."

"Then why are you sitting here, taking on the responsibility?"

She sat back. "She riled him up, is what she did. Pushing him, pushing him to corroborate her story, to save her own skin at the expense of his. 'I'm your mother. You owe me life.' I can fucking hear her saying it, and him listening to her, understanding — finally — he'd be sacrificed. That he wasn't important enough to her to save, to love."

"And still, knowing that, here you sit."

"I wanted her to go down, go down the hardest. That's why I saved her for last in Interview. Let her sweat. That's why I didn't hammer at her any harder than I did — let her sweat some more, go back at her again tomorrow. I didn't offer her a deal, and I was cleared to. I could have closed it up with a decent deal, and enough hammering. But I let her know I was going to see her fry. I let her see it. I wanted her to."

"And why not? She was responsible for all of this, for murder, for misery. You wanted justice."

"No, or not only. I wanted to give her pain and fear. He did the killings, and he enjoyed doing them. But she twisted him, right from the beginning. She made him what he was, and used him as her tool, she abused him like —"

Roarke lifted her hand, pressed it to his lips. "As you were."

"I saw my father when I went at her in the box. I felt him, and I felt what he'd done, wanted to do, with me."

"She was a monster, as he was. But regardless, Winfield Chase was a grown man. He could have escaped her. He could have gotten help."

"You don't believe in help, or escape, when they're done with you."

"He wasn't you, Eve. And you could never, no matter what, have been like Chase. You could never have made his choices."

"No. I know that. And yeah, he had choices, we all do, but she limited them. She skewed them."

"And that's what your father would have done, was trying to do, to you."

"He comes back, in my head, in my dreams. So I saw him in her. I saw him when I looked in her eyes, and I wanted her to pay. I wanted her to suffer and to pay and to *know* why. Now she has paid. I don't know if she understood why."

"Did you want her dead?"

"No. No, because then it's over, and that's not payment enough." She drew a breath, shaky, then another, stronger. "Whitney said it happened fast. They're talking, and Chase just reached over, snapped her neck. He didn't even try to resist afterward, just let them haul him away. They've got him on suicide watch."

"Look at me, listen to me." His tone was brisk and firm. He wouldn't have it, wouldn't have her carrying this load. "Can't you see whatever you wanted, however you played this, it would have ended the same? She wouldn't have been satisfied with a deal. She would still have tried to use him, he would still have killed her."

"Maybe. Maybe."

"Eve, you saw that child moments ago, that tiny new life that carries part of your name. There's a beginning for you, and you helped bring it to be. It's pure. We can't be, you and I, and he won't stay that way. But by doing what you did, by being what you are, you gave him his family."

"So close it up where it belongs." She closed her eyes, nodded. "You're right, I know you're right. I will."

"Dallas? Sorry." Peabody stiffled a yawn. "Mavis is asking for you. Oh, and she's up to seven. Some of us are heading down to get a bite to eat. We're taking Leonardo, because the midwife said we've got time."

"But —"

"She said she'd really just like a little quiet time, with you."

"Okay, okay. Wipe that relieved look off your face, ace," she warned Roarke. "You're still going to be there for lift off."

"God pity me." But he rose, put his arms around her, brushed his lips over her brow. "Think of what's been saved," he murmured. "Think of the look on Tandy's face when she held her son. There's no place for the dark here."

"Right again." She held onto him one more moment. "Thanks."

Eve thought Mavis was starting to show a little wear when she went back in. "Something happened." Mavis pushed a little straighter in bed. "Tandy? The baby?"

"No, no, they're fine. Something on the job." Close it up, she reminded herself, and remember what's begun. "It's not important."

"You don't have to leave?"

"Mavis, I'm not going anywhere till you get this job done. How're you doing? And are you sick of having people ask you that?"

"I'm pretty okay, and no. It's kind of frosty, being the focus, you know? It's not like when I'm performing. This is so real, like primal even, and I'm the only one who can do it. Can you just sit here, be with me?"

"At your beck."

Because Mavis patted the bed, Eve sat on the side of it. "I wanted . . . Oh, here it comes again. Getting stronger. Shit, damn, fuck."

"You gotta breathe. Where's the focus thing?"

"You are, right now. I'm sick of looking at fucking sunshine."

Mavis puffed, staring so hard into Eve's eyes, Eve wondered she didn't lance right through to her brain. Then she remembered one of the options from the class, and laid hands on Mavis's belly, rubbing light circles on what now felt like a mound of concrete.

"Easing back, isn't it? Yeah, it is," Eve said with a glance toward the monitor. "Coming down, leveling off, good work. Blow it out."

When she had, Mavis managed a grin. "You were paying attention in class."

"I'll remind you I'm a cop. We hear and see all. You know, they have drugs for this."

"Yeah, and I'm thinking about it. It's just I've never done anything like this before. I think I'm going to go a while longer first. Right now, I wanted the just-you-and-me time. Look."

She held up her left hand, and Summerset's ring glinted.

"Yeah, I'm happy for you."

"Couple of old married ladies now. Who'd've thought it? Pretty soon, I'm going to be a mother. I want more than anything to be a good one."

"Mavis, it's in the bag."

"There are so many ways to screw up. I used to be such a screwup. But I came around, right?"

"Yeah, you did."

"I wanted to say something to you, before everything changes again. Because I know this is going to change everything. A good change. An abso mag change, but still. Dallas, you're the best person I know."

"Are you sure you haven't had drugs already?"

Mavis gave a watery laugh. "I mean it. Leonardo, he's the sweetest, but you're the best. You do what's right, you do what matters, whatever it takes. You're the first of my family, and you really started me on the road. I wouldn't be here, wouldn't be doing this except for you."

"I think Leonardo had more to do with it."

Mavis grinned, rubbed her belly. "Yeah, he had the fun part. I love you. We love you." She took Eve's hand, laid it on her belly. "I wanted to tell you."

"Mavis, if I didn't love you, I'd be a thousand miles from this room."

"I know." Now she hooted out a wicked laugh. "It's kind of a kick to know. But you do what's right. You do what matters, so you are so completely stuck. Oh, shit, damn, fuck, here comes another one."

Two hours later, with a little something to take the leading edge off, Mavis was pronounced "ready to push."

"All right, team." Randa lifted the tent between Mavis's legs. "Positions."

"Why is this my position?" Eve demanded when she was maneuvered to the bottom of the bed.

"Mavis, I want you to take a long deep breath on the next contraction, hold it for the count of ten, and push. Dallas, give her resistance. Leonardo, on the resistance, pull. Roarke, on breathing."

"It's coming!"

"Get your breath, and go. Push! One, two . . ."

"Mag! You're amazing," Leonardo declared when the contraction passed. "You're a miracle. Breathe slow now, sugarcake. You don't want to hyperventilate."

"I love you," Mavis said with her eyes closed and her face slack. "But if you tell me how to breathe one more time, I'll yank your tongue out of your mouth and strangle you with it. Here it comes again."

During the next hour, Leonardo bathed Mavis's face with cool cloths, gave her ice chips, hunched in shame when she snapped at his overcheery encouragement.

For herself, Eve did her job and looked anywhere but at what was going on below.

"I think we should switch." She narrowed her eyes at Roarke as Mavis sucked in for the next round.

"There's no power in heaven or hell that could make me go down there."

"That's the way, Mavis," Randa encouraged. "See, the head."

Instinctively Roarke glanced at the mirror angled for Mavis. "Oh, God! My eyes."

Pulling on the bright red strap Leonardo held, pushing strongly with her foot against Eve, Mavis let out a nearly inhuman growl, then plopped back and panted.

"A couple more," the midwife told her. "Just a couple more."

"I don't know if I can."

"You can do it, starshine!"

Mavis bared her teeth at Leonardo. "You want to switch places? Shit, shit, shit." She reared up, grabbed the strap, and dug her free hand, nails first, into Roarke's.

"Head's out. What a great face!"

With one eye shut, Eve looked down, and saw the wet, slack face that was vaguely human poked out of Mavis's crotch. "Is that even possible? Can that be right?"

"One more, Mavis, and you've got yourself a baby."

"I'm so tired."

Eve blew the hair out of her eyes, waited until Mavis's glazed ones met hers. "One more time, for-the-money shot."

"Okay, okay, here it comes."

It slid out, slippery, wriggling as Mavis pushed with a vengeance. Its cry was raw and irritated, in counterpoint to Mavis's weeping laugh. "My baby! Our baby! What is it? I can't see that part. Does it have a dingle or not?"

Eve cocked her head as the midwife held up the now-wailing baby. "Dingle-free. It's a girl. Got some serious lungs on her."

Leonardo wept as he cut the cord, wept as the baby was laid on Mavis's belly. "Look at my beautiful girls. Look at my girls." He spoke it like a prayer. "Do you see them?"

"It all right, Daddy." Mavis crooned, stroking his hair with one hand, the baby's back with the other. "Hello, my baby. Hello, true love. I'm going to do everything I can so the world doesn't suck for you."

"We'll need her for just a minute," Randa told Mavis. "Just to clean her up, to weigh her. Dolly's going to take her and bring her right back to you. She's a real beauty, Mom."

"Mom." Mavis pressed her lips to the baby's head before Dolly lifted her. "I'm a mom. Thank you." She reached for Roarke's hand, then smiled down at Eve. "Thank you."

"She is beautiful." Roarke leaned over to kiss Mavis's cheek. "Like a perfectly beautiful doll."

"She'll suit her name." Leonardo wiped tears from his eyes.

"We went all over the place on names, remember, Dallas?"

"I think Radish was the last you ran by me."

"Apricot." Mavis rolled her eyes, and simply glowed. "But we decided to go with something softer, if it was a girl. Something sweet. She's Bella. Bella Eve. We'll call her Belle."

426

The beautiful Belle was wrapped in a pink blanket, her pretty bald head covered in a pink hat, and placed in her father's big arms. "Now," he whispered, "I have everything. I have the world."

Hours later, Eve stood in the quiet of her own bedroom, and pulled off her boots. "Hell of a day."

"Hell of several."

"We did okay, didn't we? Coach Roarke."

"Some shaky moments, but I think, yes, we did just fine. And thank all the gods it's done."

"It kind of looked like that vid — the pod people vid, before they're fully formed."

Tunneling his fingers through his hair, Roarke frowned at her. *"Invasion of the Body Snatchers?"*

"Yeah, that. It — I mean she — kind of looked like that when she came out, then she didn't. She looked mostly real. I never thought I'd hear myself say this, but I'm glad Mavis cornered us into doing this. It meant a lot, to see this through with her."

"It did." He crossed to her, put his arms around her. "And you've two lives, two new beginnings, carrying your name. That's quite a tribute, Lieutenant."

"Hope I never have to arrest them."

He laughed, swept her up. "I want you in bed."

"I want to be there, too. Be glad if you came along." She pressed her lips to the side of his neck. "I've got to clean up the mess tomorrow, on the job. Tie up the last of it. Might take two days, but no more than. Anyway, the new mother will sulk if we don't come in and ga-ga over Belle. But then, it's just you and me, pal. Dancing naked under the tropical sun."

"Hallelujah."

When she was wrapped around him, she let it all go, the questions, the answers, life and death. They'd all wait for her until the morning.

Elegy For April

Benjamin Black

As a deep fog cloaks Dublin, a young woman is found to have vanished. When Phoebe Griffin is unable to discover news of her friend, Quirke, fresh from drying out in an institution, responds to his daughter's request for help.

But as Phoebe, Quirke and Inspector Hackett speak with those who knew April, they begin to realise that there may be more behind the young woman's secrecy than they could have imagined. Why was April estranged from her powerful family, the Latimers? And who is the shadowy figure who seems to be watching Phoebe's flat at night?

As Quirke finds himself distracted from his sobriety by a beautiful young actress, Phoebe watches helplessly as April's family hush up her disappearance. But when Quirke makes a disturbing discovery, he is finally able to begin unravelling the web of love, lies and dark secrets that April spun her life from . . .

ISBN 978-0-7531-8774-6 (hb)
ISBN 978-0-7531-8775-3 (pb)

Fourth Day

Zoë Sharp

The cult calling itself Fourth Day is well-funded and fiercely guards its privacy. Five years ago Thomas Witney went in to try and get the evidence that the cult's charismatic leader, Randall Bane, was responsible for the death of Witney's son, Liam.

Now, Charlie Fox and her partner, Sean Meyer, have to get Witney out, willing or not. After five years on the inside the man who comes out has changed beyond all recognition. Can Witney be trusted when he says Bane is innocent and, if he is, who was behind his son's demise?

With Witney's ex-wife demanding answers, Charlie agrees to go undercover into Fourth Day's California stronghold. No real danger for someone with her mindset and training. But Charlie has her own secrets, even from Sean, and she's unprepared for the lure of Randall Bane, or how easily he will pinpoint her weaknesses . . .

ISBN 978-0-7531-8782-1 (hb)
ISBN 978-0-7531-8783-8 (pb)

Memory in Death

J. D. Robb

For once detective Eve Dallas can look at her latest murder victim and feel absolutely nothing. For Trudy Lombard awakens memories in Eve she'd rather forget. A seemingly ordinary middle-aged woman, Lombard was also one of Eve's foster parents and Eve was one of many traumatised children placed in her haphazard care.

But now — only a few days after showing up in Eve's office — Lombard is dead. A cop to the core, Eve is determined to solve the case, if only for the sake of Trudy's grieving son. Unfortunately, the list of suspects should probably include every child who ever passed through Trudy's home. And Eve and Roarke will follow a dangerous path to find out who turned the victimiser into a victim . . .

ISBN 978-0-7531-8686-2 (hb)
ISBN 978-0-7531-8687-9 (pb)

Dark Country

Bronwyn Parry

For 18 years most people in the small town of Dungirri have considered Morgan "Gil" Gillespie a murderer, so he expects no welcome on his return. What he doesn't expect is the discovery of a woman's body in the boot of his car.

Wearied by too many deaths and doubting her own skills, local police sergeant Kris Matthews isn't sure whether Gil is a decent man, wronged by life, or a brutal criminal. But she does know that he is not guilty of this murder — because she is his alibi . . .

Between organised crime, police corruption, and the hatred of a town, Gil has nowhere to hide. He needs to work out who's behind the murder before his enemies realise that the one thing more punishing than putting him back in prison would be to harm the few people he cares about.

ISBN 978-0-7531-8728-9 (hb)
ISBN 978-0-7531-8729-6 (pb)

Finger Lickin' Fifteen

Janet Evanovich

The spiciest, sauciest, most rib-sticking Plum yet

Celebrity chef Stanley Chipotle comes to Trenton to participate in a barbecue cook-off and loses his head — literally. Bail bonds office worker Lula is witness to the crime, and the only person she'll talk to is Trenton cop Joe Morelli. Chipotle's sponsor is offering a million dollar reward to anyone who can provide information leading to the capture of the killers. Lula recruits bounty hunter Stephanie Plum to help her find the killers and collect the moolah.

Stephanie Plum is working overtime tracking felons for the bonds office at night and snooping for security expert Carlos Manoso, aka Ranger, during the day. Can Stephanie hunt down two killers, a traitor and five skips, keep her grandmother out of the sauce, solve Ranger's problems and not jump his bones?

ISBN 978-0-7531-8632-9 (hb)
ISBN 978-0-7531-8633-6 (pb)